Mike Jefferies   rs
in Australia.   of
Art and then
keen rider, he
in the Belgian   he now lives in
Norfolk with his   e, working full-time as a writer
and illustrator.

By the same author

Voyager

MIKE JEFFERIES

Citadel of Shadows

HarperCollins*Publishers*

Voyager
An Imprint of HarperCollins*Publishers*
77–85 Fulham Palace Road,
Hammersmith, London W6 8JB

A Paperback Original 1996
1 3 5 7 9 8 6 4 2

Copyright © Mike Jefferies 1996

The Author asserts the moral right to
be identified as the author of this work

A catalogue record for this book
is available from the British Library

ISBN 0 00 648218 X

Set in Goudy by
Palimpsest Book Production Limited,
Polmont, Stirlingshire

Printed in Great Britain by
HarperCollinsManufacturing Glasgow

TO MY WIFE, SHEILA,
who has guided me through the dark side
of morning into the sunlight.

Swanwater

Granite City

Gildersleeves

Woodsedge

The Black forest

Clatterford

Mussle

Meremire forest

Deepling

Endless Grasslands

The Tower on
Stumble hill

Underfall

The Runegate Gorge

The Emerald Mountains

Manterns Mountain

The Petrified Forest

Motley Marsh

Cawdor

The Dark Side of Morning

ELUNDIUM

N

Prologue

Once, long ago when history was being forged upon the anvil of time, Elundium existed in two perfect parallels, one above the ground at peace with nature, in perfect harmony with the sunlight, while the other dwelt in darkness beneath its surface, a place of unnatural things and nightmare images that hated the light.

The Mason Kings, who ruled Elundium, lived in ignorance of the things that dwelt beneath their world of sunlight and stripped the surface of Elundium bare in their search for the purest silver-veined marble, gradually weakening the ground and drawing the darkness closer until, with one final, fateful hammer blow, King Mantern's chisel broke through the earth and from that tiny hole Krulshards, the Master of Nightmares, rose shadowy and terrible. Black winds screamed around him and savage storms tormented the land, laying waste everything the Mason Kings had built, tearing up trees and robbing the world of its colour as the darkness spread.

But out of the howling night a light blazed and a figure appeared wrapped in a rainbow cloak. 'Know me, Krulshards,' a strong voice cried out. 'Know me, for I am Nevian, the Master of Magic, the Lord of Daylight and the Keeper of the Sun.'

Nevian created the Granite Kings out of the living rock to drive Krulshards and all his unnatural creatures back into the City of Night, but each time, just as the seal across its black gates was almost complete, Krulshards fought against the trap and broke free. It was a time of giants when great mountains and valleys were formed from the debris of their battles but slowly Nevian's magic weakened and the age of the Granite Kings came to an end. King Holbian suffered a terrible defeat between the black Gates of Night when his fear of the dark, a secret he had kept from the Master of Magic, allowed Krulshards to escape into the City of Night to spawn more of his evil creatures, the Nightbeasts.

In anger and frustration at his own weakness the King turned on Nevian and raised his sword to strike the magician down but that moment of reckless anger cost the King dear. Orundus, the Lord of Battle Owls, snatched the sword from his hands and Grannogg, the Lord of Dogs, snarled and bared his fangs ready to attack the King. Equestrius, the Lord of Horses, reared up, thrashing the air above his head with his razor-sharp hooves. Nevian stepped in, for he would not have the King harmed, but because of his anger the bonds were broken between the King and the Warhorses, the Battle Owls and the Dogs of War who had gathered beneath his standard to drive Krulshards back into the darkness.

Nevian saw the King standing alone in his despair and was overcome with pity. He took the King's hand and told him that he had not foreseen the tragedy of battle's end but knew the bleak road that lay ahead for him because of the bond breaking. He gave him a cloak of a thousand jewels which caught the light and would comfort him in the darkness and then Nevian predicted that chaos and desolation would spread across Elundium and a new King, as yet unborn, would renew the bonds that had been broken and old legends would spring to life.

'A King?' Holbian cried out. 'But how will I know him?'

Nevian whispered, 'You will know him because he fears nothing in the dark.'

I

A Conspiracy
of Whispers

IRONPURSE, THE disgraced Chancellor, lifted his head. His watery eyes narrowed as he caught a faint, unfamiliar sound amongst the noisy hum of conversation that filled the great, smoky hall of the wayhouse inn at Deepling. He twisted and tilted his head, listening intently, trying to ignore the villagers' mutterings as they told each other of their dissatisfactions and grumbles. The sound was getting louder. Suddenly he glanced anxiously across his shoulder and looked through the haze of blue smoke towards the outer door.

'Listen, I can hear horses – there are more than just a couple and they're coming along the greenway,' he hissed in alarm, dropping the bone-hard cheese rind that he had been gnawing onto the table as he hastily rose to leave.

'What's getting under your cloak tails all of a sudden? You're so nervous you'll be jumping at your own shadow next. Sit down, you've got nothing to be afraid of!' Snatchpurse gripped his father's arm and forced him back into his seat before lazily swallowing the last dregs of ale from his jug and wiping his dirty sleeve across his mouth. 'It's early yet and we're in no hurry.'

'I'm telling you I heard horses outside on the greenway and I'll bet a Chancellor's purse-string it's a squadron of those cursed Gallopers come back to start snooping and prying into honest folks' business again. They'll be turning everything upside down in their search for those wretched

Tunnellers, you know, the ones who escaped from the Granite City when in.'

The outer door of the inn burst open putting a stop to Ironpurse's mutterings and he shrank back as far as he could into the shadows as seven of the King's Gallopers hurried in over the threshold calling for the landlord, cursing the foul weather and bringing with them a swirling flurry of snowflakes. An icy wind came in with them that made the reed lamps dance and flicker as it fanned the embers in the hearth into a blaze and sent smoke billowing out into the hall and a ribbon of bright sparks roaring up the chimney before the last Galloper had slammed the door shut behind him.

The noisy hum of conversation gradually died away and the crowd grudgingly shuffled apart to let the horsemen make their way through to the hearth to thaw out. They kept in a tight bunch, stamping their feet and shaking the weather out of their cloaks, each one aware of the silent, hostile atmosphere that surrounded them. Snatch grinned, watching them with his quick, cunning eyes.

'Landlord Masterwort – come here this minute – you have King's men, Gallopers, in your inn and they are cold and hungry after a long, hard daylight in the saddle patrolling the greenway. Bring us hot food and jugs of mulled ale, and be quick about it! Masterwort! Where the devil are you?'

The leading horseman was impatient as he glanced around at the villagers who crowded around them in the inn but was careful to avoid their eyes.

'That's another seven mouths we have to feed tonight and precious little to do it with!' somebody complained over-loudly from the back of the crowd.

'Patrols!' another voice scoffed bitterly. 'What I'd like

to know is where is all this patrolling and searching getting us? It's certainly not catching those wretched Tunnellers is it? It's not stopping them robbing and killing honest folk while they travel the greenways is it?'

'It's getting so bad now that the merchants won't travel anywhere without an escort, no matter how high the barter. I've nothing left in the forge, nothing at all,' an ironmaster added hotly.

'Who cares about iron, you fool, it's food we're desperate for!' another voice cursed.

'Just listen to them whispering behind our backs. That's all the thanks we get for riding out in all weathers searching for those treacherous Tunnellers!' one of the young horsemen complained angrily as he threw another log onto the fire. He rubbed his numb hands together and held them out towards the flames.

'They're right, you know, these patrols are a waste of time. Those Tunnellers are making a laughing stock of us, it's like chasing shadows trying to catch them. It's just as if they know exactly where we are and they're just staying one jump ahead,' another frowned, looking slowly around the smoky room. 'You know, I sometimes wonder if somebody isn't informing them of our movements.'

'Well, I don't really care, I've got better things to do with my time than waste it searching through these miserable villages along the greenways' edge. I'll be glad to get back to the Granite City and see the back of them!' an older horseman complained.

'Orders are orders,' their leader reminded them curtly as he sent the older man out to check that the horses were being stabled for the night. 'You should think yourselves lucky you weren't detailed to search through the lower circles of the city for those Nightbeasts! Remember some of them helped the Tunnellers escape and they must be still in the city – it's a warren of dark cellars and rat holes down there. At least we don't have to deal with any Nightbeasts!'

'My lords, forgive me for not being with you sooner but I have been run off my feet . . .' Masterwort exclaimed, appearing suddenly in the room, bustling through the kitchen archway and anxiously wiping his fat hands on the front of his voluminous apron.

'Bring us mulled ale, landlord, hot and spiced with the fruits of the forest. Yours is the best for miles around, if I remember rightly from my last visit. And food – plenty of it, and make it quick, my men are half-frozen to death from patrolling the greenway. And send a boy out with fodder for the horses: there's a blizzard on the way and they'll need plenty to eat.' The horseman turned away and faced the fire again.

'Oh, yes, my lord, I would, indeed I would, I know it is my duty to serve the King and I would bring you steaming broth piled high with dumpty puddings and there would be ale that frothed in the jug – but I am afraid that all we have in the kitchens are a few rancid scraps of meat and dry, stale crusts, and the only ale is the bitter dreg-ends of the barrels. You see, it has been an age of daylights since the victualler's wagons last stopped here, what with all the troubles and everything. All the murdering and robbing that's going on has made people too afraid to travel.'

The horseman's face darkened with anger. He clenched his fist and glared slowly around the crowded room. 'It's a pity some of you don't band together and help us. We can't be everywhere at once: there aren't enough of us to defend the Granite City let alone patrol every village – they're only Tunnellers, after all, no bigger than goblins!'

What he couldn't understand, and never would, was why they had let themselves become the victims of fear so easily, why they had so willingly turned their backs on the bright new daylights that King Thane had fought so hard to win for them.

'You must understand it is not just the Tunnellers that people are so afraid of.' It was Masterwort who spoke.

'Well, what else could it possibly be?'

Masterwort hesitated and swallowed, sweat glistening on his forehead and trickling down in sticky rivulets to be lost in the deep creases and wrinkles of his heavy jowls. He glanced at the sullen faces of the villagers and then looked anxiously towards the outer door before continuing in a lowered voice, 'It is the Nightbeasts that most folks are afraid of.'

'Nightbeasts? I've heard the rumours: but we haven't caught sight nor sound of any of them.'

'Oh, yes, there are Nightbeasts,' Masterwort continued quickly. 'We know the Tunnellers have awoken them from deep in Meremire Forest. It's more than a rumour. Out here, you know, merchants and journeymen have been attacked by them. Oh yes, they've even seen them together on the greenways and they are enough to frighten the bravest fellow. They are as thick as thieves, it is no wonder they helped the prisoners escape from the cellar beneath Candlebane Hall. Although it beats me why the King needed to judge them: everybody knows they're guilty, that's why nobody around here will go into the forest harvesting and gathering any more. The crops are going to ruin because everybody's afraid of the Nightbeasts.'

'We've been abandoned!' somebody shouted from the back of the room, banging his empty ale-jug on the table.

'Things wouldn't be as bad as they are if King Thane hadn't got rid of the old ways so quickly. "Change is always for the worse" – he should have remembered that saying and not disbanded the Marchers, Gallopers and Archers so hastily after the great Battle of the Rising. There should still be warriors to protect us and to escort the merchants and journeymen along the greenways!'

Another voice interrupted, 'It's not only caution King Thane needs, he needs wise heads to advise him, good Chancellors to help him rule in Candlebane Hall and then we wouldn't all be in this sorry state.'

A ghost of a smile hovered on Ironpurse's lips and his ears pricked up, but he stayed hidden in the shadows, afraid of attracting the horseman's attention.

'That's right, it's all the King's fault!' somebody else shouted recklessly. 'If he hadn't given those Tunnellers the freedom to roam wherever they pleased in all Elundium the moment the battle was over they wouldn't be causing all this trouble now, would they? I'm sure the Chancellors wouldn't have allowed it to happen in King Holbian's daylights. The Chancellors would have kept them firmly in their place instead of letting them come and go as they please. And giving them the right to live off the backs of honest folk! Why, it's scandalous. And for what? Doing a bit of gardening, that's what, mowing a bit of grass whenever they feel like it!'

'Anybody with enough sense to know one daylight from another would have known that they were bound to throw their lot in with the Nightbeasts at the first opportunity; they probably even used the excuse of all that messing about with the trees and greenways to search for them in the depths of the forest. Remember, they can't have spent as long as they did as slaves to Krulshards tunnelling and enlarging the City of Night without forming a lasting bond with his Nightbeasts, can they now! And what else could you expect from ugly little creatures like that anyway?'

'I can't for the life of me see what the King saw in them,' somebody muttered just before someone else called out darkly, 'There was magic at the bottom of it. The King was beguiled and enchanted into befriending them by that magician Nevian. And that's not all he did, is it, remember how he turned all those warriors into trees when old King Holbian died and turned back into stone, and all because they refused to accept King Thane and pledge their allegiance to him. You can never trust magic, look what it did to those old Marchers Berioss and Ustant: they never were quite the same again – that tree magic turned them bad, didn't it? Look how they threw their lot in with the Tunnellers.'

Grumbles and mutterings of discontent began to rise through the smoky room.

'That's enough!' the leading Galloper cried out angrily, his hand on the hilt of his sword. 'I've a good mind to burn this inn to the ground for the treacherous mutterings I've heard in here tonight! Thanehand is a good and just King and I won't hear another word against him!'

He took a step forward and the crowd scrambled out of his way. 'King Thane won a great victory for all of you at the Battle of the Rising and he destroyed the last of the Nightbeasts. I should know, I was there, I saw them perish and shrivel away to nothing: they were just dust in the snow when we left.'

'So who was it who helped the Tunnellers escape from the Granite City if it wasn't the Nightbeasts? Go on, tell us that!'

'I . . . I . . . I don't know,' the horseman stuttered. 'They may have looked like Nightbeasts but they couldn't have been . . .'

Another of the Gallopers intervened, 'Whatever those creatures were we'll capture them. The lower levels of the city have been completely sealed off.'

'Just like you caught the Tunnellers, I suppose?' Snatch asked loudly, tapping his empty mug on the table.

The horseman swung round towards him, his face livid. He swept his sword from its scabbard. Utter silence spread throughout the watching villagers. Flames hissed and crackled in the hearth and the wind howled mournfully along the darkened greenway outside. Then the atmosphere in the wayhouse changed abruptly and fists were knuckled as the crowd edged forward, closing in threateningly around the seven Gallopers. King's men or not, the villagers wouldn't stand by and see any harm come to Snatch. He might have been a Chancellor's son but he and a few of his friends had risked their lives only recently to escort a small band of merchants safely into the village. Admittedly there was little in their wagons and few could afford to pay the ridiculously high barter that was demanded, but it had helped to save the village from starvation.

A sudden movement in the smoke-blackened rafters high above Snatch's head, a whirr of white feathers and the shrill voice of Squark, his white magpie, startled the horseman.

'Catch the Tunnellers! Catch the Tunnellers!' it shrieked, flying down and alighting on Snatch's shoulder, where it started to preen and ruffle its feathers.

The horseman took a moment to regain his composure and he stared at the magpie in anger. 'How dare you teach a bird to mock me! What is your name, boy?'

Snatch stared back at the rider with an insolent grin across his mouth. 'My name is Snatchpurse,' he replied casually. 'Squark is just a magpie I found sitting on a branch along the greenways' edge. There is no crime in teaching it to speak, is there? I can't help it if it steals the words out of your mouth and mimics them, now can I?'

A snigger rippled through the crowded room and some-body called out, 'Perhaps you had better wring Squark's neck for treason!'

The horseman was pricked by the insult and turned round in anger but he swallowed his feelings as he saw the hostile faces of the villages pressed in around his men. There were only seven of them and he couldn't trust them all to put up a good fight; he knew that some of them secretly hated the Tunnellers and they were a long way away from the safety of the Granite City. He shrugged and smiled stiffly as he resheathed his sword and returned his attention to Masterwort who was hovering anxiously at his side.

'We'll have whatever you can manage to rustle up for us in the kitchens, landlord.'

'Yes, yes, of course, we'll do our best, we always do for the King's men. Go and sit down by the fire – I'll ask that group of tallow-makers to move.'

The horseman turned slowly and looked down at Snatch who was sneering back at him as he stroked the magpie's long tail feathers. Then he glanced across at the wizened old figure sitting opposite the insolent boy. He was wrapped up in a filthy cloak of the coarsest hessian sacking and he shrank back quickly, looking away as if trying to avoid the Galloper's eyes. But in that moment the horseman caught a glimpse of his shrunken, weatherbeaten face with its watery, half-hooded eyes and its thin, bloodless, puckered lips.

'You!' he cried out. 'You, look at me! Who are you?' There was something familiar about him, something that tugged at forgotten memories, and he took a step closer, reaching out to grasp Ironpurse's shoulder when the magpie's shrill voice suddenly mocked him again, making him draw back.

'Find the Tunnellers! Search! Search! Har har har.'

The horseman's eyes snapped back to Snatch and the white magpie perched on his shoulder with its head tilted slightly to one side as it mocked him. It was staring up at him, fixing him so accusingly with its bead-black eyes. I won't forget your name in a hurry, boy, that's for sure.' His voice was hard with controlled anger as he turned on his heel and crossed the crowded room.

The villagers parted in silence as they let him through.

'You fool! You stupid idiot! What do you think you're doing letting that miserable bird mock that Galloper? You'll get us both arrested for treason – or worse – if you carry on like that!' Ironpurse was furious. Yellow bubbles of spittle erupted from the corners of his mouth. 'I'm not staying here to watch you get us into trouble: that horseman was getting too nosey for my liking!' He grasped at the mouldy cheese rind that lay beside his dirty, cracked ale-jug and made to rise, cramming the precious piece of cheese into his torn jerkin pocket. Snatch leaned quickly forward and caught hold of his wrist, gripping it tightly until his nails cut painfully into his father's skin, forcing the old man back into his chair.

'Sit down, you old fool! And stop looking so furtive: you'll make that horseman think you really do have something to hide if you carry on like that. Relax and drink some more ale, we can't leave yet, I've promised Huxort and Girrolt that I would meet them in here. Landlord – bring us some more of that excellent ale!'

Snatchpurse glanced around until he saw Masterwort bustling about near the hearth serving the group of riders. He caught his eye and winked knowingly as he raised his jug and made sure the landlord had seen it before returning his attention to his father.

'But . . . but . . . you must have seen how that Galloper looked at me,' Ironpurse whimpered, squirming in his seat. 'I'll swear he thought he recognized me – I was only saved by that wretched bird of yours distracting him. It's dangerous in here: he might come back at any moment and then he might not be put off so easily. What am I supposed to do then? We've got too many enemies – too many – and there'll be no end of trouble for us – for all the Chancellors' families – if I'm forced to reveal where we've built our settlement. There'll be Marchers, Gallopers, everyone swarming all over the place, turning everything upside down!'

'Is that all you're worried about – saving your own miserable skin?' Snatch sat back and roared with harsh, bitter laughter. He waited until Masterwort had refilled their jugs with ale and then leant across the table. 'Listen to me, and listen well, nobody cares one jot about you or your precious Chancellors except, perhaps, to sneer and laugh at your petty plotting and your incessant self-pitying mutterings. Your daylights of meaning anything in Elundium were over the moment you fled from the Granite City when the Nightbeasts closed in to attack during those last glorious daylights of King Holbian's reign. Don't forget, I was old enough to remember the disgrace as we shrank away beneath the cover of darkness.'

Snatch's face hardened into a mask of contempt. He was sick of listening to his father's whines and to all the other disgraced Chancellors as they bemoaned their fate and whispered and muttered about taking revenge, for they were never going to do anything about it. 'It's no wonder Thanehand found it so easy to steal the throne once the smoke of battle had cleared: you had all run away to hide here in exile. You're all so weak, so frightened of your own shadows, you almost jump out of your skins whenever you catch sight of anyone else.'

Ironpurse's watery eyes glittered momentarily as he raged at the intended insult. Forgetting where he was, he shouted, 'We'll seize it back one daylight, just you see! I'll make you eat your words, you insolent boy!' And he raised his hand to strike Snatch across the head. Startled faces began to turn in their direction.

'Sit down! I won't tell you again, sit down and stop making such a spectacle of yourself. That horseman, the one who was so interested in you, is looking over here,' Snatch squeezed his father's bony fingers, crushing them until they began to crack in his powerful grip and made Ironpurse gasp with pain.

'I'm sick of listening to you. That throne-stealer and his treacherous friends will be long dead and turned to dust before you or any of the other Chancellors have found the courage to do anything about it. If I were you I would keep very quiet and drink your ale, and leave all that talk of getting back what is rightfully ours and its full measure of revenge to those who do have the courage and the cunning to do something about it!'

Ironpurse suddenly sat bolt upright and his thin, mean mouth split into a knowing sneer as he realized what was at the bottom of his son's insolent, rude and disrespectful behaviour. Leaving across the table, he lowered his voice, but it did little to disguise the ridicule he felt at the sheer absurdity of what he guessed Snatch was suggesting. 'So you're the one who is going to get our revenge and tip Thanehand off the throne for us. Well, that's nice isn't it, and how do you propose to do it? Go on, why don't you tell me, boy!'

'Yes, that's right,' Snatch grinned. 'And it's already started. All that trouble with the Tunnellers is only the beginning.'

'What do the Tunnellers have to do with it?'

'Why, everything!' Snatch laughed. 'Look at the chaos they are causing – and everyone is blaming the King! Have you heard anybody say a good word for him lately? Soon he'll be too afraid to leave the Granite City without an escort, and I don't think that many of the Gallopers and Marchers that he disbanded after the Battle of the Rising will be in a hurry to go back and serve him. Don't you remember how it all started, here at the inn at the rag-end of autumn? We had delivered a cartload of logs for Masterwort, it was pouring with rain and we came in here to have a drink and dry out by the fire before we went home, when a noisy group of those ugly little creatures burst in through the door demanding food and shelter. Then I became really angry and beat one of them up for singing or something – don't you see, I started it, and everybody in here thought I was such a hero and they helped me chase them all out of the village into the forest! Then we burned down that hovel belonging to one of those two old Marchers who foolishly befriended them and tried to protect them.'

Ironpurse sadly shook his head and rubbed his hand wearily over his face. 'I don't see much cheering going on in here now, and I wouldn't remind anybody that you started these Tunnellers rampaging through the countryside if I were you,' he looked anxiously around the inn before continuing. 'You haven't listened to anything I taught you about the art of politics have you? You have forgotten what you have learned about manipulation and the intrigues of government. Beating up that Tunneller did us more harm than good, you stupid fool! It's made them turn against the ordinary folk, I call it biting the hand that feeds them, and everything has got much worse since they fell in with those Nightbeasts and started robbing and murdering the merchants and journeymen. Remember, boy, it is us who are starving and going without, not that wretched throne-stealer, Thanehand, who doesn't care one jot what becomes of us.'

Ironpurse paused and sucked in a dribbly, shallow breath. 'By my reckoning, boy, you've got it all wrong, these troubles are benefiting the King, not harming him. The truth of it is that he probably never liked those Tunnellers much either, ugly little goblins: he was probably only using them to clear the greenways – after all, it was the cheapest labour he was ever likely to get, especially when you take into account that it was the village people like us and old Masterwort here who had to feed and house them.'

Ironpurse laughed, a sound that creaked and wheezed in his narrow chest, 'He'll be as pleased as everybody else to be rid of them and it won't be long, I'll be bound, before those Gallopers of his catch up with them, what with the winter closing in. Come on, boy, let's go home before the snow gets too deep and those Nightbeasts start roaring through the trees: this is just the sort of night you'd be likely to meet them. You've been saying you've

26

'got friends to meet in here for more daylights than I care to remember and they never show up, so come on, let's go home.'

'You can go if you want but I'm staying put. It's warm in here and there's plenty more ale where this lot came from,' Snatch replied, supping from his jug and fixing his father with a hard, mocking stare. 'Go on, what are you waiting for? Those Nightbeasts won't ever hurt you, I promise.'

Ironpurse muttered and mumbled and stared down at his son. He was afraid of the dark and the thought of the Nightbeasts hiding amongst the trees forced him to wait. Morosely he watched as Snatch swallowed the dregs from his jug and called for more ale. He began to wonder where he had got the barter to pay for it, for he had never actually seen any change hands and he certainly would never have enough to sit here eating and drinking every night. Where was it all coming from? He muttered his thanks to Masterwort as he refilled his own tankard and then drank deeply, belching and wiping his mouth with the ragged, frayed cuff of his sleeve as he looked across suspiciously at Snatch. It wasn't only the barter that bothered him: he was up to something, he was sure of that, but what? The boy wouldn't tell him anything, he had become very secretive lately and often vanished for whole daylights, sometimes two or three at a time, and he never had a word of explanation. If he complained of all the work he had been left to do on his own Snatch would merely laugh and tell him to be patient, that he soon wouldn't have to work at all. And he wasn't the only one to be behaving strangely: he had overheard some of the other Chancellors voicing the same concerns about their sons and daughters. But he knew there wasn't any point in trying to riddle out the answers — he never got a straight reply to anything these daylights.

Ironpurse took another gulp of ale and settled deeper into his chair. What did it matter anyway, the boy was never going to amount to much with his petty intrigues. He'd had his chance to kill Thanehand in the Learning Hall and he had squandered it because he had been too full of himself, far too clever to slip a silent strangle around the cursed candlecur's throat and pull it tight. Too cocky to use a quick dagger thrust between the crowded desks when he'd had the opportunity. Ironpurse sighed and yawned, exposing the blackened stumps of his teeth. The warmth of the fire and the strong ale was making him drowsy, his head slowly nodded forward and his mind began to wander. Gradually, he thought he was back in those glorious daylights when the Chancellors had held power in Candlebane Hall. His fingers were busy pinching the coarse hessian of his cloak, except that now, in his dreams, it felt like rich velvet.

Snatch glanced across at his father with contempt and muttered, 'You silly old fool, it's better that you don't know what's going on. If anyone took the trouble to ever listen to any of your mutterings . . .'

The sharp click of the latch on the outer door and an icy draught of air on his cheek made Snatch look anxiously across the crowded room. 'At last!' He pushed away his drink and signalled urgently to Huxort and Girrolt to join him as they slipped in through the door.

'Landlord, bring two fresh jugs of mulled ale for my friends, and make it quick — they look near frozen to death,' Snatch called out, catching at Masterwort's apron tails as he hurried past.

'At once, at once,' the landlord replied breathlessly,

turning and vanishing in the direction of the kitchens. He was well aware of how much Snatch and his friends were doing to make sure that at least a few of the victuallers' supply wagons got through to the village, and at great risk to themselves too. He was especially grateful for the barrels of best ale that Snatch made sure he got on the side.

Barely a head was raised or a curious glance cast at Huxort and Girrolt as they removed their cloaks and shook the snow off them. Everybody was so used to seeing them slip into the inn at the oddest times as they came for a quiet drink near the fire.

'I think there's a blizzard on the way,' Girrolt informed a group of weavers playing marchers' crowns near the door as both the young men quickly threaded their way through the smoky, crowded room to where Snatch was waiting with two brimming, frothy jugs of freshly mulled ale already on the table for them.

'Well?' he asked in an impatient whisper as they sat down. 'You've been so long I had almost given you up for dead. Tell me everything – are the others safe? Which road did the Tunnellers take? Did they ride into the Emerald Mountains after passing the last lamp of Underfall? Did they try to find the lost road to Cawdor, the one that Loremaster Grout guessed they would be searching for? Have you covered their tracks to confuse the Gallopers as I instructed?'

'We've sent the others home, they will slip into the settlement as quietly as possible, and won't arouse suspicion,' Huxort paused and shivered slightly, clasping his hands around the jug of warm ale and nodding towards Ironpurse. 'What about him? Wouldn't you prefer it if we told you somewhere else – somewhere more private?'

Snatch laughed softly and reached across and prodded

the old man quite hard in the chest. Ironpurse grunted and twitched but stayed lost in his dreams, his shallow, snoring breaths hardly altering at all. 'He's asleep so you needn't worry about him. Anyway even if he does wake up and try to eavesdrop on us he won't be able to make much sense out of what he overhears because he thinks the Tunnellers really are causing all the troubles and have thrown their lot in with the Nightbeasts – the silly old fool!'

. Girrolt and Huxort both grinned and moved their chairs closer to Snatch. 'We did exactly as you told us,' Girrolt whispered, his grin widening as he caught sight of the small group of Gallopers sitting close to the fire. 'We managed to get in between that squadron of Gallopers and the fleeing Tunnellers as they were sent out of the Granite City, although it took some hard riding to do it and at times they were so close behind us we could almost hear the rattle of their horses' bit-rings!'

He paused and took a deep swallow of ale, licking the froth from his lips before he continued, 'Anyway at the first opportunity, just where the ground was really soft, we sent a couple of the boys galloping off the greenway into the forest; they left a really clear trail for the riders to follow.'

Huxort laughed. 'We confused them all right: by the time we'd done that half a dozen times those Gallopers were all over the place following the false trails. We must have lost at least half of them in Notley Marsh! I see we've got some of them in here too! None of them were following by the time the Tunnellers had passed the last lamp at Underfall.'

'And the Tunnellers – what happened to them? Where did they go?' Snatch asked impatiently.

'They were heading for Cawdor all right, just as Grout

said they would. We followed their tracks into the Emerald Mountains but we had to turn back when the blizzards closed the high pass that they had taken ahead of us. In fact we've had to ride hard all the way back just to stay ahead of the storm – it will be here by morning. But tell us what's been happening here? Who has been stirring up all this trouble while we've been away? We've heard reports of more murder and robbery than we're capable of doing. What news is there of the Granite City and all that uproar when the Tunnellers escaped? Were we missed?'

Snatch grinned and shook his head, 'There were a few questions but no, you weren't missed, not really, everybody's been far too busy worrying about being attacked or murdered in their beds! But you won't believe how many people have begged to join us. They've been arriving every daylight asking to meet the hero who stood up against those Tunnellers. They want to help him protect the people!'

'But surely you haven't let them join us have you? That would mean revealing who we are and they would know our real purpose.'

Snatch merely laughed at him, 'Yes, of course I've let them join our Honourable Company of Murderers: I've ensnared them in such webs of intrigue and dishonesty that they'll never be able to leave us reveal who we really are without revealing themselves as traitors. But on top of that you won't believe what that Galloper sitting over there said earlier this evening – just listen to this! Everything has worked out a thousand times better than I had ever imagined; the city's in uproar, the villagers are terrified out of their wits, they believe that the Tunnellers really have awoken the Nightbeasts deep in Meremire Forest, nobody is in the slightest doubt that it was real

Nightbeasts who broke into the Granite City. We fooled them all! Everybody has been duped by our disguises and to cap it all the King is convinced that they're still somewhere in the city waiting for a really dark night so that they can escape. He has sealed the lower circles so tight that even the rats' holes have been blocked up with stone choke and stay-safe candles and lamps are burnt continuously on the walls to light up the darkness each night.'

'So now we can really start terrorizing everybody with all these extra murderers to help us and turn all that killing and stealing into real profit!' Huxort laughed and the three of them surreptitiously drew the middle fingers of their right hands silently across their throats in the sign of the Honourable Company of Murderers.

Suddenly Snatch gripped hold of Girrolt's arm. 'That crippled boy! The clumsy sweep – was he in amongst the Tunnellers? Did you see him?' he hissed.

'Why yes, I'm sure he was, we only saw them at a distance but there was no mistaking the way he sat so crookedly in the saddle. And that girl, the small, ugly one we almost captured, helped him to escape down Tallow Finger Alley where they broke out from the armoury. She always rides at his side.'

'When the snows have melted and we go to Cawdor we'll get them all – but those two are mine, mine, do you understand?'

Snatch's eyes had narrowed to murderous slits as he spoke and his voice shook with rage as his nails dug painfully into Girrolt's arm. 'Do you understand!' he growled.

Ironpurse stirred and opened his eyes, bewildered and confused by the anger that had woken him. Both Girrolt and Huxort drew back, afraid of the sudden gleam of near-madness in Snatch's eyes but Snatch just laughed and blinked and suddenly the madness was gone, masked by cunning.

'I think it is time we paid our friend, Grout, another visit – don't you? We'll stir things up a little in the Granite City.'

II

Wise Counsel in Candlebane Hall

THANEHAND, KING of Elundium, threw up his hands in an impatient gesture at the seemingly fruitless, repetitive arguments that surrounded him and turned abruptly away from the council of trusted friends. He was beginning to doubt the wisdom of summoning them into Candlebane Hall

'I know what you are all thinking secretly – even you, Breakmaster!' he accused them, angrily. 'But you're wrong. The Nightbeasts are all dead, the last of them perished in the Battle of the Rising when I stabbed that fragment of Krulshards' black malice into Kruel's footprints. I gave him a shadow and reduced him to a helpless infant. I don't care what those guards thought they saw in the courtyard near the armoury that night when the Tunnellers escaped but they were certainly NOT Nightbeasts!'

Thane paused and glanced up. A smile softened his face as he caught sight of Mulcade, the Battle Owl, sitting silently on a high rafter beam listening to the debate. 'Anyway,' he continued, 'it's more important to find out where they're hiding in the city than to keep on arguing about what they are.'

Mulcade stooped silently down, his outspread wings fanning the thousands of candle flames that illuminated the hall, making them dance and sway, jumbling up the council's shadows as they leapt up across the sooty walls before alighting on Thane's shoulder. 'What can I do,

Mulcade? The city is in turmoil and dark rumours stalk the countryside – fear is everywhere. Where are those creatures that looked so much like the Nightbeasts? Surely they cannot evade your sharp eyes – they can't have vanished into thin air.'

There was a hint of hurt in Breakmaster's voice. He was devastated that the King might doubt his loyalty:

'Lord, I do not doubt you, I too saw the last Nightbeasts die, but there can be no denying the guards saw something remarkably like those creatures. The gates of the city were slammed shut and sealed only moments after the last of the Tunnellers escaped on the Nighthorses. We know the creatures weren't with them and there haven't been any claw prints in the dust outside the city, not a single one. And there have been none since then. That can only mean they are still hiding somewhere in the lower circle of the city.'

'That's exactly why everybody is so afraid, and why the city folk are in such an uproar,' Arach, the master mason, interrupted heatedly. 'Everybody is terrified of being attacked or murdered in their beds – and not without good reason. I mean, think of it, the creatures must be getting hungrier and more dangerous with every daylight that passes since they were last seen.'

'Well, it is not our fault they haven't been caught, my Archers and every Galloper and Marcher we can muster have been searching, no scouring, every cellar and dark hole, every house, every alleyway . . .' Greygoose the Captain of Archers retorted quickly.

'Yes . . . yes . . . I know how hard you have all searched but standing here arguing about it doesn't get us anywhere,' Thane sighed wearily, reaching up and ruffling Mulcade's chest feathers as he strode over to the open window. The owl had been with him since the very beginning, long before he had become king. Thane remembered how it had been, so long ago, when one sunny morning in the Learning Hall he had dared to stand up, he a mere candleman's son, and challenge Loremaster Pinchface, accusing him of telling lies about his grandfather, the last errant rider for the Granite Kings. He remembered how Nevian, the master of magic had suddenly appeared and forced the Loremaster to tell the truth. It wasn't until long afterward's that he had realized that this had been the beginning, the real beginning, when the enraged Loremaster had set the Chancellors' sons after him, hunting him through the city, crying out for his blood. He recalled how he had been forced to seek shelter in the breaking yards. Thane glanced briefly back at the old horseman who had risked everything, even the wrath of King Holbian, the last Granite King, when he had taken him in and hidden him from the Chancellors.

Breakmaster and the others were now bent over a yellowing parchment showing the lower circles of the city, and were muttering and mumbling amongst themselves as they checked and re-checked that they had not left a single stone unturned. They traced even the narrowest of alleyways and hidden culverts with careful fingers. He had been wrong to doubt their loyalty or become impatient with their fears. Thane inhaled a deep breath of the chill, evening air and rested his hands heavily on the ornate stone balustrade, feeling the frost prickle his fingers as he watched the night draw in across the city following the dark, relentless tide of nightshapes gliding across the surrounding countryside to shroud the bare, bleak, winter fields. The trees and hedgerows that bordered the vanishing greenways began to dim and soften their stark, frosty outlines as the dark covered the first hint of snow that lay hidden in the ditches.

Mulcade hooted suddenly, squeezing his talons into the rich weave of Thane's long, flowing winter cloak as his sharp eyes picked out a horseman, a Galloper, riding hard towards the city through the thickening gloom. Thane leaned forward to stare out into the gathering darkness.

'There is a rider – a messenger – approaching on the greenway. Perhaps he carries news of the escaping Tunnellers, or maybe he can at least tell us if the other creatures have been sighted. Send word down to open the outer gates to let him into the city, but make sure the guards are extra vigilant. Nobody must leave until we get to the bottom of this mystery.'

A rush of iron-shod boots echoed down through the city.

Thane looked out for a moment longer as the darkness deepened. The nightshapes were swirling and drifting up over the sheer granite walls that encircled the city, filling the steep, winding lanes and blind alleyways and slowly smoothing the weather-bleached roofs and forests of tall chimney pots with the colour of night. One by one the thousands of lamps and stay-safe candles that he had ordered be set upon the parapets of each of the lower circles of the city were being lit, a measure that he had hoped would calm the people's fears and reassure them as they illuminated the dead hours of the night in those troubled times. But, more importantly, the light thinned out the shadows in the darkest places where those creatures might try to hide.

Thane smiled to himself as he remembered his own humble beginnings. Faintly, from every quarter of the city, far away voices of the candlemen sang out the hours as they lit the lamps, their voices floating up to him on the cold night air as the glow of the lights steadily grew stronger, dispersing the encroaching darkness.

'Who calls the candlemen to light them to bed?

Who calls the candlemen to weave dreams in their heads?'

Somewhere from the gloom below he heard the shout of the guards at the Stumble Gate as it was pulled open and bumped and rumbled across the cobbles. The sound was immediately followed by a sharp clatter of quick hoof beats echoing beneath the gate arch as the messenger cantered up through the narrow, winding lanes of the city and made his way towards Candlebane Hall. The hoof beats grew steadily louder until Thane caught a fleeting glimpse of the rider's helm, the flying tails of his cloak and the horse's outstretched head and sweat-soaked neck. Bright, blazing sparks danced beneath its feet as it passed through the archway that led into the courtyard below.

'Now perhaps we will find out if those Tunnellers really were trying to find the lost road to Cawdor . . .' Breakmaster began.

Footsteps accompanied by a musical jangle of spurs sounded as the messenger approached.

Thane turned quickly towards the old horseman, his eyes flashing a veiled warning for him to keep a check on his tongue, for careless words fell all too easily into listening ears. He had agreed with Errant before he set out in pursuit of the Tunnellers that he was on no account to attempt to recapture them, to bring them back for Judgment would be as good as condemning them to death. The people were so enraged, so convinced of their guilt that nothing but death would satisfy them and Thane had serious doubts as to whether the Tunnellers were capable of any of the atrocities of which they were accused. He sighed: how he hated the intricacies of politics.

Nobody but Breakmaster, Errant and himself had heard Silkstone's cry in the shadow of Stumble Gate moments after the Tunnellers had fled. Nobody had heard him telling them that the Nighthorses were going to seek the wild, forgotten road to Cawdor. Grout, the Loremaster, had dredged deep into his memory of the Lore of Elundium to tell him that Cawdor had once really existed although it had now sunk into myth and legend. He had told them how once it had lain somewhere beyond Underfall behind the distant heights of the Emerald Mountains shrouded by the dark side of morning. He told them how it had been a wild and dangerous place where the Nighthorses were first gathered to serve the Granite Kings, how it had been guarded by many-headed serpents and armoured, lump-backed beasts that spat boiling steam and fire from their mouths. He had told tales of a tangled, petrified, impenetrable stone forest full of frozen orchids that shut it away from the dark margins of the known world and had voiced doubts that the Tunnellers had much chance of finding a way through the high mountain passes with the winter approaching, let alone finding Cawdor itself.

Thane frowned and returned his attention to their present predicament. He was becoming convinced that somebody, or some secret group, was conspiring to make the people of Elundium think that the Tunnellers had become treacherous rebels and that they had awoken the Nightbeasts and formed a murderous alliance with them to wreak havoc and destruction along the greenways. But why? What could they possibly gain from such a conspiracy? And, more importantly, who were they?

Breakmaster broke into his thoughts by noisily clearing

his throat indicating that the messenger was now at the doorway of the Candlehall, his travel-stained cloak thrown back across his shoulders, his metal helm emblazoned with the emblem of the sun tucked securely beneath his arm as he knelt to offer his king the leather dispatch pouch that he was carrying. 'Lord, I bring word from Errant, First Captain of the Nighthorses that he has safely reached the fortress of Underfall.'

'Yes, yes, but what real news do you bring, I wonder?' Breakmaster muttered beneath his breath. His cheeks were still hot-flushed by the embarrassment of forgetfully uttering the forbidden name of Cawdor, and he welcomed the arrival of the rider to divert the curiosity and attention of the other members of the council, hoping it would help them quickly to forget his indiscretion.

'Servers – bring hot food and mulled ale for our weary traveller and make haste, a ride on a night such as this must have frozen him near to death.' Thane reached out to grasp at the messenger's battle-gloved hand to pull him to his feet. He took the pouch and beckoned to the rider to walk beside him and stand close to the great hearth where two huge, twisted tree trunks burned as they rested on a bed of ash between black iron fire-dogs. The crackling flames were leaping half way up the chimney.

'Now, come and tell us everything, leave nothing out, how do things really stand in the villages along the greenways' edge? Are the rumours we have received true? Do the people really fear that the Nightbeasts have awoken in Meremire Forest? Are the merchants refusing to travel without escorts? Are the people beginning to go hungry?'

'Lord, lord, there is fear, a terrible fear and it is stalking the whole countryside . . .' The rider fell silent. Errant had warned him to choose his words carefully and to say

43

nothing of where the Tunnellers had fled to. He was to tell that only to the King in private. But now he was at journey's end and he was in fear and awe of the majesty in Candlebane Hall, the eyes of the whole council were upon him and he was standing before his king with only black news to tell. He did not know how to continue.

Mulcade hooted and rose from Thane's shoulder in a gale of feathers, startling the rider and making him shrink back. The owl hovered for a moment in front of his dirt-streaked face, searching his eyes, making him feel as though the bird was looking right down inside him, then Mulcade suddenly released the messenger from his pitiless, unblinking stare and flew up amongst the swirling nightshapes that wove between the high rafter beams where he perched, silently overwatching all the comings and goings in Candlebane Hall, listening to every word and whisper that echoed in the still, smoky atmosphere.

'Come, speak, man: the owl obviously saw some truth and honesty in your eyes. Have you completely lost the use of your tongue? Quickly, messenger, your king and his council are waiting!' Breakmaster demanded impatiently as he took a step closer, briefly studying the rider's gaunt and weary face which was pinched and blue with the cold, despite the glow of the flickering firelight. Arach and Greygoose and the other council members crowded closer.

'Have patience, Breakmaster, and all of you, let the poor man draw breath,' Thane chided softly, but as he returned his attention to the rider he sensed the fear he carried and could feel the terror in his heart and a troubled shadow crossed his eyes.

'You have nothing to fear in Candlebane Hall, messenger, providing you speak the truth and tell us now how

44

things stand in Elundium. What did you see on your long ride from Underfall? Remember that we are siege-locked with the burden of politics and government here within the city, so you must be our eyes and our ears. Now, tell us everything that we may begin to set things right and restore law and order to the land.'

The messenger swallowed and glanced up into the gloomy rafters overhead in fear of the owl.

'Lord, the situation is far worse than you had imagined. The countryside – especially in the more remote areas – is close to chaos, much of the harvest still lies rotting in the fields. The ironmaster forges are cold and choked with ash and clinker and the weavers' looms stand idle and unused. Many of the villages are close to starvation because the merchants and the journeymen flatly refuse to travel to them without an escort. It seems not to matter how high they are willing to barter, for escorts are hard to find in these dark daylights. To make matters worse the greenways are fast becoming overgrown and dangerous to travel on now that the Tunnellers have all disappeared and no one mows them or cuts back their wildness.'

'But . . . but . . . what about the Marchers and Gallopers who used to live in the villages and wayhouses along the greenways' edge? Tell us, messenger, why are they sitting idly by? Surely they have not forgotten the pledges they swore to me upon the Causeway Fields! Surely they can't forget how they kept the roads open and provided escorts for the merchants and journeymen, how they defended the villages during the darkest daylights of the Granite Kings when all Krulshards', foul creatures plagued the dead hours of the night? What has become of these once-proud warriors, messenger? Why are they now so incapable of restoring law and order?'

Thane frowned and added, 'Surely their swords haven't grown so blunt and rusty that they cannot bring a handful of trouble-makers – most of them no taller than my belt buckle – to heel.'

The rider shuffled his feet uncomfortably and the sharp rowels of his spurs jingled through the smoky, shadowy silence of the Candle Hall. He looked down at the smooth, tallow-stained flagstones, avoiding his sovereign's eyes and those of his council. The king might have reassured him that he had nothing to fear by speaking the truth but what shade of the truth should he tell? It wasn't easy picking and choosing his words and it was even more difficult to find the courage to utter them.

The owl hooted softly from high up in the raftered darkness above his head demanding that the colour of the truth be pure. The messenger inhaled a nervous, shallow breath and bravely tried to continue. 'Lord, there is no law and order on the greenways now, nor are there warriors to enforce it, because . . . because . . .'

His voice faltered and he stumbled into a frightened silence. He could not find the words to tell his King that it was his own bold proclamations and changes that had heralded the new Elundium at the death of King Holbian that were at the root of all these troubles.

'The warriors gone? But why – where to?' Thane exclaimed. 'What could have happened to them?'

'Well, I would have thought that it was as plain as daylight why those warriors have turned their backs on you, my lord,' Greygoose, Captain of Archers, muttered. He had enough problems of his own without trying to shoulder the burdens of Elundium, for Eider, his eldest son, was getting headstrong and had become almost impossible to control, and having got himself into trouble with

Loremaster Grout he had now gone and run off with those wretched Tunnellers and that crooked sweep's scuttle, Drib. The shame and disgrace of it were almost too much to bear, so he really did understand why the messenger felt so afraid and tongue-tied. Nobody would welcome the task of laying the bare bones of the truth in front of the king except perhaps Nevian, that wizened old master of magic, all wrapped up in the voluminous folds of his rainbow cloak. He had never seemed to worry about how sharp the truth cut, but he hadn't been much help to the King since the Battle of the Rising. And that was just like him, weaving spells and then vanishing, melting away into thin air and leaving all the hard work of actually running the kingdom for others to do.

'What was that, Greygoose? What did you say?' Thane's voice made the archer blink and jump, the spines in the quiver slung across his shoulder rattling noisily. 'No . . . nothing, my lord,' he stuttered, the colour rising in his cheeks as he looked helplessly from face to face of the silent council, hoping that the King wouldn't press him for an answer.

'Nothing!' Thane's voice hardened with anger. 'You should know better than most men, Greygoose, that I will have no muttering and whispering behind my back in Candlebane Hall. You felt the need to say something so speak up, Captain of Archers, illuminate us with your wisdom. Come, now, the council awaits.'

'Surely, my lord, you haven't forgotten that you disbanded all the warriors after the Battle of the Rising; you sent them home to their homes and families as free men and proclaimed that the daylights of fear and darkness were finally gone forever?' Greygoose tried to continue, his mind racing as he tried to find the words that would blunt the

47

truth. He hadn't the courage to tell the King that the warriors had felt betrayed and dishonoured in their hour of victory.

'Surely you haven't forgotten what a wonderful sight it was, my lord? The great battle crescents stretching away into the distance, the cheering as the sunlight drove away the shadows, the clash of swords and spears upon the thousands of upturned shields echoing like the rolling sound of thunder as the ranks of proud warhorses stamped their iron-shod hooves in the bloody, trampled snow and tossed their silken manes in their impatience for the road? I can still see the stoops of Battle Owls wheeling and turning, hovering in the bright new rays of morning sunlight above our heads while the savage, sable-coated Border Runners snarled and barked as they crowded at Esteron's heels while you rode across the battlefield to thank them all for the part they had played and the sacrifices they had made to win the sunlight.'

'Yes, of course I remember: how could I forget such a parting of true friends – but you still haven't explained why or where all those warriors have disappeared to?'

Greygoose wrung his hands wretchedly; there was no escaping, he had to tell the King the whole truth.

'Many of the Marchers and Gallopers, indeed most of the Archers and Armourers who had served you so faithfully, my lord, who had helped you rid Elundium of the shadows, did not see battle's end as a parting of true friends, they felt betrayed, stripped of their rank and honour, deserted by the freedom you gave them. You sent them back to their homes to forage whatever living they could from the land because you no longer had a use for them. To make matters worse, that same morning, before the new shadows had grown a handspan longer, you gave Lord

Willow and those Tunnellers of his their freedom, the freedom to roam Elundium as they pleased, gardening and mowing the greenways as they travelled, living easily off the fat of the land with the right to demand a clean bed and a roof over their heads and as much food as they could eat wherever they chose to stop for the night. That, my lord, is the truth and the reason why so many of those warriors have disappeared since the Battle of the Rising. That is why the wayhouses have fallen into neglect. These people were proud fighting men, not innkeepers: they could not turn to everybody's beck and call. That is why there is nobody to keep law and order on the greenways' edge!'

'Then I say it is good riddance to them and all their treacheries . . .' Breakmaster began, only to have Thane cut him short with an angry glare.

The King clenched his fist and called down Mulcade from his perch high up amongst the rafters. He ruffled the owl's chest feathers and let his gaze travel across the silent, uncertain faces of his council. Why, he frowned, why had they kept him in ignorance, why had they allowed these lies and rumours to grow? There wasn't one of them in the Candlehall whom he wouldn't call a friend and yet they had left so much unsaid. Surely they were not afraid to speak out? How he hated the complexities of government, in which every word and gesture, no matter how well-intended, could so easily be misunderstood.

'Is it true, messenger?' he asked, quietly, turning on the horseman who stood before the roaring fire. 'Is it true that the warriors who helped me to win the daylight think that I have cast them aside? Is it true that the people of Elundium are envious of the meagre handfuls of food and shelter that I offered to Willow's people in return for their labour in clearing away the ruin and wildness that had run for so long unchecked, choking our beautiful land?'

Reluctantly the messenger nodded his head. 'Yes, my lord. Many of them speak out openly against your generosity to the Tunnellers. They say it has made them greedy, that they covet everything that doesn't belong to them. But their greatest fear, and I have heard this echoed in every wayhouse along the greenways' edge, is that the killing and stealing will escalate now that they have taken up with those foul Nightbeasts. They say that the Nightbeasts have been hiding, lurking deep in Meremire Forest ever since their defeat at the Battle of the Rising. The villagers fear for their lives now that there is nobody to protect them, except in Deepling. As I passed through the village I overheard somebody offering to protect travellers, but the villagers were very secretive when I pressed them on the matter.'

'Fools! These people don't need protection. Stupid, ignorant fools!' Thane cried angrily, making Mulcade shriek and spread his wings. 'Nothing could be further from the truth. The villagers should know that the Tunnellers have no need to steal from them. Why the daily clutter of our lives would only be a burden to them. It is their freedom, messenger, that they value above all things. Tell the villagers that. Tell that to the villagers as you journey back to Underfall . . .' Thane paused momentarily, distracted by the thickening nightshapes that were silently drifting into the Candlehall to swirl and dance around the flickering candle flames, intensifying the shadows. Lowering his voice, he continued uneasily, 'You must also try to make them understand that there is no truth in all these wild stories of nightcreatures roaming deep in Meremire or any other forest for that matter. Such rumours are nothing but fairy tales. Remind those rumour-mongers of battle's end, prompt them to remember how the last two Nightbeasts along with Arbel, Queen Elionbel's black-hearted brother, perished and shrivelled into nothing but dust when I stabbed Durondel's sword and the remnant of Krulshards' black malice into Kruel's footprints to give him a shadow. Let them cast their minds back and delve deep into those memories they so easily forget, let them find that moment when the winter sunlight first broke through the shadowlight. Remind them of that moment when I trapped Kruel with his own shadow and how he was reduced to an innocent baby, how his armies quailed then as they were defeated! Let them all remember how I lifted up that helpless infant from the bloody, trampled snow and everybody looked upon him. They will recall how I named him Krann and spared his life. Surely the people cannot have forgotten that this was the true end of all Krulshards' night creatures and a new beginning for us all?'

The messenger glanced uncomfortably around Candle-bane Hall. 'Lord, I know it to be true as do those few Marchers, Archers and Gallopers who have remained loyal to their pledges, but there are many who did not witness the triumph of battle's end and do not believe it truly happened like that. It is their doubt that has now been fuelled by rumours, ugly lies that say the end of the battle was steeped in magic, that trees came to life and shadows grew in the snow where none had existed before. They say that magic beguiled you from slaying Kruel and that he now lives simply disguised as Krann. They say that Elundium cannot be free of Krulshards' long shadow of terror until Krann is dead.'

For a moment the messenger's words seemed to drift slowly away until silence surrounded them. Thane stared at him, speechless, unable to believe what he had just heard. 'But . . . but . . . that is ridiculous! Absurd!' he stuttered. 'How could such an abomination of the truth have come about? Who would have spread such terrible lies? Surely the warriors who were there must have seen that the evil, the darkness, had left Krann's body, that he lay cradled in my hands in all innocence? The owls saw it, they saw it and welcomed my gesture of mercy towards the infant.'

'Lord, I do not know where those ugly lies had their beginnings but it was clear to see wherever I stopped to rest that they had shaken the people's belief in the new Elundium and filled them with terrible doubt. In the more remote villages I overheard many voices complaining that change is always for the worse and there were whispers everywhere calling for a return to the old ways when the Chancellors ruled in Candlebane Hall. That is the truth, that is what you have requested me to reveal.'

'So the people have chosen to shun and cast aside this new world free of fear that I have laboured so hard to give to them? They would rather eke out a shadowy existence beneath the Chancellors' cruel tyranny in which their lives are owed in barter from the moment they are born to the daylight they die? Well, I am sure that a Chancellor or two can be found lurking in some dark corner of Elundium who would be more than willing to yoke them into servitude. I am sure there is a Chancellor somewhere who would be quick to impose crippling taxes and grow rich and fat on their labour if that is the kind of world they would prefer to live in. If that is what they really want then they should have it!'

Thane's voice had hardened with anger and a sense of betrayal as he turned towards the waiting council.

'No, no, my lord, please do not abandon the people of

Elundium. Many of them are weak and afraid: they fear to speak out against these black lies. Lord, I beg you, find forgiveness in your heart for them, for there are many who love the world you have created from the ruin and chaos of the shadowlight but they dare not speak out openly in these troubled times. They fear being cast out of the villages, they fear they would have to fend for themselves in what is rapidly becoming a hostile and dangerous world.'

'What would you have me do, messenger? Would you have me ride out surrounded by the few Marchers, Archers and Gallopers who serve me in this city to give these doubting villagers a mock show of strength? Haven't we enough problems to cope with as we try to get to the bottom of this trouble? Has Errant entrusted you with any private messages for me? Has he told you anything relating to the Tunnellers' escape? I fear they may be the victims of some dark plot but I can't see how or for what purpose – unless . . .?' Suddenly Thane paused and strode away into the shadows. 'Unless . . .' he frowned, but no, it wasn't possible, it couldn't be that the Tunnellers were really causing all this trouble. It was ridiculous even to consider that they could be trying to undermine everything they had worked so hard to create. It didn't make any sense. He shook his head, but a new worry pressed in on him. What should he do about Krann? Now that he knew that the people feared him and wanted him dead he had to do something.

'Lord, a moment please!' the messenger called, breaking into his thoughts. Errant had cautioned him to speak only to the King and he wondered how sharp the councillors' ears were in the odd, echoing silence of the Candlehall or how much they could be trusted to keep to themselves anything they might overhear. He was certain he could trust Breakmaster and Greygoose but there were others, faces in the shadowy background, that he did not know or recognize. He lowered his voice conspiratorially to a whisper and kept his back to the others as he spoke.

'I do bring private messages from Errant, my lord. The written dispatch in my pouch reports that the Tunnellers evaded capture and vanished and tells that they are somewhere in the wild grasslands to the east but Errant is certain that they are trying to reach Cawdor. It is just as the owl who flew with them foretold as they escaped from the Granite City. But he warned me to tell you that it is anybody's guess whether they ever reached their journey's end or found that lost road through the Emerald Mountains which legend tells leads to Cawdor. They will be very lucky to survive the savage blizzards that sweep down through the high passes they will have to cross.'

'Is there anything else Errant told you to report? Did the Tunnellers try to stop or ask for help in any of the villages?' Thane asked as the messenger caught his breath.

'No, my lord. I rode with the pursuing Gallopers so I know that they kept well away from everybody and used only the wild and overgrown paths. Errant marked their path clearly but we kept well back throughout the pursuit as you commanded, which raised more than a few comments I may add. The Gallopers under his command were puzzled when on more than one occasion he could so easily have closed the gap and captured them but he had to refrain. We all knew that the old Marcher who was riding with them would not have surrendered without a fight, but it was that small crippled boy, the sweep's scuttle, who slowed them down. He looked so awkward perched in the saddle, hanging on for dear life. He wouldn't have managed it at all if one of the Tunnellers hadn't constantly been at his side helping him.'

Thane smiled at the messenger as he mentioned Drib. He remembered quite clearly coming upon the boy as he lay injured in the gutter, bullied and persecuted by the other boys in the Learning Hall because of his wild, impossible dreams that one daylight he would be able to ride upon a horse. It had been so easy for him to make that dream come true that morning as he lifted him up and set his crooked legs across Esteron's saddle but now, by escaping with the Tunnellers, Drib had really made his dream become reality. Esteron, the Lord of Horses, would never have allowed him to fall, but riding one of the Nighthorses along the greenways was a different thing altogether. There had been a strength and determination in the boy, a straightforward honesty, that he had glimpsed through the layers of dirt and grime that morning: perhaps if he survived the winter, he would have some part to play in the troubled daylights ahead.

'And you are sure that nobody saw which road they took beyond the last lamp at World's End, save for Errant of course?'

The messenger nodded and drew closer. 'Errant broke off the pursuit within sight of the doors of Underfall but early the next daylight, before the grey hours had left the sky, he selected four of his most trustworthy Gallopers, and I was lucky enough to be one of them. We picked up the Tunnellers' tracks on the edge of the heather meadows and followed them up across the bleak shoulders of Manterns Mountain close to the ruined Gates of Night and into the wilderness beyond until they disappeared into a deep ravine walled in by sheer, wind-cracked crags and towering spires of ice. It looked like the beginning of what once must have been a very ancient road leading directly into the heart of the Emerald Mountains. The weather was worsening with the scent of blizzards in the bitter, winter wind and Errant wisely called off the pursuit after carefully marking the entrance to the ravine. That, my lord, is all there is to tell.'

Thane murmured his thanks to the messenger and signalled the servers forward with the hot pottage and mulled ale they had brought for the weary horseman. He turned towards the waiting council, at a loss to know what to do. It seemed that the whole of Elundium was turning against him.

Breakmaster interrupted his thoughts: 'We must find somewhere safe for Krann while we search for the treacherous troublemakers who have been spreading these slanderous lies.'

Thane looked up at the old horseman, his own face drawn and tight with the sudden realization that it would probably be impossible to find a simple, straightforward answer. It wasn't just the envy and jealousy the people of Elundium felt against the Tunnellers, or the various misunderstandings of the freedoms he had bestowed upon them, or any one of all the other rumours, or even the mutterings of discontent that the messenger had faithfully reported to him. No, these were only symptoms, they were not the true malady that was strangling Elundium and drawing it back down into chaos. The real cause of the sickness ran much deeper and he had been a fool not to see it in the beginning or realize its significance at once. The sunlight he won at the Battle of the Rising and his new way of doing things just wasn't enough to have prevented this. It never could be, not while night still followed daylight and he could never change that. It was the people's ingrained fear of the dark he had foolishly ignored. From the beginning of time itself they had been taught that beasts inhabited the night. The people thought they were as much an essential part of the fabric of darkness as the nightshapes who carried it in their silent, swirling, gliding forms, only they believed them to be much more terrifying as they stalked and prowled the dead hours of the night beyond the door.

Thane sighed. Had he done the wrong thing when he had spared Kruel's life by sewing his shadow into his footprints and renaming him Krann? The more Thane turned the thought over in his mind the more convinced he became that he had been right to show mercy and spare Krann's life. But it was easy to see now why the people doubted his promises of a world free of fear. It had been easy for him: he feared nothing that moved in the dark . . .

Perhaps, he pondered, perhaps he had been too quick to strip away the old rituals. The people lived by them, perhaps he should have spent more time trying to riddle out the structure and rhythms of their lives before he turned them upside down. After all, he could hear them say, kings come and go but . . .' Chancellors!' he muttered grimly. They had kept the curfews and rhythms of the people's lives firmly in check and it had worked, though in a hard and cruel way. They had grown fat and greedy in the process but they had ensured that there were always Marchers garrisoned in the wayhouses and Gallopers enough to patrol the greenways. The people had paid dearly for their safety then and he had tried to sweep away the burden of the old system with bold promises but he obviously hadn't been able to keep them. Thinking back, he could see his first error. It had been when the proclamation of his kingship still echoed across the Causeway Field and he was heady with victory. He had been naïve to promise the people a world free of fear as he had held up the severed head of Krulshards, the master of nightmares. It had seemed the right thing to do then. He had thought he could hold the world in the palm of his hand and yet before the ashes of Krulshards' funeral pyre had the chance to blow away, Kruel, his bastard offspring, had risen up out of the shadows to spread the terror of the shadowlight across Elundium.

Thane shook his head. He had no intention of going back on that act of mercy; Krann was innocent of any blame. He would not sacrifice the boy to appease the people's fears. The child was as pure as the driven snow they had fought upon, and anyway, he reasoned, the Battle Owls were sharp-eyed – they could hunt the Nightbeasts, especially Mulcade, the chief loft-master, who had stayed with him long after the other owls had returned to their wild freedom. He would surely have spotted the slightest hint of darkness in the child as he grew up – or would he? Thane twisted his head and looked hard into Mulcade's blinkless eyes and doubt clouded his thoughts. What if, with the passing of King Holbian, the last of the Granite Kings, and the end of Nevian's magic, the owls had lost their power to root out the dark scent of Krulshards' evil? Just because they could no longer sense it would not necessarily mean it was not there. What if there was a grain of truth in the people's fear? What if a single seed of that dark evil he thought he had destroyed had, in fact, survived and was now growing, spreading its tentacles unseen inside the child. What if there was a malignant growth so secret that even he wasn't aware of its existence?

Another thought suddenly struck him so hard it nearly took his breath away. What if, by some wild improbability, the darkness that might dwell in Krann had given off the scent of evil that could have drawn the surviving Nightbeasts into the Granite City and not, as everybody had so wrongly guessed, their desire to break out the Tunnellers. It would certainly explain why night creatures had emerged from deep in Meremire Forest and the guards who kept watch over the Tunnellers swore they had seen Nightbeasts swarming in the courtyard of Candlebane Hall and in the alleyways below the armoury. Much as he had no desire to believe in their existence he had inspected the scuffs and scrapes that their feet had made upon the cobbles and he couldn't deny that some foul creatures had certainly breached the gates of the city. He had been bewildered about why they had made no attempt to escape with the Tunnellers or why they had not left the city during the dead hours of the night but perhaps the real purpose, once awoken, was to stay as close to Krann as they could, waiting for the moment when the darkness would suddenly flower?

The faint sound of running footsteps and childish laughter came from the corridor outside the Candlehall and broke into his thoughts, and then he heard his wife, Elionbel, calling out his name and he spun round just in time to see the two of them appear – her and little Krann – hand in hand, in the open doorway. Elionbel smiled and gently reminded Thane that the bell summoning everyone to evening fare in the banqueting hall had been rung some time ago and his guests were waiting for him at the tables. 'You haven't forgotten, have you? Surely you must remember we have a merchants' feast?'

Mulcade hooted a welcome and rose from Thane's

shoulder to swoop between the tall, flickering candle flames that illuminated the hall, scattering the swirling nightshapes before settling on Krann's outstretched arm, making the boy laugh with delight as he ruffled the owl's feathers. Thane watched for a moment and a smile softened his face as doubt fled from his heart. He knew he had made the right decision when he had spared the child's life at battle's end, and he would lose no more time worrying about it. If there was the slightest echo of Krulshards' evil still within him then Mulcade would most certainly have sensed it long ago.

Krann advanced into the Candlehall, the owl upon his arm and his eyes wide with curiosity as he spotted the dusty messenger. 'Have you ridden all the way from Underfall?' he asked, staring at his travel-stained clothes.

Before the messenger could answer, the boy continued, breathlessly, 'Errant brought me a pony from Underfall, he's called Fleetfoot. He is really beautiful but I can't ride him yet. Some horrible people – nightcreatures or something – broke into the stable and hurt him. But Breakmaster says he'll be better soon. When he's well I'm going to . . .'

'That's enough, Krann,' Elionbel chided the boy gently, taking his hand in hers. 'I'm sure the council has a thousand important matter to discuss. Come, I'll ask if the messenger can be seated beside you at supper time.'

'Guests? Yes, of course, it's the Honourable Merchants' Feast. I am sorry, my dear, it had been driven from my mind completely. Please beg their indulgence and ask them to forgive my temporary absence. Tell them we will not be many more moments dealing with affairs of state and then we will follow in your footsteps.'

Thane's face grew serious as he watched the two of

them leave the Candlehall but he hesitated to speak until the echo of their footsteps had faded into the night. He quickly drew Breakmaster and the other members of the council around him and called the messenger to attend. 'You are right, Breakmaster,' he spoke quietly, keeping a wary eye on the shadows that lurked in the corners of the Candlehall. 'But it isn't only Krann we must get away from here: I fear for Elionbel. You must remember Arbel, her brother, was consumed by Kruel's evil as the shadowlight spread and there are blood-ties that bind her to Krann. We must get them both to safety.'

'But where? Where can we find such a place? If the messenger has told us the truth and all those warriors who once manned the wayhouses have really deserted, then where can they go?' asked Arach.

'There is always Underfall, my lord,' the messenger offered quickly. 'And there would be no safer place in the whole world: Thunderstone and Errant would see to that.'

'Yes, yes, of course, I know they would defend the two of them with their lives,' Thane murmured reluctantly. 'But I would have preferred somewhere closer to the Granite City, and slightly more.' he paused, searching for the words that would describe that cold, bleak fortress perched high above the Causeway Fields, where the tomb of the Granite Kings lay in the shadows of the storm-racked shoulders of Manterns Mountain and guarded the ancient road that led up across the heather meadows to the ruined Gates of Night. He did not wish to offend those who lived and served there and he knew well that Thunderstone, the keeper of the great lamp, would not take too kindly to the fortress being called inhospitable, but Thane knew from experience that there wasn't a draughtier or colder place in all Elundium. But there were other reasons why he would hesitate to send Elionbel and Krann to Underfall, no matter how safe they would be there. Elionbel had once been held prisoner in one of its darkest dungeons during the worst of the daylights of the shadowlight when Kruel's shadowrats had overrun the fortress. He doubted that she would welcome being sent there. And there was another reason. He didn't want Krann going to Underfall, because of its proximity to the Gates of Night and the vast, empty, echoing City of Darkness where Krulshards' Nightbeasts had been spawned. Just in case there was a single seed of that darkness still lying undiscovered somewhere within the boy.

'I am sure you would prefer somewhere more homely for the lady Elionbel, my lord,' Breakmaster suggested, his voice filling the expanding silence.

'Yes, yes, you're right, somewhere more homely. Perhaps where there are children for Krann to play with. I sometimes worry that his life has become very isolated here in the Towers of Granite. But where can we find such a place?'

The members of the council looked blankly from one to the other, murmuring names and places only to shake their heads as they tried to think of somewhere else.

'You could send them to the Wayhouse Tower on Stumble Hill, my lord,' the messenger suggested. 'The Archers there have stayed loyal to a man. Lord Kyot and Lady Eventine would not have a bad word said against you. In fact, on the night I stopped to rest my horse there the talk at evening fare was full of how the three of you fought side by side and I lost count of the times a glass was raised in your honour.'

'Why yes, of course, the Wayhouse Tower! How could

I have forgotten? Kyot and Eventine would keep them both safe. There are no truer or better friends in the face of adversity!' Thane exclaimed.

'And there is Fairlight, their daughter. She is younger than Krann by one sun but by all accounts she bubbles with life just like her mother.'

A smile tugged at the whiskery wrinkles around the old horseman's mouth as he wistfully whispered Eventine's name. His eyes misted over with the memories of that special daylight when all Elundium had been summoned to witness Nevian, the Master of Magic, bind the love ties between King Thane and the Lady Elionbel. He remembered the noise, the bustle and the splendour of the occasion when everybody had dressed in their finest silks and gowns. There had been the glitter of sunlight on polished mail and sounds of laughter and shouts of joy from the crowds that lined the way leading through the city. The horses had pawed sparks from the cobbles as they tossed their heads and showed off their silver-threaded battle-plaits that had been so proudly woven into their manes by the Gallopers who rode them. Warhorses and Border Runners had thronged the great doors of Candlebane Hall and stoops of Battle Owls had wheeled and turned above the waiting crowds.

Breakmaster laughed softly, the sound chuckling deeply in his throat, the memories of that wonderful daylight were still so sharp. He remembered the city folk as they began to shuffle and grow impatient in the shafts of dusty sunlight that shone through the Candlehall. Their voices had risen in whispered mutterings of fear and curiosity because none had dared openly to question Nevian who stood wrapped in his rainbow cloak as to why he hesitated to start the King's wedding. Thane had already led Elionbel into the hall and her trailing dress had held the daylight, capturing it in each tiny, sparkling thread as they waited close to the great doors. The bright morning sun seemed to burn upon the bodice and cool starlight seemed to have been threaded into the flowing hem. Lace so delicate and spider-fine had been etched across the blue velvet, telling the story of Thane's triumph over the darkness, and with each halting step she took countless peacocks' eyes that had been needled into the weave of the gown appeared to stare out at the waiting crowds.

Nevian had looked up suddenly, staring over the heads of the crowd towards the open doors and a smile had broken out on his ancient face. Breakmaster remembered how he had instinctively turned his head as he caught the faint sound of hoofbeats rising to a gale of thunder as they raced across the bridge that spanned Swanwater and arrived at the doors of the Candlehall. Then the crowds had shrunk back in fear as Tanglecrown, the Lord of Stags, Eventine's mount, had passed between the great doors to halt before Elionbel. He knelt and swept his huge stand of antlers, each tip encased in crystal, in a huge arc and then held them statue-still for Elionbel to place her hand between the razor tips on his soft forehead.

'Tanglecrown lead us forward. Lord of Stags, light the shadows of Candlebane Hall,' she had said. 'Eventine, I feared you would come too late.'

Before she could continue Nevian had appeared by her side and taken her hand to lead her up onto the high dais where Thane waited and the ceremony had begun.

Breakmaster smiled at the memories. Eventine's clothes had been travel-stained by the hard ride from Clatterford but they could not diminish her beauty and as she clasped Kyot's hand and whispered something to him, pulling him close to her, her face had shone with some inner light that had made it difficult for Breakmaster to pull his eyes away. The people had already begun to chant the wedding ties as Nevian joined Thane and Elionbel's hands together when the Master of Magic had suddenly paused and brought the crowds in the Candlehall to complete silence before he called out, 'There are two others who should be love-bound. They are here in the Candlehall.' He slowly turned his head, searching the crowd and his eyes had smiled as he caught sight of Eventine. 'Come forward, Lady of Clatterford, bowmaiden of Elundium.'

'Lord I . . . I . . . I . . .' She had stepped backwards in confusion and clutched at her dusty, travel-marked clothing. Breakmaster remembered so clearly seeing her look of panic and he had hurried forward, deftly unbuckling her dirty cloak and casting it aside, and its place he had spread the steel-silver battlecoat that King Holbian had once pledged into his keeping. It was the most precious thing he possessed and as it spread across her shoulders it made her beauty shine out in the shadowy hall.

'Go, go forward now,' he had whispered to her. 'There is none more worthy, my beautiful Lady of Clatterford, no one has more right to wear this gift from a king that I have put about your shoulders. It shimmers with all the colours of a summer's day. Listen and as you move lark song and meadow thrush music will be with each graceful step you take.'

Kyotorm, the first bowmaster of Elundium and Keeper of the Tower on Stumble Hill knew the measure of the gift and had gripped Breakmaster's arm in silent thanks before leading Eventine forward to where Nevian waited with Thane and Elionbel. Breakmaster sighed and smiled as his memories faded. The tower on Stumble Hill would probably be the safest place for Elionbel and Krann until they got to the bottom of the troubles.

'Yes, Stumble Hill it will be,' Thane decided. 'We will journey there without any delay. Breakmaster, gather what escort you can and have Esteron, Stumble and the safest pony you have ready to ride in the courtyard of the Towers of Granite one hour before daybreak. The sooner they are away from here the better it will be. We'll ride out as the criers herald a new daylight.'

'But surely, my lord, such a procession is bound to arouse suspicion amongst the people, especially if all these rumours are true. They are sure to think the worst if word gets out that you are escorting Lady Elionbel and Krann to somewhere safe. The people are close to rioting as it is and it is so soon after the Tunnellers escaped that they are still worried about the nightcreatures and you wouldn't want them to get wind of what you are doing would you? They might follow you to Stumble Hill and then . . .' the old horseman fell into silence.

Thane turned angrily but he saw the sense in Breakmaster's words. 'Well, what would you have me do? Do you want me to sit here idly while a handful of Gallopers escort my family to Stumble Hill? Why, anything might happen and I want to be with them.'

Thane threw up his hands in helplessness as he paced backward and forward between the tall, fluted candlestands.

'But yes, you are right, Breakmaster,' he conceded eventually. 'But how would you propose to spirit them away without anybody noticing? Can you tell me?'

Breakmaster thought for a moment, stroking his whiskers, and then he laughed, 'Why that's easy, my lord. We will travel in disguise, just the three of us, and we will go when the Stumble Gate is at its busiest, at noon, when it is thronged with merchants and journeymen nobody will take much notice of us amongst all that hustle and bustle.'

'Such a plan would be madness – utter madness! How could you hope to protect them on the journey if you are on your own? Haven't you listened to what the messenger has told us of how wild and dangerous the greenways have become? No, I will not hear another word of such a venture!'

'Stumble Hill is on my way back to Underfall and there are others who would protect Krann and the Queen, my lord. Greygoose, the Captain of Archers, would ride with us and if you ask Mulcade will fly with us and use his sharp eyes to watch the road and there will be Border Runners and Warhorses. I'm sure they will come to our aid if Mulcade calls to them.' Breakmaster was keen and the scent of adventure was fresh in his nostrils.

Reluctantly Thane nodded. 'I will speak privately to the Lady Elionbel and if she is in agreement with this wild scheme then you will ride out tomorrow at the noonday bell and we will create a diversion with every loyal guard we have.'

Thane turned on his heel and hurried towards the doorway that led to the great banqueting hall but the last thing on his mind was entertaining the honourable merchants. He stopped abruptly in the entrance and turned back, holding the members of the council with a hard look as they prepared to follow him. 'Not one word of this will be uttered beyond these doors. Remember, Elionbel and Krann's lives will depend upon your secrecy and their safety will hang in your silence.'

Greygoose's attention had sharpened as the messenger

suggested that he ride with the escort to Stumble Hill. Perhaps now he would find out more about where his son, Eider, had disappeared to. He fell into step with the messenger and drew him aside as the council members began to hurry after the King. 'A moment please, I beg you. Will our journey take us anywhere near the route the Tunnellers took?' he whispered, glancing anxiously over his shoulder to ensure they could not be overheard. 'You rode with Captain Errant – do you know which way they went?'

The messenger nodded curtly, his eyes narrowing as he wondered what the Archer wanted of him and then he remembered that Errant had pledged him to secrecy.

Greygoose wrung his hands together and asked, 'Did you see anything of my son, Eider – only the stupid boy was reported as having being seen fleeing with those wretched Tunnellers. I'm so worried about him, he is so headstrong and there's no knowing what trouble he will get himself into if he's mixed up with that bunch of ruffians and villains.'

The messenger could see the anxiety and distress etched deeply into the Archer's face and hesitated for only a moment before deciding it could do no harm to tell him what he knew about the boy since they would soon be riding in escort together. 'He was carrying two bows and quivers full of arrows. For all the hardships they had suffered on the road he looked fit and well. You shouldn't worry yourself about him.'

'But he must know I'll forgive him whatever he did wrong. Why doesn't he come back? Why does he stay with them? How will they survive the winter?'

The messenger leaned closer and tried to ease Greygoose's fears. 'We followed their tracks to the entrance of an ancient road that led up into the Emerald Mountains. Errant told me that it leads to Cawdor, a place that is wrapped in old legends. There is a good chance that they will be able to weather out the winter there if they reach it before the blizzards close the road. But tell nobody what I have just told you – none but the King knows of its existence.'

'Cawdor – Cawdor, will our journey take us anywhere near it?' Greygoose asked. The messenger hurried to catch up with Breakmaster and shook his head. But Greygoose turned the name over and over in his mind until it touched a hidden chord deep down in his memory and he thought back to his dusty daylights in the Learning Hall and once more he caught the Loremaster's words. He paused, alarmed by the messenger's revelation about Eider's possible whereabouts and let the other council members get well ahead of him on their way to the banqueting hall. He needed a moment to think. He realized that the name of the place wasn't enough: he had to know where it was and if his son would be safe there. But how could he find out?

He hurried to the closest tall, narrow casement window and stood peering out into the vast, empty darkness before slowly letting his gaze drop to the thousands of frost-glittering roofs and the flickering lamps set out on the city walls. He looked at the chaotic forest of smoking chimney pots and to the city spread out below Candlebane Hall. Where did Cawdor lie? Who would know? Suddenly he picked out the steep, gabled roof of the Learning Hall shuttered and wrapped in gloomy shadows as it stood towering over the houses that crowded around it. The fountainhead of all knowledge! Of course, Loremaster Grout would know! Surely it wouldn't do any harm to ask him, after all he must know if anybody did. He was the wisest and most learned man in all Elundium and who else but a Loremaster could be trusted with secrets? Why, they had a fingertip on everything that happened, they were the confidants of kings whose ancient guild had written the books of lore that governed their lives. Yes, he decided with a slight nod of his head, he would ask him at the first opportunity.

Krann had barely been able to contain his excitement all morning, especially when Elionbel had brought him some thick, homespun winter-warm riding clothes with a grey woollen cloak that had a large hood that almost completely hid his face. She had put her finger to her lips to stop his stream of questions and told him to change into them and to keep away from the windows. He'd got the first hint that something special was going on that involved him the previous evening during the banquet. The messenger had been sat next to him, as Elionbel had promised, but he had refused to be drawn by his questions about the great ride from Underfall and all the wonderful things he must have seen along the way. He had merely laughed at the boy's barrage of questions and had told him to be patient, drawing close to him and whispering conspiratorially that he would find out for himself probably much sooner than he imagined. Sleep had taken its time to come to the boy that night and he had tossed and turned beneath his feather quilt listening to the crackle of the frost spreading its icy fingers across the walls and windowpanes of his sleeping chamber and tried to imagine what was going on. There had been hurried footsteps in the darkness outside his door and urgent whispers. Once he thought he had caught the sound of his name on Elionbel's voice. She had sounded close to tears and he was sure he had heard Thane trying to calm her.

Krann hesitated in the shadows of the huge ironwood doors of the Towers of Granite. The cold morning wind ruffled his snow-white hair and he was afraid, unsure of what was happening as he held on tightly to Elionbel's hand. It was one thing wanting to have an adventure but quite another being drawn into one, knowing it was beginning all around you, but nobody would tell you what it was all about. He heard voices in the courtyard below, which sounded like those of Thane and Breakmaster, and they were talking in urgent undertones and there was a clatter of horses' shoes on the cobbles. Curiosity quickly got the better of his apprehension and he stepped forward, his pale blue eyes round and shining with excitement. There, at the bottom of the broad granite steps, he saw Breakmaster mounted on Beaconlight and Thane on Esteron engaging the old horseman in last-minute instructions. Stumble, Elionbel's horse and a small, sturdy, dark bay pony stood ready-saddled and waiting beside Greygoose and the messenger who had the reins of their horses gathered and held easily in his left hand. Krann could see at a glance that the horses were ready for a long journey. There were thick, fur-lined rugs bound into tight rolls and securely strapped with leather thongs behind the cantle of each saddle and each horse carried a bulging saddle-bag of fodder for the journey. Drinking flagons hung down against the horses' flanks. Breakmaster caught sight of Krann at the top of the steps and laughed as he beckoned him to come down.

'So, we are going on a journey! Is that pony for me? Why, he's so beautiful – what's his name? Where are we going? You must tell me, you must. It's so exciting!' he cried, breaking free from Elionbel's hand and running down the steps towards the waiting party.

'One thing at a time, one thing at a time!' Thane laughed as he vaulted lightly to the ground and caught Krann up in his arms, lifting the boy off his feet and swinging him around. 'Yes, you are going on a journey, my boy, it's high time you saw the greenways' edge, but one thing at a time!' He set the boy into the pony's saddle and his face grew serious as he fitted the child's feet into the small, ornate stirrups. Slowly he gathered up the reins and pressed them into Krann's hands. 'You are going to accompany Elionbel, Breakmaster and the messenger on a long journey but first you must promise me that you will do everything they ask you to do, and you must stay close to them at all times. First winter's snow is on the hedgerows and the greenways are no place to . . .' He paused, what could he tell a child of the dangers he might be facing once he rode beyond the great gates of the city? What could he say of the vile rumours and gossip that he was trying to protect him from? He sighed and glanced anxiously around the courtyard. It was probably best to tell him nothing, enable him to make his escape from the city a game and keep his innocence for as long as possible. Tell him nothing of the black, malignant growth of mistrust that dwelt in people's hearts.

A movement from high up in the tower caught Thane's eyes: the striker was raising his hammer to strike the noonday bell; he knew the journey must begin now if it was to start at all, for they had to leave while the city gates were thronged with the noonday crowds. Thane smiled at

Krann and gently pulled the hood of his cloak up over the top of his head so that it hid his tousled, white-blond hair and almost concealed his face in shadow. Lowering his voice he said, 'I want you to play a game of hide and seek with me. I shall follow you on Esteron and will try and spot you leaving the city. You must try to slip out unnoticed between Elionbel and Breakmaster. The messenger will ride a pace behind you and tell me if you try and look round to see me. He will judge who wins this game!'

'Oh yes, what fun, of course I'll play!' Krann cried, eager to start as Breakmaster spurred Beaconlight in close beside him, clipping a lead rein onto his pony's bridle. 'But where are we going? And what is my pony's name?'

'Patience, Krann. Your pony's name is Larksong, ride him well and I will tell you where we're going once we're clear of the city,' the old horseman grinned with a conspiratorial wink as he led the procession slowly forwards beneath the archway.

Krann glanced up at Breakmaster and saw the flash of a mailshirt and the hilt of a long Galloper's sword and dagger hidden beneath his cloak. The boy guessed that this would be no ordinary game of hide and seek and he watched as Thane helped Elionbel onto Stumble and grasped her hand, entwining his fingers in his as he drew her hood down over her head and quickly kissed her forehead. The noonday bell struck the hour and Stumble fretted to follow the other horses beneath the archway.

'Send word as soon as you can to tell me you are safe. I shall be thinking of you every moment.'

Elionbel turned slightly in the saddle and kissed her hand in parting, her eyes full of tears as she drew her cloak back to reassure him that she was carrying the same long dagger that she had worn at her belt at the Battle of the Rising, and beside it she had the small pouch of nightflower seeds should darkness overtake them on the road. Mulcade swooped silently to Thane's shoulder but kept his wings outspread as the party disappeared beneath the archway. 'Go, follow them, great bird of war. Fly high and watch over their journey lest danger lurks in the shadows. Forewarn the Border Runners and the warhorses that Elionbel and Krann are in need of their protection. Fly . . . fly . . . keep them both safe for me.'

Mulcade rose hooting shrilly as Esteron neighed and reared before surging forward to follow the other horses but Thane held the Lord of Horses still. 'No, dear friend, we must stay, they must make this journey alone.'

He turned and cantered up to the highest battlements of the city where he stood, statue-still to watch the small group ride into the distance as the afternoon shadows gathered.

Thane shivered as the first evening stars twinkled in the sky and the nightshapes began to draw the early winter darkness across dyke and hedgerow but as he turned Esteron and urged him to retrace his steps to Candlebane Hall his eyes paused, for a moment, and gazed at the far horizon line that was merging into the darkness. He couldn't help wondering if the Tunnellers accompanied by that old rebellious Marcher, Berioss, and that crooked chimney-sweep's boy had ever managed to reach Cawdor. He smiled, remembering that the Master Armourer had informed him that they had stolen a collection of mock armour pieces made by the apprentices some hundreds of suns before. There was enough for each one of them to wear during their escape but he couldn't see what use it would be to them. The Tunnellers were not knights or warriors: they were peaceful gardeners. Drib, for all his dreams, would never be able to twist and turn and wield a blade with those crooked legs. And then he remembered Nevian's words of warning, as his translucent shape wrapped in the melting rainbow colours, had appeared briefly in his chamber just as the troubles began. 'Beware of false friends. Be slow to judge those who are brought in chains before you.'

Thane wondered about the Tunnellers, were they really his allies? Were they really the innocent ones in all this chaos and turmoil?

III

Hunting
Nightboar

CROOKED DRIB shivered, his fingers numb from the bitter cold as he looked dubiously ahead at the still gaunt, winter trees which were shrouded beneath their glittering layers of frost and snow. A heavy, oppressive silence seemed to be closing in all around them, muffling the rhythmical jingling of the horses' bit-rings and the soft creak of their harness as they rode through the snow towards the petrified forest. Drib sensed that they were being watched. There were eyes in the shadows between the trees but they vanished as soon as he tried to get a better look at them. He was beginning to get a really bad feeling about the Nightboar hunt and wished he hadn't so readily volunteered to go with Eider. It was beginning to dawn on him that they were both likely to get more than they bargained for but the others were depending on them to find food and bring it back to Cawdor. They would all starve it they failed – it was too late to turn back now.

Suddenly he remembered those stories that Loremaster Grout had woven in the dusty, noonday light of the Learning Hall, stories of the great Nightboar hunts during the time of the Granite Kings, stories of how whole companies of Gallopers and strikes of Archers would pursue the creatures through Manterns Forest until the exhausted beasts, their hides pierced through with dozens of broken spear shafts and arrows, were cornered. He remembered hearing how that then they would sometimes turn and charge at their hunters, goring the horses, trampling and scattering the archers before they were eventually killed. Bleakly Drib wondered if Eider remembered any of the stories and if he had any idea how they were supposed to kill one of those enormous, savage creatures.

Drib swallowed nervously as he crouched low in Sparkfire's saddle, keeping a tight hold on the bow that Eider had given him, while with his other hand he hung onto the pommel of the saddle to keep his balance. His crooked legs were sticking out at odd angles and he tried to draw them in to prevent them from striking the trees as the horse surged forward following Eider's mount beneath the dark, forbidding eaves of the forest. The heavy quiver of arrows cut painfully into his back but there wasn't time to adjust it. He caught sight of a dark shape out of the corner of his eye and heard an almost silent flutter of wings as Silkstone, the owl who had helped him to escape from the Granite City, flew down to his shoulder.

'I'm not really cut out for this!' he whispered, happier now that he had the owl with him.

Silkstone hooted softly, rubbing his beak reassuringly against the boy's cheek before staring out into the thickening gloom beneath the trees. Suddenly the owl gave a warning hoot and squeezed his talons onto Drib's shoulder before lifting silently and flying on ahead.

The horse snorted, its ears flattening, and Drib caught the strong, pungent odour of the beast they were hunting for the first time. A knot of fear tightened in his stomach. 'I must be mad! Why didn't I tell the others that I am no archer? Why did I pretend?' he muttered to himself as his horse pushed its way through the undergrowth and he only just ducked his head in time to avoid the brittle vines and razor-sharp flowerheads of the frozen orchids that trailed in profusion from the overhead branches. The lowest vines grazed lightly across the top of his head, sprinkling a fine shower of frost and ice crystals down his neck. He shivered as he took a last, quick look over his shoulder back through the trees towards the ruins of Cawdor, now a distant, misty silhouette crouching beneath the shadows of the endless clouds of crying seabirds that wheeled and circled above it. He caught a glimpse of the ancient Marcher, Berioss, who had been falsely accused of high treason for helping the Tunnellers and who had helped them all escape from the cellars beneath Candlebane Hall. The old man was still standing between the riven doors of the ruined fortress where they had left him. He had looked so worried as they rode away that, for a moment, Drib had expected him to stop them. At the time the boy would have been disappointed if the Marcher had sent them after easier quarry – but now he wished that he had.

He also wished that he'd had the courage to tell the others the truth about that lucky arrow he had loosed at the Nightbeast. The creature had appeared so suddenly, snarling and drooling, crowding the staircase above the cellar, blocking off their escape – in truth, a blind man couldn't have missed that hideous creature. He should have told the others that he had never handled a bow before. Archery wasn't a skill that ragged, chimney sweeps' apprentices were allowed to acquire, especially crippled ones. But it had been so wonderful to hear Berioss praise him as the Nightbeast went crashing backwards into the courtyard. Nothing like that had ever happened to him before, but he doubted that he could aim another arrow at an enraged Nightboar which may be charging at them through the undergrowth. He doubted if he could nock an arrow onto the bow-string correctly in the first place!

Sparkfire took him deeper into the trees and his view of the fortress of Cawdor vanished from sight. Drib concentrated, staring ahead. He had to think more positively; it was no good worrying about failing before they had even sighted the creature.

'Eider!' he called out, trying to dredge up his courage. 'Nobody in the Learning Hall will ever believe that we actually reached the dark side of morning will they? And to think that the sound of all those voices crying in the wind was only birds . . .!'

'Shut up and pay attention if you want any supper! Your infernal chattering is enough to frighten away the deafest animal!' Eider hissed at him.

Suddenly the older boy slipped his reins down onto his horse's neck, his heartbeats quickening as he reached for an arrow. With expert fingers he nocked it onto the bow-string. There was something moving through the undergrowth: he could hear its muffled, snuffling snorts. He knew he had to be careful, he remembered the stories his father had told him of hunting the Nightboar; how, without a moment's warning the creature could turn and charge at its attackers, savaging and killing anyone it could reach.

Drib heard the sound of the creature grunting and crashing through the trees ahead of them and his heart sank into his boots. He could imagine its enormous, muscular body with its rough, prickly, armoured hide. He could almost see its ugly head with its two, small, mean, murderous eyes set well back on either side of its long snout and the two huge tusks curling up out of its lower jaw.

'Halt, Sparkfire!'

His voice was a dry whisper as he reached back into the quiver with fumbling fingers for an arrow.

Eider hesitated, remembering something else that his father had told him about hunting Nightboar. Something really important. He had said that it didn't really matter how many arrows were loosed at one of these savage, short-sighted creatures, or what number of spear blades were driven into its sides as it blundered away from the huntsmen to hide in the forest, there was only one, small, vulnerable spot in its enormous, prickly, armoured hide where it could be killed – but that place was no larger than the King's smallest silver finger bowl and it was set high up in a shallow well-protected depression between its powerful shoulder blades. And that spot was usually visible only to the hunters as the beast turned to charge its pursuers.

Cold sweat began to bead on Eider's forehead as he drew the bow-string taut. He didn't know if he would recognize the place to aim the arrow at let alone have the courage to stand his ground if the creature charged at him. With a knot of fear winding itself tighter in his stomach he listened to the sounds of the animal's approach and watched the thick, tangled undergrowth that fringed the clearing only a few paces ahead as it swayed and shifted. Eider forced himself to sit statue-still, his legs pressed tightly against the knee-rolls of Nightshade's saddle, as the feathered flight of the arrow held between his first two fingers of his right hand brushed lightly against his cheek. His toes were curled with the tension of the moment and his breaths were short and ragged. Time seemed frozen and he felt lightheaded with fear. He could feel his horse's heart pumping between his thighs and smell the sweet scent of its sweat drying on its shoulders.

The undergrowth rustled and suddenly the bushes were forced roughly apart. Vines and branches snapped and were tossed aside, but some remained hanging, entangled with leaves and flowerheads, from the two, long, yellowing, curved tusks as the beast emerged snorting and scenting the ground, oblivious of the two riders. It stopped and pawed the ground with its cloven hooves, churning up the snow in its search for the tender roots that lay hidden beneath the icy, winter shroud. Still ignorant of their presence the creature advanced erratically towards them.

Eider's horse whinnied in alarm and reared, its neck arched as it shied sideways, almost dislodging its rider and spoiling his aim. The boy cursed under his breath as the arrow slipped from the bow and he had to grip tighter with his knees to stay with his mount as he nocked another arrow. The Nightboar stopped abruptly in the centre of the clearing and looked up, blinking its small, mean eyes and twitching its bristly ears towards the unfamiliar sounds. It snorted, wrinkling its muddy snout and turning its head from side to side as it scented the air. Eider suddenly saw the depression that his father had told him about, a dark, shadowy dip between the creature's shoulder blades. He had the perfect shot! His fingers tightened on the feathered flight as he took careful aim, holding his breath. But before he could loose the arrow he heard Drib give a muffled shout from somewhere close behind him and felt the draught of another arrow fired wildly at the beast. Drib's flight sang through the air, missing Eider's arm by a finger's breadth and struck the Nightboar's armoured body in a blaze of sparks a handspan behind its shoulder. Drib had watched in horror as the undergrowth was torn apart and the huge creature had lumbered into the clearing towards them. It was much bigger than he had imagined, and it looked so much more mean and dangerous than the stories had led him to believe. He

84

couldn't understand why Eider just sat there watching it; why didn't he loose his arrow? Suddenly he saw Eider's horse rear as it shied away. He thought Eider would fall beneath the creature's hooves; he had to do something. He called out and fired his arrow.

The Nightboar bellowed in rage as the arrow struck its side and it turned towards Drib. It lowered its head ready to charge, snarling and grunting as it stamped its feet, shaking the ground and dislodging an avalanche of ice and snow from the branches overhead. It churned up deep, muddy furrows in front of it with vicious jabs of its solid, curved tusks. The thick, prickly skin that covered its body rippled and twitched violently as it rushed forward. The shaft of Drib's arrow snapped as easily as though it were a stalk of straw against a tree trunk, leaving the sharp steel barb embedded in the creature's hide.

Drib sat mesmerized by the enormous creature, paralysed with terror. The Nightboar's eyes fixed and held him with a murderous stare. The boy was unable to speak, incapable of spurring his horse away to safety, and his hands were too weak to reach back for another arrow. But it wasn't just the Nightboar's imminent charge that terrified him; there was something else even more fearful than being gored and trampled to death. The sensation of being watched had intensified ever since they left the edge of the forest. Figures, dark, indistinct shapes, were moving through the trees towards them. They had appeared the moment his arrow had stuck the Nightboar and it had snarled and bellowed with rage.

'Eider! Look, all around us, look!' he wanted to cry to warn his friend, for thin, wispy, elongated shapes and squat, distorted shadows of darkness were gliding and moving effortlessly through the trees, converging on the enraged Nightboar. But Drib couldn't move, couldn't even blink his eyelids as the wraiths scented rage and hatred as the murderous fury erupted inside the beast. The power of the anger that the arrow strike had released would feed them, giving them substance and new life.

The Nightboar quivered as they crowded around it with tortured voices that echoed the wind wailing through the crags. They moved closer, touching and caressing the prickly flanks, melting and merging with its body through its armoured hide. Slowly the creature began to darken and shimmer, its colour changing through darkest indigo. It began to swell, fuelled by the evil melting through its skin, and gradually it grew more menacing, more brutally savage. It spread a defensive shroud of shadows around itself and smoke and fire crackled in its mouth as the snow beneath its feet turned to slush, boiling up in clouds of choking steam as the creature surged forward across the clearing towards Sparkfire.

Eider blinked, unable to believe his eyes. He saw the danger Drib was in and loosed his arrow, hoping it would knock the creature off-balance and slow it down while Drib spurred his horse to get out of its way. But the spine skidded harmlessly away as it struck the Nightboar's flank. Sparkfire neighed in panic, the whites of his eyes showing as he shied violently away, plunging into the undergrowth and sending Drib toppling out of the saddle. The bow flew from his hand as he struck the ground and his breath was knocked out of his body as he landed directly in the path of the charging Nightboar.

'Get up! Get out of the way!' Eider shouted, but Drib couldn't move. One of his crippled legs was twisted, trapped underneath him. All he could do was look up helplessly as death charged towards him.

The ground trembled and shook as the Nightboar grew larger and larger, filling the boy's vision, blocking out the gloomy winter daylight that filtered down through the canopy of branches overhead. Silkstone hovered and hooted a shrill warning call of alarm from high up amongst the still winter branches as he saw the wraiths weaving silently between the trees, converging upon the Nightboar, infusing the beast with the strength of their shadowy evil. The owl's voice rose into a shriek of alarm as he called for help for Drib. With feather-stripping speed he stooped to earth, his talons outstretched.

Drib heard the owl's call and saw a movement above his head as the Nightboar's shadow threatened to engulf him. He felt the cold draught of Silkstone's wings on his face and saw a blur of feathers and talons as the owl struck the charging Nightboar's long, prickly face, raking his sharp talons across its eyes, gouging, cutting deep into his leathery skin as he gripped and hung on grimly. The tiny owl momentarily blinded the charging beast, making it stop and arch its back as it began flinging its head violently from side to side in an effort to dislodge him, bellowing and snarling with rage. Eider shouted to Drib, urging him to scramble backwards away from the creature but before the crippled boy could look around for some- where to hide, the clearing was full of barking, snarling Border Runners, huge, wild hunting dogs, who had heard and answered Silkstone's desperate call for help.

Six, seven, eight – Eider didn't have time to count as the enormous, long-coated dogs leapt upon the Nightboar. It seemed to be magical the way they had appeared quite suddenly through the undergrowth, snapping at the creature's legs, biting at its prickly, armoured hide and clinging onto its back as they tried to pull it down.

Silkstone let go and flew erratically across the clearing to Drib's shoulder and watched as the Nightboar wallowed and plunged in an effort to spear the dogs with its sharp tusks. Shadowy shapes erupted from the creature's flanks, swirling and winding themselves around the attacking dogs, surrounding them in shrouds of night and making them yelp and scatter in confusion. But each time the wraiths reached out to drive the dogs away their evil power weakened and the blanket of menace they had woven to envelop the beast became more and more transparent. With a wailing cry of rage the wraiths shrunk back into the Nightboar, consolidating their darkness once more. The Nightboar appeared to grow in size and menace as it gored one of the Border Runners, tossing it high into the air but its action seemed to spur the other dogs into a renewed attack and their fury made the creature turn and flee into the depths of the forest.

The Border Runners had its scent in their nostrils and they followed immediately, baying and snapping at its heels and the sound of their hunt receded quickly between the trees. Eider saw that their only chance of supper was vanishing and an idea suddenly formed in his mind. He would help the dogs: he would give chase. If he followed them and tried to ride level with the Nightboar perhaps the dogs would drop back and let him drive an arrow down between the creature's shoulders and find the killing spot. He would willingly share the Nightboar meat with them.

'Come on, Nightshade, gallop – gallop faster than the wind – don't let that creature get away from us!'

Eider spurred his horse recklessly forward, nocking another arrow onto his bow-string as they left the clearing.

Drib barely had the time to stagger to his feet in order

to make a grab at Sparkfire's reins and stop him from following Eider's mount without his rider.

'Follow! Follow!' Silkstone hooted, rose from Drib's shoulder and flew after Eider.

Thin twigs and branches, brittle vines and creepers whipped and scratched at Eider's face, grazing his hands and arms as Nightshade galloped between the trees, following the trampled path that the Nightboar had made with the pack of Border Runners at its heels. But Eider didn't care how scratched and bruised he became: the heat of the hunt had consumed him – he wasn't going to let the Nightboar escape.

Suddenly the trees became more spread out and the air was lighter as the ground began to rise. Eider had a glimpse of distant mountains and narrow, rock-choked valleys; he could hear the roar of waterfalls and the cry of eagles. Immediately ahead of him snow-drifts lay between the trees, frozen into ice-white waves. The Nightboar hesitated as it reached the open ground and then it turned and charged to the right, back to the impenetrable undergrowth of the woods.

Eider saw the creature's doubt and anticipated the direction it would take. Turning Nightshade with his left spur he deftly cut off its escape and galloped through the trees towards it. He knew there would be no time for a second shot. He sat deep in his saddle as the galloping horse drew level, the flight of his arrow drawn back and ready. Silently the Border Runners dropped back, almost as if they sensed what he was about. They fanned out on both sides of the turning Nightboar and Nightshade galloped into their midst, gradually drawing level, moving in closer and closer with each lengthening stride.

Eider pressed the balls of his feet down into the stirrups

to keep his balance as he stood up and tilted the bow to look down the arrow shaft. Suddenly he saw the small depression between the creature's shoulders. He leaned out of the saddle as far as he dared, gripping tightly with his knees; his fingers tensed instinctively, curling around the bow-string, drawing it tighter ready for the killing shot. Hard clods of snow and frozen earth, twigs and lumps of leaf mould were flying up all around him, kicked into the air by the beast and Nightshade's flying hooves. The dogs were baying and the wind, stirred up by the speed of the chase, tugged at his hair and pulled blurring tears from the corners of his eyes. But nothing, nothing was going to distract him now, nothing was going to spoil his aim.

The wraiths, infesting the creature with their evil power, suddenly sensed what the galloping archer intended to do: they heard it in the wailing voices of the pursuing dogs and saw the weak glint of light reflecting on the steel arrow-blade aimed at that one, small, unprotected spot between the creature's shoulders. They shrieked and drove the beast faster, making the thick, prickly skin across its back and flanks stretch and jerk as it fled towards the safety of the impenetrable undergrowth that lay only twenty paces ahead. Black, shadowy fingers, wispy claws of darkness boiled up from the Nightboar's body and reached out for Eider's leg. Threads of shadow tried to claw at him and distract his aim as other pieces of darkness tried to weave a shroud across the creature's shoulders. But it was too late. With a shout of triumph Eider released the arrow and watched as it cut through the shadows and found its way into the soft patch of skin deep into the Nightboar's flesh, shearing through muscle and sinews, splintering bone until it pierced the creature's heart.

Nightshade neighed wildly, tossing his head and veering

away as the enormous beast floundered, wavering from side to side as its careering charge slowed and it churned deep, erratic furrows into the frozen ground. Its front legs buckled suddenly underneath it and it staggered, bellowing and snarling, each cry weakening it further. And then it collapsed, rolling slowly over onto its side before its legs twitched and convulsed. The blood from the fatal wound spread out from between its shoulders and flowed across the snow.

The wraiths erupted in thin, wailing wreathtails of darkness which oozed out of the beast's trembling flanks and flowed out of the soft, bristling skin of its belly, deserting the dying creature. They swirled across the snow to gather above the stricken Nightboar in a dense, black cloud of hatred that began to shimmer and move, blending and folding in upon itself until it formed into the shape of a long spear that moved towards Eider. The wailing cries and screams of the wraiths within it grew louder as it gathered speed. Nightshade crouched back, sinking defensively onto his hocks, his ears flattened along the sides of his head as the darkness approached. Eider raised his bow hand in a helpless gesture to ward it off. For an instant he was surrounded, immersed in wraith-blackness. He felt the ice-cold touch and he caught the briefest glimpse of the strange, tall translucent warriors, beasts with armoured scales, some with the look of giants and others lump-backed and misshapen. They all crowded forward to touch and scald him with their rage and hatred, searching for a way into his soul, for the whisperings of evil, for the corruption of greed and envy that they were sure always dwelt in men's hearts, but they could find nothing to feed upon. Eider shuddered, crying out in pain and fear and suddenly the Border Runners were all around him, leaping up to snap and tear at the blackness. He could hear Silkstone's voice from high above his head and feel the draught of the wind beneath the owl's wings as he swooped onto his shoulder, bringing the daylight to his side. Then Eider laughed and shouted with relief as the shrouds of night melted away and he could see the Border Runners pulling at the carcass of the Nightboar. He called out to Drib, calling for him to hurry and come and see the great beast they had killed.

Drib felt ashamed of himself. He had let Eider down by loosing the arrow without taking proper aim. He had fallen from Sparkfire's saddle and Silkstone had had to risk his life to rescue him. His face blushed scarlet as he limped wearily along at Sparkfire's shoulder looking for a fallen tree or a rock that would help him climb back into the saddle.

'I'm sorry, Sparkfire, I know I'm slowing us up but I can't go any faster. This armour is so heavy and difficult to walk in.' He was breathing heavily, keeping a tight hold on the reins and accidentally making the bit-rings jag and pull at the corners of the horse's mouth, breaking the rhythm of his stride as he tried to forge ahead through the undergrowth and follow the fading sounds of the hunt. Drib was really afraid of being left behind and becoming lost in the forest.

Pushing aside a thick tangle of vines that trailed down in front of him, he almost collided with a fallen oak that lay buried beneath a drift of leaves and snow. 'Sparkfire – halt!' he called, stumbling to keep his balance and clutching at the reins as he swept the armoured glove he was wearing on his free hand through the crust of ice and snow that covered the tree, clearing a place so that he could stand and remount the horse. But suddenly he snatched his hand away and stepped back, a gasp of startled surprise on his lips as puffs of bright purple dust exploded beneath his fingertips. For an instant the dust hung in the air, drifting around him, releasing a strange, pungent perfume before settling on the untouched snow, staining it with small purple patches.

'Of all the wonders in the world what have I found? What have I touched?' he whispered in alarm, turning over his hand to see that the leather fingertips of his gloves were stained a deep violet colour. Tentatively he brought his hand up to his face and sniffed, the same heady scent filling his nostrils.

Sparkfire stood patiently, unperturbed as he listened, ears pricked, to the sounds of the distant hunt. After a moment's hesitation Drib's curiosity got the better of him and he carefully brushed away some more of the snow from the tree trunk. At a glance he couldn't see where the puffs of brightly-coloured dust had come from but a closer inspection showed him that the rotting bark of the tree was covered with hundreds – no, thousands – of tiny, bell-shaped toadstools whose slender stems and white, fibrous roots clung to every crease and wrinkle in the ancient skin of the oak. They were so brittle, so fragile, that they shattered into clouds of purple dust at the gentlest of touches.

Drib wondered what the fungus was. Clearly it was far too delicate to be edible and he rubbed his fingers together and brought them to his nose again to savour the earthy scent of the forest, only to find that it had faded. He glanced down and found that the bright patches in the snow around his feet were dissolving slowly away. He sighed and clambered awkwardly onto the fallen tree, careful not to disturb the thick carpet of toadstools if he could help it. There was so much beauty, so many strange and wonderful things out here in the wildness of Elundium, things that Loremaster Grout had not woven into the stories that he had told them in the Learning Hall.

Drib laughed softly as he thrust the toe of his armoured boot into Sparkfire's stirrup, shortening the reins and gripping the pommel of the saddle as he remounted his horse. It suddenly occurred to him that perhaps the Loremaster hadn't told them because he didn't know about half the marvellous things they had already experienced on their flight from the Granite City. Perhaps the Loremaster had never ventured beyond the gates of the city himself, for he had never seen the Loremaster go further than the steps of the Learning Hall. But then the idea dissolved as quickly as it had formed. Drib knew that in reality the Loremaster was the wisest, most clever man, the keeper of all the lore of Elundium.

'Come on, Sparkfire, we had better try and catch up with Eider,' he whispered without any enthusiasm as he pushed all thoughts of Loremaster Grout and the stories from the Learning Hall to the back of his mind. He wasn't looking forward to seeing Eider. He kept expecting the young archer to reappear at any moment anyway, angry and empty-handed. And it wasn't difficult to imagine how cross the others would be when they eventually found their way out of the forest and were safely back in the ruins of Cawdor. He could almost hear Eider telling them all how stupid he had been, how he had lost them their supper by loosing off that arrow so wildly and then falling from Sparkfire's back into the path of the charging Nightboar. He had been so lucky that Silkstone had come to his rescue.

Drib sighed and an irrepressible smile crinkled the corners of his mouth. It hadn't been all bad: he realized he had been stupid, but if he hadn't fallen off Silkstone wouldn't have had to stoop to blind the beast as he had called out for help. Those magnificent Border Runners would never have come, breaking through the undergrowth, snarling and barking as they leapt on the creature, chasing it away, driving it back. He remembered the stories he had heard in the Learning Hall about how the Border Runners had saved the King's life when he had been lost in the black forest, how they had sat and guarded him throughout the darkest watches of the night. He remembered learning how Grannogg, the Lord of Dogs, had become King Thane's friend and had run at his stirrup, leaping up at the marauding Nightbeasts who had attacked them on the road to Underfall. They had looked so huge, so ferocious as the gloomy light had dappled their coats while they sprang at the Nightboar.

Suddenly he heard Eider's voice. He was somewhere very close and he was calling to him. He could hear him shouting at him to hurry up. Sparkfire neighed and surged forward, breaking through the last of the undergrowth that hid the rising ground. Drib caught his breath as he saw the enormous Nightboar lying on its side with Eider's arrow protruding from between its shoulder blades. The seven Border Runners were savaging at its stomach, trying to tear open its soft underbelly. Eider was sitting easily in Nightshade's saddle, his feet dangling free of the stirrups, his bow resting across his knees. He turned his head when he heard the sharp snap and crack of twigs beneath Sparkfire's hooves as the small horse approached and a grin widened across his face at the look of shocked surprise on Drib's face as the boy stared down at the pack of dogs noisily pulling and biting at the Nightboar's carcass.

'You must be the best, bravest archer in all Elundium – you've killed that huge creature with only one arrow! How? How did you do it?' Drib was full of excitement.

Eider laughed and waved his hand dismissively. 'The secret is where you aim the shot, not how many you loose. Now come on, dismount and help me cut off the Border Runners' share before they tear the carcass to pieces. And then we have to think of a way of getting the rest of it back to Cawdor. Come on, stop your daydreaming – it will be dark soon.'

Eider sprang lightly to the ground, hanging his bow on the pommel of the saddle before taking the long, bone-handled dagger from his belt and calling to the Border Runners to move away. One of the dogs looked up, snarling and baring his bloody teeth, the hackles ridged along his back.

'They won't hurt us, will they?' Drib asked anxiously as he slipped awkwardly to the ground.

Eider hesitated, the laughter dying from his face. One by one, as if alerted by the dog who snarled, the Border Runners had stopped worrying at the bloody carcass. For a moment they seemed to watch as he approached, staring at him with unblinking, yellow eyes and, as he hesitated, they seemed to scent his fear. Slowly they began to spread out, silently padding around him, keeping their stomachs low to the trampled, bloody snow, growling softly as they advanced.

'Drib, do something, talk to them – quickly!' Eider hissed in panic. He hadn't given a moment's thought as to how the dogs would react to him taking the carcass, and he certainly hadn't thought that they would turn on him.

The closest one was already less than three strides away, and it looked so large, so menacing. As it stalked towards him his legs felt as though they were turning to jelly: he couldn't move, to turn and run was out of the question.

'Drib! Make that owl call the dogs off! Conjure up that magician you're always talking about! Do something – anything – just stop this pack from tearing me to pieces!'

Drib stepped back hastily and banged against Sparkfire's shoulder. The cold hand of fear was tightening around him, for he knew the Border Runners were wild and free, but he couldn't remember them attacking anyone in any of the Loremaster's stories. No, they had befriended the King and had fought beside the Marchers and Archers. He didn't understand what was happening now. He looked around desperately for Silkstone amongst the stark winter canopy of branches. He called the owl's name; he called out for Nevian, the Master of Magic, begging him to come to their aid, but his voice floated away, unanswered, lost in the oppressive, gloomy silence beneath the trees. He knew he couldn't just stand there doing nothing but he didn't know what else to do.

'Perhaps they're growling at you because they sense you're afraid, Eider. Try talking to them, tell them you'll help them by cutting up the Nightboar.'

'I know I'm afraid, you idiot: talking to them will only make them even more sure of that! *You* talk to them, *you* try and get near the carcass: I'm too terrified to move!' Eider said in a small, tight voice.

Drib looked helplessly around him through the trees. He didn't know if he could summon up the courage to do what Eider was asking. He had never been afraid of the mangy dogs that scavenged through the rubbish that the merchants and traders left lying in the gutters beneath their stalls in the shadows of the Stumble Gate where they bartered their goods across the cobbles. Those dogs had growled and barked as they tried to protect the mouldy rinds and scraps they foraged for between the merchants' feet, but it had all been show and a shout or a wave of his fist had usually been enough to make them scuttle away with their tails tucked tightly between their hind legs. But to go in amongst these savage Border Runners – to go in whilst they still had the scent of the kill in their nostrils – that was a different matter. He didn't know if he could find the voice that wouldn't betray the doubt, the apprehension – the fear he felt inside.

Something moved in the shadows between the trees, a momentary swirl of soft rainbow colours, a stolen glimpse of the sunlight, an indigo hue that sparkled on the snow. Soft laughter filled the air around Drib's head and made Sparkfire snort and arch his neck. Drib blinked and rubbed the back of his armoured glove across his eyes. 'Nevian! Nevian, is that you?' his voice was a halting whisper. 'Please help us. The Border Runners are so savage and they're about to attack Eider – I don't know what to do!'

The colours between the trees began to melt away before the words had left Drib's lips and ghosted the frosty air but they left him with the sensation that the Master of Magic had been standing there close beside him, watching him. He could almost see his ancient, wrinkled face creased into a smile and he had the impression that he was mocking his indecision. He heard the faintest echo of Nevian's voice: the laughter had gone and now he was chiding him, scolding him.

'You don't need my magic to find your courage, Drib. Go to the Border Runners – they will not harm you. Tell them who you are and they will understand.'

'Drib – for goodness sake do something!' Eider gasped.

The leading dog was so close to him now that it was stretching out its muzzle towards him, and he could feel its hot breath on his face.

'But . . . but . . .' Drib stuttered, taking a clumsy, crooked step forward. He held out his open hand in a gesture of greeting.

The advancing semi-circle of Border Runners paused and watched him with low, snarling growls rumbling in their throats. Their breaths erupted from their open mouths in vaporous clouds that hung in the still, cold air.

'We didn't mean you any harm, we were only hunting for something to eat. We . . .' Drib fell silent. His limping, twisted strides had taken him in amongst the dogs and they were all around him now. The largest one's head was almost level with his shoulders.

'Drib . . . tell them who you are . . . make friends . . . they will not hurt you . . .' The magician's words echoed in his head and with barely a pause for breath he started to talk to them.

'Berioss said that you helped him find Oaktangle and the other Tunnellers when he was lost in the forest. He told us lots of stories about how you fought beside the Marchers, and the Loremaster told us hundreds of other stories about how you saved the King's life . . . and . . .'

Drib was talking so fast that he stopped being afraid as the words blurred together. Suddenly he stopped and felt a cold, wet nose against the back of his neck; the largest dog, the leader of the pack, was scenting him, sniffing at his face and hands, pushing his nuzzle against his crooked legs. At last the dog lifted his head and barked, almost deafening poor Drib, and then he licked his face. Drib laughed with relief as he patted the dog, rubbing his hands through the thick, winter coat. The dog closest to Eider sniffed him suspiciously and Eider let out a sigh of relief as the other dogs turned and padded through the snow back towards the carcass of the Nightboar.

'Slit open the belly – go on, do it quickly before these dogs rip the meat to ribbons!' Eider urged Drib.

Drib glanced at the Nightboar dubiously. It was one thing pretending to be brave and making friends with these wild dogs, it was quite another barging in amongst them while they were eating.

'Go on, Drib, one of us has got to do it and you're the closest! You can use my knife, it's probably sharper than the one you've got.' Eider tossed him the dagger that he carried in his belt.

Drib caught the knife and reluctantly walked towards the carcass, trying to keep up a continuous line of chatter to the dogs as he approached as much to give himself courage as anything else.

'Come on, give me some room, I'll help you with that if you'll just let me through,' he called out.

The dogs snarled and snapped furiously as they worried at the tough, prickly skin but they moved apart and let him get in close to the soft underbelly of the Nightboar. The creature smelt so strong that he caught his breath: he had never done anything like this before.

'Can you see where the rib-cage ends and the softer skin of the creature's belly begins?' Eider called out. Drib nodded. 'Well push the point of the blade in as deep as it will go about two fingers' width below the rib-cage and then draw the blade backwards along the centre of its belly towards the hind legs. It's easy, I've watched my father do it dozens of times. Go on!'

Drib struggled for a moment to overcome his revulsion and then took a deep breath. He could see where the Border Runners had already torn small bloody weals in the Nightboar's skin, exposing pieces of white bone, but none of them had managed to open the carcass up. He tossed aside his armoured gloves in order to get a better grip on the knife and dropped to his knees. Clenching his teeth he tried to push the point of the blade into the pink, prickly skin below the rib-cage but it was thick and tough and he only managed to get the point of the knife in so that a tiny pin-point of blood welled up.

'You'll have to push harder than that,' Eider urged as Drib tried again, gripping the handle of the knife with both hands and putting all his weight behind the thrust.

Suddenly the blade punctured the tough skin and sank deep into it. Blood oozed up, wetting Drib's knuckles and making the knife slippery and difficult to hold as he tried to drag it back towards the Nightboar's hind legs. The prickly skin bulged and sagged heavily, tightening against his hands as the blade slowly cut through it. Drib gasped for breath as an overpowering stench wafted up from the widening gash he was making in the beast's stomach. The Border Runners stopped worrying at the creature's head and legs and crowded around him, drawn by the smell and the spreading pool of blood that was beginning to gush out of the deep cut Drib had made, soaking his hands and forearms.

Suddenly, without any warning, the belly split wide open. Drib cried out in disgust as the creature's intestines spilt out onto the ground in front of him. The Border Runners surged forward, pushing him roughly out of the way as they snarled at each other and tore at the sweetmeats he had just released. Drib staggered dizzily to his feet, clutching at one of the creature's forelegs for support as the dogs milled around his feet. He felt Eider's hand on his arm as he helped to pull him away and watched in horror as the Border Runners devoured all the entrails, gorging themselves before sloping off into the undergrowth. The large dog who had scented Drib and licked his face trotted up to him, blood and gore dripping from his tongue, and barked before rubbing his head against Drib's hand. Then, without a backward glance he followed the other Border Runners into the undergrowth and vanished.

'What did he say – that last dog? Wasn't he the one who barked in your face?' Eider asked. The relief that the pack of dogs had gone and that he and Drib were alone again showed in his voice as he walked slowly around the Nightboar, wondering how they were going to get it back to Cawdor in one piece.

'How should I know? He just barked at me,' Drib replied, crouching down to try and clean away the dark, sticky stains of blood from his hands and forearms with the help of handfuls of snow. It made him shiver and his teeth began to chatter.

'That's obvious, I could hear that!' Eider answered, harshly. 'You're always talking to that owl – and the horses – you're always telling us that they mean this or they're saying that. And you see magicians. You must have understood that dog just now – you made friends with it didn't you?'

'Well, yes, I suppose I did, but that doesn't mean I can understand what they were saying. And I couldn't have made friends with them at all if . . .' Drib hesitated and frowned as he limped crookedly back to where Sparkfire was waiting patiently and took a scrap of rag from under the saddle flap to dry his hands. He was on the verge of telling Eider that he wouldn't have been able to find the courage to approach the dogs if Nevian, the Master of Magic, hadn't suddenly appeared between the trees, but he thought better of it. Eider had been all for him calling on the magician when he thought the dogs were going to attack him and he wanted Drib to ask for Silkstone's help when they were in a tight spot, but the moment he thought they were safe he seemed to mock him, telling him that his imagination was running away with him.

'Magicians . . . owls . . . it's a pity you don't pay more attention to what you're supposed to be doing and then you wouldn't be falling off your horse and dropping the bow I lent you,' Eider muttered in disgust.

'I'm sorry . . . I'm really sorry about that beautiful bow, I didn't mean to drop it,' Drib began to apologize as he felt his cheeks flush scarlet with shame but Eider dismissed him with a glare.

'You want to concentrate on what you're doing in the future and not go wandering off into your daydreams. Now, come over here and help me try to work out a way to get this creature's carcass back to Cawdor.'

Drib limped back reluctantly and looked down at the enormous creature. He was going to ask Eider what he thought the dark, shadowy shapes were that he had seen converging on the Nightboar before it charged but he thought better of it. Instead he asked, 'How do you suppose the hunters usually carry the Nightboars out of the forest after they killed them?'

Eider laughed harshly, 'That's easy – there were always dozens of them when my father used to hunt and they had strong carts each pulled by two horses upon which they used to lay the bodies.'

'Sparkfire and Nightshade could pull the Nightboar along if we made a sleigh out of branches and creepers couldn't they?' Drib suggested tentatively.

To his surprise Eider was quick to agree and sent him scouring through the trees for fallen branches while he climbed up into an ancient oak that was festooned with vines and creepers and began to cut down the youngest, most supple ones he could find.

They were both hot and tired as twilight thickened beneath the trees but they barely noticed the light flurries of snow that were beginning to fall before they had finished cutting, notching and lashing the fallen branches they had gathered and formed into a crude sledge that was large and strong enough to carry the Nightboar.

'Well – what do you think?' Eider asked proudly as he stepped back. He had finished knotting the traces that he had woven from strong, supple creeper and formed into a collar that was tied with the stirrup leathers to the saddles. He rubbed a dirty hand across his forehead and admired their handiwork before gathering up the woven traces ready to tie them to the sledge.

'It's excellent – really wonderful. I've never done anything like this before: we've really made something! But ...' Drib hesitated as he reached up to stroke Silkstone's downy chest feathers.

'But what?' Eider frowned, wondering what the sweep's boy could have spotted that his sharp eyes hadn't seen.

'Oh there's nothing wrong with the sledge, nothing at all, it's perfect, but I was wondering how we are going to get that huge carcass onto it – it's far too heavy for us to move on our own.'

Eider had to agree, Drib was right; he hadn't given a moment's thought to getting the beast onto the sledge after they had built it. Silkstone hooted softly and flew from Drib's shoulder onto the pommel of Sparkfire's saddle and then up onto a stout branch above where the Nightboar lay. Eider followed the owl's flight and then laughed suddenly as he saw a way to lift the carcass.

'It's simple, Drib, we'll use the horses' strength to lift the Nightboar!'

Quickly he devised a plan to throw the traces up over the branch above the body and secure them to the Nightboar's legs and then as Drib led the horses forward the creature's carcass would be pulled off the ground. 'And then I'll push the sledge in underneath once there's room. As soon as I tell you, you can rein the horses back and it'll lower the Nightboar down onto the sledge!'

Drib nodded doubtfully and reached up on tiptoe to catch hold of the horses' bit-rings with both hands, stroking the velvety softness of their nostrils and feeling their breath on his knuckles as they tossed their heads. He looked back to where Eider was knotting the creeper traces around the Nightboar's legs. Drib watched him raise his hand and he urged the horses forward.

'Come on, pull – pull hard both of you!'

Sparkfire and Nightshade snorted, arched their necks and surged forward, muscles rippling along their flanks and up across their powerful shoulders as they threw their weight into the collar. Their hooves churned up mud and snow and the traces of woven creeper drew as tight as bow-strings. Then the huge carcass began to turn, inching up first a finger's span and then a hand's span above the ground.

'Pull! Pull harder, come on, you've almost done it!' Drib

called out in excitement as a sheen of sweat glistened on the horses' coats and steam rose into the cold air.

Eider manhandled the sledge in beside the Nightboar, watching as the gap between the sagging body of the beast and the ground began to widen. At last he thrust the sledge in beneath it, pushing it carefully in place before he gave a shout.

'Back! Rein back!'

Drib almost slipped over in the mud and snow as the horses threw up their heads and obeyed his voice, stepping backwards over the churned ground. The carcass sank back onto the sledge, rolling slowly over onto its side. Eider quickly untied the traces and fixed them to the front of the sledge.

'Come on, Drib,' he laughed, putting his arm around the little crippled boy's shoulders. 'Let's take our supper home – I'm starving!'

IV

A Touch
of Magic

MARCHER BERIOSS stood between the riven doors of Cawdor shivering from the bitter cold and fidgeting, shattering the frozen tangles of icicles in his beard with numb fingers as he watched Eider and Drib ride away beneath the dark, forbidding eaves of the forest in search of food. He knew he shouldn't have let the two boys go off on their own to hunt something as ferocious and dangerous as a Nightboar but he couldn't do everything and be everywhere as the same time; and it seemed unlikely they would encounter a Nightboar anyway. Besides, he thought that they would stand a better chance of surviving the fresh storm he noticed gathering over the Emerald Mountains if he stayed with Oaktangle and the other Tunnellers to help them erect some sort of shelter in one of the derelict towers. He had to hope that the tracks that Damask had spotted in the snow as they left the forest earlier belonged to easier game.

Berioss drew his cloak more tightly around him, pulling the collar up around his ears as he listened to the wind howling mournfully through the broken walls of the gate house behind him and felt overwhelmed by the burden of despair. Fate had driven them on a hard and cruel road to this journey's end and yet he knew that there was nowhere else in all Elundium, not one single village, town or wayhouse along the greenways' edge, where they could have sought shelter for the winter, where the people would not have stoned them and cursed them, believing them to be traitors to the King. They had been falsely accused of such despicable crimes that he could have wept. Instead he clenched his fist in anger at the frustration of not being able to see a way to prove their innocence. He felt so alone, so helpless without his friend, Marcher Ustant, who had given up his life so that they would escape from the cellars beneath Candlebane Hall. How were they to survive? Cawdor was a ruin, an empty, desolate ruin that stood wrapped in its own, forgotten dereliction on the dark side of morning, battered by a wild and restless sea that boiled along the margin of the world and mocked by the pitiless cries of the wheeling, soaring seabirds that gathered in the stormy sky above it.

A noise in the courtyard behind him, soft laughter and singing voices made the old Marcher glance around to see the Tunnellers hard at work. Mistletoe was gathering anything that looked as though it might burn while Sloeberry and Damask were manhandling a large, old fire-scalded cauldron they had discovered in the ruins and were pulling it towards one of the towers where Mistletoe was making a pile of firewood. Oaktangle and Blackthorn were kneeling and trying to repair the broken pulley of the well in the centre of the courtyard. A smile replaced the frown on Berioss' face as he combed the remnants of the ice and frost out of his beard with his fingertips. The Tunnellers were such an inventive, hard-working people who seemed to thrive on adversity; it was a tragedy that they were hated so much, just because they were different from the other people in Elundium. He sighed as he remembered how it had all begun on that stormy night in the Wayhouse Inn at Deepling. It seemed an age ago now when he had been sitting there with Ustant as they warmed themselves by the fire, talking about old battles and listening absently to the rumours and gossip going on around them. Thinking back, it struck him that there had already been an atmosphere of dissatisfaction in the smoky room that night. A group of merchants and journeymen had been airing their grievances noisily and one of them had told some ridiculous story about seeing Nightbeasts in the woods and how the King no longer seemed bothered about protecting them, how he had disbanded the Marchers, Archers and Gallopers who had helped him finally defeat the darkness at the last great Battle of the Rising. They had been unhappy about the way the King never seemed to leave the Granite City and seemed to have no idea how the common people lived. He remembered how there had been mutterings at almost all the tables in the inn before Oaktangle and his small company of Tunnellers had burst in, shaking the rain off their clothes and asking for food and shelter.

Yes, he remembered the very moment it had all begun. It seemed that the discontent and dissatisfaction that had been rife all around the inn had finally found a focus. Berioss' face darkened with anger as he remembered. It had been Snatchpurse, the exiled Chancellor's son, who had started it all. The boy had started to mutter loudly, making sure that plenty of people were listening to him as he went on about his dislike of the Tunnellers, telling everybody that they were barely taller than goblins and so ugly, with their bulging eyes and peculiar shell-shaped ears. He had gone on to say that all their misfortunes were the Tunnellers' fault and he criticized the King for giving them their freedom to roam Elundium and allowing them to live off the backs of honest folk. He had derided the hard work they did, pruning and keeping the greenways open for everyone to travel down. Gradually one thing had led to another and suddenly everybody in the inn had been crying out for the Tunnellers' blood. They had been lucky to escape alive. From then on everything seemed to have gone from bad to worse and every mishap, accident and disaster had been blamed on them. They had been hounded, hunted and persecuted all over the land and wherever they showed their faces they had been cursed and called traitors. Even the Tunnellers' own people had turned against Oaktangle and his small company and they had been cast out.

Berioss looked anxiously back to the silent, stone forest that pressed in around the ruins of Cawdor and from there towards the distant peaks of the mountains that were now completely wrapped in storms. He knew that as soon as the roads were passable the King would send out Gallopers to pursue them and bring them back as prisoners to the Granite City ready to stand trial for the treacheries and atrocities of which they were falsely accused and he felt despair as he realized that no one believed in their innocence. The King's men had pushed them hard and they had been lucky to get through the mountain passes before winter closed the road behind them. He sighed, wishing that Ustant was still with them as he examined the riven doors and ran his cold fingers over the ancient, wormy wood. Perhaps they would survive, perhaps they could somehow fortify the ruins of Cawdor and make it their home. He had until the spring melted the snows to teach Oaktangle and the others how to defend themselves: after all they had taken all that mock armour from the armoury in the Granite City before making good their escape on the Nighthorses and it would be silly not to put it to some use.

But doubt was quick to draw cold fingers around Berioss's heart and weaken the spark of his resolve. These gentle people who gardened the greenways of Elundium were not warriors. Eider would, perhaps, make a fine archer one daylight and Drib, he knew, would stand his ground bravely if asked to, but he was a crooked boy, cruelly twisted by nature, who for all his trying could barely keep his seat in Sparkfire's saddle. Berioss shook his head sadly. He would stay with them, protect them until his last breath and would teach them everything he knew, but he didn't hold out much hope of turning them into warriors.

A faint movement in the darker shadows beneath the broken gate arch, a swirling glow of soft rainbow colours, showed up against the wind-smoothed stone. Berioss stepped hastily backwards and gasped in fear as the translucent figure of the Master of Magic began to appear.

'What is it? What do you want from me?'

Berioss's lips were trembling so much he could hardly speak as he shrank back away from the shimmering figure. The last time the magician had appeared before him and all the other Marchers who had fought beneath King Holbian's banner, it had been on the Causeway Fields. The old King had died and they had doubted the boy, Thanehand, believing that he did not have the makings of a king and had refused to pledge their allegiance to him. Nevian had cursed them all and his rainbow cloak had seethed with violent colours; lightning had crackled from his fingertips as he had used a magic so powerful that it trapped them all, catching each one of them unawares long after they had forgotten his words. They had all been turned into trees to stand and bide their time upon the greenways' edge to watch and wait until they knew the full measure of Thane's kingship; to wait until they had grown to love him as they had the last of the Granite Kings. And they were to remain as trees until Thane had great need of them, for only he could break the spell and call upon them.

Berioss shivered, remembering only too clearly standing parched and thirsty in the hot sun, recalling how the straggling leaves had hung from his fingertips shrivelled and spinning in the wind; remembering, too, shivering with icicles clinging to every crease and wrinkle in his skin as the bitter winter blizzards blew along the greenways. He would never forget how he had waited for the King to call for them. He glanced down at his crooked knuckles that had never quite straightened and noticed how the rough texture of the skin on the backs of his hands had never smoothed away after the spell had been broken. He had much to fear from the magician's sudden appearance.

'Be not afraid, Berioss,' Nevian smiled, reaching out and warming the old Marcher's hands with a gentle touch. 'You have learned through a long and hard life to hold honour and justice above all things and I pledge you now to use those virtues to make this company strong. Forge them into the Knights of Cawdor. Prepare them to ride out in the name of justice and honour into the dark daylights that lie ahead, for King Thane will have great need of them. Prepare them well, for they know nothing of the shock and sway of battle.'

'Nevian, wait! Tell me how? Tell me who it is we have to fight – who were those creatures that attacked us when we tried to escape from the cellars beneath Candlebane Hall? Are they still pursuing us? How much time do we have? Nevian . . . Nevian . . .' Berioss cried out, trying to hold onto the melting colours of the rainbow cloak, but the magician's voice faded, blending with the mournful cries of the seabirds that wheeled overhead in the darkening sky. He looked down at his gnarled old fingers where the soft colours of the rainbow were still infused with his skin, smoothing the rough texture and straightening his knuckles, strengthening his hands. He spread his fingers in wonder, then reached beneath his cloak and drew his sword before striding out between the broken doors. Then he laughed, it seemed for the first time in ages. He felt proud that the Master of Magic had entrusted him with such an awesome task.

'They will be ready – you have my pledge on it!' he cried against the thunder of the surf that was boiling up against the rocks below the grim fortress. He swept the sword in a glittering arc, which caught and reflected the last rays of the low winter sun as the storm clouds drew across it, momentarily lightening the dark side of morning.

'Berioss! What's the matter? Have you seen somebody? Are the King's Gallopers approaching – or is it those beasts that attacked us in the city?' Sloeberry called out in alarm, loosing the dagger that hung at her side as she heard the old Marcher cry out a challenge and saw him sweep his sword above his head where he stood between the broken doors of the gatehouse.

Berioss turned slowly towards her, resheathing his sword, and his ancient, weatherbeaten face creased into a smile. He took another glance down at his hands, flexing his fingers. 'No, no, it's nothing my dear, nothing for you to worry yourself about. I must have been daydreaming and I thought I just saw an old friend in the mist; I thought I heard his voice calling out to me but it must have been the sound of the sea –

he's gone now.' he murmured, looking back towards the forest.

Sloeberry looked up at Berioss uncertainly. His serious, stern warrior's face was different: there was a light, a twinkle of laughter, a soft, far-away look in the old man's eyes that she had never seen before and she worried that something serious and strange must have happened to him. She had felt uneasy about the ruins from the first moment they had entered them but she couldn't explain why. She sensed they were not alone in Cawdor but at the same time she knew that there wasn't anybody else there.

'Did you see the ghost of Ustant? Was that who it was?' she asked, but Berioss merely laughed and shook his head.

'No, no, it was somebody far older than Marcher Ustant, older than time itself. But come: enough of this chatter, come and help me call to the others. We must erect a shelter against the coming storm or we'll all freeze to death.'

Sloeberry hesitated as he took her hand and she looked out anxiously past the long, flowing folds of his marching cloak, across the windswept, snowy headland. Out there were dark storm clouds and thickening flurries of snow that were beginning to obliterate the edge of the forest and the mountains beyond.

'What about Drib and Eider? What do you think has happened to them? They will be able to find their way back, won't they? You don't think they're lost, do you? I'm really worried about . . .' she left the sentence unfinished and began to shiver as the strengthening wind tugged at her skirts and blew through her hair.

Berioss looked down at her and smiled. He bent and warmed her hands. He had seen the first spark of love kindling between Sloeberry and Drib despite their desperate circumstances and the enormous differences between them. He had noticed how they always rode together if they could and how they talked and laughed in soft whispers long into the night after everybody else in the company had fallen, exhausted, into sleep. So he hid the worries that he felt about Eider and Drib hunting the Nightboar.

'They'll be back long before we have finished building a roof over our heads, and most probably they'll bring back something good and wholesome for us all to eat. You mark my words, the Nighthorses won't let them come to any harm.'

Berioss glanced up mistrustfully at the broken-toothed top of the ruined tower before following Sloeberry through the low door arch. He blinked and coughed, his eyes watering at the hazy blue smoke that blew up from the fire that Mistletoe had managed to light in the soot-blackened hearth that stretched across the far wall and filled the gloomy chamber. He joined the others in the centre of the room and looked at the remains of the sagging roof that left the room open to the sky above his head. Large snowflakes were beginning to swirl down through the broken roof to settle on their upturned faces.

'It's far too dangerous for us to shelter in here. The weight of a heavy snowfall will bring the rest of that roof down on top of us!' Berioss warned. 'Are you sure there isn't anywhere else in this warren of ruins that would offer better shelter? What about the gatehouse? The rotten tower there is more substantial than this one.'

Oaktangle shook his head. 'No, we've examined them all very carefully. Most of the towers look better but they are crumbling and are close to collapse. The walls of this one seem to be the strongest and it has the added advantage of having lost its upper rooms and turrets long ago. The roof you are looking at isn't really a roof at all but the remains of a floor from the chamber above. It should be easy to support it and thatch it with a new roof of turf and earth. We should be able to keep out the weather if we can find some beams amongst the rest of the ruins and haul them up to strengthen the existing joists. If you look hard enough you will see that the stone capitals are still intact: we can rest the beam ends on them and there is a narrow, winding stairway that leads up to the roof in the far corner of the chamber. It shouldn't be too difficult, really.'

Berioss stroked his beard and he shook his head doubtfully. Oaktangle seemed to be attempting the impossible and yet he knew that the Tunnellers were capable of the most extraordinary feats of ingenuity when the situation demanded it. He also knew that they would freeze to death outside without a doubt.

'I saw what looked like long beams amongst a pile of fallen masonry in the north-east tower while I was gathering firewood: they might be exactly what we are looking for,' Mistletoe offered.

Oaktangle turned swiftly to the others, sweeping his long, thin, delicate fingers out across the ruins. 'I am sure that everything we need is lying all around us if we look hard enough. We could have a roof over our heads in no time at all if we put our backs into it. Berioss if you . . .' He paused and looked up at the old Marcher and smiled shyly; Berioss was a giant of a man and stronger than the rest of the company put together, but he was a warrior, not a builder and Oaktangle hesitated, unsure of how to ask him to help with something as menial as building a roof.

Berioss sensed the question hovering on Oaktangle's

tongue and laughed, a deep, guttural sound that rumbled out from the back of his throat. 'Death won't hesitate, you know, and it won't pick and choose which one of us to take first. If we don't get a shelter built before that storm comes in we are in trouble. I know I'm not very clever with my hands but you tell me what to do and I will do the best I can to get it done.'

Oaktangle's smile widened with relief. A strong pair of hands would make all the difference. 'If you could help us to drag those fallen beams out of the north-east tower then, with the horses' help and the ropes we took from the armoury we could hoist them up into position and strengthen the floor. Blackthorn and Sloeberry could start to gather the materials we need to build a roof above that floor. Remember, we'll need long, strong lengths of wood or straight branches for the framework, vines and creeper for the bindings, and thistles, grass and fallen leaves for the covering and thatching. Damask – you go and fill a cauldron with snow and earth and while the mixture heats up and melts together go out and search close to the outer walls to see if you can find some alcanquirt roots. If you do, crush them and mix them into the cauldron with the snow and earth and we'll smear it over the thatching to make it weatherproof. The original inhabitants of Cawdor must have grown alcanquirt or something very similar, they must have weatherproofed their thatching with something, for you can see it where it still clings to the roof of the gatehouse.'

The Tunnellers hurried away into the gloomy light but Berioss paused in the doorway with his hand on one of the horse's bridles. He frowned with worry and took a last, lingering look towards the dark forest, hoping to see Eider and Drib making their way back, but the approaching storm was beginning to blur and obliterate the trees in a hazy, silent shroud.

'Come on, boys, hurry up before the storm cuts you off. We would all rather go hungry and tighten our belts another notch than lose either of you.'

All thought of the boys' plight was quickly driven from Berioss's mind as he worked beside Oaktangle, putting all his strength into manoeuvring the two heavy beams that the horses had dragged across the courtyard into the tower into position. He was soon hot and sweating from the effort of scrambling up and down the narrow, winding stone stairway and hauling on the ropes until his fingers bled as they tried to get the beams up into the roof. Oaktangle called out, gesturing and giving directions and inch by inch the beams grated against the rough walls and slipped into position on the stone capitals. He was vaguely aware of the others working hard above him, singing and talking as they balanced precariously on the outer rim of the wall and built the framework of the steep, conicle roof. They were knotting the skeleton of poles and branches that they had found in the ruins, forming them into a strong structure with lengths of vine. Damask and Mistletoe were working from the outer edge that overhung the wall going over the framework and around and around towards the top, working with thin strands of vines, sticks, thistles and leaves to form a thick covering that shut out the last of the gloomy daylight.

The light of the fire had ceased to shed sufficient light and Berioss had to light his spark to see what he was doing as he used the hilt of his sword to hammer at the four wooden wedges that Blackthorn had so expertly split from a broken piece of wood and fitted them into the wall to hold the beam ends securely in place upon the capitals.

The voices of the Tunnellers working on the roof above his head were gradually becoming muffled.

'Are you all right out there?' he called out anxiously, cursing as the spark burned his fingers and went out. 'What's going on? I hope none of you have fallen off!'

He stood up slowly, straightening his aching back and feeling his way across the remains of the floor that he had just strengthened, taking care to avoid the holes in the rotten boards. He climbed the last three stone steps that protruded up through the side of the new roof. The air was full of swirling snowflakes that stung his eyes: the wind had got up while he had been pulling the beams into place and now it tugged fiercely at his beard. Blinking as he looked up, he searched around for the Tunnellers, gasping and crying out in panic as he saw them silhouetted against the last of the daylight.

'What on earth are you doing up there? One slip and you'll all fall to your deaths! Come down at once!'

Damask merely waved and laughed back, 'We're almost finished, it'll soon be weatherproofed.'

Berioss was uncertain as he gripped at the slippery, icy stone balustrade where the stairway ended abruptly in broken masonry. Weatherproofing looked like a very dangerous occupation from where he was standing. The Tunnellers had taken off their boots and were moving quickly and sure-footedly across the steep thatchwork, curling and gripping with their toes as they rubbed handfuls of the glutinous mixture of mud, melted snow and crushed roots that had been boiled up in the cauldron and spread it into the weave of the thatch, working it in evenly as they moved down, around and around the roof. Oaktangle and Blackthorn were slightly ahead of the others and moving more slowly as they carried a heavy earthenware vessel between them, ladling out the mixture for the others to spread.

'Don't worry, Berioss, we've done this before. We're almost finished – and not a moment too soon!'

Oaktangle climbed down from the roof and came to stand beside Berioss. He pointed up to the sky as it darkened and the storm grew suddenly heavier as the snow began to settle on the Tunnellers' backs and cover the thatching with a thick, white carpet as they worked, blotting out everything around them.

'Quickly! Get inside everybody!' Oaktangle cried out and the Tunnellers scrambled down, squeezing past Berioss as they ran down the stairway.

Berioss followed their example, pulling shut the make-shift trap-door that one of the Tunnellers had fixed over the stairhead to keep out the worst of the weather and slamming it shut behind him. His marching boots slipped and kicked up dancing sparks in the darkness as he slowly descended the smooth, well-worn stone steps. The storm was strengthening and beginning to howl around the tower, rattling the trapdoor above his head and sending thick flurries of snow and gusts of wind against the outer door of the chamber, threatening to tear it off its hinges at any moment. The noise of the storm was frightening the horses who were whinnying and fretting where they had been picketed near the door. Berioss went to them immediately and herded them into a quieter corner, calming them with his voice and caressing their necks the way he had seen the Gallopers do when they needed to soothe their horses as they waited nervously in the great battle crescents ready to take the shock of the charge.

The chamber felt bitterly cold despite the new roof and he turned from settling the horses to find that the

Tunnellers were huddling around the embers of the fire, shivering and blue with the cold they had suffered from working on the roof. They were talking in whispers and trying to warm their numb fingers and toes. Berioss strode across the chamber towards them and was about to ask why they hadn't built up the fire when he saw that only a handful of sticks still remained from the pile of firewood that Mistletoe had begun to gather before he had climbed up on the roof to help the others.

'This won't do, this won't do at all. We'll all be frozen to death by morning,' he muttered to himself, realizing that he would have to do something about it – and quickly. He stooped to gather the few remaining pieces of wood that lay close to the hearth and threw them onto the fire. 'This chamber's colder than King Holbian's tomb. What we need is a good fire roaring up this chimney!'

And before any of them could get to their feet or call out to stop him he had pulled on his marching cloak, settling it tight around his shoulders and pulling up the hood before forcing open the outer door, fighting against the howling wind. He opened the door just wide enough to squeeze through and it slammed shut behind him, sending flames leaping up the chimney as the icy gale blew in the snow and rushed through the chamber.

'By all the magic in Elundium help me now, Nevian . . .' he shouted against the fury of the storm as he struck out for where he thought the eastern towers should be. He shielded his face as the snow stung and blinded him and the wind buffeted against him, threatening to knock him over. But his words were sucked away, unheard, as he struggled forward, veering away to the north and passing through a maze of broken-down walls and bumps of masonry that had been softened and blanketed by the snow making them unrecognizable as landmarks. But Berioss was too intent on finding fuel to notice that he had lost his way.

He stumbled, his foot snagging on an object that had been buried by the storm, and as he fell he threw his hands out in front of him to save himself. Snow forced its way inside his armoured gloves, up his sleeves and inside his boots, chilling him to the bone, but then he felt the sharp edges of what he had been looking for – broken pieces of wood. He had found the wormy, rotten remnants of a carved balustrade, some columns, posts and pillars that had once graced the walls and towers of Cawdor. Frantically he scraped the snow away to find the fuel they so desperately needed was frozen, stuck to the ground by the frost. He cursed, his teeth chattering from the cold as he unsheathed his sword to smash and hack at the frozen wood, sending up showers of brittle splinters.

Gathering together as much as he could carry in a bundle across his shoulders he turned to retrace his steps, shaking off the thick layer of snow that had settled on his hood. He frowned as he looked from left to right. The tower had disappeared completely from sight: the blizzard hid everything – even his footprints had been smoothed out by the falling snow. He was lost, utterly lost and with no idea of which way to go. He took a faltering step and halted, cursing his own stupidity, wishing he had paid more attention to the direction he had taken. It wouldn't matter how much firewood he gathered if he couldn't find the way back. He had been such a fool, first for letting the two boys go off hunting on their own and now for blundering out into the storm without a moment's thought as to what would happen to the others if he didn't return.

He began to wish that Ustant was there with him:

he would have stopped him from making these stupid mistakes. He reached out with his free hand as though he could part the thick, black, swirling shroud of wind and snow that had enveloped him. He had to find a way: it was no good standing there whining and feeling sorry for himself for the others couldn't survive without him. Suddenly he felt something touch his hand and then he heard a voice, laughter riding in the shriek of the wind. He spun awkwardly around, his fingers tingling, burning, and snatched his hand back to bring it up to his face. Faint, soft, rainbow colours were spreading between the fingertips of his gloves making the armour glow and sparkle as it illuminated the snowy darkness. He heard the voice again. This time it was calling out to him, commanding him to follow, follow and be quick before it was too late.

'Nevian?' he whispered, peering ahead, taking another uncertain step as he tried to catch at the vanishing words. He held up his gloved hand and it lit the way. He thought he could just see the shape of a ghostly figure and then one, two, three footprints appeared as if on their own. They formed slowly at first and then more quickly, spreading out ahead of him, curving slightly to the right, leading him back through the ruins towards the dark bulk of the tower with its steep new roof now hidden by a thick blanket of snow.

Berioss burst through the door and let the heavy load of firewood fall to the floor as he shook the snow from his cloak. The Tunnellers crowded anxiously around him all talking at once. Sloeberry grasped his hands and drew him closer to the fire to thaw him out.

'We were so worried – the storm became so violent!' Oaktangle began. 'We tried, but we couldn't open the door: we wanted to go out and search for you.'

'We could hear strange noises in the wind – high-pitched screams and shrieks of laughter. It upset the horses and was making us really frightened,' Damask added excitedly, betraying her relief at Berioss's safe return as the other Tunnellers began to break open the bundle of firewood and drag it towards the fire.

'How can Drib and Eider possibly survive this storm without proper shelter? They are still out there in the forest. They'll freeze to death. I wish they hadn't gone . . .' Sloeberry began in a tearful voice but then she stopped and stared up at the faint rainbow colours that still clung wetly to the fingertips of the old Marcher's battle glove and dripped into glowing pools on the floor at his feet.

'Berioss – look at your hand! Your glove is glowing – it's on fire!'

Berioss looked at his gloved hand and laughed softly, flexing his fingers and making the colours fizz and sparkle. 'It's nothing to be afraid of – it's magic, just magic.'

Sloeberry shrunk back with fear in her eyes. 'Magic?' she whispered, looking nervously into the corners of the gloomy chamber. She had sensed something around them, something moving in the shadows, floating around them in the firelight.

'Yes, it has to be magic, that's the only way to explain it!' Berioss smiled. 'I'm not sure what it was but something came to me out there in the blizzard. I was lost, completely lost when something touched my hand and then the light suddenly began to glow between my fingertips. Footprints started to appear quite magically in the snow and they led me back here. And . . .' he paused as the purpose of the words and the beautiful light that still lingered between his fingertips suddenly became clear. It wasn't only there to help him find his way back to the tower but to guide

Drib and Eider back to Cawdor. He knew he had to go out and find them quickly before the light failed, before they froze to death.

He wrapped the heavy, wet folds of his cloak around him and stamped the thick crust of snow from his boots as he turned towards the outer door, pausing only to comfort Sloeberry. 'You need not fear for their safety, child: there is a powerful magic in the air tonight, such wonders as I have never witnessed before. Build up the fire – have the flames leaping up the chimney warming this chamber for their return. I will go out and find them, and guide them home with this magic light.'

'No, no, Berioss, you can't go out there again, your clothes are soaked through – you'll freeze to death, and you'll be lost forever if you venture beyond the gates in this blizzard. It would be madness to go out now: surely Drib and Eider will have the sense to find somewhere to shelter beneath the trees and wait out the storm rather than try to get back. You can't go out there!' Oaktangle cried, dropping the armful of fuel he had gathered from the floor and hurrying across to intercept the old man before he reached the door.

Berioss laughed and gently pushed Oaktangle aside. 'You forget I am Marcher-born and that I am pledged to protect and watch over all of you.'

His eyes took on the far-away look that Sloeberry had seen in them earlier and his voice shrank to a whisper. 'I am the watchkeeper, Oaktangle, and my sword arm is my strength. My hand will be their guiding light in the darkness. I must go out and find them, I must.'

'Then let me come with you, Berioss,' Sloeberry pleaded, running to the hearth to snatch up her cloak and throwing it quickly around her shoulders. 'Please, let me come: you know our people can see far better than you can in the dark, and anyway two sets of eyes are better than one – and it doesn't need all of us to build up the fire.'

Berioss looked down at her and shook his head. 'It would be too much of a risk, I will not hear of it.'

He lifted the latch and braced himself to force the door open against the fury of the storm but Sloeberry's voice made him hesitate. 'What if you miss them? What happens if you don't see them and blindly pass them by – they may be only a footstep from safety!'

Berioss frowned and rubbed his gloved hand across his face, leaving a faint halo of rainbow colours clinging to his eyebrows and the grey, straggly end of his beard. There was truth in her words but he knew it would be madness to let her come with him. The first, violent gust of wind howling around her would probably lift her off her feet and carry her away, but then Drib might perish and the fear that she might never see him again was visible in the tears of helplessness that were brimming in her eyes.

'Come on, look sharp, be quick if you expect to come with me,' he growled suddenly as he made up his mind. 'Hold tightly to my hand and don't let go whatever you do. Stay very close to me and tread in my footprints.'

His voice became a shout as it fought against the fury of the wind when the door was forced open and they stumbled out into the blizzard. Sloeberry gasped for breath as the wind and snow struck her, combing savage fingers through her hair, stinging and scouring her face and tearing at her clothes with a violence she had never thought possible. She lost her grip on Berioss's hand.

'Stay close, stay very close!' Berioss shouted and she made a desperate bid to catch hold of his cloak.

Slowly they forged ahead, bent double against the wind

as they made their way towards the gatehouse. Berioss thrust the battle glove above his head, where it burned with brilliant colours and lit their way as he forced a passage through the snow-drifts that blocked their path.

Sloeberry clutched onto the flying tails of Berioss's cloak as the blizzard engulfed them. The darkness was suddenly full of sinister shapes and the wind wailed and shrieked, scratching painfully at her ears. She looked frantically about her as the shadowy figures closed in, threatening to isolate her from the old Marcher. The blizzard was filling his footsteps faster than she could keep up and he seemed to be getting further and further away with every step, the tails of his cloak slipping through her fingers. The shadows – they had to be the same ghostly forms she had glimpsed in the firelight – seemed to be violent, menacing shapes and she could sense a hatred, a rage in them as they swirled faster and faster around her, smothering her in their shrieking shroud of darkness.

'Berioss! Berioss!' she cried out, but her voice was lost in the fury of the storm. The hem of his cloak was finally snatched from her grasp as she tumbled to her knees. Thin, wailing shrieks of laughter spun around her, cruel and pitiless faces rubbed coldly against her cheeks. She buried her face in her hands and hid her eyes, trying to shut out the twisting, tortured shapes that seemed to scour the deep drifts of snow, feeding on her fear, whipping the stinging snowflakes up into huge forms that towered over her. Instinctively she flinched, raising both hands to protect herself, but she could feel nothing, only a thousand icy prickles striking her skin as the shapes collapsed on top of her, dissolving back into snowflakes which were sucked away by the wind. A huge, dark shape, more solid than all the other ghostly figures, suddenly loomed over her and reached out, trying to seize her. Shards of brilliant light broke through the swirling snow and strong hands lifted her.

'Oh Berioss, it's you – oh Berioss, I thought I was going to die!' she sobbed.

'I told you to hold on tight! I told you to stay close to me!' Berioss was frowning with concern, but Sloeberry was crying with relief as she saw Berioss' face, his beard and eyebrows thickly covered with frozen snow.

'I saw huge monsters – figures in the snow – horrible creatures all around me, in the air, tugging at me, pulling my hair, and my arms. They stopped me keeping up with you,' she tried to explain through chattering teeth but Berioss silenced her with a shake of his head.

'You're letting your imagination run away with you, girl. Snowstorms can play strange tricks on your mind. Now concentrate, look ahead and try to find that gatehouse. Come on, I'll carry you.'

Sloeberry felt safe in the old Marcher's arms and let the demons that had terrorized her fade into the back of her mind.

'It's there! It's there! Look, to the left,' she shouted suddenly, wriggling and pointing as the bulky outline of the crumbling gatehouse suddenly seemed to loom ahead of them.

The fury of the storm appeared to dwindle as Berioss stepped into the scant shelter beneath the broken archway. He stamped the thick snow from his boots and gently put Sloeberry down. He beat his gloved hands together to try and get some life into his numbed fingers and once more lifted the blazing battle-glove up above his head to examine the old building.

'That's odd, it doesn't seem to have been snowing

anywhere near as much around here. The snow has barely drifted up the walls!' He turned back to look through the ruins at the way they had come.

'Look, the tower is still wrapped in the centre of the storm, it's trapped by it. How is that possible?' Sloeberry was bewildered.

Berioss frowned darkly. 'I really don't know, there is much about this place that I don't like.'

He shivered and turned to stride out through the riven doors onto the causeway that led across the bleak headland towards the petrified forest. 'Yes, there seems to be so much strange magic in the air tonight, magic that I do not understand.' He sighed, blinking as he tried to shield his eyes from the sharp, stinging snowflakes that struck his face. 'Now, where shall we try to look for Drib and Eider? Which way do you think the hunt might have taken them?' Berioss stamped his feet. 'This driving snow makes it almost impossible to see anything properly, even with the light on this battle-glove – and the infernal silence is unnerving, it's so unnatural.'

Sloeberry hurried out to where he stood and reached up to take his hand as she peered out into the swirling darkness. She blinked and turned her head slightly to one side, listening intently.

'Come on, let's get on with the search! Standing here freezing to our deaths isn't going to do anybody much good is it?' Berioss grumbled impatiently, although he was uncertain which way to begin.

'No, wait!' Sloeberry cried as she tightened her grip on his hand. 'Wait and listen – can't you hear it?'

'Hear what? No, there's nothing – I can't hear a thing!' Berioss frowned and fell silent.

'No, wait, there's a sound – a faint noise on the edge

of the silence – it sounds like . . .' Sloeberry paused, throwing back her hood and twisting round, turning her head this way and that as she tried to catch the elusive sound with her shell-shaped ears. 'It's bit-rings! I can hear the jingle of the horses' bits, that's what it is, and the sound is coming from directly in front of us!'

Berioss stood in silence and eventually he too could hear the far-off, muffled sound of harness. He quickly gathered Sloeberry up in his arms and took two giant steps along the causeway, lifting the blazing battle-glove as high as he could above his head. 'Look ahead, girl, use your sharp eyes, tell me what do you see?'

'I can't be sure but it looks like two horses yoked together, they're pulling something, a sledge I think. It looks as though there is somebody with them, staggering, floundering – being dragged along beside them.'

'Could it be Drib or Eider?' Berioss asked, his voice full of hope as he hurried forward.

'I don't know, they're still too far away for me to see properly through this blizzard. I don't think there are two of them, I can only see one. I don't think it's Drib, he walks too straight.' Sloeberry's voice ended in a sob as misery and despair flooded over her.

'We'll find him, we'll find him if we have to search the whole of this petrified forest, you have my pledge on it.' Berioss strode purposefully forward through the snow, the battle-glove thrust high above his head, scattering bright rainbow drops of colour onto his hair and beard as it shone out, a beacon in the darkness. His strong voice boomed through the roaring wind as he shouted, trying to draw the stumbling figure with the two horses towards them. It had to be Eider, it had to be, and he forced his mind to shut out the pitiful picture of Drib lying frozen to death somewhere in that gloomy wilderness. Sloeberry was mistaken: the two boys were together, she couldn't see from this distance, there were two of them, there had to be.

V

A Vision in the Blacksmith's Forge

THICKENING SNOWFLAKES were swirling silently down through the bare, winter trees that bordered the greenway and hemmed in the small, isolated village of Muddle. The sky was dark and foreboding, heavy with fresh winter snow which, as it fell, was quickly settling on the thatched roofs of the houses and spreading a fresh, white shroud over its dirty streets. Smoke curled up from the chimneys and here and there a candle flame flickered from behind a shuttered window. There was no welcome for travellers in Muddle and the only sound to be heard in its deserted streets was the mournful wail of the wind as it combed its icy fingers through the branches of the trees.

Quencher, the village blacksmith, stooped to rub clear a patch in the feathered patterns of frost and grime that coated the small windows of the forge and looked out at the frozen winter.

'It's no good, Quencher, we can't go on like this, the children are starving,' grumbled Malthera his wife as she stood by the cold forge. She was at her wits' end as she tried to comfort the two, thin children that clung to her apron tails and looked up into her face with pleading, tear-filled eyes. There seemed to be no end to the winter, no end to the despair.

'There's no need to tell me that, woman,' the big man replied gruffly. 'There's not a scrap of iron here for me to work with in the forge, nor coal for the fire. There's nothing I can barter with. I don't know what we're going to do: I can't conjure food up out of thin air.'

Quencher's huge shoulders shook with despair as he pressed his forehead against the cold window.

'I blame it all on the King for giving those Tunnellers the freedom to roam where they pleased. Mark my words, it wouldn't have happened in King Holbian's daylights. Oh no, the Chancellors would never have allowed it: they would have kept those wretched people in their place. They wouldn't have encouraged them to wander deep into the forest where the nightcreatures lurk. Any fool could have seen that they were bound to fall in with those vile Nightbeasts and start thieving from honest folk. And that's not the worst of it. You know as well as I do, Quencher, that all this chaos and disruption has gone to the heads of the youths in the village – just when they should have been settling down to learning their family trades. Well, now they've just used this as an excuse to turn wild!'

Quencher nodded as his wife fell silent. He knew what was behind his wife's outburst and his face was gaunt with worry as he worried what had happened to his eldest boy, Crimp. He had disappeared three daylights ago, having left the house in a fit of temper. The forest was no place to wander lost after dark, especially with winter closing in. 'Stupid young fool!' he hissed under his breath. His worry began to turn to anger when he thought about the anguish the boy was putting them through, as if they didn't have enough to worry about. He threw down the pair of rusty, long-handled forging tongs he had been gripping in his right hand and they fell into the cold bed of the fire sending up a fine shower of ashes and making the other two children cry out and hide behind their mother.

Crimp had disgraced him and the family in front of the whole village when he had openly defied him, refusing to sweep out the forge and make everything ready to start work. He had shouted and raged that there was no point in doing it, that there was no work to do, that there would never be any work again. He had cursed Quencher and called him a weak, silly old man who was scared of a handful of Tunnellers. He had accused his father of jumping at his own shadow and had spat at his father's feet and laughed in his face. He had sneered at him and said that he wanted a real life, full of adventure. He wanted to do more than skulk behind his mother's apron tails like his father.

Quencher had been too startled by his son's outburst to reach out and clip him firmly behind the ear, too shocked to reach out and stop him as he ran off through the village calling out to his friends and urging them to follow him if they were as sick of living a half-life as he was. Three, maybe four, other youths had followed him. The last thing he had heard was the words Crimp flung over his shoulder as he disappeared into the forest. He had said that he was going for good and he would never come back, that he was going to join the Honourable Company of Murderers if he could find them. That had all happened a worrying three daylights ago and no one had had sight nor sound of the youths since.

'Honourable Company of Murderers indeed! What a lot of silly nonsense! What will people dream up next?'

The air was thick with rumours and the talk in the wayhouse was of nothing else but the troubles, not that some of it didn't have some thread of truth in it he was sure. He remembered a while back when the merchants and journeymen still tried to travel he had overheard a noisy group of weavers complaining bitterly to Landlord Hawksplenty that they had been robbed of everything they possessed, even the tools of their trade. All their harvesting baskets, lobster pots, eel hives, everything they had ready for barter, even the fresh bundles of willow and the clothes off their backs had been stolen by a mob of violent Tunnellers and large, snarling nightcreatures who had attacked them less than a league from the village of Deepling. They had been lucky to escape with their lives. But the interesting thing was – and Quencher distinctly remembered hearing one of them say this – that somebody had approached them in the inn at Deepling only moments before they had set out and had offered them the services of some company or another who had promised to protect them on the road. But the barter for their services had been too high and they had refused. Perhaps, on reflection, there was some truth to this Honourable Company of whatever they called themselves. Perhaps Crimp had managed to join them. Those weavers had certainly been convinced of their existence and had lamented their foolishness in not scraping together everything they had to pay for their protection. By the time they had reached the inn at Muddle they had been in a sorry state, forced to beg and survive on charity. Those had been better daylights with only a hint of the troubles to come and there had still been plenty to eat and iron in the forge; he had forged them new beating irons and a dozen bodkins and they had promised to pay him when they next visited Muddle with new baskets for barter.

Anger darkened the blacksmith's face again. All the rumours in the world were no excuse; these troubles should never have been allowed to happen – the Tunnellers should have been kept firmly in their place and the night creatures should have been banished to the dark depths of Meremire Forest. He wasn't against the people being rewarded for their part in winning the sunlight, and they were excellent gardeners. He had been at the Battle of the Rising, had worked tirelessly at his forge singing out as he repaired battle gloves and breast plates and made new swords and arrow heads. He had seen how bravely the Tunnellers had fought with pick and shovel side by side with the warriors of Elundium. What could have gone wrong since then?

'It's no good you standing there daydreaming, husband, it's about time you started thinking out where our next meal's going to come from!' His wife's voice broke sharply into his thoughts as she bustled the children towards the low doorway that led into the small room at the back of the forge where they all ate and slept. Although she dropped her voice her next comment was still loud enough for him to hear. 'I would like to give that King a piece of my mind for causing all these troubles. How could he let those Tunnellers loose to plague us honest folk? And then with Crimp running off like that . . .'

'No, you're wrong!' Quencher broke in hotly, making his wife pause and glance back in surprise. 'It's not the King's fault, I'm sure he would do nothing to harm us intentionally. If you had been at the Battle of the Rising – if you had seen the misery and torment that the Tunnellers had suffered as slaves to Krulshards, locked away in the darkness for time beyond counting as they were forced to hollow out the City of Night. If you had only seen the way they fought for the King to win the sunlight then I am sure you would have wanted to give them their freedom as well.' Quencher paused and lowered his voice as he glanced at the door. 'And there's another thing – I don't think they really are the ones who are stealing from the villages along the greenways' edge and causing all this trouble, despite what everyone says. They called in here often enough in better times for me to put a keen edge on their scythes and hoes and they never so much as stole a horseshoe nail. No, I don't believe they are thieves: quite the contrary – they more than compensated me for the little I did shaping their tools when they left us those baskets of forest fruits and garlands of flowers – or had you forgotten? The Tunnellers are honest, I tell you.'

'Well that may be so, husband, but thoughts like that won't put food in our bellies will they? They won't bring Crimp back. You had better start thinking about how we're going to eat, for we can't eat horseshoe nails even if we had any and that IS the truth.'

'Yes, I know, and I'm thinking as hard as I can. There's no need to keep going on like this,' Quencher's voice was tight and tense with worry as his wife swept the children away and pulled the door shut behind her. He rubbed a tired hand across his face as he turned towards the cold forge and reached down to retrieve the long-handled tongs that he had thrown down in anger. He sighed helplessly, knowing full well that there wasn't any way he would ever be able to earn the barter he needed to feed his family. Forging hot iron was his trade, it was all he knew, he was too old to change, too old to start again and his family faced starvation. It had been difficult enough after the King had released him and all the other craftsmen from their pledges at the end of the Battle of the Rising. To change from being an armourer tempering swords and spears upon the huge, oak anvils that had been transported to the battle fields, grinding razor sharp edges on new-forged arrow heads and spending hours of patient work linking and weaving the heavy steel rings on the Marchers' chainmail shirts; that had been difficult enough but finding work and toiling as the village blacksmith of Muddle had not been easy. He had learned how to forge coarse ploughshares, hoes and hooks; he had learned how to haggle with the villagers and passing travellers, but the work had seemed a mockery of his skills with swage, hammer and anvil. He had swallowed his pride and he had not looked back on those better daylights, but what on earth could he do now? Could he barter his tools for food? They were all he had left. His thick, calloused fingers lightly touched the smooth handle of his tongs: he could not bear to think of being without them, for then he would feel naked and completely worthless. There had to be another way.

The ashes of the cold forge suddenly billowed up without the slightest breath of air from the set of leather bellows that stood beside the fire. Quencher gasped in fear and snatched his hand away from the tools as a haze of soft, transparent rainbow tones began to glow in the bed of ashes. It rose and swirled, filling the gloomy, grey morning light with a myriad of colour, changing and shifting, blending together and forming the faint outline of a man, old beyond time, heavy with wisdom. He had gathered about his shoulders a flowing rainbow cloak and Quencher knew immediately who he was.

'Nevian!'

The blacksmith stepped hastily backwards and brought his troubled hand up to his mouth. He was afraid, so afraid that he could barely utter the Master of Magic's name and he dared not ask what was wanted of him. Like most ordinary folk Quencher had grown up with a fear of magic and had kept well away from it, especially the power that dwelt beneath Nevian's rainbow cloak. He had good reason to fear that, for he had seen the power at work and knew it to be more than idle inn gossip. He had stood beside his anvil on the Causeway Fields and had heard the Master of Magic curse the thousands of warriors who had refused to pledge their loyalty to King Thane after King Holbian, the last Granite King, had died. He had seen them bound with a fearsome spell that had turned them to trees the first moment they had tried to cross the greenway. They had been forced to stand there as punishment for their defiance, wretched sentinels watching through sweltering summers and bitter, freezing winters until they had learned the error of their disloyalty and King Thane had forgiven them. Quencher had heard the King's shout as it rose above the roar of the battle: 'Warriors, brave men who love the sunlight, I have great need of you.' And then, quite by magic, all the dense groves of trees that had been following the King's beleaguered army through the snow, protecting and gathering up the weak and falling warriors in their branches, began to sway and crumble. Their gnarled, old trunks had broken into hollow strips of bark and they had broken and shattered into a fog of splinters and suddenly in their place stood those thousands of warriors who had once abandoned King Thane.

Quencher's mind was racing as he tried to riddle out what the magician could possibly want from him. One thing he knew for certain: he would have to be very careful not to incur Nevian's anger. Rumour had it that the magician could hear a thousand whispered conversations all at the same time and that he could be in a dozen different places all at once. So maybe he had heard his wife berating the King for causing all the recent troubles. She had been a fool to speak out like that, especially since it was common knowledge that Nevian had groomed Thanehand for kingship and it was he who had placed the crown on his head on the death of King Holbian. And it was well known that he was particularly fond of the Tunnellers. Quencher could remember hearing stories that once, long ago, the Master of Magic had discovered the Tunnellers deep inside the City of Night. He had found them to be slaves of Krulshards' darkness and it had been he who had given them their names and had painted pictures of the sunlight in their prison and foretold of the daylight when they would be free. Yes, his wife had been a fool to speak so loudly out of turn.

'I . . . I . . . I'm sure Malthera didn't mean any disrespect to the King, my lord. Nor does she know the part the Tunnellers played in winning the sunlight.' Quencher found himself pleading, barely pausing for breath. 'Only you must understand she is worried, we're both worried and that's the truth of the matter, what with our son, Crimp, suddenly turning so wild and disappearing like that and me with no work. And the whole village is on the verge of starvation. We're at our wits' end. On top of that . . .

'Enough! Enough, Quencher, I do not come in anger.' Nevian smiled as he lifted his hands and filled the forge with shimmering light. He brushed his long, translucent fingertips across the blacksmith's lips to bind him in silence and then began to paint pictures of the great battles all around them where his hammer had rung out on the anvil and the air around him had been full of sparks.

'I have travelled far, my good blacksmith Quencher, in search of an armourer with your excellent qualities who still holds truth and loyalty in high esteem.'

Quencher swallowed and was at a loss to understand what the magician could possibly mean but he exhaled a shallow breath of relief. At least Nevian had not suddenly materialized to punish Malthera or turn him into something nasty: all was safe so far – but what was this talk of an armourer? Surely as the wisest man in all Elundium he must know that there wasn't a scrap of iron in the forge, nor anywhere else in Muddle for that matter. And even if he could, by magic, conjure up bright metal out of thin air Quencher doubted his ability to work it to the satisfaction of the Master of Magic. He didn't have the skill of Durondel or the Master Armourer of the Granite City who could forge the finest battle coats and weave chainmail shirts so light and yet so strong they could turn the sharpest blade and yet be held in the palm of your hand. No, he feared that Nevian would be sorely disappointed with anything he hammered from his anvil.

'Lord, I could not forge what you desire. I am not worthy,' he stuttered, keeping his eyes fixed on the rough earth floor at his feet.

Nevian laughed softly. 'How wrong you are, Quencher. Look into the fire and see in the flames the strength and quality of the armour you forged. See how men clamour for its protection.'

'But the fire is dead!' Quencher began, only to gasp as Nevian swept out the folds of his rainbow cloak and the cold ashes burst into bright flames. Smoke billowed up without a breath of air and in the fire he could hear the clash and sway of battle and see the battle gloves and helms he had forged. He rubbed his eyes in amazement and watched those battle daylights mirrored so clearly in the fire. Mystified, he turned slowly to the Master of Magic.

'Why are you showing me this? Surely, my lord, the King

does not need my armourer's skill now? It was a different life we lived then and now there are few warriors left who would need what I can forge.'

Quencher paused, racking his brains. He was terribly afraid of upsetting the old magician and the palms of his hands were beginning to bead with sweat despite the bitter cold. Suddenly the reason for Nevian's visit became clear to him: surely he must be seeking some special weapon . . .

'Lord, as you can see there is nothing here save dust and ashes, but I will direct you to the armoury in the Granite City if it is weapons you seek.' When Nevian stayed silent the blacksmith carried on breathlessly, 'King Thane ordered that all the gear belonging to the war that was left over at battle's end upon the Rising should be brought into the city and stored in the armoury. He proclaimed that there would be no need for swords and spears in the new Elundium, nor would there be warriors pledged to bear arms. I am sure that if there is a special sword or battle coat or even a set of spurs, a saddle or a bridle that you have set your heart upon you are bound to find it in there. I doubt if anybody's disturbed those racks and spear-stands, save for oiling and polishing, since then.'

Nevian smiled and then slowly shook his head. 'No, my simple blacksmith, it is not weapons that I seek. You misunderstand the purpose of my visit.'

'Then what can you possibly want from me?' Quencher asked in bewilderment, spreading out his empty hands. 'I have nothing I can offer you, not even a mouldy crust of bread to eat. I do not even know where my children's next meal is going to come from, and all that I have left to barter with are my tools, which will bring precious little in these troubled times.'

'You are wrong, blacksmith, very wrong. Now listen to me,' Nevian ordered, the laughter dying from his face. He drew Quencher close to him, smoothing the flames in the bed of the forge with the tails of his rainbow cloak. He lowered his voice until it was no louder than the wind that ruffled to stir the brittle autumn leaves lying thick upon the forest floor. When all else was silent he continued.

'I fear the people of Elundium are turning against the King: even the few who remain loyal to him are doubtful. Yes, the very people he fought so hard to lift above the shadows are turning traitor. Soon, Quencher, everything he sought to achieve will lie in ruins.'

Nevian paused and looked deeply into the blacksmith's eyes, searching for the strength that he knew had once been there, that he thought he had heard in his voice when he had chided his wife for speaking ill of the King. Surely time had not dissipated his deeper qualities. 'Everything King Thane fought for will be destroyed unless those who hold loyalty and honour in high esteem come forward – people like you, blacksmith. People like you have to make their voices heard. It is time you started doing something to stop this destruction – each and every one of you must do something.'

'But . . . but . . . what can I do? What can anyone do? Surely you know my forge is cold and empty and if you stay longer than half a daylight in Muddle you will find out how much the villagers hate the King and blame him for all their troubles, so nobody here is going to lift a finger to help him. Why, if I was to do so much as to whisper about my love for the King – if I so much as hinted that I had my doubts about the Tunnellers' guilt, they would stone me; they would burn down my forge and drive my family out of the village. I know that would happen, believe me. I have listened to stories of the two old Marchers from Deepling who threw in their lot with the Tunnellers right at the beginning of all these troubles and look what happened to them. Look what the people did to them for interfering: one of them had his house burned to the ground and they were both hounded out of the village.'

'Yes, blacksmith, they were driven out, that much is true; but they were brave men, not swayed by the mob, they followed truth. That part is always left out of the telling, I'll wager. But are they the only ones who remember what part the Tunnellers played in the winning of the sunlight? Are they the only ones who will stand up and defend them? It cost Ustant more than the destruction of his home, for he laid down his life for truth in the courtyard of Candlebane Hall. Berioss protects the Tunnellers still and is pledged to make them strong and ready to serve the King in the dark daylights that lie ahead.' Nevian held the blacksmith's gaze. 'Would you do as Berioss and Ustant did? Would you protect the weak, or have you lost the courage that once coursed through your veins? Will you once again let your hammer ring out on the anvil for justice? Will you help Berioss and forge armour for the Knights of Cawdor?'

'Why yes, yes, of course I will, my lord.'

Nevian's eyes softened. He had not been wrong in judging Quencher's courage or testing his loyalty to the King, and he grasped the blacksmith's arms. If my guesses are right your skill to forge helms and battle gloves will be great demand before the spring sun has thawed the winter snows. You will be needed in Cawdor when the rough and tumble of practice has broken and worn out the few pieces of mock armour that the Tunnellers took from the armoury in the Granite City before they fled. Yes, your skill and the skills of those you can gather with you as you travel along the greenways' edge will be needed in Cawdor. Remember, there will be a place for everyone who holds truth and loyalty in high esteem and would see justice done to those who helped to win the sunlight.' Nevian gathered the folds of his rainbow cloak about his shoulders and his translucent image began to fade and merge with the shadows

'Nevian, wait!' Quencher cried in panic. 'I don't understand, which way do I travel? Where is Cawdor? How can I make such a journey in winter? What will happen to my family? I thought you meant that I was to forge arms and armour here in my forge in Muddle, to use metal conjured up by your magic.'

'Magic?' Nevian snapped angrily. The thin colour of his cloak sharpened and intensified and seemed for an instant to fill the forge with a brilliant, blinding light. 'If there was real power in my magic, blacksmith, Elundium wouldn't be in this sorry state and there would be no need for arms and armour.' Nevian sighed and let his anger sink into sadness. 'But my magic belonged to the time of the Granite Kings and it was never meant to linger on into this new age of man.'

Nevian paused. Then he almost chuckled. 'What you see, blacksmith, is a small magic trick, just an illusion which can only influence little things. I am, in short, my good Quencher, merely a shadow of my former self. I have been reduced by circumstances to helping a crippled sweep's scramble to find truth and now I look for blacksmiths, saddlers and cobblers to find the proper use for their talents where once I used to mould the destiny of Kings! But still I would not stand idly by and watch this chaos and destruction ruin everything. It is to Cawdor you must journey. Your family and all those who still love their King that you can gather along the greenways' edge, they must join you. If my perception is anywhere near the mark it will be on the dark side of morning, far, far away from here, that the fate of Elundium shall be decided.'

'Cawdor?' Quencher whispered, shaking his head in dismay. 'But what of my forge? My family's life is here in Muddle. No, I can't go: you ask too much of me to abandon everything we have worked so hard to create. And anyway I know Malthera will never agree to such a journey in the depths of winter: the greenways are dangerous places and we would starve on the road. The children, especially, are already in a sorry state and are weak from hunger. They would drop to the ground before we reached Underfall. No, no, I cannot do it!'

Nevian's face grew grave and serious. 'And so you will turn your back on your King. You have changed much, Quencher: you are no longer the true-hearted, brave armourer who manned his anvil at the Battle of the Rising. Do you for one moment think that I would let you starve on the road?'

'But I am afraid,' whispered the blacksmith, blushing with shame.

Nevian watched him for a moment and then gently put the fingers of his right hand beneath the blacksmith's chin and lifted his face until their eyes met. 'There is no shame in fear and I will not now ask of you what you cannot offer with a brave heart. Be at peace, Quencher, but remember this: for all the dangers that might have lain ahead of you upon the wild road that leads to Cawdor, a greater darkness is gathering here in Muddle ready to engulf you all. You and your family be warned: famine and death are stealing closer to the village with every daylight and following closely on their footsteps are ruin and decay. They will not pick and choose: they will smother everything that lies in their path. Remember, there is still time, a little time, if you find your courage and decide to follow the great greenway beyond the last lamp at Underfall. Do it in secret and take the high pass through the Emerald Mountains. The Warhorses, Border Runners and Battle Owls will watch over you, I promise, and the fruits of the forest will feed you on the road. Remember everything I have told you.'

Nevian's touch upon the blacksmith's face grew feather-light as the magician's image began to fade away.

'Nevian, Nevian, I am so sorry, so sorry . . .' the blacksmith whispered, sinking onto his knees beside the cold forge. Tears brimmed in his eyes and memories of the courage he had once taken so much for granted welled up.

Kneeling there, his head upon his hands, he did not hear the click of the latch as Malthera opened the door and peered into the gloomy interior of the forge. 'Quencher,' she called as she took a hesitant step inside to search the shadows. She thought she had heard voices, except that now she could see he was all alone and the only sound was his muffled sobs. 'Quencher, what is it? Has the boy been found? Has somebody brought news of his whereabouts? Tell me, tell me!' she cried, grasping hold of one of his large hands and shaking it fiercely to try to get his attention.

'Mother, what's the matter?' a small, fearful voice called out.

Malthera glanced down to see Roenia and Blick, their two younger children, anxiously crowding the doorway. 'Go back, go into the kitchen, both of you, go on now and shut the door!' she ordered loudly before turning back to Quencher and shaking his hand again, 'Tell me what you've heard!'

Quencher blinked, the sound of her voice scattering the memories as he stared into her face. 'Nevian was here, only moments ago, he was here – the Master of Magic. He stood where you are standing now, Malthera . . .' and then, with barely a pause for breath he recounted everything that the magician had said. He left out nothing, especially about the revelation that destruction, famine and death were soon to overwhelm the whole village. 'I was really afraid of the thought of leaving here, of stepping out into the unknown. Even after he told me of the disasters that would befall Muddle I couldn't do what Nevian asked: no, Malthera, I just couldn't risk your life, nor the children's for that matter. Nevian only gave the vaguest hint that the forest would feed us anyway and I wouldn't know where to begin such a journey. And, for all that, how would we find a place that probably only ever existed in the Loremasters' stories that we heard in the Learning Halls? I'm not saying it doesn't exist, I wouldn't dare, not after everything that Nevian told me, but . . .' he paused, glancing furtively around the forge and letting his voice sink to a whisper. 'Mixing with magicians isn't for the likes of you and me: thank goodness he's gone, I was terrified that he was going to turn me into something horrible for refusing to help the King. I felt so ashamed of myself. I would have forged anything he'd wanted here in the forge, if only I'd had the metal; I might have even considered starting on the journey if I had known somebody, anybody, who had the slightest idea where Cawdor lay; but in all my daylights and all the travels I've made Cawdor was only ever somewhere far, far away beyond the edge of sight, somewhere beyond the last lamp of Underfall, beyond the wildness of the Emerald Mountains.'

'Cawdor? I remember hearing something of that place in fireside tales told when I was a child,' Malthera exclaimed, raising her eyebrows in curiosity. 'That's where the Nighthorses were gathered in the time of the Granite Kings, wasn't it?'

There was a slight movement as she spoke, a faint swirl of colour from the gloomiest corner of the forge behind where her husband knelt. It caught her attention: it was as if weak beams of sunlight were briefly finding their way in through the dirty window, trapping and illuminating the minute specks of dust that floated in the frosty air. Except that she knew it couldn't really be sunlight, for the sky was winter-dark and heavy with falling snow.

'Nevian!' she gasped, clutching at the hems of her apron as she whispered his name. She knew then that the Master of Magic had not disappeared, that he was still there, dwelling in the shadows, listening to them, watching them.

'Oh yes, there were plenty of stories about the Night-horses being gathered from Cawdor on the dark side of morning but that's all myth and legend: it's not going to help us now, is it? It won't help us any more than my hammer and anvil can help the Tunnellers. Anyway, I don't see why you're so interested: the magician's gone, vanished back to wherever he came from, and there's no point in regretting being unable to help him. The shame will eventually go away. There are more important things to think of for now, and we will have to riddle out what to do for the best. Clearly we would be fools to stay here after what he revealed to me about what disasters will befall this village. Perhaps we should make our way to the Granite City: at least I might be able to find enough work to feed us if somebody will employ me in one of the forges near the Breaking Yards, if they're still working. There must be someone there who remembers me from my battle daylights. We could ask if anybody's seen Crimp on our way: he must have stopped somewhere, even if only to beg for food.'

Quencher climbed slowly to his feet and brushed the dirt from his knees. 'Yes, that's what we'll do,' he murmured as he began to sort through the racks of tools that hung beside the forge. He turned abruptly to his wife, 'Well, what are you waiting for, woman? Go and gather up whatever you need and collect the children. Take whatever you can carry: we haven't got time to stand around here daydreaming.'

Malthera hesitated, her eyes drawn irresistibly towards the shadows. She could still make out the faint outline of Nevian's rainbow cloak. The air around her was suddenly filled with soft, elusive whispers foretelling their journey if they followed the greenway towards the Granite City. She heard the tramp of endless feet growing louder and louder and saw hundreds of other desperate souls converging on that same bleak, empty road seeking food and shelter within the city walls. She heard the wailing of the dying and the curses of the villagers as they passed by on their journey. She saw how they were to be shut out and stoned as they were driven away and then she heard Nevian's voice.

'That is not your road, Malthera, not unless you wish your children to be counted among the dead. Listen to my counsel, good wife, and take the wild road to Cawdor. Let me guide your footsteps and all those you gather along the way. Have faith. The forest will feed you all. I do not come here lightly, for your King has great need of you and all who still hold him in honour and loyalty. No skill, no matter how slight, will go unused within the walls of Cawdor.'

'What was that? I thought I heard voices.' Quencher dropped the striker he was about to push into the heavy, bulging sack of tools he had gathered. He looked anxiously around him, searching the shadows. He felt wretched and wanted to get away from the scene of his disgrace as quickly as possible.

'Hurry up, woman, what are you waiting for now? Do you think the magician will reappear? Go on, get the children: this place is cursed and the sooner we are out of it the better it will be for all of us.'

He slung his sack up over his shoulder and strode towards the door.

'No, wait, Quencher, you mustn't go rushing off, wait a moment and listen to me before you do something you might regret for the rest of your daylights.'

There was an urgency in her voice that made him hesitate before he turned slowly back to face her.

'Your King has great need of your skills, husband: you cannot refuse him no matter how hard the sacrifice. You know in your heart that you must make this journey to Cawdor.'

'You would have me try to find this road, this desolate and secret road to Cawdor?' Quencher gasped as he stared into her eyes. 'What? Have you gone mad, woman? What would happen to you and the children if I do that? How will you survive if I go? Who would protect you on the road to the Granite City?'

Malthera smiled. 'We will not be on the road to the Granite City, we will be with you, husband. Nevian said that all would be welcome at Cawdor and two sets of hands pulling the handcart will make the journey easier.'

'Well of course it would, but there is no way of knowing if we'll even be able to find a road through the Emerald Mountains, especially in winter, and who knows what dangers we'll meet on the way? I know that the Master of Magic promised that the forest would feed us, but we don't know if there will be enough to keep us all alive. Surely it would be safer to head for the Granite City?'

Malthera shook her head. 'My guess is that everybody who can will be seeking food and shelter in the city and the greenways will be crowded with starving people. No, our best chance of survival lies in the direction of Cawdor: we will gather with us all those who are loyal to the King as we travel.'

Quencher paused and asked in a slow whisper, 'Do you think Nevian will ever forgive me for refusing to help the King?'

Malthera glanced back into the corner of the forge and thought she caught a glimpse of the rainbow cloak as it melted into the shadows.

'I'm sure he already has. Now go and put on your warmest clothes and we will load up the cart.'

VI

Creatures in the Snowstorm

EIDER TRUDGED along silently behind the crude sledge they had made. The laughter and euphoria of killing the Nightboar was long forgotten and he was becoming increasingly worried that they were lost and was beginning to believe that the horses and the owl, who was still with them sitting on the pommel of the saddle, were taking them in the wrong direction. He found it difficult to believe Drib's assurances that the animals knew the way to Cawdor and that they were taking them by the shortest route. He didn't altogether trust Drib's flights of imagination and all this talking to animals and magicians had been irritating enough in the safety of the Learning Hall, let alone out here where a wrong turning could lead to their deaths. He glanced back impatiently to where the small, crippled boy was stumbling along, making heavy weather of the rough terrain and the deep snow – he had already fallen back more than a dozen paces behind the sledge.

'Come on, Drib, can't you try and hurry up a bit – or at least let me help you. Why don't you ride on the sledge or even on Sparkfire's back? At this rate we'll never get back before the storm swallows us up. Look!' He pointed anxiously up through the treetops towards the darkening sky and the silent white wall of the blizzard that was sweeping relentlessly down the steep mountainsides towards them, obliterating everything in its path.

'No, no, you go on ahead,' Drib called back, gritting his teeth and trying to smile reassuringly through the pain. He knew his feet were blistered and bleeding inside his armoured boots but he dared not take them off and his twisted knee joints were burning from the effort of forcing a path through the snow, but he wouldn't give up, he wouldn't become a burden to the others. He remembered only too well how reluctant Berioss had been to let him join the company when they had all escaped from the cellar – Sloeberry had been the only one who had said that he should be allowed to come with them, the only one who had seemed to notice his legs, but he had promised the others that he would be able to keep up with them and fend for himself despite his disability and he wouldn't give up now.

'I'll be all right – stop making such a fuss. I'll catch up with you in a minute. That sledge is already heavy enough for the horses without adding my weight: go on and get back to the others, go as quickly as you can and get that Nightboar roasting over the fire. Everybody is hungry so go on. Don't let me slow you down, go on . . .'

Drib's words trailed off in mumbling breathlessness. He couldn't take another step, he staggered and caught hold of an overhanging branch in an effort to keep his balance, dizzy and light-headed with exhaustion. 'Just go . . .' he gasped, his legs buckling helplessly under him as he sank to his knees.

Silkstone hooted in alarm as he saw Drib collapse in the snow and the horses stopped abruptly, tossing their heads and the sledge slid to a halt. The owl flew from his perch on the pommel of Sparkfire's saddle and past Eider in a whirl of feathers before stooping to hover over Drib, fanning his face with the beat of his wings. His voice rose to a shriek as he pecked at his hair and clawed at his cloak with his outstretched talons.

Drib looked up into the owl's face; everything was swimming in and out of focus. 'It's no good, Silkstone, I just can't get up – not yet – I must rest. Make Eider hurry back to get the others, show him the way, tell Sloeberry, tell . . .' the words slurred together as the boy's head sank slowly forwards.

Eider looked at the boy and the owl helplessly and cursed softly under his breath as he ran back, his boots crunching through the snow, leaving deep footprints back to where Drib lay. He knelt and gathered him up in his strong arms. 'Oh no, I'm not leaving you here, you can think again, you'll freeze to death. Anyway, Berioss and the others would never forgive me. You are going to ride back on the sledge whether you like it or not!'

Silkstone flew to Eider's shoulder and watched carefully as he carried Drib to the sledge and made him as comfortable as possible beside the carcass of the Nightboar, wrapping him up snugly in his cloak.

'Anyway,' Eider muttered thickly, glancing dubiously sideways to the owl perching on his shoulder, 'you're the best friend I've ever had, despite all your irritating chatter and make-believe, I couldn't leave you out here to die – could I?'

Drib's eyelids fluttered at the sound of his voice and he opened his eyes, frowning in an effort to focus and struggling weakly as he tried to get up.

'No! You are staying where you are – no arguments!' Eider insisted firmly as the horses strained at their harness and jolted the sledge forward as they slowly churned a path through the snow between the trees. He hunched his shoulders and pulled his hood down over his head as it began to snow heavily.

'Look! There's something moving – look up the mountain!' Drib whispered, pointing out into the darkness.

'What are you talking about? You're always dreaming up something new!' Eider muttered, yet unable to resist the urge to turn his head and look to where Drib was pointing.

The blizzard was sweeping all around them, enfolding everything, but he thought he could catch a fleeting glimpse of something light up amongst the trees. 'You've got me at it now!' he grumbled crossly, gripping at the back of the sledge as the full force of the storm hit them.

Silkstone flew down and burrowed beneath Drib's cloak for shelter. The horses arched their necks, turning their heads away as much as they could from the stinging snowflakes as they forged slowly on. The snow became deeper and deeper, built up in huge drifts so that Eider could barely keep pace with the sledge and staggered past it, grasping at Nightshade's reins in desperation and knotting them firmly around his wrist so that even if he fell he would be dragged along rather than be left behind. The fury of the blizzard buffeted and roared around them, enveloping everything in a thick, black shroud of stinging darkness. The huge, gnarled tree trunks, the hanging vines and creepers, the sprays of brilliant, frozen orchids, the drifts of snow and all the undergrowth vanished abruptly under the force. Suddenly he couldn't see a hand's distance in front of his face and quickly lost all sense of direction. His only comfort was the muffled jingle of the horses' bit-rings and the constant sharp tug from Nightshade's reins around his wrist. At least he knew that the sledge was still there beside him.

As the storm intensified and the snow fell thicker he found it harder and harder to keep up. He began to stagger, overwhelmed with tiredness. His armoured boots felt as heavy as lead, the snow was stinging and freezing his face and finding its way into every gap and fold, every buttonhole in his clothes. His mind began to wander, to shut out the nightmare of the journey and dull his fear of being lost to die alone in the snow. His thoughts began to blur and lose their focus; memories began to take the place of thoughts; scenes from the past began to crowd in around him. He heard the harsh cackle of the Loremaster's voice and the mumbling chant of the boys in the Learning Hall as they learned by rote. He thought he was in his father's house, warming his feet and fingers by a roaring fire where a suckling pig hissed and crackled above the flames, its blackened skin glistening with basting oils. He could see a cauldron of pottage bubbling on the flames beside it and his father came towards him with laughter in his eyes, his arms open to embrace him. He was holding out the great bow he used in all his battles and was offering it to him. His mother was standing in the background, warm with smiles. Eider tried to thank his father, tried to reach out towards Greygoose and take the bow, but his face was stiff, frozen with snow, and his cold hands only struck the flank of the horse bringing back all too sharply the bleak reality of his desperate plight. He sobbed, cursing as he stumbled heavily against Nightshade's shoulder. His father would never give him that bow, not in a thousand suns. He despised him for being different, for not living up to the example he had set. He knew he had disgraced his family and his father, by now, had probably cast him off completely for falling in with bad company. It was too late to make amends now with death stalking him in this blizzard, waiting to smother him with the thick, white mantle of snow. It was too late to do anything about it at all.

Eider sobbed, overcome with self-pity. He had been so stupid – what had made him escape with Berioss and the Tunnellers? What had made him listen to the wild intrigues of a crippled boy? Nothing could save them now: they were hopelessly lost and nobody, not even the Nighthorses, could find their way through a storm like this. By running away from the Loremaster's accusations he had as good as admitted that there must be some truth in them. But what did it matter – one, maybe two more steps and it would all be over. There wasn't any point in stumbling on: they were never going to get back to Cawdor. Regrets weighed as heavily as the flakes that had piled up on his shoulders as he sank slowly down onto his knees. Frozen tears welled up in his eyes as the white shroud of snow quickly began to cover and soften the crumpled outline of his body. He shivered from the intense, numbing cold and lay still, his mind shutting out the bleak reality of death. He thought he was back in his tiny bedroom high up in the fourth circle of the Granite City, safe and warm, cosy beneath his feathery sleeping rug. Sleep was beginning to blur his senses and enfold him, he was sinking, drifting, and yet thin streams of sunlight seemed to be keeping him awake. They were pouring through the gaps and cracks in the wooden shutters that covered his window, breaking up the darkness, and a breeze was rising, making the shutters rattle and preventing him from falling asleep. Far away he could hear other noises, the sound of street criers heralding in the new morning and he could just make out the familiar, dry, rusty rumble of the merchants' carts being dragged up through the steep, cobbled lanes with their bright awnings flapping and snapping in the strengthening wind. He tried to snuggle down deeper and let the sounds wash over him, let them blend with the darkening waves of sleep that were slowly smothering him.

Eider was completely unaware of the three huge, hairy figures that were following them. Dark, slow-moving creatures whose curiosity had made them follow the sledge-tracks in the storm, pausing only to forage for roots and berries hidden beneath the snow or to search the fallen tree-trunks, scouring the rotten bark for the rare, rich, purple fungus that they prized so highly. The Yerrak, whose people were once rulers of Cawdor long before the time of the Granite Kings, had been reduced to shy, nomadic gatherers, simple, gentle creatures who now existed by harvesting the fruits of the forest. They knew each tree by name and all the secrets it hid amongst its branches. They moved slowly with each season, travelling from the high, inaccessible passes of the Emerald Mountains down through the petrified forest to feed on the black, slippery seaweed thrown up by the restless surf that thundered and boiled along the dark margin of their world. But for all their size they moved with stealth, leaving barely a trace of their passing, a broken twig or a footprint in the snow. They feared the shadow of the Eretch – the wraiths that infested Cawdor and the huntsmen who dwelt in the high mountain fastnesses and hunted them for sport. Umm, the leader of the small group, moved carefully closer to the sledge, glancing furtively through the trees for any sight or sound of the wild dogs who had been hunting with the two humans. They didn't look like any of Largg's hunting people. He listened to the empty howling sound of the wind to make sure that the dogs were far away and sniffed the air to be certain there were no other humans close by. As he hesitated, the figure stumbling along beside the horses suddenly collapsed and fell to the ground and Umm felt that it was the right moment to move in. He wrinkled his squat nose, scenting the swirling darkness; there was no doubt, he could smell the earthy odour of the purple fungus. It had to be coming from somewhere on the sledge. Despite his fear of the humans and the danger his group were in if they came too close he wetted his lips in anticipation. He motioned to two of his companions, beckoning them to follow and lumbered forward, reaching the sledge in three enormous strides and gripping the back of it with the strong, hairy fingers of his left hand.

Nightshade felt a hard tug on the reins as Eider fell and he snorted and stopped. Sparkfire whinnied, tossing his head and fretting at the bridle as he sensed danger. Nightshade shook the ice and snow from his mane and stretched his head down to gently nudge Eider back onto his feet. The horses tensed and their nostrils flared: there was a strong, unfamiliar odour, a smell of earth and trees, all around them. Suddenly three dark shapes emerged through the swirling storm; huge, hairy creatures whose thick coats glowed slightly in the darkness and who were wreathed in billowing clouds of steam where the settled snow was melting from their backs. Nightshade neighed and threw up his head but the traces and collars attached to the sledge prevented him from turning and attacking the beasts. The Nighthorses reared and churned up the snow, pulling hard against the traces in their efforts to get away. The sledge rocked wildly and slewed sideways, pushing up a mound of snow and almost overturning before jolting to a stop.

The leader grunted, gesticulating at the horses and calling out to them in his deep, musical voice, begging them to be still, telling them that they were in no danger, and the horses slowed and rolled their eyes, still anxious. The creature ran one hand down Nightshade's neck and slowly eased his grip upon the sledge. Then he slowly bent down and sniffed at the carcass of the Nightboar, expecting to find the crushed remnants of the bright purple fungus caught between the prickly hairs on its armoured skin or ground in along the sides of its long tusks where it had rubbed against a fallen tree trunk. But the fungus wasn't there. The smell was getting stronger but it wasn't where he had expected to find it. He frowned, his low, wide forehead creased into deep furrows as he sniffed and moved around the sledge, carefully brushing away the snow that had covered Drib's cloak. Umm caught hold of the hood clumsily and pulled it back. The sight of Drib surprised him and he jumped back. He called to his two companions and pointed down at the boy's smooth face and pale skin. Gingerly they touched Drib's cheeks and then combed their stubby fingers through the tufts of orange hair that grew thickly over their own leathery faces. They had never been so close to a human before; they had seen the occasional fisherman from a distance and watched him casting his nets before they had been chased away from the seashore; and they had been hunted through the forest – but those men had long beards and grim-looking, reddish-brown faces coarsened by the wind and weather. They had never felt skin so smooth and so soft.

The heady scent of the fungus was overpowering now and they pulled the cloak further back and sniffed at Drib's clothes, following the pungent, earthy odour down to his gloved hand. Drib felt hot breath on his face and felt something lift and pull at his hand. He stirred and opened his eyes. For an instant he just stared up, disorientated and confused as he looked into the creature's hairy, deeply-furrowed face. Drib blinked and tried to focus on the gentle black eyes set above the large, loose-lipped mouth and the flattened nostrils. Suddenly he realized that he wasn't dreaming, that the creature leaning over him and pulling at his hand was real – terrifyingly real.

Drib gasped and cried out, striking out wildly in his fright. The glove that the beast was holding onto suddenly loosened and came off Drib's hand and Umm stepped back in surprise to stare at it; at the same time Drib fell back in a dead faint. Silkstone, who had been sheltering from the storm beneath the cloak between Drib's crooked legs, was awakened by the sudden jolt of the sledge and the warning neighs of the horses and he flew out, erupting in a whirr of feathers, hooting and shrieking with his talons outstretched, ready to drive the attackers away. The Yerrak easily warded off the owl's attack and sent the bird fluttering across the snowy ground before hastily dropping the glove and turning away. They had never meant to harm the humans and Umm would never have meant to tear his hand off. Their leader stood perfectly still, gripping the sledge as he wondered what to do as the other two began to scour the ground beside it before quickly losing interest. They scraped the snow off Eider's clothes, eager to see another human, and cleaned it away from his face before scenting him, gently stroking the soft skin of his cheeks. One of them lifted him up to take a closer look, turning towards their leader as the owl shrieked and flew out from beneath the cloak on the sledge.

The reins were still knotted securely around Eider's wrist and they became taut, cutting painfully into his skin. The images of warmth and safety inside his head rapidly changed, the shafts of sunlight vanished abruptly and a chill wind began to blow, rattling the shutters in his mind violently. He became shiver cold and the sleeping rug turned to a crumpled sheet of ice and snow as the wind grew louder and more persistent. He felt the tug on his wrist and at once he could hear the sounds of the horses neighing somewhere near him but there were other noises, odd, unfamiliar, strangely musical sounds, voices he had never heard before. He could smell something too, a strong, earthy smell like rotten leaves and moss. The pull on his arm became sharper and sent a hot stab of pain through his fingers as he felt himself being lifted up. Somebody was swinging him around.

Eider abruptly snapped back into full consciousness as the storm howled around his head and the blinding sting of the blizzard struck him full in the face. He knew he was awake but he felt there was somebody, or something, with him in the swirling darkness. He could feel himself trapped, lifted above the ground, his body encased by an enormous, hairy arm. He could see, faintly, the glowing silhouette of the creature that was holding onto him – the outline of its gaping mouth and its large eyes staring curiously at him. Eider screamed in shock and fear, then kicked out, flailing at the beast's chest with his free hand, twisting and wriggling in his effort to break free. The creature stared down at Eider with surprise as he struggled violently and let go, backing away from him.

Silkstone, who had recovered from being knocked to the ground, swooped in between the horses. He flew back to circle once around the creatures' heads and raked his talons through the leader's hair as he tried to drive them away.

The horses neighed and snatched at their bridles, sensing Eider's fear as he drew his dagger, shouting at the top of his voice and stabbing and slashing wildly at the Yerrak as they backed away from him. Umm released his grip on the sledge and it jolted forward, quickly gathering speed and ploughing a furrow through the snow as it raced through the trees.

'Faster! Can't you go any faster?' shouted Eider, whipping Nightshade's flank with the loose ends of the reins as he ran, stumbling and scrambling along beside the sledge. He was too terrified to look back and was expecting at any moment to feel one of the creature's huge hands reach out and grab him. All thoughts of tiredness, of giving up and lying down to die in the snow, were forgotten in his panic to get away. Fear gave him the strength to run and twice, in huge leaps and bounds, he got ahead of the horses only to be pulled up short by the reins that were stilled knotted around his wrist.

He cursed the Nighthorses' slowness, urging them again and again to pull harder. Eventually his racing heart slowed down and he eased his pace and dropped back beside the sledge to check that Drib was all right. He rearranged the cloak, tucking Drib's bare hand into his jerkin.

'You were lucky you had those thick gloves on or one of those creatures might have bitten your hand off!'

Eider glanced up at Silkstone who was perched on the high cantle of Sparkfire's saddle watching the darkness behind them. 'Do you think they're following us? Do you know what they were?' he asked, reaching for his bow and taking a quiver of arrows from the sledge and slipping them back over his shoulder. At least he would be ready if they did appear again.

Silkstone tried to explain to Eider in hoots and whistles that they had vanished from sight but he would watch and warn him if they reappeared but Eider shrugged, none the wiser. He couldn't understand anything the owl was supposed to say, but it was comforting to have something to talk to.

The Yerrak squatted down in the trampled snow and stared at Drib's glove long after the sledge had vanished. They whispered to each other in sad, frightened whispers foretelling the hunting and the burning of the forest as they imagined the retribution that would be demanded of them for tearing the hand from a human.

'We must keep it: we must try and return it. It will be dangerous but we must return it to them,' Umm murmured softly.

One by one the others nodded slowly. Umm picked up the glove gingerly and cradled it in his hand. Then the Yerrak retreated deep into the forest, weaving its branches neatly back into place behind them, leaving nothing to show of their passing.

Eider kept close to Nightshade's side, gripping tightly to the empty stirrup iron for support as they forged a path through the deep snow. In all his life he had never been so frightened by anything as much as by the appearance of the Yerrak and he kept glancing back over his shoulder with his spine tingling and his heart racing with every rising howl of the wind or groan and creak from the canopy of branches in the darkness above his head. After what seemed to be a numbing age of blundering against unseen trees and tripping over hidden roots, they reached the edge of the forest and passed out onto the bleak, windswept headland. The fury of the storm seemed to be abating but it was still snowing hard, although now and again a star appeared through ragged tears in the cloud cover.

Ahead, the snow lay in wide, frozen, wind-driven ridges that sparkled with millions of ice crystals in the occasional starlight. Eider sobbed with exhaustion but fear of what lay behind them still gave him the strength to keep going.

'Come on, we've got this far: Cawdor must lie somewhere just ahead of us,' he whispered breathlessly to the horses as they began slowly to force a passage through the deep snowfield.

His mind started to wander again: no matter how hard he tried to concentrate, he thought he could see a light ahead, a tiny, point of light that glowed with all the colours of the rainbow. He tried to shut it out but it seemed to grow stronger with every step he took. Then there was a voice, a familiar voice hanging on the edge of the wind, and it was calling out his name. Gradually he thought he could see the figure of Berioss striding forward, holding a blazing glove above his head. He knew he had to be dreaming, for surely nobody would venture out to find them on such a night.

Slowly Drib regained consciousness. He felt warm and snug beneath the pile of rugs and cloaks that had been laid over him. Soft firelight danced and flickered on the sooty walls and worn, crumbling stonework of the vast chimney that climbed up into the darkness somewhere high above his head. There were voices laughing and talking in the background, familiar voices, only he couldn't remember who they belonged to. Then he could smell meat roasting on a spit over an open fire and hear the hiss and crackle of hot fat bubbling and hissing as it dripped into the flames below. He began to lick his lips in anticipation but then he stopped and frowned: something was terribly wrong. He couldn't remember who he was or why he had been allowed to lie so close to the fire; he couldn't think who had taken the trouble to put the rugs and cloaks over him. Was he injured? He tried to sit up and cast the rugs aside but he couldn't find the strength and his head throbbed and made him feel dizzy as if he had hit it on something. He sank back in confusion and looked up into the unfamiliar chimney trying to remember which inn his master, Sweepscuttle, had sent him to sweep. He imagined that he must have slipped and lost his footing, wherever he was, and knocked himself out as he'd fallen. It wasn't the first time he had fallen, nor would it be the last, especially when the landlord was impatient to light the fires. But what he couldn't understand was why he had been covered with rugs. Usually if he fell the landlord or Sweepscuttle would grab him by the scruff of his neck and curse him for all the mess and trouble he had caused before throwing him into the gutter.

Drib struggled and, using both hands and elbows, managed to raise himself into a sitting position. He blinked and stared at his unfamiliar surroundings, from the haunches of Nightboar crackling as they roasted over the fire so close to him, over to the wider circles of the tower where what remained of the Nightboar's carcass was suspended by a stout rope from the rafters in the roof. There were horses picketed in one corner and an owl perched, statue-still, on the cantle of one of their saddles; at the other end of the great hearth there was a group of people squatting or sitting, laughing and talking, gathered around an ancient Marcher who was listening intently to an Archer in the centre of the group, his bow held easily in his hand as he described how he had felled the Nightboar with one well-aimed shot between its shoulders. Drib listened as the young man told how he and his companion had been attacked during their long journey back through the storm and then he frowned as the memories began to come back.

'I don't know where they came from . . .' Eider spoke softly, crouching slightly and glancing behind him into the shadows, 'but suddenly they were all around us. The horses were rearing and going mad with fright and the huge, lumbering, hairy creatures seemed to be swarming all over the sledge. I didn't have time to see how many there were – they were so strong the horses couldn't escape, couldn't break free from the grip the beasts had on the sledge. I'm telling you – they must have been twice, no three times, as big as Berioss and they grunted and snarled in the most terrible way. One of them made a grab at me and tried to tuck me underneath its arm while another one tore the cloak from Drib – they tried to bite off his hand! He's lucky he was wearing those thick, armoured battle gloves, for one of the monsters managed to tear one of them off! I've never been so frightened in my life – I was terrified! I don't know what would have happened to us if I hadn't managed to break free and unsheath my dagger!'

'Eider! Berioss . . . Sloeberry . . .' Drib whispered as he recognized the group of Tunnellers sitting around the old Marcher at the far end of the huge hearth. Suddenly his memory flooded back and he remembered loosing the arrow at the Nightboar and spoiling Eider's aim; and then falling from his horse in front of the creature just at the moment of its charge, and having to be rescued by Silkstone and the Border Runners – and then, to cap it all, he had lost the beautiful bow that Eider had lent him. He hadn't been able to walk through the snow with his crooked legs and had become a burden to Eider and the horses and had slowed them up. He should have been helping them to bring back the Nightboar's carcass not being such a nuisance. He realized why he had been put at the far end of the hearth – away from everybody else: it was to separate him from them because he had been such a liability. His face flushed scarlet with shame.

'I'm sorry, I really am so sorry . . .' he began, wanting to crawl away and hide in the darkest corner he could find. He could imagine the whispers. The laughter he had heard as he awoke must have been in response to Eider's description of his clumsiness and his stupidity during the hunt – well, he fully deserved it, no matter how much it hurt to hear it.

Eider paused for breath and glanced across the hearth to see Drib stir and regain consciousness. Immediately he remembered how Drib had dropped his precious bow and for a second anger flared up in him. He was about to tell the others how the boy had fallen from his horse when he saw Drib's face flush scarlet and become a mask of misery and despair. Eider fell silent and echoes of the Learning Hall filled his mind. He remembered all the jibes and taunts, all the humiliation Drib had suffered from the other boys because of the way he walked and all the constant, cruel teasing. They had mocked his poverty and had shunned him because of his dirty, ragged clothes. They had derided all his efforts to do the things they could all do so easily. Eider averted his eyes, ashamed suddenly of all those taunts, for Drib was a better friend to him than any of the others had ever been. His eyes softened as looked across at Drib.

'So, you've decided to wake up at last – and about time too! Come on, come over here, we've kept the warmest seat for you here by the fire. Come and tell the others how you went in amongst those savage dogs and slit open the belly of the Nightboar for them to feed on. Come on, supper's almost ready!'

Drib blinked and could hardly believe his ears. Sloeberry scrambled to her feet the moment she realized that Drib had regained consciousness and ran to his side. 'I was . . . I mean we were so worried about you when Eider brought you back on the sledge. You looked half frozen to death – you were hardly breathing. And that horrible bump on the back of your head looked so large – and your hand, how cold it was without the glove – it was turning blue. We put you as close to the fire as we dared to and we piled all our clothes and sleeping rugs on top of you. We tried to keep you warm – were you warm enough?'

'No, no, I don't understand – YOU don't understand . . .' Drib muttered in confusion. 'I let Eider down – I dropped his beautiful bow, the one he lent me, and I almost lost us the Nightboar – I was so stupid, so . . .'

His stumbling words trailed away into silence as he saw Berioss climb stiffly to his feet and walk toward him with Eider at his side. Silkstone flew across from the corner of the chamber and alighted on his shoulder, hooting softly and pulling at a stray curl of his untidy hair. Eider stopped in front of him and reached down, clasping his hand and gently pulling him to his feet. He spoke softly and privately so that nobody else in the company could hear his words.

'You dropped the bow by mistake: it was an accident – anybody would have done that if their horse had been spooked the way yours was. We killed that Nightboar together. I couldn't have done it on my own – I couldn't have done it without you.'

'But . . . but it wasn't . . .' Drib protested in surprise.

'No buts!' Eider grinned, putting his arm around Drib's

shoulders and turning him towards the others. He raised his voice. 'Now that Drib has got his strength back he can help me carve the meat. It must be ready by now – I'm starving!'

Oaktangle and the others laughed in agreement and began to pull a broken table they had found in the corner of the tower in front of the fire, close to the hearth.

Berioss gripped Drib's arm. 'Well done, lad, that Nightboar is one of the largest I have ever seen. It will feed us for a good part of the winter.' The old Marcher paused and glanced anxiously across at the door to check that it had been securely bolted before he lowered his voice and asked, 'Tell me, what did you think of those enormous creatures that attacked the sledge? Do you think they were after the carcass of the Nightboar? Do you think they will follow the tracks of the sledge and attack us here?'

'I don't know – I'm not really sure. How can you tell?' Drib replied slowly as the others gathered around him listening eagerly. He looked past them into the gloomy shadows of the tower and listened to the sound of the wind howling through the ruins outside. He could hear the thunder of the surf breaking on the rocks below and he shivered, remembering suddenly waking up to find himself lying on the sledge, the freezing snow flurries striking his face as one of those huge, hairy figures loomed over him.

'I was really so scared when I first saw them but . . .' he paused, shaking his head, 'but now I'm not really sure if they meant to harm us. The ones leaning over me didn't really seem very interested in the carcass of the Nightboar – they were touching my face and pulling at my clothes – one of them seemed intent on my sleeve. They were sniffing me all the way down my arm, trying to get at my hand. It was as if they were looking for something, I don't think they were trying to bite it off. The strange thing is that although they were so big they didn't hurt me at all and it really seemed to frighten them when they pulled my glove off, almost as if they were afraid of what they had done. And there's something else, their voices were deep but they were oddly musical. They gave me a feeling of sadness, real sorrow that seemed to echo before it went away in the stormy darkness.'

Eider laughed loudly and slapped Drib on the back. His voice made the Tunnellers jump in the flickering firelight and Sparkfire whinnied softly as he kicked up sparks from the cobbles where he had been picketed with the other horses. 'Sadness in their voices! Whoever heard of such a thing! That's typical of you, Drib: no wonder you were teased and taunted in the Learning Hall, you're always trying to see the best in everybody – even those savage creatures. Why, you'll be wanting to make friends with them next! You'll want us all to go out and search for them!'

'Now now, that's enough of such talk!' Berioss interrupted sharply. 'I don't want any of you wandering off on your own, not until we know a lot more about this place.'

'But why?' Oaktangle asked, following the old Marcher's gaze around the chamber and out toward the bolted door. 'Surely there can't be anything really bad here, can there? The Nighthorses wouldn't have brought us here if there was, surely? And we know it's completely deserted.'

'Is it? I'm not so sure, not after hearing about those creatures that attacked Eider and Drib's sledge,' Berioss answered gravely, leaning forward and resting his large, weatherbeaten hands upon the table. One of them still held the faintest hint of the rainbow colours between the fingertips and it seemed to dance in the flickering firelight. He lowered his head so that he was level with the rest of the company. 'There's something strange about this place, a feeling of magic in the air that makes me uneasy, and there's no knowing what dangers may be hidden out there in that petrified forest. Trees that grow like that just ain't natural. And who knows what may lurk unseen amongst those ruins waiting to pounce? Remember, it's been a very long time since the forefathers of those Nighthorses who brought us here were gathered on the dark side of morning to serve the Granite Kings and I for one would like to know a lot more about what brought about the ruin and devastation of this once great fortress. What happened to the people who used to live here? I want to know that before I'll sleep easy in my bed.'

'Why yes, that's right!' Eider was quick to agree with the old Marcher. 'We've got to be on our guard – they could attack us at any moment. I suggest that we take it in turns to stay awake and keep watch.'

The Tunnellers began to look anxiously around the room and Sloeberry moved closer to Drib.

'No wait!' Drib cried, seeing fear steal amongst them, making them grip the hilts of the swords and daggers that hung at their sides. 'I don't think those creatures meant us any harm . . .'

'That may be the case but we won't take any chances. Eider's right, we've got to be prepared. We'll mount a guard. Mistletoe, Damask – you two take the first watch . . .'

Berioss began to organize a rota for guarding the tower.

'Why won't Berioss listen to me? It's not those creatures we should be worrying about . . .' Drib muttered in exasperation as he turned towards Sloeberry. He felt her gently squeeze his hand, entwining her fingers briefly with his.

'I'm listening, you can tell me – if you want to,' she whispered.

Drib smiled shyly, feeling the colour rising in his cheeks. 'Well, yes,' he stuttered, pushing his untidy hair out of his eyes. She looked so beautiful in the flickering light that he had to think hard to remember what he had been saying.

'There was a real gentleness in that creature's eyes, the one that leaned over me. I could see it when he sniffed my clothes and pulled off my glove. I don't know how to explain it but I had the distinct impression that it was a lot more frightened of me than I was of it.'

Drib paused for a moment and watched the others gather around Berioss. 'Berioss is right to set a guard but it should be to watch out for those other dark, sinister, shadowy figures, the ones I caught a glimpse of following us through the trees when we first found the Nightboar's tracks in the snow.'

'What figures?' Sloeberry's fingers tightened on his. 'What did they look like?' Her eyes grew wide with fear as she remembered the huge, monstrous shapes that had wailed and shrieked in the storm, threatening to engulf her when she became separated from Berioss.

Drib searched for words to describe what he had seen. 'I don't know how to tell you about them: in a way they weren't real, and I'm not sure that Eider saw them at all. At first there was just a sensation, a feeling that something was following us, eyes in the shadows between the trees. But whenever I looked they just seemed to vanish. If I say anything Eider's bound to say that I imagined it, but the moment I loosed the arrow at the Nightboar and it glanced off its side it was really strange. The Nightboar turned around and began to charge at me, it was really angry, and those ghostly shapes seemed to crowd around it and merge with it, making it swell up and darken . . .'

'Come on you two, stop whispering together. Drib, help me carve the meat – everybody's starving,' Eider called out.

Drib turned to go to the fire but Sloeberry caught his sleeve. 'I think I've seen these creatures as well, when I went out with Berioss to look for you. But he didn't believe me when I told him either.'

'There's a strange feeling here, I just can't quite make it out. I don't just mean in the ruined fortress but everywhere, all through the petrified stone forest, in the sounds the birds make as they wheel and soar above the surf,' Drib replied as he watched the flames flickering in the hearth. 'It feels as though we're being watched by something evil wherever we go and whatever we are doing.'

VII

Woodsedge

BREAKMASTER SPURRED Beaconlight out ahead of the others, fiercely shaking the snow and icicles from his beard and bushy eyebrows as he peered anxiously through the worsening storm for any sight of the wayhouse at Woodsedge. Silently he cursed his own impatience for wanting to press on with the journey. He had been more worried about getting Elionbel and Krann away from the hostile atmosphere and furtive whispers on everybody's lips than he was afraid of the threat of the Nightbeasts. Talk of these creatures was rife and they had encountered veiled glances and nervousness wherever they stopped to rest or ask for shelter: he almost wished that he had listened to Nebran, the messenger, who had offered to accompany them and guide them to the safety of the tower on Stumble Hill.

The old horseman twisted stiffly in the saddle and glanced back across his shoulder, past the silent figure of Greygoose hunched forward in his saddle, through the swirling snowstorm to the dark, barely visible silhouette of the messenger who was riding a pace behind Elionbel and Krann, bringing up the rear of their small company. He wished he'd had the good sense to listen to him in the courtyard of the Three Horseshoes Inn in Thrift. Nebran, like all good Errant riders, had a nose for weather and had warned him of a fresh storm bringing a blizzard onto the road from behind them, but Breakmaster had been more concerned by the hostile faces that were staring out of every window and doorway and their angry mutterings as they cursed the coming of strangers to their village and he had not heeded the rider's warning; he should have demanded lodgings for the night.

Thrift was the last village and the Three Horseshoes Inn the last hostelry, but they had ridden too far to turn back now. Breakmaster scoured the hedgerows on either side searching through the swirling snowflakes for a familiar landmark, anything that would tell him where they were. It was a long time since he had journeyed this far beyond the gates of the city in the depths of winter and the countryside all looked the same beneath the thickening mantle of snow. He glanced up into the darkening sky and then back to the others. Krann was shivering and crying from the cold and Elionbel had drawn his pony in close to hers with the lead rein. She was doing her best to comfort the child as she brushed the settling snow from his shoulders and wrapped his thick travelling cloak more tightly around him in an effort to keep out the icy wind. Breakmaster didn't want to alarm Elionbel but if they didn't reach her father's house within the hour they would be forced to spend the night on the greenways' edge, sheltering as best they could beneath whatever crude canopy he, Greygoose and Nebran could build from the fallen branches. He feared that if he could not light a fire Krann might not survive such a night.

'Mulcade, where are you? I need your sharp eyes to find Woodsedge,' he muttered irritably under his breath, but he could hardly blame the owl for seeking shelter as the storm had worsened.

'Elionbel, I am so cold, is it much further? Why aren't we there yet?'

Krann's cry broke through the old horseman's fears and he reined Beaconlight back beside the boy's pony and smiled down at him, brushing the snow from the top of his hood with a broad sweep of his battle glove as he tried to raise the child's spirits.

'Take heart, Krann; we can't be more than half a league from Woodsedge. Why, you would be able to see the chimneys if it wasn't for this infernal storm.'

'But I'm so cold, my fingers and toes are burning, I want to go home,' Krann wept, trying to huddle deeper inside his cloak. All his enthusiasm for this adventure had evaporated. He had lost track of how long he had sat there being rubbed raw by the saddle and frozen stiff by the weather.

Breakmaster could see the boy's pinched, blue face beneath his hood and saw that he was so cold and shivering so violently that he would have to do something quickly if he was to stop him freezing as he sat in the saddle. Distant memories suddenly filled his head and again he heard the thunder of the iron trees battering on the outer walls of the armoury where King Holbian and all those who had survived the battle had retreated when the Nightbeasts had overrun the Granite City. He remembered how the King had hesitated on the threshold of the secret road that would have led them down beneath the city, his fear of the dark having completely consumed him. That was the moment when Breakmaster had heard Nevian's voice urging him to wrap the King in the precious steelsilver battle coat that he had found hidden beneath a pile of forgotten, rusting spears and shields. It was the last steelsilver coat in all Elundium and he had so dearly wanted to possess it himself.

'Keep him warm,' the magician had whispered through

the shouts of chaos and the roar of the Nightbeasts who were assaulting the armoury. 'Cloak him with something you value above all else.'

Breakmaster smiled as he reached down to unbuckle the two leather straps on the flap of the saddle-bag where he had stored the coat, his most treasured possession. He remembered how he had given it up to wrap around the King, ashamed by his desire to keep it, and as he had draped it around his fragile shoulders even after all the time it had lain forgotten in the armoury it had had a touch of sunlight hidden in its folds and as he had wrapped his King in it the sound of meadow larks and the first blackbird of morning had whispered from its shimmering, silken weave. It had not only kept the King warm but had given him the courage to walk in the darkness and King Holbian had known the measure of his gift when he had bequeathed it to Breakmaster, making it his forever once they had reached the daylight at the end of the hidden road.

'Hold still, Krann, and I will wrap you up in this coat of kings,' Breakmaster called, slipping it over the boy's head. 'It is large enough to wrap three times around you and I promise it will keep out the cold until journey's end.' He laughed as he felt its silken softness even through his thick battle gloves as he threaded the fine silver buckle beneath the child's chin.

'It is really strange, look at the colours, they change as I move. Listen, I can hear music . . . oh, it's really warm and look, the snow's not settling on it at all, look. Can I keep it, can I, please?'

Breakmaster hesitated, not knowing how to say no, but Elionbel quickly came to his rescue. 'Oh, no, you mustn't ask to keep that, Krann, you see it's a very special coat that King Holbian bequeathed to Breakmaster at the end of a long, dark journey. I am sure that Breakmaster will tell you the whole story if you ask him nicely.'

Breakmaster frowned and brushed away the settling snowflakes from his nose as he shook his head in refusal. He had promised King Thane to escort Elionbel and Krann to the safety of the tower on Stumble Hill and place them in the care of Lord Kyot and the Lady Eventine, to take them away from all those stories of the Nightbeasts and the troubles that were driving Elundium into chaos. It hardly seemed the right time or place, while they were lost upon the greenway in a blizzard with night drawing in around them, to retell how the Nightbeasts had overrun the Granite City and forced King Holbian to flee by way of that dark and frightening road beneath the ground.

Elionbel leaned close to the old horseman and whispered above Krann's head, 'Tell him of the magical caves that you saw, the ones hung with jewelled stalactites; tell him of the singing fish that swam in the underground rivers and leapt up through the sparkling waterfalls.'

'But . . . but . . . we didn't see any of those . . .' he tried to interrupt the Lady Elionbel only to feel her cold fingertips silence his protest.

'I know you didn't – just as clearly as I know that we will perish out here on the greenway if we don't reach Woodsedge by nightfall. Just make it up,' she urged. 'Weave such a tale of magic that the wonder of it will distract him from our desperate plight.'

Reluctantly Breakmaster agreed although he knew that he was no storyteller. He beckoned Nebran and Greygoose to ride ahead and told them to keep a sharp lookout for somewhere to stop and build a shelter before it got too dark. The messenger nodded grimly, tightening his cloak around his shoulders as he spurred Remus out ahead of the others, keeping to the righthand side of the road while Greygoose searched the left. Both vanished into the swirling storm. Nebran thought he knew the road as well as anyone but by his reckoning they should have come upon the wayhouse of Woodsedge a good hour or more before: he couldn't understand why the journey was taking so long. Unless the child's pony, Larksong, had slowed them, and then there was the storm, of course. He looked ahead through the snowflakes and saw a vague outline of trees growing close together, bordering the greenway. They became clearer as he rode towards them and he realized that they were coming to the eaves of the Black Forest. Now he was certain that the ancient wayhouse of Woodsedge stood beside the road less than a league ahead of them. He urged Remus into a trot and the Archer drew in close beside him as he called back to Breakmaster telling him that they would ride ahead and get help, but his voice was snatched away by the storm.

Breakmaster didn't hear the messenger's shout as he moved Beaconlight in close beside Larksong and leaned down. Raising his voice above the howl of the storm he started to tell Krann the story of King Holbian's escape from the armoury and the journey along the secret road.

'But who was the King running from?' Krann asked, his eyes wide with interest, interrupting the old horseman before he had really got into the spirit of the story.

Breakmaster hesitated, at a loss for a way of describing the Nightbeasts that wouldn't terrify the child or reveal the truth of his beginnings. 'Oh, they were just some nasty creatures – hobgoblins and the like – nothing for you to be worrying yourself about. Now, listen carefully and I will tell you of the great winding stairway that we descended: it was

lit by millions of glow-worms that hung from the ceiling
and the narrow, cobbled road that we followed for leagues
underground had, at some time in the distant past, been
inlaid with magical stones that sparkled and shone when
we stood on them.'

Krann yawned as the story unfolded. He felt warm and
drowsy inside the steelsilver coat and the old horseman's
voice grew faint and far away, mingling with the sounds
of a summer's day as he drifted into a deep sleep.

A dark shape suddenly fluttered and hovered in front
of Breakmaster's face, startling him and making him reach
for his sword. 'Mulcade!' he cried, letting the blade slip
back into its scabbard as the owl hooted and stooped to
his perch on his shoulder.

Elionbel, in her frozen misery, heard the owl's voice and
sat up straight to stare around her. She saw two figures
emerging through the storm ahead of them and realized
they were running towards her. She thought she could
hear familiar voices calling her name.

'Father! Rubel!' she cried out in joy as she recognized
them and realized that they had reached the safety of
Woodsedge at last.

Tombel, breathing hard, stopped beside Beaconlight
and rested his broad marching sword across his shoulder
before taking the horse's frozen reins in his hand. 'Need
must have driven you on a hard road, old friend, for
you to be out in a storm like this one. Mulcade arrived
hours ago and made such a fuss that we knew somebody
must be in trouble upon the greenway but it was only
when the messenger arrived with Greygoose that we
knew for sure who it was and from which direction
you were coming. We don't get many travellers these
daylights – ' He paused to glance over his shoulder towards

the silent trees before adding darkly, 'Not since these new troubles began.'

Tombel's greeting suddenly faltered and he took a sharp intake of breath as he caught sight of Krann warmly wrapped up in the steelsilver battle coat fast asleep in Larksong's saddle, his head resting against Breakmaster's calf where he was sandwiched between Stumble and Beaconlight. Tombel's ruddy face paled and his lip began to tremble as painful memories of the child's black beginnings flooded back. There had not been a waking moment since his wife's death when the horror of what she had suffered as Krulshards' prisoner wasn't with him, or a night when the nightmares of it didn't come back to haunt him. If only his duty to King Holbian had not called him and every Marcher under his command away from Woodsedge to fill the ranks of the battle crescent massing before the Gates of Night. Their victory over the Nightbeasts had indeed been hollow and he had been a fool not to have guessed that Krulshards, having escaped capture, would journey across Elundium to exact revenge for that defeat. And he had done that by overrunning his home at Woodsedge and taking Martbel and his daughter, Elionbel, prisoners.

Hatred – revenge? He would probably never know what had caused the Master of Nightmares to capture them or what had driven Krulshards to rape Martbel in the ruins of the Granite City before he took them back to the City of Night. Tombel had never been able to find the words to talk to his daughter about the terrible daylights they must have suffered in captivity or to ask her about the vile offspring of that evil coupling that had been torn from Martbel's womb as she lay dying in the City of Night. King Thane might have been able to forgive the bastard, that vile half-creature of light and darkness who had spread the terror of his shadowlight across Elundium, but he had never seen the sense in what Thane had done when he had plunged the sword of Durondel bound with a fragment of Krulshard's black malice into Kruel's footprints to give him a shadow. Never mind that he had been reduced to a helpless baby that now slept so easily in Larksong's saddle, he would not – could not – have forgiven him. He would have plunged the sword not into his tracks but into his heart.

Breakmaster saw the pain and the anguish in his old friend's eyes and he reached down to him. The brittle layers of ice that had formed in the joints of his battle gloves shattered as he gripped Tombel's arm. 'The past is over and is gone forever,: your anger cannot bring Martbel back. Krann is not to blame, let it go.'

'You are wrong!' Tombel replied, his voice rising as the anger flashed in his eyes. He broke away forcefully from the old horseman's grip and took a threatening step towards the child. 'I know you are wrong because I have heard the sounds of the Nightbeasts as they reawaken in the depths of the forest. I have seen the damage that the marauding Tunnellers have done as they steal from honest folk and I have seen the way they murder travellers at every opportunity. I say it is happening because the King spared Kruel's life at battle's end. Changing his name from Kruel to Krann won't wipe away the dark stain of evil that dwells inside him. Shrinking back into the form of a snivelling, innocent baby doesn't fool me: he will always be Krulshards' vile offspring no matter what the rest of you call him.'

'Father, stop it!' Elionbel cried out in distress as her father's raised and angry voice made her turn sharply towards him. There were tears in her eyes as she spoke. 'It was I who begged Thane to spare the boy's life. It was I who took the sword out of his hands as he was about to make the killing stroke because I saw in that moment when he planted the shadow into Kruel's footprints that he had destroyed Krulshards' black seed. He had purged the evil forever. The small, helpless infant lying in the snow was a part of my mother; his likeness to her was so strong and there was such a look of innocence and gentleness in his eyes that I could not let Thane kill him.' Elionbel paused to look down at the sleeping child and reach a protective arm around him, 'In that instant I saw him for what he truly was – my brother.'

'Brother!' Rubel spat out the word as though the taste of it scalded his tongue. 'I could never in all my daylights call him that.' And he moved in close beside his father, his hand on the hilt of his sword.

'Enough!' Breakmaster cried, casting back the folds of his heavy winter cloak to reveal the hilt of his own sword.

Mulcade shrieked from the old horseman's shoulder and spread his wings in preparation for the attack. 'I will not stand here as we argue the rights and wrongs of what the King did when he spared the life of this infant. I know Krann and I know him as an innocent child, pure of heart, and I will not let you or anybody else stand in my way or make me break my promise to King Thane. I swore that I would escort your daughter and Krann to the safety of the tower on Stumble Hill where they will be safe from such talk. Now either you can offer us the hospitality of Woodsedge and keep faith with the pledges you once made, Marcher Tombel, or you can stand aside and let us seek shelter from others who do not doubt their loyalty.'

For a moment Tombel stood his ground defiantly and stared up into Breakmaster's face, oblivious to the howling storm and snowflakes that were swirling around them both. All the hurt and rage he felt about Martbel's torment, all the suffering she had endured, boiled up in his heart.

'Father, stop it – stop!' Elionbel cried out. 'Krann is a part of us: Martbel's blood courses in his veins just as it does in mine and Rubel's. If you don't believe me come and look at the likeness in his face. Come and look, both of you.' Elionbel's voice faltered and dropped into a sob. 'You mustn't hold him responsible for mother's death: he didn't ask to be born, he doesn't deserve to carry the burden of hatred, the hard, cold looks, the masked whispers that he encounters at every turn. He is just a child, an innocent child. Come here, come here and look at him.'

Tombel's broad shoulders sagged as the truth in what his daughter said cut deeply into his anger. He had seen little of the child since Thane spared his life at battle's end, for he had rarely visited the Granite City despite a constant stream of invitations. He had shrunk further and further into himself as he allowed himself to be consumed by the tragedy of his loss.

'Father, I love you,' Elionbel whispered as she saw the broken old man who had once strode so boldly out amongst the shadows to rescue her from the Nightbeasts. Through her tears she reached out her free hand toward him.

'Come now, son, lend me your arm to give me the strength to face my demons. It is time that I faced the torment of my soul,' Tombel muttered, grasping his son's arm for support and moving closer to the child who was still fast asleep on the pony. Tentatively he brushed away the settling snow from the top of the child's hood and gently drew it back to look upon Krann's face. He caught his breath as he saw the likeness to Elionbel and his son and gasped as memories of those better daylights came flooding back with the echo of Martbel's voice.

'Forgive my anger,' he whispered as Krann stirred and opened his pale blue eyes to look innocently and trustingly into Tombel's face before smiling and drifting back into sleep. 'Quickly, follow me, you shall weather out this storm at Woodsedge.'

Tombel stepped hastily back away from Krann and caught the look of understanding from his daughter's eyes before leading them along the greenway.

Rubel hesitated for a moment longer, staring down at Krann. 'Brother?' he whispered, trying to fit his understanding around the word before turning on his heel to fall into step beside Elionbel's horse. She reached down and touched his shoulder, clasping the thick weave of his cloak in silent thanks. She had feared this meeting from the very first footsteps of their journey but she had known no shorter or easier route to the tower on Stumble Hill than this one that passed the door of Woodsedge.

Krann stirred, warm and secure in the steelsilver coat, and opened his eyes, blinking them at the flickering candle-light as Breakmaster carried him in over the threshold of Woodsedge. The child looked around, wide-eyed, at the low-beamed room with its rich, dark oak panels set with firmly sculptured lamps and the huge fireplace big enough to seat a dozen people. A huge log lay between the twisted bars of the fire-dogs glowing red and hissing and crackling as it sent flames and ribbons of bright sparks up the blackened chimney and illuminated the polished, stone-flagged floor. Then he heard an unfamiliar voice saying, 'Krann, you shall have the guest room.'

Immediately Elionbel interrupted and said, 'No, Krann will sleep in my room. He will be more content that way and less afraid of unfamiliar surroundings.'

Krann yawned as he felt himself being carried upstairs. He glanced backward, saw Elionbel and reached out for her hand.

Breakmaster shivered and stamped the snow from his boots as he hurried back into the wayhouse and stood with his back to the roaring fire after checking that the horses were safely stabled for the night, warmly rugged and well fed.

'What news do you bring from the Granite City? Tell me, is there any substance to these black rumours that are on everybody's lips? Are there Nightbeasts loose in the city? Is that why my daughter is fleeing from Candlebane Hall? And why, for goodness sake, can they not stay here? Doesn't Thane think I am capable of protecting my own family?'

Tombel offered Breakmaster a brimming jug of mulled ale and the old horseman warmed his hands around the jar, drinking deeply before he answered. 'Oh, yes, there are rumours all right, the city is alive with them but, as you well know, rumours are just the gossip-mongering of the uninformed. You remember the saying surely, the one about idle tongues?'

Breakmaster laughed uneasily, unsure about how much to say and whether he could trust Tombel or his son, Rubel, with the King's confidences. There was no knowing who the real enemy was in these troubled daylights. He hadn't originally intended to stop anywhere for very long during their journey to Stumble Hill, especially

Woodsedge: they were here only because the weather had forced them to stop. There had been enough whispers in the Towers of Granite telling how Tombel had spoken openly against the King, calling him a fool, throwing his glass down in anger and storming out of a banquet soon after the great battle. But Breakmaster always hesitated to believe such rumours and Tombel was one of his oldest friends, they had fought side by side so many times. In better daylights he would have trusted him with his life.

Breakmaster was in a quandary as he lifted the tankard to his lips and slowly drained its frothy contents. He glanced over the earthenware rim at the keeper of Woodsedge and his son: had Tombel's grief poisoned him enough that it would force him to seek revenge for Martbel's death? He was glad that Elionbel had the good sense to insist the child spend the night in her room, at least he should be safe enough until morning.

'Come, old friend, tell us more. Surely every rumour contains a thread of truth? We have heard tell that the Nightbeasts killed a hundred guards to free the Tunnellers and that they escaped on the Nighthorses after sacking half the city. There must be some truth in it because we have heard the creatures themselves roaring from the forest – or at least something that sounds remarkably like the Nightbeasts. We have even seen their tracks in the snow . . .'

Tombel paused, sensing the frigid atmosphere in the room. He frowned and glared at Breakmaster, Greygoose and the messenger. 'What ties your tongues? Surely they are not still frozen with the cold? What makes you all so reticent, so guarded? Come, Greygoose, tell me, how is that boy of yours? Still up to his old tricks, I'll be bound. Relax, you're amongst friends. I'll call for more ale.'

Greygoose looked hastily away to avoid answering and Tombel hesitated, realizing that Breakmaster was still wearing his sword and Greygoose had not laid down his bow. Tombel's face blanched as he remembered his friend's accusation, how he had doubted his loyalty when he had first set eyes upon Krann asleep in the pony's saddle and how he had openly vented the anger that had been stored in his heart.

'Surely you don't think that I would abuse my high office as Keeper of Woodsedge? You don't think that I would seek revenge for Martbel's death by harming the child, or hurting my daughter in any way? If you harbour such fears then take my sword – bind me in my chair – lock me up in the stables – banish me!' Tombel was devastated by the doubts that he now saw so clearly in Breakmaster's eyes and turned towards the outer door.

'No, wait, come back!' Breakmaster called after him. He unbuckled his sword and placed it upon the table, relieved to hear such sincerity in Tombel's voice. 'You must forgive my caution, old friend, but we live on the edge of such dangerous and uncertain times. It is difficult to know whom you can really trust. It was different in the daylights of the Granite Kings: then we knew who our enemies were.'

Tombel retraced his steps and embraced the old horseman in relief. 'Now, tell me everything and leave nothing out.' He motioned the two men towards the chairs now set near the fire.

When Breakmaster had finished talking Tombel looked thoughtful. 'But these troubles don't make any sense. They don't seem to profit anybody, well no one that I can see. Somebody's got to be behind them though, somebody's got to have started the rumours and be doing all the murdering and stealing.'

'What about the Tunnellers? Surely they started it!' Rubel interrupted hotly. 'Feelings have been running pretty high against them for some time even before the troubles began: I've been hearing mutterings and gossip in all the villages around here – everybody is accusing the Tunnellers of living off the fat of the land, coming and going as they please, demanding the best lodgings and eating everything they could lay their hands on. It is said they ate the landlords out of food and for what? Just for doing a bit of gardening, mowing the greenways and trimming back the forest edge. Not that I've got anything against them personally but I think the King spoiled them by making their lives so easy. It stands to reason, doesn't it, that they wouldn't be satisfied with all that, that they would become greedy and want more? It's obvious to me that they wandered off into the forest and woke the Nightbeasts.'

'Oh, no, no, no, no, no, you've got it all wrong,' Breakmaster exclaimed, rubbing a weary hand across his face. 'Don't you realize that what you have just said is all a lie? The Tunnellers value their freedom above all else: they are a gentle people, not robbers and murderers. They're not interested in possessing things. If only we could find out where all these rumours started!'

Rubel thought for a moment and then nodded. 'Yes, you're right, come to think of it they have never asked for anything when they've stopped here for the night.'

'I should think the rumours have grown from fear and jealousy,' Tombel added, thoughtfully. 'You have to remember that they look very different to the rest of us with their tiny stature, bulging eyes and shell-shaped ears. I think a lot of people were afraid of them and suspicious when they first started turning up in their villages.

Remember, Thane made so many sweeping changes once he had won the daylight at the Battle of the Rising and if my memory serves me right the saying around here goes – "change is always for the worse". Well, for a lot of villages the changes came much too fast and they found it difficult to accept the new Elundium; for them the shadows of their fears were still very real.'

'But that doesn't explain why the Tunnellers stirred up the Nightbeasts, does it? It doesn't make sense at all when you think of what the Nightbeasts did to them in the City of Night,' Rubel said defiantly.

Breakmaster glanced over his shoulder towards the storm-dark windows and drew his chair closer to the others, lowering his voice to a whisper barely louder than the crackling firelight. 'We don't think they are Nightbeasts – not real ones. The King is certain that they didn't break into the city to try to rescue the Tunnellers: he thinks they were trying to kill them.' The old horseman barely paused for breath before telling everything that had happened since the Tunnellers had been brought to the city in the prison cart and locked in the cellar beneath Candlebane Hall. He told of their escape on the Nighthorses and the persistent fears that the Nightbeasts had not only helped them but were still hidden inside the Granite City. Greygoose sat on the edge of his chair listening intently, hoping to hear something of his son amidst all the talk of the Tunnellers' escape.

'The worst of it is we can't seem to flush the creatures out no matter how thoroughly we scour the alleys. Our guess is they have escaped somehow, or somebody is hiding them, but who would do such a thing? Who could abide to be that close to such vile beasts? The longer they remain at large lurking in the shadows and evading capture the more panic it stirs up amongst the people, the more it fuels ridiculous rumours. They even say that Krulshards' black seed must still dwell somewhere deep inside Krann and that it is his presence that keeps the night creatures within the city as they wait for him to grow in power. But that is clearly a lie: those of us who know the child, who have watched him grow, know him to be innocent and free from this evil. This is why the King fears for Krann and Elionbel – he feels they are unsafe staying within the city, there are too many doors and secret passageways in the Towers of Granite, too many opportunities for enemies to attack from the shadows. That is why we journey to the tower on Stumble Hill despite this atrocious weather.'

'But why didn't he send them here? Doesn't the King think us capable of protecting our own family? Has he forgotten so quickly how I entered the City of Night all alone and tore free the sword of Durondel from Krulshards' rotten heart? Has he forgotten how I carried it half way across Elundium wrapped in a fragment of the Master of Nightmare's black malice so that the King could use it to sew a shadow in Kruel's footprints?' There was hurt pride and an edge of anger in Rubel's voice as he rose accusingly from his chair.

'No, no, of course the King has not forgotten,' Break-master began, but Tombel interrupted him quickly.

'It is not our place to question his orders, Rubel, and if my knowledge serves me correctly then Stumble Hill is more of a fortress and much easier to defend than this wayhouse. He has chosen wisely.'

He turned to smile at Breakmaster. 'Then we shall accompany you, old friend, and ensure that they arrive safely. It is time we stopped living in memories and did something to help the King; goodness knows there are few who still serve him in these troubled times. We will leave by first light, if it has stopped snowing.' Tombel rose slowly to his feet and nodded to the servers, indicating that it was time to serve evening food.

'Not true Nightbeasts you say? Tell me more about this,' he murmured with interest, linking his arm with Breakmaster and leading the way through to the dining hall.

VIII

Rock Pools
and Seaweed

COLD, SALTY mist swirled through the snowy, desolate courtyards before clinging thinly to the ruined, frost-glittering battlements of Cawdor softening and shrouding its gloomy, crumbling dereliction in the strengthening daylight. Drib didn't have the time to glance around at his surroundings or to listen to the surf boiling and thundering up amongst the rocks below the jagged remains of the curtain wall that surrounded the fortress and edged the sheer, black, marble cliffs it stood upon. He didn't notice the soaring flocks of sea birds as they rose on the icy morning breezes, for he was too busy screwing up his courage as he sat in Sparkfire's saddle making ready to make another galloping sword attack on the heavy, straw-filled sack that Berioss insisted he call a quintain and had suspended from a crude scaffold close to the archway of the large inner courtyard.

Berioss was doing his best to fulfil the pledge he had made to the Master Magician and was determined to make warriors out of them before the snows melted, but for Drib with his crooked legs it wasn't coming easily and he spent more time nursing his bruises and struggling back into Sparkfire's saddle than he did stabbing with his sword or spear. Much as he would never let it show to the others, all the dreams he'd had about how he would one day become an accomplished horseman were slipping through his fingers. He felt he was letting everyone down:

he just couldn't keep his balance in the saddle unless he clung onto the pommel and then he couldn't steer Sparkfire. The horse did everything it could to help him but unless he could hold the reins in one hand and the sword in the other he would never manage to do this. Sloeberry and the others kept giving him encouragement but in his heart he felt he would never master it, never be more than a passenger on his horse's back. All those jibes and taunts from the other boys in the Learning Hall had been true: he was a useless crippled boy whose only talent was scrambling up chimneys and knocking the soot out of the corners with his bent knees.

Eider cantered past him, sitting tall and erect in the saddle, controlling the horse so easily with his knees as he nocked an arrow onto his bow-string and aimed it at the sack. The arrow sang through the air and struck the target with a thwack, hitting it dead centre.

'Oh well done, good riding, excellent shot!' Berioss called out after him as he pulled the arrow out. The old Marcher looked at Drib waiting at the far end of the courtyard. 'Are you ready?' he shouted, signalling that it was time for him to make his attack. Berioss smiled: he had to admire Drib's courage – for all his bumps and bruises the small boy never once gave up trying.

Drib took a quick glance around the courtyard as he prepared to canter towards the quintain that swung and twisted in the icy morning breeze. He was really beginning to hate that apparatus and, even on the rare occasions he had managed to strike it, his sword blade had glanced harmlessly off because without a secure seat in the saddle there was no weight or strength behind the thrust. But at least Sloeberry wasn't there to watch his futile attempts at swordsmanship, which was something to be grateful for.

Sloeberry and Damask were busy searching beneath the walls of the outer ward and in all the hidden corners of the ruins for any signs of the ancient kitchen gardens that once must have been cultivated to feed a fortress as large as Cawdor. There was still plenty of meat on the huge Nightboar's carcass but despite the bitter cold it was spoiling and becoming maggoty and the stink of it was overpowering. They would have to find something else to eat very soon or starve to death.

'Come on, Drib, you're daydreaming again!' Eider called out as he rode back beneath the archway into the courtyard with another arrow held loosely on the string and he grinned as he watched Drib clumsily grip his sword.

Gritting his teeth Drib avoided Eider's eyes – one daylight he would get it right, then he'd show them. He would be as good as anybody else. He let go of the pommel of Sparkfire's saddle and tightened his hold on the reins. This time it would happen, this time. Silkstone the owl hooted and rose from Drib's shoulder to watch. Sparkfire snorted, arched his neck and pranced as he felt Drib shift his weight in the saddle and pick up the reins. The horse charged across the courtyard, sending balled lumps of snow flying from his hooves. Try as he might he just couldn't keep the small crippled boy on his back: once Drib let go of the saddle it became a race to reach the straw-filled dummy before he fell off. Sparkfire had kept the boy safe on the long journey through the Emerald Mountains, but keeping him in the saddle during battle was beyond his skill. Drib's voice rose in a startled cry as the horse surged forward, his crooked knees tried to grip and then skidded on the saddle flaps as his feet flew uselessly out of the stirrups. The reins became taut as he used them to balance and pulled on Sparkfire's bit making him throw up his head in pain and veer away from the target. Drib slowly began to topple sideways with his sword arm flailing wildly, thrashing at the empty air. He let the reins slip through his fingers and crashed unceremoniously to the ground. The sword flew out of his hand and fell without sound onto the mud and snowy slush that covered the cobbles.

Berioss sighed and shook his head as he hurried towards the boy. Reaching Drib in three huge strides, he caught hold of him by the collar and hauled him to his feet. 'It's balance, Drib, just balance. You have to concentrate, boy.'

Drib blinked and shook his head. Everything around him was spinning and blurring out of focus; for an instant he wasn't even sure where he was and he half-expected his master, Sweepscuttle, to loom above him with his leather strap taut between his knuckled fists. But there wasn't any soot on his clothes and one of his hands was snugly fitted inside a strong, armoured battle-glove while the other was raw and exposed to the biting cold wind. He frowned as he tried to remember. He looked up when he heard a faint, familiar voice above him and peered through the dizzy haze of pain to see the old Marcher, Berioss, and then the memories flooded back. He knew exactly where he was and why he was dangling by the collar from Berioss's strong hand. The old Marcher's voice was telling him to concentrate on keeping his balance, telling him to sit upright and square in the saddle, and most importantly to sit still. Drib tried to smile through the pain and tried to nod his head in agreement but it wasn't that easy.

Berioss seemed to become distracted by the noise of impatient hoofbeats coming from the far end of the courtyard and he set Drib gently back onto his feet before calling out to Mistletoe to make his pass at the quintain.

The Tunneller spurred his mount forward, sweeping his sword arm down to stab enthusiastically at the straw-filled sack. The point of the blade struck the body dead centre so forcibly that it sent a violent shiver through the sack and the sword pierced right through the coarse hessian and reappeared through a tear in the other side. With a cry of dismay Mistletoe felt his sword stick fast and the hilt twisted sharply, almost breaking his wrist as it jerked free of his fingers. With a burning hand he rode out beneath the archway.

'No, no, no, not like that! How many times do I have to tell you!' Berioss shouted in exasperation. 'Follow the sweep of the blade with a slightly bent arm – and keep your wrist in line with the blade or the force of the thrust will break your wrist easier than you can snap a stalk of straw. Remember, there is no point in skewering your enemy so savagely that you lose your sword! You don't want to be disarmed and surrounded by foes, so come back and do it again, properly.'

Drib bent down gingerly to retrieve his sword from where it lay in the trampled snow. The nicks and chips splintered out of its cutting edge clearly marked the number of times that he had accidentally dropped it or let it fly out of his hand as he had tried to charge at the dummy. With his head bowed he cleared the slush from the hilt with the tail of his cloak and started limping to where Sparkfire stood waiting for him to remount. The reins were in a tangled knot high up his neck near his ears and the horse nickered softly as Silkstone stooped to perch on the cantle of the saddle. With a grim face Drib reached for the reins and began to untangle the knot.

'I think that's enough bruises for you today, Drib. Go and unsaddle Sparkfire and rub him down. If there's time after that you can practise those unmounted fencing moves I showed you yesterlight. Eider will go through them with you.'

Drib felt his cheeks flush with shame. He had failed again: every daylight it was the same.

'No, no, no, you're moving much too slowly. Try and remember what Berioss taught you about parrying an attack; you have to try to keep your opponent in sight – at least try to anticipate which way I'm going to move instead of just standing there rooted to the spot!'

Eider's voice had an edge of impatience to it as he tried hard not to laugh openly at Drib's clumsy attempts at fencing. Why Berioss persisted in trying to teach the boy how to fight was a mystery to him. Eider easily side-stepped the blow and slipped behind the small crippled boy as they practised swordsmanship in the trampled snow. Eider had a hundred other, much more pressing, things he would rather be doing – scouring the ruins for anything suitable to whittle or split for arrows to replenish his diminishing supply was the most urgent, not that any of them ever flew very well; or to see if anything edible had wandered into any of the traps he had set beneath the outer walls – but he carried on with good enough grace. Drib grunted with the effort, stabbing at empty air where moments before Eider had stood. Trying to stay on his feet in the armoured boots was difficult enough: he had never worn shoes or boots of any kind before escaping with the Tunnellers, for Sweepscuttle his master had said they were far too good and certainly too expensive for the likes of him. He hadn't yet grown accustomed to their restriction, but his toes were warm and snug no matter how cold it got and he was grateful for that. Twisting and turning and changing direction had never been easy with his crooked legs and trying to keep his quick, light-footed opponent in sight seemed almost impossible. Eider seemed to wait, almost to hover until he had started to turn and then changed direction in the blink of an eye. And then he would laugh and tease him, prodding and pricking him with the point of his sword for being so slow.

'I'm here,' Eider laughed, scything his sword through the air a handspan above Drib's head, making it hum. 'And you would be dead, as dead as that Nightboar I killed, if I was a real enemy,' he muttered, already tiring of the game.

Drib heard the hum of the blade above his head and instinctively raised his own weapon to protect himself. There was a bright blaze of sparks and a loud clash of steel as their blades met. The force of the blow sent Drib staggering forward and Eider was so surprised by the sudden contact of their two swords that he was unable to prevent his blade skidding along the back of Drib's sword and riding up over the hilt to nick at the exposed skin on the knuckles of his ungloved and unprotected hand. The boy cried out with the pain.

'I'm sorry – I'm really sorry, it was an accident!' Eider hastily stepped back and lowered his sword.

Drib regained his balance, gasping with pain, and turned awkwardly towards Eider, hot tears of agony welling up in his eyes. But he felt more than pain: he was sick of being so easily defeated by his own clumsiness; sick of being made to look a fool. And he was angry that he had allowed that creature in the forest to steal his battle glove – the blow would have glanced off harmlessly if he had still been wearing it. He tried to ignore the trickle of blood oozing between his fingers as he shouted back at Eider.

'Fight on! Fight on! I didn't say you could stop did I?'

Berioss and the others were drawn across the courtyard by Drib's cry of pain only to come to a shambling halt in the shadow beneath the archway as they watched Drib face up to Eider and beckon him on to continue the fight.

'Stop that! Drib's hurt!' Sloeberry cried, searching beneath her cloak for something to staunch the flow of blood as she started to hurry towards him but Berioss caught her by the arm and stopped her.

'No', he whispered. 'You must not interrupt. Don't you see, it's his pride and dignity that have suffered a greater hurt than his hand, and that is something only he can redress.'

Berioss frowned with concern and he muttered to himself, 'I only hope that Eider has the good sense to let him win back something.'

Eider hesitated. He could see blood dripping from the wound on Drib's knuckles and he didn't want to hurt him any more. He felt that they were friends, almost brothers, or would be if it wasn't for the boy's irritating habit of daydreaming and constantly chattering on about everything and anything.

'Come on! What's the matter? Are you afraid? Are you afraid that I might fight back for once?' Drib shouted, lunging angrily at the taller boy.

The doubt and concern died from Eider's face. He hadn't wanted to continue the fight but he wasn't going to back down. He raised himself on the balls of his feet and prepared to attack, sure that one or maybe two of the moves that Berioss had taught him would easily disarm the boy.

Drib gripped the hilt of his sword. All the anger and frustration of his helpless inadequacies centred on the lithe, elusive figure of Eider. This time he would show him! He would show them all that he wasn't just a useless cripple. But before he had completed that first angry lunge Eider had stepped neatly aside and parried his stroke, and was already disappearing somewhere behind him. Which way should he turn? Where would the next attack come from? He was already regretting his momentary burst of anger.

Silkstone had been watching the incident from the top of one of the crumbling walls of the courtyard and he suddenly decided it was time for him to come to Drib's aid and redress Eider's unfair advantage, but that he would do no more than any Battle Owl helping the warrior he accompanied into battle. He would be Drib's eyes and ears.

'Turn right, turn to the right . . . step forward two strides . . . listen for the squeak of Eider's armoured boots and follow the sound of his breathing – now attack!'

Drib heard the owl's instructions and acted quickly, doing exactly as he had been told. Turning sharply to the right he strode forward and brought up his sword. Eider suddenly appeared directly in front of him and was caught off-guard. Drib lunged forward and again there was a clash of steel and bright sparks flew in the gloomy morning light, except that this time it was Eider who staggered backward, startled and surprised by Drib's reactions. He barely had time to recover and parry Drib's thrust which almost twisted his own sword from his hand before the boy attacked again. This time Drib's aim was closer and it struck sparks off the knuckles of his armoured glove, the force of the blow making him wince and numbing his hand.

Eider cursed and jumped defensively away. He had never

known Drib fight like this. He was aware of the owl's hoots and shrieks but the sound meant nothing to him, for he couldn't understand a thing the owl said.

'Attack again, lunge forward, follow up your advantage of surprise and disarm him,' Silkstone hooted.

Drib leapt forward and didn't give Eider a chance to recover. There was a scream of metal skidding against metal as he attacked, their blades locking together briefly and Drib stepped in close, twisted his sword arm sharply to the right, bringing it up and over so fiercely that Eider didn't stand a chance of parrying the move. The hilt of his sword was wrenched from his hand and sent flying away across the courtyard. Eider stared at Drib in dismay before scrambling backwards with uncertainty. He had been left standing, a complete fool with his sword hand numb and throbbing and could barely believe what had just happened. Drib had never done anything like that before.

Drib was almost as surprised as Eider as he stood there breathing hard. He realized that the point of his sword was raised and pointed at his friend's throat. Blushing, he let it drop and trail in the snow near his feet as Silkstone stooped and settled on his shoulder. He glanced sideways at the owl, knowing full well that he couldn't have done this without his help.

'Well done, boy, that was an excellent display of swordsmanship!' Berioss called out from the entrance of the courtyard, breaking the startled silence, and adding as he strode forward to congratulate Drib. 'It's just as I'm always telling you: perseverance always pays off. You see, some of that training must have sunk in, mustn't it? Keep on like that and you'll become a proper warrior.'

'Oh, Drib, I was so worried that you were hurt!'

Sloeberry called out as the old Marcher turned away before Drib could tell him the truth. She ran to his side and began to dab at the wound on his ungloved hand, quickly stemming the trickle of blood.

'It's nothing, nothing,' he muttered, pulling his hand away from her and walking across to where Eider stood. He wanted to say that he was sorry, that he shouldn't have lost his temper and that it was all a fluke. He wanted to tell him that without the owl's help he would have been stumbling about as usual. He couldn't let Eider or the others believe that he had disarmed him so easily on his own: what would happen if they really were under attack and Silkstone wasn't there to help him? He had already almost got Eider and himself killed when he had loosed that badly-aimed arrow at the Nightboar they were hunting, and he knew Berioss would never have let him go on the hunt if he had been more truthful about that lucky arrow he had fired at the Nightbeast on the stairhead of the cellars beneath Candlebane Hall. His swordsmanship, in truth, was about as good as his archery which didn't amount to much. Nevian's words came flooding back to him. 'Truth, Drib, is a quality to value above all others.'

He opened his mouth to speak but Berioss's deep voice boomed out from behind him, 'You had better watch out in future, Eider: Drib's learning fast.'

'No, you've got it all wrong! It was just a fluke, I didn't disarm him on my own, Silkstone helped me, he told me which way Eider was going to move and when to press home my attack!'

Eider just laughed and shook his head. 'Don't be silly, I know the owl helps you a lot and we all know you can understand some of what he says but he couldn't have done that. What do owls know about fencing?' Eider pulled the

219

small crippled boy off his feet and swung him around. 'Take some credit when it is due – goodness knows you get it wrong often enough. You beat me fair and square this time but I'll be ready for you next time. Now forget about that and come and help me and Oaktangle to strengthen the outer doors.'

'But I didn't do it on my own!' Drib cried out angrily as he wriggled free of Eider's grip and stumbled before he could regain his balance. He turned to Berioss for help. 'Tell him, please – you saw what happened. Tell him how Silkstone helped me, tell him!'

Berioss frowned, unsure of what he could say. It was true that he had heard the owl making a tremendous fuss throughout the duel and he remembered the stories he had heard from the great daylights of the Granite Kings about how the Battle Owls used to ride to war upon the warriors' shoulders and fight side by side with them against the darkness. But that was a long, long time ago in the days before King Holbian, the last of the Granite Kings. Holbian had been so enraged by his own terror of the dark, which prevented him from pursuing Krulshards into his lair that he had been persuaded that Nevian the magician had caused his fear of the dark and legend told how that foolish surge of anger had broken the bonds that tied together all the creatures of Elundium in their struggle against the powers of darkness and the evil that dwelt there. Oh yes, Berioss remembered the stories all right: he remembered hearing how Orundus, the Lord of Owls, had stooped and snatched the sword from the King's hands and Grannogg, the Lord of Dogs, had leapt to the magician's defence with his fangs bared. Equestrius, who had so proudly carried the King into battle, had reared up to thrash the air above his head with his razor-sharp hooves and would have killed the King had not Nevian called out, ordering them not to harm Holbian. But his punishment had been great, for from that daylight on all creatures were free and men had to stand alone against the terrors of the night. Berioss knew that things had changed for the better since that fateful night, for he had seen Mulcade, the Chief Loftmaster owl, perching upon King Thane's shoulder and fighting beside him in the thick of battle; and Esteron, the Lord of Horses, had carried him to victory with the Border Runners at his stirrup, bringing old legends to life. But he found it hard to believe that the hoots and shrieks that Silkstone had made during the duel had anything to do with its outcome. The owl knew nothing of the art of swordsmanship or how to use such skills, for he couldn't have been more than a nestling at the time of the Battle of the Rising. And anyway, Drib was no great warrior in the old tradition.

Berioss smiled down at Drib. 'Eider is right, boy: take the credit where credit is due and forget all this talk about owls' voices. You won fairly. Mind you, I didn't say there wasn't room for improvement. Keep your guard higher next time and try to take a little more weight on your twisted foot.'

'But you're wrong, completely wrong! I wouldn't have known which way to turn or when to twist and parry without Silkstone helping me. Why don't you believe me?' Drib let his words trail away and bleakly shrugged his shoulders. He could see the disbelief in Berioss's eyes; like so many of the things he seemed to say, his explanation was falling on deaf ears. The old Marcher began to remind Drib that out here in the wilderness he had to learn to separate fact from fantasy, stories like that were perfectly all right for telling in the safety of the Learning Halls but . . .

Drib ceased to listen. He resheathed his sword and

turned angrily away, pushing through the others as he limped out of the courtyard. He wanted to be on his own where nobody could tell him he was making things up – and even if he did indulge in daydreams it wasn't a crime. He threaded his way absently through the ruins, avoiding the deeper drifts of snow that masked the extremes of the dereliction, drawn by the restless thunder of the surf breaking over the rocks below the fortress and the haunting cries of the seabirds that wheeled through the drifting mist of salty spray to soar high into the sky. He suddenly felt a sharp, painful tug at the stray, untidy strands of his hair that had escaped unnoticed from beneath his helm. He glanced sideways to find that the owl was still perched upon his shoulder and was pulling playfully at his hair.

'See what you did by helping me!' Drib muttered crossly. Everybody's calling me a liar and telling me I'm a dreamer. They're complaining that I'm always living in the stories I heard in the Learning Hall – that's what I get for telling the truth! It's all your fault for intervening: it would have been a lot better if you had just let me get beaten as usual. Anyway, if I hadn't let that creature steal my battle glove in the first place my hand wouldn't have got cut and . . . and . . .' Drib began to sob with self-pity.

Silkstone ruffled his feathers with indignation and hooted shrilly before flying away to perch on the conicle roof of the tower that the Tunnellers had rebuilt, keeping his back to Drib. To begin with he had only helped him to fulfil a nestling pledge he owed to Esteron, when the Lord of Horses had made him promise that he would watch over the boy. It had all started when he had shown Drib a way down from the roof of the Prancing Horse Inn when one of the drinkers had lit a fire in the hearth while Drib was still cleaning the chimney. But there had been something so likeable about the boy, and by some strange quirk he could understand almost everything he said. So he had stayed close to Drib and helped him and the Tunnellers to escape from the city, all the time hunting grassland hares and rodents on the long journey through the Emerald Mountains. Gradually, he thought, a friendship had grown up between them – until now.

'I'm sorry – I didn't mean what I said, I really didn't, please forgive me. Silkstone, come here, I didn't mean it,' Drib called up to the owl, ashamed of his cruel and unnecessary outburst.

Silkstone maintained his stance upon the roof, staring out across the frozen countryside for a long moment, and then, without warning, he swooped back to Drib's shoulder and pecked painfully at his ear.

'I'm really sorry, it wasn't you I was so upset with,' Drib gasped, trying to ignore the pain and overjoyed that Silkstone seemed to forgive him. 'It's just that sometimes it's so difficult trying to keep up with the others and, apart from you, Sloeberry is the only one who doesn't get impatient with me.' Drib paused and smiled as he mentioned her name and then his face grew serious as he remembered how he had snatched his hand so rudely away from her when she had hurried across at the end of the duel to staunch the blood that was oozing from his injured knuckles. He turned towards the archway to go and apologize and then hesitated – he couldn't do it in front of the others. He would speak to her privately after their evening meal and hoped that she would forgive him as quickly as Silkstone had done.

Thinking of Sloeberry started him wondering if she'd had any luck finding the remains of the old kitchen gardens. Food, or the lack of it, was becoming a serious problem: even the horses were becoming gaunt and thin on the meagre grass and low, wind-riven bushes that they were forced to forage from amongst the ruins. Drib had thought they would manage to survive the winter on the Nightboar they had killed soon after their arrival and on the other game they had assumed would inhabit the forest but the carcass had become foul and black, crowding with maggots in no time at all despite their efforts to clean it thoroughly. They had even hung it outside where it had become stiff and frozen solid in a matter of hours but it made no difference. They had tried rubbing sea salt scraped from the outer walls into its decaying flesh and hanging it up to cure in the smoke of their fire but that, if anything, just made it rot quicker. And the stench was becoming horrible. Drib wondered if it wasn't the place itself that was having this effect on the carcass. Far-fetched as it might seem there was definitely something eerie about the ruins, something he couldn't quite put his finger on. Sloeberry had felt it as well but talking about it had made it seem more real and frightening, especially after dark and it always made the others uneasy. Berioss and Eider had said that their fears were ridiculous, that, as usual, he was daydreaming, but he knew they sometimes sensed it as well even if they wouldn't admit it. He could see it in their sudden, unexpected glances over their shoulders and the startled look in their eyes; he could see it when their fingers tightened around the hilts of their swords as they left their sentence unfinished, the words dissolving upon their tongues as they searched the shadows as if expecting to find somebody, or something, lurking there. He guessed that everybody had experienced the feeling of being watched at some time or another since they had arrived: even the horses whose forefathers had been gathered here on the dark side of morning to serve the Granite Kings would suddenly become restless in their picket lines, snorting and neighing and showing the whites of their eyes. And then there was Silkstone; the owl would hoot and fly protectively around him for no apparent reason and whenever he asked what the bird had seen he just said that there were Eretch, shadow-spirits, lurking and it left him none the wiser.

They had been completely wrong about being able to supplement their diet with grassland hares and rabbits. The thought of rabbit stew made his mouth water, but the whole area seemed to be deserted of life for leagues around the ruined fortress save for the flocks of seabirds, some of whom seemed as large as eagle owls and more menacing with their screams and long, curved beaks. They wheeled and soared between the crumbling walls of Cawdor and were very different from the birds he was used to seeing within the Granite City or hunting along the Lunduran River. These winged creatures were more vicious than the huge, black carrion crows that roosted in the shadows of the Buriers' Yard and squabbled over the dead. The seabirds had unexpectedly flocked to the Nightboar carcass the moment it had been hung outside the tower and greedily pecked at the rotten meat, and recently the largest birds had grown bold enough to start mobbing the smaller Tunnellers if they wandered away from the others, although they hadn't seemed to bother Berioss and Eider. Even Drib had been fairly safe as long as Silkstone was there to protect him. But the Tunnellers had started to arm themselves with spears or stout staves to keep the birds away.

Drib suddenly had the feeling he was being watched and

he twisted awkwardly around, knuckling his sore fist, but as usual there was nothing to see save the faintest hint of shadows melting into the snow or vanishing into the cracks in the walls. A cold, tingling sensation crept up his spine. He shivered and returned his attention to the restless waves beating between the rocks below and the real reason he had come to the edge of the cliffs. For the last couple of daylights he had begun to get an idea of where they might find a source of food. It was Silkstone who first brought it to his attention, and then only accidentally. The owl had continued to look well-fed despite the scarcity of game and the other morning Drib had found out why when he had suddenly appeared with a strange, small, armoured creature in his talons. It had an almost flat, circular body and was obviously still alive. It had five, jointed legs on either side of its body, and was moving its two armoured pincers in vicious snapping movements as it tried to catch hold of the owl's legs. The creature resembled a flat, odd-shaped spider with armour. The owl proceeded to batter it against a stone until it had killed it and broken into its protective shell to reach the flesh inside. Silkstone had held up a sliver of the meat for him to taste and Drib had taken it gingerly into his mouth. It was chewy and very salty but it hadn't made him sick and when he had excitedly asked the owl where he had found it he had told him that there were thousands of them, some of them much larger and far too heavy for him to carry, scuttling over the rocks and all along the seashore.

'Are there fish? Have you seen any fish?' Drib had asked him, his enthusiasm mounting. He remembered the rare morsel of fish he had tasted from the Lunduran River when he had been given the leavings from Sweepscuttle's plate.

Drib had been about to go and tell the others when he

realized that these fish might just as well be a hundred leagues away unless they could find a way down the cliffs, and there was none that he could see. But the possible lure of food had brought him back and he had climbed up, squeezing himself into a broken gap in the curtainwall that edged the sheer rocks, ignoring the cries of the sea birds who hovered closely to his face. He had brushed them away as he stared down, watching the sea water surge up over the rocks, lifting the glistening, dark swathes of seaweed that clung in thick tangles to the wide, sloping shelves of stone and the jumble of huge, irregularly-shaped slabs of black marble at the base of the cliffs. The waves broke in measured rhythm against the rocks and then retreated with a sigh, draining slowly out of the thousands of holes and fissures, channels and gullies leaving countless deep pools brimming full of water. Drib rubbed his eyes and stared hard. Yes, Silkstone was right: there were fish down there, hundreds of them, trapped in the rock pools until the next tide surged up to free them. He could see the flash of their silver scales in the blue-green water, the ripple and splash of their barbed fins and tails as they swam backwards and forwards.

'I'll bet the people who once lived here had a way of getting down to the sea. Silkstone, could you scour the cliff-face and see if any of the path remains?' Drib whispered, lightly running his fingers over the owl's talons where they dug into the thick, warm weave of his cloak.

Silkstone hooted softly and lifted effortlessly into the icy, salty breeze and flew slowly along the seemingly sheer rock-face. The seabirds rose from their roosts in their thousands and, voices screaming, they wheeled and dived in a black, angry cloud around the owl. Drib gripped at the crumbling wall on either side of where he knelt and leaned out as far as he dared to watch Silkstone search. There had to be a way; there just had to. Silkstone hovered away to the right where part of the cliff face must, at some time in the past, have fallen away, taking with it a corner tower of the fortress. He had noticed seaweed-encrusted slabs of masonry littering the rocks at the base of the cliffs while exploring the ruins soon after their arrival but he had barely given them a second glance. But why, he wondered, was Silkstone taking so much interest in the route they must have followed as they had plunged unexpectedly into the sea? Suddenly the owl disappeared and Drib blinked and rubbed his eyes. He craned his neck anxiously, calling out the bird's name, and breathed a sigh of relief when he reappeared a moment later out of a dark hole close to the bottom of the cliff immediately above the broken remains of the tower. The owl alighted on a rock on the edge of one of the rock pools and let the sea water wash over his talons as he pecked at one of the smaller fish that had been trapped there, pulling it out onto the seaweed beside him before flying back up to where Drib knelt in the gap in the wall.

'There was once a way down: there are crude steps hewn into the cliff beneath the tower, but the entrance is choked with rubble and little remains of it . . .'

'Would I be able to climb down? Can you show me?' Drib interrupted, his excitement almost getting the better of him.

Silkstone sqawked and shook his head. 'All that is left is a narrow crack, a sheer crevice of slippery rocks no wider than a chimney.'

At the mention of a chimney Drib laughed and his eyes lit up. Scrambling up and down chimneys had been all he had known before throwing his lot in with the Tunnellers and escaping with them from the cellar beneath Candlebane Hall. He wasn't afraid of heights. If there was a way down where the steps once used to be then he would find it, but how was he to reach that natural chimney in the rock-face? He took a moment summoning up his courage: there was nothing else for it, he had to try to traverse the cliff-face: it was the only way to get down to those rock pools and the fish that were still trapped in them until the tide rose. He glanced over his shoulder to check that none of the others had come looking for him: he didn't want them to risk their lives as well, especially Sloeberry. Then he carefully removed his armoured boots, his helm and mailshirt, in fact everything that might encumber him. Then, dressed only in his breeches, undershirt and cloak, which he would have left behind but for the bitter wind, he began to climb out through the broken gap in the wall. Swallowing hard, he wriggled his toes and felt for hand and foot holds on the slippery rocks, then slowly began to edge his way towards the place where Silkstone had first disappeared.

Traversing the cliff-face was much more difficult than Drib had imagined and where his crooked legs had been an advantage in the narrow confines of a chimney, giving him a purchase in the most unlikely places, out on the rock-face it was almost impossible for him to get a toe-hold with both feet at the same time. Twice he almost slipped and fell and bitter, cold beads of perspiration began to trickle down his forehead and into the corners of his eyes. His fingertips and toes were sore and had begun to bleed from the sharpness of the rocks. Silkstone did everything he could to help, hovering slightly above him to keep the seabirds away and calling out to tell him where the next crack or fissure was. Once Drib had foolishly looked down and almost lost his grip, dizzy from the sight of the sea crashing up amongst the rocks so far below. But handspan by handspan he edged his way across and squeezed himself into the top of the vertical fault in the cliff where the steps had once been. He stopped and took a moments' rest as he sobbed with relief.

Scrambling down the dark chimney and squeezing through the gaps in the boulders was easy, or would have been if it wasn't for the eerie wails and screams that echoed around him. He could have sworn that he felt the touch of those same ghostly figures, the elongated shapes and squat, distorted shadows, that had glided effortlessly through the trees to converge on the enraged Nightboar when he and Eider had hunted it. He remembered the way they had merged with the creature, making it swell and grow even more menacing. The ghostly shapes swirled around him, brushing roughly against him in the gloomy darkness, giving him the distinct impression that they were trying to prevent him from reaching the bottom of the cliffs and the fish that swarmed in the rock pools. But, much as their presence terrified him they couldn't stop his gradual descent and he discovered that if he waved his arms and shouted back at them they melted away, their voices seeming to merge with the cries of the seabirds.

'I'm not afraid of you!' he shouted, his voice echoing up and down the chimney, but in truth their cold touch made him shudder with revulsion and he was glad to wriggle out of a gap between the huge blocks of masonry and slabs of black marble that had fallen away from the cliff-face and now lay with their feet in the water.

Drib scrambled quickly between the last huge slabs of marble and the debris of the fallen tower and walked out onto the wide shelf of rock where he had glimpsed the fish in the rock pool. He laughed and shouted over the thunder of the waves breaking up against the far edge in huge white plumes of spray as Silkstone showed him where the best fish were trapped. 'Come on, we have to catch enough to feed everybody. I'll carry them back wrapped up in my cloak!' he laughed as he scrambled over the rocks.

'Beware, the tide is turning,' Silkstone hooted in alarm, watching the water wash a little closer across the shelf with each wave that broke. But Drib, eager to catch the fish, ignored him and ran out towards the rock pools, slipping and sliding on the thick carpet of seaweed, the freezing water oozing up between his toes.

Silkstone stooped low and flew a stride ahead, guiding him to the largest shallow pool and again urging him to be quick and get back to safety before the rising water cut him off, but Drib merely laughed, barely even hearing the owl's warning. He had found enough food to feed them all for an age of daylights and he cast his cloak down onto the seaweed before falling to his knees at the water's edge and stared with delight into the greenish, translucent pool. Through the waving fronds that grew there he could see the fish: he had never seen so many in one place before and the water seemed alive with their long, sleek bodies. The whole pool was a mass of shimmering, silver-blue scales, armoured spikes, fins and tails, but the moment he touched the surface of the water the fish darted away in every direction, the water seeming almost to boil as they collided, dived and skimmed along the bottom to evade him. He had never tried to catch a fish before and without a moment's hesitation he plunged both hands in amongst them and tried to grab at their elusive, slippery bodies. There were so many in the pool that he had little difficulty in grabbing hold of one but it wriggled so violently, thrashing its tail, that it slipped through his fingers and swam away.

'Grasp them more firmly behind the gills – I'll help,' Silkstone called out, anxious to hurry Drib away from the rising tide and he swooped across the surface of the water and plunged his outstretched talons into the shallows hooking them securely into the side of a large, silver sea-trout, but being strong and heavy it fought against the talons, slowly starting to drag Silkstone beneath the surface of the water. Drib saw that Silkstone was in trouble and, making a grab for the fish, he hauled it out. Silkstone released his talons from the fish and shook his feathers dry as Drib tossed the trout flapping onto his cloak. Drib quickly became an expert at grasping hold of the fish and jerking them out of the water before they had a chance to wriggle free and a small, flapping pile began to grow on his outspread cloak. Silkstone kept a watchful eye on the rising tide and repeatedly urged Drib to retreat to the higher rocks only to be completely ignored.

'Drib, you must stop at once!' he shrieked and eventually had to flutter his wings in the boy's face and begin to peck at his hair.

'Just one more; let me get that really big one that keeps escaping to the bottom of the pool. There! That one!' Drib exclaimed, pointing down into the water.

He was rapt, intent on catching the last fish, when a surge of icy water suddenly washed up around his knees and ankles where he knelt and swirled in over the lip of the pool. The coldness of the water made him gasp and twist around. He gave a cry of surprise to find that the waves were beginning to wash in across the shelf of rocks and lift the thick carpet of seaweed that he had crossed to reach the pool. He realized that it would only be a few more moments before the rising water would cover the rock he was fishing from as well.

'Quickly, follow me,' Silkstone hooted, flying back towards the cliffs.

Drib snatched at the hems of his cloak, now heavy and soaked through, just in time to prevent it from being washed away by the next large wave, but not quickly enough to prevent half his catch from flapping their escape back into the rock pool. He cursed his own foolishness for not listening to the owl and quickly knotted the wet tail-ends of the cloth together, securing what remained of his catch into a tight bundle that he slung across his shoulders.

'Come on, hurry, run as fast as you can and head straight towards that fallen block of masonry at the base of the cliffs,' Silkstone urged.

Drib staggered slightly beneath the weight of his catch but he didn't need telling again. He struggled through the rising water, fighting to stay on his feet. The waves surged around his legs threatening to knock him over as they rushed in across the rocks, and then they almost sucked him backwards as they retreated, making him totter and sway. The water rose up his calves and covered his knees, making each step harder and slowing him down. His feet skidded and he became entangled in the seaweed: he couldn't see where he was treading and the rocks had become treacherously slippery.

'Come on or you'll never reach the cliff. You must hurry or you'll be swept out to sea. Throw away the fish, it's your only chance!' Silkstone shrieked, flying back and pecking at the knotted end of the cloak.

'No! I am not throwing them away. I am not giving up now!' Drib shouted angrily, tightening his grip on the heavy bundle and driving the owl away with his other hand.

The sky had darkened with storm clouds and the wind was strengthening, bringing with it fresh flurries of snow. Behind him the thunder of the surf breaking over the last few remaining outcrops of rock not yet submerged seemed to grow louder and more threatening. The water was almost up to his waist and the pull from the ebb of the waves was stronger, but he wasn't about to give up. He had caught enough fish to feed everybody and he grimly surged forward, reaching beneath the water with his free hand and clutching at the rocks and tangles of seaweed, using every hand and toe hold he could find.

'Go more to the left, the left, you're veering away from the cliff!' shrieked the owl.

Drib staggered with exhaustion, barely managing to keep his footing as larger waves struck his back and almost dislodged the precarious bundle.

'I am not giving up – I'm not!' he repeated over and over again through gritted teeth and with sheer determination he forced a way through the battering waves until, sobbing with exhaustion, his numb fingers found and clawed at the rocks that stood above the tide-line. Breathing hard, Drib pulled himself up and out of the water onto a rocky outcrop and lay his precious cloakful of fish beside him. He kept a tight hold on the knot of the cloak as he looked back out to sea, a triumphant grin widening across his face. The gentle sloping shelf of rock where he had fished in the pool had vanished completely beneath the restless, white-capped waves, but he had succeeded. He had beaten the tide!

His grin quickly faded as he looked up and searched for the way he had climbed down. He hadn't given a moment's thought as to how he was going to get back up the cliff, having been so intent on catching the fish. But now one glance was enough to show him that climbing up was not going to be as easy as getting down – even without his precious catch he wasn't sure he could do it. He sank down realizing what a fool he had been. Why hadn't he had the good sense to bring some of the ropes they had taken from the armoury in their escape from the Granite City?

He shivered with fear and cold. Berioss was always telling him to wrap up warmly before going out and warning him to keep as dry as possible in this cold weather, so he knew the cold was likely to kill him quickly and now he was trapped on a rocky ledge dressed in only undershirt and breeches, soaked through to the skin.

Suddenly Silkstone reappeared and stooped quickly to his shoulder. The owl had discovered the remnants of a causeway that ran along the base of the cliff away from the fortress of Cawdor and eventually ended in a small, stone stairway that led to the cliff-top half a league from the gates of the fortress. The owl urged him to get to his feet and find his way back to Cawdor before he froze to death.

Drib shouldered his catch and did his best to follow the owl as he clambered awkwardly over and between the masses of huge rocks and boulders that littered the base of the cliff. He traversed narrow ledges, some barely a finger's span wide above the crashing waves, until they had slowly rounded the headland clinging precariously to any purchase he could find. Buffeted by the wind, his face stung by the snow flurries, he came to a sudden halt in the shelter of a cavernous, overhanging rock that had been hollowed out by the weather. Ahead of him lay a vast bay that stretched away into the gloomy distance. Its sheer cliffs fell abruptly into steep, densely-wooded chines and eroded wind-cracked outcrops of rock that he could see at a glance would be impossible to climb. The tangle of trees and blackthorn bushes grew right down to the wide beach of azure sand and were broken only by swift-flowing streams and deep, treacherous-looking gullies that flowed down through the sands to vanish into the sea. Most of them looked far too wide to wade across safely. Thick swathes of black, glistening seaweed edged the thundering surf as far as he could see along the deserted beach. The sky darkened as the wind began to howl across the bay, whipping the sand up into swirling eddies that raced and chased each other along the winter beach.

Drib would have found the way ahead impassable and would have had no alternative but to huddle in the shelter of the overhanging rock and wait for death to claim him if it wasn't for the wonderful sight of the causeway that had brought him to such a sudden halt. The owl had found him a road and he stood there marvelling, following it with his eyes. It curved sharply in front of him, running out to sea for more than sixty paces before stopping at a squat, ruined tower. In the other direction it led away from him in massive blocks of black marble, laid so cleverly that there was no more than a fingernail's gap between them. They stretched in a wide, unbroken road hard against the cliffs that tunnelled through the outcrops of rocks and bridged the chines in soaring viaducts until vanishing from sight, curving gently inland through a huge archway into the trees about half a league from where Drib stood. The surface of the causeway had been worn smooth by time and the rub of wind and water, and gave little hint of the busy thoroughfare it had once been before the rise of the Granite Kings. The only signs were faint ruts that the iron-shod wheels of the merchants' carts had scored in its surface and the rusty, eroded stumps of the huge rings and shackles where the ships of Carth, Minios, Gnarlsmyre and Elundium had tied up before Krulshards' darkness had spread its shadow across the world.

Silkstone hooted at him to hurry and pecked painfully at his ear. Drib laughed with relief and slung the heavy bundle of fish across his shoulders but as he prepared to move forward the wheeling, angry cloud of seabirds that had followed since he had climbed down the cliffs swooped down and tried to peck at the cloakful of fish. Silkstone shrieked and lifted from Drib's shoulders in order to drive them off and Drib clenched his fist to strike at the bolder ones, sending them spinning away amongst the waves as he hurried through the milling swirling shapes. The seabirds' attack lasted for only a few minutes before, as one, they soared up and away, retreating to their nests on the sheer black marble cliffs below the fortress of Cawdor.

Drib watched the dark, angry cloud of birds vanish round the headland and heard their haunting cries grow fainter and he wondered if they had anything to do with those ghostly figures and distorted, eerie shadows that had assaulted him as he had climbed down, for their voices were similar. He shivered and cast the dark thoughts aside as he concentrated on the road ahead, hurrying as fast as his crippled legs would carry him.

IX

The Tower on Stumble Hill

KRANN YAWNED sleepily as Elionbel shook him gently awake and persuaded him to eat and be strong, ready for the journey ahead, but he wished she had left him wrapped warmly in the battle coat with his dreams. He wished he could stay safe from the storm that still battered against the shutters of the wayhouse and the wind that was howling in the chimney instead of leaving his bed and going with her down to the crowded feasting hall. The moment they entered the long, low-beamed room the noisy hum of conversation fell into whispers and he felt embarrassed. Everybody seemed to be watching them as Elionbel took him to the head of the table where she introduced him to an ancient, ruddy-faced Marcher with a straggly beard and fierce, penetrating eyes. She called him Tombel and told him that he was her father, the Keeper of Woodsedge.

Krann smiled awkwardly and extended his hand in greeting as he had been taught to do but the old Marcher's unwavering gaze made him feel uncomfortable. Suddenly the old man laughed and grasped his hand, squeezing it painfully as he cried out a shout of welcome and the hum of table talk resumed. Elionbel hurried him along the table, smiling and nodding to people she knew, stopping when she reached a tall, serious-faced man who bore a striking resemblance to her. She called him Rubel, embraced him and told Krann that he was her brother, and then, after a small moment of hesitation, she stooped and whispered in his ear that Rubel was also his brother.

Krann frowned and looked up into Rubel's face. He knew Elionbel was his sister but nobody had ever told him that he had a brother before. He glanced curiously along the table to where Tombel was deep in conversation with Breakmaster as they discussed the state of the road and wondered if he was his father as well. Nobody ever said anything about any of this in the Towers of Granite. He started to ask, but Elionbel averted her eyes and quickly changed the subject as Rubel stared coldly at him and she hurried him away to take an empty seat at the far end of the table.

'No, Tombel is not your father, but one daylight I will tell you everything, I promise, but now you will have to be patient and eat your food, no more questions.' Elionbel's voice was firm as a server put a plate in front of him but Krann was not hungry. He kept glancing along the table to Rubel, his mind alive with questions he was forced to suppress, and he barely touched the rich, dark meats that smelled of the forest or the sticky mound of fruits that had been preserved in summer oils. He wanted to be alone in his room upstairs, to burrow beneath Breakmaster's beautiful battle coat and listen to the music in its weave. He waited patiently until Elionbel became engrossed in conversation with the woman sitting opposite her before pushing his plate away and slipping quietly, and he thought unnoticed, from his place at table. He pulled the door of the feasting hall shut behind him and hurried along the gloomy stone-flagged corridor, turned a corner and realized that he was lost. Somewhere ahead, around another turn in the passage, he could hear what sounded like the noise and bustle of the kitchens and the hurrying footsteps of a server approaching. He didn't want to be caught wandering through the wayhouse without permission: he got into enough trouble in the Towers of Granite when he was caught playing where he shouldn't be, and he had promised that he would be good on the journey. Light spilled through the gap around a large oak door that stood ajar on his right and without a moment's hesitation he slipped through into the room. He gasped in wonder at the bright banners that hung from the beams and the dozens of swords and battle helms that were heaped in the corners or hung up on chains. There were scrolls and books and thousands of trophies and trinkets that crowded every shelf and surface. There were so many magical, wonderful things that he didn't know where to look first, but his eyes were drawn irresistibly to the myriad of bright colours he could see in the edges of a huge block of crystal that was partially concealed by a thick, black cloth. It stood on its own upon a table close to the fireplace. Krann picked his way through the untidy clutter to the table, grasped a corner of the cloth and pulled it off the crystal.

A silent scream gripped his throat, for he was paralysed by the terror of what he had uncovered. He was unable to move or tear his eyes away from the horror of the severed Nightbeast head that stared blindly from the crystal. His heartbeats drummed in his ears and a darkness seemed to envelop the crowded trophy room. He couldn't seem to blink or tear his eyes away from the hideous, hairy, armoured head of the creature trapped in front of him. Its blackened nostrils overhung a snarling mouth and its lips were stretched back into a soundless snarl exposing its needle-sharp yellow teeth. But it was the blind-dead eyes, red-veined and huge, glistening in the firelight that seemed to come alive and hold him in such menace, boring pitilessly into his soul as if searching for an echo of a black seed of darkness deep down within him.

'No, no, no, let me go,' he whispered, backing away and raising his small, helpless, trembling hands as if to ward the creature off. He was desperate to escape its penetrating gaze. 'No, no you shall not have me!' he cried, snatching up a dagger from amongst the discarded weapons that lay all around him. He stabbed wildly at the block of crystal, almost sending it toppling onto the floor. But still the blind eyes seemed to stare at him and follow his every move.

Suddenly he heard a sound from behind him in the doorway and he imagined other creatures of the darkness swarming towards him. He spun round and stumbled over a pile of shields. He cried out in panic and the dagger flew harmlessly from his hand as he fell. A huge shadowy figure was blocking the doorway and moving towards him, its shadow leaping up across the low ceiling and rushing around the walls, smoothing over books and banners, threatening to engulf him. He glimpsed another small figure behind it and heard what he thought sounded like Elionbel's voice raised in anger from far away. A merciful tide of oblivion swirled around him, blotting out the horror of what he had just seen and two strong hands reached out to catch him as he slumped into unconsciousness.

Tombel had caught sight of the boy yawning and had watched him slip out of the feasting hall. He guessed that he was intending to go back to his room but he rose to follow him in concern as the boy had left by the wrong door, which could only lead him to the kitchens, the trophy room or the empty, disused part of the wayhouse that had been shut up for the winter. Tombel had heard a muffled cry from inside his trophy room as he hurried after Krann, and as he pushed open the door he had found the child standing, transfixed, staring at the severed head of the Nightbeast encased in crystal

Tombel's lips began to tremble with anger and, his fingers tightened around the hilt of the dagger that he kept concealed beneath his cloak. He had been right all along to doubt that Thane could purge the dark evil of Kruel by seeding him with a shadow at the Battle of the Rising, but nobody had listened to him, nobody had heard him when he had insisted that when Kruel had shrunk into the form of a helpless baby it was nothing more than a clever ruse used to escape death and ensure that Krulshards' evil seed would survive and once more have the power to grow strong. But now he had the proof. Krann must have sensed the presence of the severed head and been drawn to it. What else but its brooding presence would have led him directly to it? How else would he have found it amongst the almost-forgotten clutter that filled the trophy room?

'Your evil shall haunt us no more!' muttered Tombel under his breath as he began to unsheath his dagger, but he hesitated in confusion as Krann cried out and staggered backwards, as if trying to escape from the creature's blind stare. Suddenly the child snatched up a rusty blade from the floor and used it to flail and stab wildly at the beast's head, feebly shouting threats. Tombel could see the terror and panic etched into the boy's face as he tried to rush towards the door and it convinced the old Marcher of his innocence. He put his own weapon away and reached out to catch him.

'Father – how could you do such a thing? What on earth were you trying to prove by showing him that disgusting old head?'

Tombel heard the accusation in his daughter's voice as he caught the child and he spun round in surprise to see her standing in the doorway.

Elionbel had noticed that Krann's chair was empty and had seen him slip from the room with her father close on his footsteps and she had risen to follow them, remembering her father's anger when they had first met on the greenway: she feared for Krann's safety.

'Father, I'm ashamed of you!' she cried before he could speak, snatching Krann out of his arms and turning away from him.

'But . . . but . . . but surely you don't think I brought him in here to test him in some way do you?' he protested but the accusation had been made and the hurt was clear on Elionbel's face.

'No, no I never would, you misunderstand. Surely you don't believe I would stoop so low, daughter? I saw the child slip away from the table and take the wrong door, you must believe me. He found his own way here and when I followed him in he had already uncovered the Nightbeast's head by himself.'

Tears were brimming in Elionbel's eyes and her lips were pressed tight as they trembled. She retreated away from her father with Krann held protectively in her arms. 'We have gone to such trouble to shield him from his dark beginnings, to protect him until he is old enough to understand . . .' she sobbed. 'And I trusted you, father, I believed that enough of the love that you once had for me still dwelt deep down inside your heart and that it would prevent you from betraying that trust. I thought that for one night we might find rest and safety here with you.'

'Wait! Stop, please, listen to me, daughter,' Tombel

reached out and gripped her arm fiercely in his desperation to make her understand and Krann began to stir. 'My heart brims with love for you, child, from those first moments when you were cradle-wet to my last breath I will always love you, but for too long I have dwelt in the darkness of the memory of your mother's death and I have laid the blame of it upon Krann. I will admit that now, but out there in the blizzard you healed much of that pain when you challenged me to look upon Krann's face. You were right, Elionbel: there really is an echo of Martbel in the child and I cannot betray that part of her . . .' Tombel swallowed, searching for words that would not come easily.

Slowly Krann began to regain consciousness to the sound of Tombel's deep voice. He wriggled in Elionbel's arms and blinked in confusion, uncertain of where he was or how he had got there, unsure if he had dreamt of the sinister, formless creature with the hairy, armoured face who had pursued him through the darkness. He shivered and looked up at the ceiling of the room and saw that it was festooned with bright banners and the walls were crowded with rows of books, and swords and battle helms were heaped in disorder on the floor. Fragments of memory began to flood back. There was something in the room that had terrified him, something so horrible that it had filled him with loathing. It stood upon the table behind Tombel.

'Elionbel – there's a creature in here – don't let it get me, please, don't let it get me!' he cried out, struggling to break free from her arms.

Elionbel held onto him more tightly to comfort him and carried him out of the room. She looked back over her shoulder and caught her father's eye and gave him a cold, accusing look before she turned away. He followed her out of the trophy room and quietly shut the door. 'We will speak no more of this until we have safely reached journey's end,' she muttered as she carried Krann up to the safety of her room and securely bolted the door.

Krann was woken up by the noise and bustle of preparation as the company got ready for the continuation of their journey. He yawned and threw aside the steelsilver coat, trying to shake off the dark dreams that clung to the edges of his memory as he ran to the window, rubbed a hole in the thick, frosted patterns on the glass and looked out across a brilliant, sunlit landscape of smooth white snowdrifts that stopped in frozen lumps and bumps beneath the eaves of the sombre black forest. It looked so different to how he had imagined it in the stormy darkness of the night. Shouts and movements below his window caught his attention and he stood on tip-toe to peer down. Tombel was giving orders to a group of servers who were piling a cart high with provisions. Breakmaster, Greygoose and Nebran suddenly appeared leading their horses and his pony out of the stableyard ready-saddled for the long ride ahead. Suddenly he became worried that they might leave without him. He dressed hurriedly and had barely finished stamping his feet into his boots when Elionbel brought him in a steaming bowl of broth, urging him to be quick in breaking his fast as Breakmaster was impatient to take to the road while the weather was so good. Krann picked up the hot bowl with both hands and blew on its dark, steaming surface in his effort to cool it and swallow the spicy gruel. He frowned, hardly listening to Elionbel as she told him that her father was shutting Woodsedge for the winter so that he and Rubel could bring the handful of faithful Marchers who had not deserted their posts and accompany them to the tower on Stumble Hill to ensure they arrived safely. Krann was trying to remember what it was that had frightened him so much in the night. He clearly remembered slipping away from the table before the meal was over, and getting lost in a maze of corridors but after that it all became a blur of bright banners, swords, shields and helms, but in amongst the fragments of memory there was a persistent image of a dark, formless figure, a face, a hideous snarling mask that he had glimpsed in the firelight. But where had he seen it? Had it been a dream?

'Elionbel?' he asked, interrupting her as she gathered the thick, winter cloak around her shoulders and threaded the buckle at her throat. 'Elionbel, did you see anything last night? I think I was somewhere I shouldn't have been and I saw something horrible after supper, only I can't quite remember it. It doesn't feel like a dream – it seems much too real for that.'

Elionbel hesitated, wringing her slender fingers together. She had hoped that he would have forgotten the incident and she looked steadily into his clear, blue eyes, torn between telling him a part of the truth of what he had seen or dismissing the whole thing. But how could she tell him? He had seen the head of a Nightbeast slain and preserved by her father an age ago, taken by him in the great battle before the Gates of Night. The boy was so inquisitive that she was sure he would deluge her with a barrage of questions and it would lead to her being forced to reveal that his father was Krulshards, the master of such creatures. Elionbel strove to find words to answer him with truth. She had never imagined the repercussions, the webs of lies and half-truths that she would have to weave if she wanted to shield him from knowing about his past so that he could be free to grow up in joy and innocence.

'It was a dream, Krann, just a bad dream, and that's what comes from not finishing your supper and slipping away from the table without asking. You went through the wrong door and I found you asleep in a storeroom near the kitchens. I brought you up here asleep in my arms. Now stop all this chattering and worrying about dreams and get ready or the others will leave without us,' she laughed, waving down to Breakmaster who was pacing impatiently around the horses, checking that every strap and buckle was correctly fastened.

This ploy seemed to work. 'Where are your horses? Surely they are not intending to walk the whole way – are they?' Krann exclaimed, watching as Tombel, Rubel and the four Marchers in the company strode out ahead onto the greenway, their broad marching swords resting easily across their shoulders, their armoured boots leaving fresh footprints in the smooth, untrodden snow.

Tombel overheard the boy. He laughed deeply and called back, 'We are Marchers born and bred, my lad, and we travel quickly on our own two feet, much quicker than if we were put into a saddle.'

The talk and easy laughter of the company fell away into a sombre silence as they trudged through the long, cold daylights towards Stumble Hill keeping more and more to themselves and stopping less frequently, dispirited by the desolation and poverty they saw in the remote wayside villages they passed through. All that could be heard as the low winter sun dropped towards the distant, misty horizon on the third daylight was the musical jingle of the horses' harness, the soft crunch of the Marchers' boots in the snow and the sway and creak of the heavily laden cart at the rear of the procession.

Krann had been afraid of the wild-looking villagers who, on their approach, had come running out of their broken-down hovels and tried to catch hold of their stirrups, stumbling along in the trampled snow beside them pleading, begging for a crumb or a mouldy rind, anything to stave off their hunger. Bone-thin children were thrust in their faces and they would have been overwhelmed and the provision cart ransacked if Breakmaster and Nebran hadn't joined with the Marchers to drive them back with the flats of their swords. It was during the first of these encounters that Krann experienced his first glimpse of death: poor, pinched, wizened bodies frozen in their last stumbling stride, half-buried in the snow. He had been so horrified that he had been unable to tear his gaze away.

Slowly throughout the first daylight the dense shadows of the Black Forest with its starving villagers and beggars at every cross-roads had given way to bleak, rolling snowfields that dazzled their eyes and stretched away to the distant, hazy, purple horizon where fresh storm clouds were gathering, dark and ominous. Now they had ridden for two more daylights and the trees had diminished until there were only broken clumps, the branches bent against each other in conspiratorial whispers beneath the weight of snow that had settled on them. Apart from this there was nothing more than untidy hedges marching away across the hills, unbroken ribbons of thorns to keep them company. Nightshapes were beginning to gather the darkness around them and Tombel, who was troubled by tracks in the snow that stretched out ahead of them all along the greenway where none should be, held a huddled conference with Nebran and decided that they could reach Stumble Hill if they pressed on. But the old Marcher was hesitant and he strode ahead to search for a suitable place to bivouac beside the greenway's edge, for he felt they were too tired to go on but was worried by the trampled snow and wondered who could have made the tracks.

Krann shivered in Larksong's saddle, wretched with the cold. Despite being well-wrapped he couldn't keep the weather out and the moaning wind that was blowing the tops from the snowdrifts and swirling into stinging, misty clouds that fogged the greenway was pushing icy fingers inside every fold of his clothes and through every buttonhole beneath his cloak.

'How much further is it?' he called to Elionbel, reaching up a flapping sleeve in an effort to catch her attention as she rode beside him, hunched against the stinging wind, her hood drawn down over her head, her high collar pulled tight to shield her face. She was about to lean down and comfort the child when she heard her father give a warning shout as he ran back to them.

Instinctively Greygoose nocked an arrow onto his bowstring and Breakmaster and Nebran closed in on either side of Elionbel and Krann. The Marchers, unsure of what Tombel had seen, pulled back around the company in a protective circle, their swords drawn and ready. The servers of Woodsedge crowded around the cart, hurriedly arming themselves with pikes and swords.

'What's the matter? What's happening?' Krann cried in alarm.

Tombel suddenly re-appeared at Breakmaster's stirrup, breathing hard. He spoke rapidly, pointing ahead through the swirling snow that was blowing across the greenway.

'I now know what is making those footprints. There is a well-trodden path on the right of the greenway ahead of us. At first I thought it had been made by the people from some of the many villages we have passed through, but the last of those was more than a daylight ago and there aren't any more before Stumble Hill. And then I caught a glimpse of what looked like a long column, dozens and dozens of people filling the road ahead of us. They are all heading in the same direction.'

'How many?' Breakmaster interrupted, lowering his voice. 'Could it be those Tunnellers? From the rumours we have heard their numbers are swelling daily. Were there Nightbeasts among them? Were they armed?' He glanced quickly towards the countryside on either side of the road; but it was too overgrown and the snow too deep to see much, especially with the light fading so rapidly.

'What are we to do? Clearly we cannot risk making camp out here in the open, and we will freeze to death, especially poor Krann and your daughter, the Lady Elionbel, if we don't light a fire. But we dare not risk lighting anything or it will reveal exactly where we stand and they could attack at any moment.'

Tombel could only nod in agreement. 'It's difficult to be certain of anything, even where we are exactly, in this infernal icy haze, but there is one thing I am certain of from the glimpse I got of them – there are a lot more of them than there are of us. My counsel is to retreat until we are sure that they can't see us and then build a fortified camp . . .'

'No, wait!' Greygoose cried, standing in his stirrups as he shielded his clear Archer's eyes as best he could from the stinging snow and peered along the road ahead. 'I think there is a light – yes, there it is again – a pinpoint of light on top of that distant hilltop, and it seems to be glowing brighter as the gloom deepens. What can it be?'

'That must be the watch lamp on Stumble Hill!' Nebran interrupted. 'I say we should make a run for the safety of the tower, it can't be more than two leagues ahead of us . . .'

'That would be madness!' Breakmaster cried. 'How can you expect Krann and Elionbel to fight their way through . . .'

'I am not afraid,' Elionbel's voice came to them clearly. 'I am sure I have faced far worse in the fight to win the daylight and I will keep Larksong close to me so you will not have to concern yourselves about Krann.'

'Rubel and my Marchers will run ahead and clear a path through the villains. Our swords will sing with sweet music while we buy you what time we can!' Tombel cried, making to turn his sword in an arc high above his head.

But Breakmaster stopped him, shaking his head, 'No, dear friend, we win through together or not at all. Darkness, speed and surprise will all be to our advantage. We will have horses front and centre, the Marchers and servers in close order on either side, their shields locked together.' But he leaned down securely knotting the lead rein through Larksong's bit-rings and passed the buckle end to Elionbel to strap around the pommel of her saddle. As his head bent toward her he whispered, 'If it looks to go badly as the forces of evil threaten us, break free if you can.'

Elionbel nodded gravely, caressing Stumble's neck. 'He is a courageous horse and he will not falter, and Larksong has a brave heart, he will follow him. If needs be we will gallop with all speed to the tower on Stumble Hill and bring help.'

Without a moment's hesitation Breakmaster unbuckled

his saddle-bags and draped the steelsilver battle coat, his most treasured possession, across Stumble's back. It glittered and shone in the thickening gloom and glistened as Stumble snorted and pawed the ground, his neck arched proudly as if he caught the scent of battle in his nostrils from the tension around them. 'There is no blade or arrowhead forged that can penetrate its weave, my lady, it will help Stumble carry you through the darkest night.'

He smiled and looked down at Krann. There was fear in the child's large, blue eyes and Breakmaster laughed and ruffled the boy's hair with one hand while unsheathing a dagger with the other. He pressed it into the boy's grip, remembering the first time he had ridden into battle with the apprentice Gallopers holding a sword he could barely lift. He couldn't have been more than a couple of suns older than Krann was now and fear had knotted tightly in his stomach then and his legs had felt so like jelly that he could hardly keep his feet in his stirrups, and his heart had beaten so loudly that he had thought it would burst right out of his chest. He remembered the captain of the Gallopers who rode in the centre of the battle crescent singling him out and entrusting the safety of the banner of the owl to him and how his task had kept his mind off his fear.

'Stay close to the Lady Elionbel, my lad, and protect her for me.'

Krann swallowed and nodded, awkwardly gripping the dagger in one hand as the small column now formed ready for battle and surged forward. The horses snorted and arched their necks as the light of battle shone in their eyes, their hooves churned up the snow and Greygoose drew an arrow back, the feathered flight lightly touching his cheek as he paused in readiness to loose it into the enemy.

Breakmaster and Nebran grimly lowered their spears as the horses gathered speed.

The tail-end of the dark mass of figures ahead of them filled the greenway and suddenly seemed to appear through the swirling snow. Startled faces turned to stare, voices cried out in terror and the long, ragged column scattered in every direction leaving the weak and exhausted with a jumble of meagre possessions littering the road. Breakmaster watched the crowds milling in confusion and called to his battle column to halt, ordering them to lower their swords she reined Beaconlight to a sliding stop. These were not robbers or villains: he couldn't see a sword or a spear amongst the scattering figures as he rode past to the head of the column. He walked back toward the crowds and looked in horror at their ragged, starving faces. People on every side were hesitantly climbing back out of the ditches or the tangled undergrowth where they had fled for protection and were brushing the snow from their rags or retrieving their possessions and helping the weak back onto their feet. As soon as they could they began shuffling slowly forwards again in eerie silence. There was something unnerving about them; they didn't beg or demand food and yet they were clearly starving, when one of them staggered and threatened to fall the others closed in and stopped to help them back to their feet. There was a pride, a dignity, in their eyes that Breakmaster had not seen for an age of daylights. It made him realize with a shock that it had gone missing in the eyes of the people of Elundium.

But who were these people? Where could they be journeying to in the depths of winter and on such a lonely road? There was nothing beyond the tower on Stumble Hill save the frozen wastes of Notley Marsh and the endless, shadowy leagues of Meremire. There would be nowhere for them to find food and shelter until they reached the fortress of Underfall that guarded the wildness of World's End and the sheer walls of the Emerald Mountains, and he doubted that they would find much welcome there.

'Halt in the King's name – halt! Tell me who you are and what business you have upon the King's greenway in this atrocious weather,' Breakmaster demanded as the leading figures bent against the stinging wind and moved slowly apart to go around him. Beaconlight snorted and retreated a step, pirouetting to block their path, his ears flattened against the sides of his head and the whites of his eyes showing.

At the sound of Breakmaster's voice Quencher halted and raised his hand and the untidy column behind him stopped, huddling together defensively. They had already been attacked by villagers and had learned by experience to keep together whatever happened. Quencher let go of the handle of his rickety cart which was loaded down with tools and reached for a long-handled forging hammer with which to defend himself. He cast aside the ragged hessian sack that served him as a hood and blinked away the frozen tear-drops that clung to his eyelashes before looking up first to see the heavily armed horseman who was blocking his path and who wore the emblem of the King upon his battle helm and then at the handful of Marchers who were protectively surrounding a woman and a small child mounted on a fine horse and pony.

'Who wants to know?' he replied warily as Tombel lit a torch and strode forward.

Quencher had learned to be cautious: his family had been stoned and driven out of most of the villages they had stopped at along the way. The villagers were wary of strangers; they had been very aggressive when he had tried to tell them about Nevian appearing to him and warning them that they had to do something for themselves to stop the ruin and desolation spreading across the countryside. He was shouted down when he tried to pass on the magician's message, and they had jeered when he tried to persuade them to follow him to the dark side of morning and the fortress of Cawdor, for to them Cawdor was no more than a place in myths, belonging to fairy tales that only a fool would believe in. Were they to follow such a vision they would all die for their trouble, frozen to death in the snow. Then they had chased him out beyond the village boundaries to perish as the weather worsened; but at each village *some* – a very few – people had listened and one by one those who had not forgotten the good King Thane had struggled to achieve would slip silently away to join him. And Nevian had been true to his word, for he had protected them, and so far none had died of starvation or frozen to death upon their journey although many were sick. Luck or chance had been with them like a silent shadow guiding them. The Border Runners had brought freshly-killed hares and rabbits to the greenways' edge and left them in their path, and the Warhorses had left clear tracks for them to follow deep into the forest where they found the fruits that had been felled by wind and weather and lay scattered in the snow. It hadn't been much but there had always been just enough.

'How dare you challenge me? I am a keeper of the King's horses and proud of it!' the old horseman replied.

'Then well met – we are both King's men,' Quencher suddenly laughed. He thought he had recognized the horseman's voice and when he saw his grim face he let the hammer fall from his cold, numb fingers back into the cart. He swept his arm back towards the procession behind him and started to reveal the true purpose of their journey.

'You mean to say that Nevian, the Master of Magic, actually appeared to you and told you to journey to Cawdor? He came to your forge and told you to go and help the King?'

'Yes,' Quencher nodded, looking over the crowds of ragged people gathered with him and feeling fresh snowflakes lightly touch his cheeks. He stamped his frozen feet in his worn-out boots. 'And he has provided for us as he promised but . . .' the blacksmith paused and frowned as he glanced up to see that the snow was beginning to fall more heavily. 'We must build a shelter and find fuel for fires or we will not survive this night.'

Breakmaster turned around and looked towards the watch lamp shining in the darkness from the tower at Stumble Hill. It was now clear for all to see and he cried out as he turned Beaconlight on a tight rein and galloped away towards it.

'Follow us, Quencher: there will be food and shelter enough for everyone in the tower on Stumble Hill. I know Lord Kyot and the Lady Eventine will not turn away those who love King Thane: they will not let you go wanting when they hear how you love him enough to trudge to the ends of the earth for him. Follow me, follow.'

Quencher smiled and lifted his hand to motion to his ragged following to move forward and for an instant he imagined he could glimpse a shadowy figure wrapped in a swirling rainbow cloak as he dragged his cart towards the single light.

*   *   *

The afternoon light had faded and the great doors of the tower were being pulled shut for the night when Mulcade suddenly swooped in through the closing door-crack hooting and shrieking. Kyot and Eventine, alarmed at the bird's appearance and fearing that an important messenger was lost and in trouble on the greenway as night was falling, both hurried to the platform at the top of the tower and began to search the snowy landscape.

Eventine reached for the glass of Orm and took it from where it stood beside the warning bell in the centre of the platform. Closing her fingers around the smooth black, ebony handles she pushed the tall, wooden pedestal topped with its slender cylinder of brass and polished crystal lenses to the stone balustrade which overlooked the greenway. The narrow wooden wheels of the contraption squeaked and left shallow tracks in the fresh snow as she pushed it carefully into position. Slowly she turned the crystal lenses in opposite directions between her fingertips and instantly made the distant landscape leap closer. Catching a glimpse of what she thought might be a long column of people spread out along the greenway, slowly approaching their tower through the deepening gloom, she stepped back to allow Kyot to look through the glass. Kyot stared carefully through it before he shook his head.

'I don't know who they are. They cannot be King's men and whoever they are they're not Gallopers – look again.'

Eventine's knuckles whitened as she gripped the glass and saw the ragged horde approaching the tower.

Then a watchman trimming the lamp beside them suddenly spotted a small company of Gallopers and Marchers on the road rapidly overhauling the mob and Kyot quickly took the glass back and swung it round. This was what the owl was warning them about. Suddenly he gave a cry of alarm as he recognized Tombel, Elionbel and Krann. Had Woodsedge been overrun? Had the Granite City fallen? And where was Thane? He must help them to outrun those ragged figures who blocked their road. Quickly he gave the order for a strike of Archers to be formed and Sprint and Tanglecrown to be saddled.

'Throw open the doors – we must rescue them!' he ordered, cutting the rope on Orm's bell as he leapt down the spiral stairway.

The warning clatter of the bell summoned every archer, fletcher, armourer and groom to attend to their battle stations and footsteps rang out in the courtyard as candlemen lit the lamps, orders were shouted, bows bent and strung and quivers loaded with new-forged arrows.

Sprint snorted, his neck arching with excitement as Kyot vaulted into the saddle and sparks danced between the horse's hooves as he champed at the bit. Tanglecrown, the Lord of Stags, lowered his huge crystal-tipped antlers and roared as he knelt for Eventine to mount. Both creatures were ready to clear the road of all foul creatures of the night as the great doors were swung open across the cobbles. The strike of Archers swarmed out to right and left and lined the road, leaving the crown of the greenway open for the King's company to gallop to safety between their ranks.

Krann had kept very close to Elionbel as the company skidded to a halt and he felt very alone and frightened as the mass of gaunt and half-starved, frozen figures shuffled closer and he saw small-boned, thin children, some no older than himself, peering out from beneath their mothers' cloaks and staring bleakly at him. He could hear Breakmaster and Tombel talking urgently to their leader but none of what was said made any sense to him and he breathed a sigh of relief when Elionbel whispered to him and told him to put the dagger away. Moments later they began to move forward again and the horses broke into a canter; he had to hold on tightly with both hands as they galloped the last uphill league towards the light that was now occasionally visible through the darkness ahead of them. But one backward glance across his shoulder was enough to rekindle his fear. The silent, ragged crowds were following, their black shapes swallowing up their hoofprints as they advanced one by one, silently.

'Krann, look at the lights on the tower – and look at the strike of Archers – they are coming out to greet us!' Elionbel called out, making him look ahead and cry out with delight, their ragged followers momentarily forgotten.

The young boy peered through the dark, overhanging branches that crowded the road on either side of the greenway, brushing at the nightshapes that swirled and glided around them as softly as the falling snow against his face. Suddenly the darkness parted to reveal a sheer tower in vivid detail. The battle-scarred walls and narrow casement slits, the overhanging platform that surmounted everything with its brilliant lamp; every window was ablaze with light and the great, scarred ironwood doors were being dragged open to reveal an inner courtyard hung with dozens of flickering lamps and crowded with Archers, who ran out through the opening doors casting long, velvet shadows across the snow as they spread out on either side of them and closed in behind the royal group in an unbroken line. As they drew back the arrow shafts they made their bows creak as the feathered flights of death touched their cheeks and they took aim at the tattered advancing hordes. Breakmaster, with Tombel at his stirrup, raced ahead shouting at the Archers, demanding that their weapons be lowered.

Quencher began to doubt the horsemen and hesitated, the lamplight of the tower reflecting on the Archers' hard, unblinking eyes and the mass of arrow heads that were aimed directly at them. The crowds around him slowed and huddled uncertainly together. 'Put your faith in Nevian, remember he promised that he would protect us and he hasn't let us down yet, has he?' Quencher tried to sound strong as he tried to give the others heart but he could hear the doubt in his own words as the wind snatched his voice away.

Kyot and Eventine spurred their mounts forward only to come to an abrupt halt as Breakmaster, with Tombel running at his side, burst through the doors. 'Do not attack the travellers nor let their appearance deceive you: they are all King's men loyal and true, and there are women and children among them. Call back your strike of Archers and welcome these people into the safety of Stumble Hill for they have journeyed a long and hard road with, I fear, little reward for their loyalty.'

Breakmaster jumped stiffly from the saddle and looked up at Kyot, who hesitated to give such an order. 'But how can such a ragged horde be loyal to the King?'

'Since when was loyalty measured by the cut of a person's cloth? Let it be enough that Nevian guides and protects them. Their leader will tell you everything over a bowl of hot gruel, if hospitality still exists in Stumble Hill,' Breakmaster replied impatiently, striding across to embrace Eventine as she dismounted from Tanglecrown.

Still uncertain, Kyot called out and gave orders to allow the travellers into the tower. The Archers holding the crown of the road lowered their bows and stepped aside as the silent crowd of figures shuffled forward to follow Elionbel and Krann through the great doors of the tower.

'I knew you would not let us down, Nevian!' Quencher muttered under his breath, trying to disguise his relief as he was slowly jostled into the flickering lamplight.

The falling snow suddenly became heavier, covering the freshly-swept cobbles as Eventine embraced Elionbel. As she gathered Krann into her arms she noticed his small, cold face. Then she looked round at the pinched, frozen faces of the beggarly crowd who were, by now, filling the courtyard and hovering silently in the background. 'What are we thinking of, keeping you all out here in the cold! Come, come all of you, follow me, there shall be hot gruel, hare and forest fruits for all. Come with me into the feasting hall; a fire roars up the chimney there.'

Krann was put carefully down beside Elionbel and was about to follow when he felt a tug on his arm and he looked around to see a girl a hand shorter than he was dressed in rich velvet and wearing a fur cloak and gown. She was holding a small bow with a quiver of arrows, fresh snowflakes had settled on her long, fire-bronzed hair and she beckoned to him. 'Come on, I've got a thousand things I want to show you. I saw you coming; I couldn't wait for you to get here. Come on, nobody will miss us at supper.'

'Who are you?' Krann frowned.

'I am Fairlight,' she laughed. 'I am Kyot and Eventine's daughter.'

'So you live here in the tower?'

'Of course. Now come on. Have you ever loosed an arrow into the falling snow or tried to split a candleflame?' she asked curiously.

'No – no I have never been allowed to do anything like that.'

'Well, you can if you stay here,' and she offered him her bow.

Krann's footsteps quickened as he followed her laughter through the gloomy, curved corridors.

'Yes, it is to Cawdor we travel,' Quencher paused from telling Kyot his tale of why they journeyed through the dead of winter. He paused long enough to sip gingerly at his bowl and savour the steaming gruel he had been given and looked around the crowded feasting hall, blinking his eyes at the smoky warmth from the fire that blazed in the hearth – yes, Nevian had indeed provided for them. But before long the barrage of questions started again.

'Cawdor? Why are you travelling to Cawdor? Where exactly does Cawdor lie?' Greygoose asked, moving closer as his curiosity sharpened. Perhaps now he could find out the whereabouts of the place that his son, Eider, had supposedly vanished to. Surely this wandering vagrant must know, nobody would be foolish enough to take such a road in this weather: he must know where they were going.

'Cawdor lies beyond the Emerald Mountains. Nevian told me to follow the great greenway past the last lamp of Underfall. He told me to have faith and believe in him and then he would guide our footsteps to the dark side of the morning.'

'But . . . but . . . but that's utter madness!' Greygoose

cried in disbelief. 'You would have us believe that you are leading all these people on such a road with little more than a whim of light – a shadow – a dream to guide you?'

'Nobody is forced to journey with us, friend. Those who believe travel of their own free will and Nevian really does guide and provide for us. We would never have got this far without his help.'

'You shall have everything we can spare, winter clothes, fuel, food – everything,' Kyot promised. Then he took out the parchment Breakmaster had given to him and slowly read through the letter that Thane had sent, asking him to keep Elionbel and Krann safe until he had resolved the troubles that were threatening to wreak such havoc throughout Elundium. Thane had written that although he knew that Kyot and Eventine would not hesitate to come to his aid, he felt they would do more good if they stayed where they were and kept the road to Underfall open.

Breakmaster yawned and climbed stiffly to his feet as he bid Kyot and the company goodnight. 'Greygoose and I will set out at first light on our journey back to the Granite City,' he said, lowering his voice so that no one but Kyot could hear him whisper. 'I worry for the King's safety: there are few who can be trusted in these black daylights.'

Greygoose glanced back at the ragged travellers as they hungrily devoured their food. For him the journey had been a fool's errand – he had learned little of Eider's disappearance that he didn't already know. He was suddenly impatient to return to the city, so that he could ask Grout, the Loremaster, the whereabouts of Cawdor. He would know if anyone did.

X

Treacheries in the Learning Hall

HOAR FROST crackled in the cold, empty, brooding silence of the Learning Hall, thinly gilding the dirty windowpanes and painting fragile feathertails of ice across the bleak granite walls. Loremaster Grout paced backward and forward, treading down the long, erratic shadow he cast from the light of a single, guttering candle amongst the discarded books and scrolls scattered amongst the upturned stools littering the floor. Grout was consumed with fear. He was helplessly caught up in Snatchpurse's intrigues to overthrow the King and there seemed to be no chance of escape. He dreaded the moment his treacheries would be uncovered and waited in fear for the hollow knock upon his door that would mean that he would be summoned to Candlebane Hall to be judged and sentenced for his part in helping the Chancellors' sons.

'Fools! You stupid, stupid fools!' he muttered under his breath, cursing Snatchpurse and his murdering friends for being so impatient, for ignoring all the lessons he had taught them in the fading daylights of King Holbian, the last Granite King. Did they not listen to any of his talks about cunning and politics? Power had to be seized carefully, plans painstakingly laid, not wantonly grasped on the bloody point of a dagger. Nobody hated this new Elundium more than he did – look at the indignities he had to suffer through King Thane's proclamation that learning was for everyone. Now, wherever he looked, all he could see were candlebrats, sweeps' boys and the riff-raff of the city crowding his Learning Hall. Nobody wanted the old ways back more than he did, but murdering and stealing from the common people and setting everybody against those wretched, ugly Tunnellers – much as they deserved it – wasn't the way to overthrow the King. The Chancellors would never have condoned this Honourable Company of Murderers if they had known about it.

Grout froze suddenly, standing statue-still, his mutterings stifled in his throat as he listened intently, trying to catch at the faint sound he thought he could hear. What was it? Was it the scuffle of a rat or the moan of the wind beneath the rafter ends, or was it the sound of footsteps? He could not be sure what it was but he knew that it came from the narrow alleyway at the back of the Learning Hall. Sweat beaded on his high-boned forehead despite the bitter cold. The one thing he feared more than being summoned to Candlebane Hall was Snatch and his murderous friends coming back as they had promised. They had sworn to spread more chaos and terror throughout the city as they dressed up in the foul, rotting armour they had stripped from the dead Nightbeasts they had found in Meremire Forest. Grout knew he could not – dared not – deny them shelter or refuse to help them in their murderous intrigues. Snatch had a terrible hold over him, for he had intercepted and kept the handful of secret letters Grout had been foolish enough to send to Ironpurse, the boy's father, in exile. They showed clearly how he had promised to help the Chancellor to overthrow the King when the time was ripe and Snatchpurse had been quick to threaten to send those incriminating letters to the King if he refused to help them. And Grout had looked into the ruthless, murdering madness that shone in the boy's eyes and had not doubted for one moment that he had meant what he said.

The Loremaster listened to the expanding silence and let out a shallow gasp of relief, sure that he was safe for at least another night. Too mean to light a lamp, he shuffled through the low archway into the darkened scullery to check that the back door into Blackbone Alley was securely bolted. He felt his way through the swirling nightshapes, cursing as he knocked his shins on the unseen bench and complaining bitterly as he fumbled for the bolts on the door. 'Why, oh why, didn't I have the sense to call the guard the moment those murderous boys came scratching at my door? Surely the King would have rewarded me! Surely he would not have punished me for my indiscretions: I could have explained those letters.'

Grout's mutterings suddenly ceased and he screamed as an ice-cold, powerful claw gripped his wrist and began to twist it violently making him dizzy with panic. The stench of decay made him sick.

'Turn us in would you, Grout? You treacherous, spineless creature!'

Snatch's harsh voice whispered in his ear as other claws pulled painfully at his hair and scratched at the dry, wrinkly skin on his face. He was spun around faster and faster. A spark flared in the darkness and Grout staggered and fell to his knees as the claws let him go. Trembling he looked up to find himself surrounded by the Chancellors' sons disguised in the skin and armour of the hideous, leering Nightbeasts.

'No! No! I didn't mean that I would betray you – I promise. It was nothing but the mutterings of a silly, old man,' he wept, his face grey and sweating, his lips trembling and dribbling uncontrollably at the sudden shock of their appearance in the scullery.

Grout was not a brave man and the menacing look in Snatch's eyes as he stared at him out of the dead creature's mask turned his legs to jelly. He knew rationally that the Chancellors' sons were only disguised as Nightbeasts but they seemed to have given new life to the beasts, and there were many more of them crowding his scullery than on their first visit to the city. Their slightest movement distorted the shadows and spread rippling webs of darkness in the fragile light of the spark that Girrolt held up between the blackened claws he wore over his left hand. Grout could barely dredge up the courage to look up into the mass of scaly, misshapen faces with their snarling mouths crowded with jagged, razorsharp teeth. They were much more frightening than anything his imagination could have conjured up for his stories in the Learning Hall.

'Get up, you snivelling fool! Get up and light the lamps. Bring us food and ale and be quick about it. We are cold and hungry after our long journey.'

Snatch's voice hissed in disgust as he looked at the Loremaster and he hooked a sharp claw into the collar of his gown, tearing it slightly as he jerked him roughly to his feet and pushed him away. Grout sobbed and fumbled in his pocket, searching for his worn-out spark as Snatch pulled off the hollowed-out head of the Nightbeast he had been wearing and brushed away the flakes of dead skin from his hair before tossing the head down upon the table beside the Loremaster, making him jump as he scuttled away to fetch the lamps and worry about how he was going to feed so many. Snatch sent Krush and Thoragrasp to check out the Learning

Hall thoroughly and make sure that all the doors were securely bolted.

'I don't think that the Loremaster can altogether be trusted do you?' Snatch called after them.

'That can easily be dealt with,' Girrolt grimaced, slowly drawing the middle finger of his right hand across his throat.

'Please, please don't hurt me, you must know I am loyal to your cause, you must realize I want the old ways back more than anybody else!' Grout pleaded as he came back into the room to place the lantern in the centre of the table with a shaking hand.

Snatch laughed out loud. 'But of course you would betray us, Grout – you would betray your own mother, if you had one, to save your own worthless hide. That's why we crept into your house so secretly, that's why we picked the lock, so you wouldn't have the time to give us away!'

'Betray your own mother . . . betray your own mother . . . har . . . har . . . har,' Squark, the magpie, mocked, imitating the Loremaster's voice, bobbing his head up and down where he perched on Snatch's shoulder, compounding Grout's misery as the rest of the Honourable Company of Murderers crowded his scullery, laughing at him as they stripped off the Nightbeast armour they were wearing.

Snatch suddenly leaned forward, his dagger in his hand as he gripped the Loremaster by his collar and pulled him close. The laughter in the room died away and the crowd shuffled back, watching with bated breath. They knew how ruthless Snatch could be, how his moods could change so suddenly – and how he enjoyed killing, especially those who doubted his cause. Few of them had realized to what lengths he would go to exact his revenge upon King Thane for driving the Chancellors into exile and all of them had been drawn too deep into the murdering and stealing to back out now. Most of them disguised their revulsion at what he forced them to do, covering it with pretence and boasting, eager to lure others into the Honourable Company to take their places. Except that it never seemed to free them, for no matter how much they stole it never seemed to be enough. Nothing would sate Snatch's lust for power.

'But you won't have time to betray us, Grout, or time to doubt your loyalty,' Snatch sneered in his face, pricking at his adam's apple with the point of his dagger to emphasize his words. 'Because I will slit your miserable, scrawny throat and pull your tongue out through the bleeding slit at the first sign of a hesitation or another treacherous whisper against me – do you understand, Grout?' Snatch sneered and continued mercilessly, 'And remember, I will always be watching you, listening to you from the shadows, especially when you least expect it.'

Grout nodded helplessly, his frightened eyes and short, ragged gasps for air revealing the terror he felt as Snatch let go of him and he slumped across the table. The sight of him made the Chancellor's son laugh.

'Now tell us everything that has happened in the city, good Loremaster, while you pour our ale and fill the table with all the delicacies you have hidden in your larder. What has been happening since those wretched prisoners escaped from us? Rumours tell us that the King thinks there are still Nightbeasts hiding within the city walls.'

Grout blinked nervously and wiped a trembling hand across his lips. A moment ago the boy was about to kill him, pressing a dagger to his throat and now he was all softness and smiles just as if the threats had never been made. He felt as though he was treading on such treacherous ground that he hardly dared to open his mouth, but Snatch stared at him, awaiting an answer.

'I am afraid there is hardly anything to eat except a few mouldy crusts and the last dregs of ale in the bottom of my barrel, and that is soured and almost undrinkable,' he muttered in a small, frightened voice but added quickly, 'The tallow houses are almost empty and there is hardly a candle to be had in the whole city. I have even heard rumours that soon Candlebane Hall will be smothered with darkness and that all food this is left can only be bought at an exorbitant barter, far beyond the means of a humble Loremaster. But the King won't be going hungry, that's for sure, not with all the food that has been hoarded in the kitchens and storerooms in the Towers of Granite. I have heard that there is so much locked away in there that it is stacked from floor to ceiling. The people are starting to mutter that if the King wasn't so greedy he would share it out, but everybody knows he is much too mean to do that. He doesn't care if we all starve to death.'

'Excellent! Excellent!' Snatch grinned, his face split with sheer delight. 'Well, well, Grout, who would have thought we could succeed so quickly, you didn't for sure, you old doubter. And to think it all started because I had the courage to stand up for the people's rights and chase that ugly bunch of Tunnellers out of the inn at Deepling and into the forest!' Snatch laughed, patting the Loremaster on the shoulder with the hilt of his dagger.

'That thronestealer, Thanehand, was such a fool not to realize how much everybody would hate the changes he has made: I knew that his undoing would be giving those wretched Tunnellers the freedom to roam wherever they pleased, giving them the rights to live off the backs of

275

honest folk – and for what? Pruning a few miserable trees, mowing the greenways! I tell you, Grout, the people were just waiting for someone to show them the way, they were impatient for a leader like me!'

Snatch's eyes narrowed with cunning as his imagination began to run away with him. Everything he wanted, the power that should have been his by right, the revenge for his father and all the other Chancellors being banished into the depths of Meremire Forest, it was all there at his fingertips, there for the taking. The countryside was paralysed with fear, controlled by his followers masquerading as Nightbeasts or marauding Tunnellers. The merchants and journeymen were afraid to travel without his protection and he had extracted such a high price for this protection that his secret barns and storehouses were overflowing and, from what Grout had just divulged about the dwindling supplies of food in the city, he sensed that the city folk were close to revolt. All they needed was a gentle push in the right direction and then they would hang the skin of the throne-stealer on top of the Stumble Gate. Snatch watched the Loremaster for a moment. There was just one thing that bothered him and nagged at the back of his mind. He cursed his own stupidity for letting the Tunnellers slip through his fingers – what if they came back? Were they responsible for the outbreaks of unrest that seemed to be sweeping through the more remote villages? He was receiving the most ridiculous rumours that somebody was stirring up trouble, talking openly about being loyal to the King and then abruptly vanishing before any of his men caught him. But each time he spoke out a handful of villagers disappeared. Where could they be going in the depths of winter? But he sighed, pushing these troubling thoughts to one side.

'But I shall forgive you, Grout, I will show you how I keep my side of a promise, or had you forgotten that I said I would reward you for sheltering us here in the city and showing us the secret way up into the courtyard of Candlebane Hall to get at those Tunnellers before they were judged? It wasn't your fault they escaped before we could get our hands on them.'

Snatch motioned to the pile of heavy sacks they had brought with them and placed in the shadows of the scullery door. Four of them were dragged forward and lifted up to be tipped out on the table in front of the Loremaster. Grout's eyes almost popped out of his head in sheer astonishment when he saw the food that spilled out of the sacks: there was too much for the table to hold and some of it fell onto the floor – dozens of crusty loaves, jars of rich preserves and combs of honey wrapped in linen strips that oozed wetly, pouches of grain, a side of smoked meat and more fruits of the forest than he could have gathered in his arms. There was enough for a feast fit for the King.

'I promised to reward you for having the good sense not to reveal my presence here in the Learning Hall,' Snatch reminded him, 'or had you forgotten how the King burst in here accompanied by that fool of a horseman, Breakmaster, on the morning the Tunnellers escaped? How else would we have discovered where the prisoners were heading if I hadn't eavesdropped from the shadows when they asked for the way to Cawdor, where the Nighthorses were gathered on the dark side of morning?'

'Yes, yes, of course, how stupid of me,' Grout quickly agreed, his eyes following a large truckle of cheese as it bounced onto the floor and rolled away between the feet of the group. Momentarily his greed got the better of him and he dropped to his knees and scrambled after the cheese, to the roars of laughter from the youths who crowded his scullery.

'Get up you fool!' Snatch hissed angrily, prising the ripe, round cheese from the old man's fingers as he demanded answers. 'You can tell us everything that has happened here in the city since our last visit before you fill your ugly face. How many men are still loyal to the King? What news is there, if any, of those wretched prisoners? Have any of the patrols found any of their bodies yet? If they are still alive we can't risk them coming back. Have you found out anything more of the road to Cawdor? Don't those scrolls and books that clutter up your precious Learning Hall tell you anything?'

The Loremaster looked frantically from face to face. There was very little to tell except that the city was in chaos and close to starvation but he knew he would have to tell them something. 'People are deserting the King in droves every daylight and some say that those who do stay with him only do so to fill their bellies. Oh yes, I did overhear somebody only the other day say that Breakmaster and that Captain of Archers – Greygoose I think his name is – had deserted their posts. At least nobody has seen them in the city for a while. But of the secret road to Cawdor I am afraid my books have yielded little save that the road lies in a high place three daylights' ride beyond the great lamp of Underfall and that it skirts the heather meadows and passes close to the gates of night before entering a deep ravine . . .'

'Oh yes, yes, we know all that!' Snatch interrupted impatiently. 'But if you can't tell us the way, what can you tell us of Cawdor itself? Who lives there? Who rules, what are their customs? Will they give the prisoners shelter or slaughter them on sight?'

Grout shrugged his shoulders helplessly. 'I'm afraid Cawdor has been lost in history, its people forgotten in the mists of time but ... but ... I could look again tonight while you rest after your long journey – perhaps there is something written that I missed. If I could just have a crumb of cheese to give me strength ...'

Snatch looked at the Loremaster in disgust, wondering what it was his father and the other Chancellors had seen in him or how they could possibly have feared him when they had been his pupils in the Learning Hall. The man was a snivelling coward.

'Take what you want,' he snapped, reaching for the hollowed out Nightbeast head and pulling it down over his head. 'Thoragrasp will stay here to keep an eye on you, Grout, while we do a little murdering and frightening in the lower circles of the city, if there is anybody fool enough to be out at this hour. But leave the door unlocked, we'll be back for some answers before the grey hours have touched the sky.'

'We'll be back ... we'll be back ...' Squark mocked as the Honourable Company of Murderers slipped out into the frozen darkness and began to swarm through the shadows.

Grout darted anxious glances at Thoragrasp as he crammed handfuls of the food into his mouth, greedily devouring it as he hurried into the Learning Hall to begin the long, fruitless search through the scrolls and books of lore. He knew he would have to find something – anything – to satisfy Snatchpurse's thirst for knowledge about Cawdor. 'It's a waste of time, an utter waste of time,' he muttered softly to himself as he gathered a pile of dusty books.

Cawdor was a place of legend, lost and forgotten so long ago he didn't even know if it had ever truly existed. Why did Snatch want to know so much about it? The Tunnellers must have perished, and even if they hadn't, they were never going to come back.

Crimp, the blacksmith's son, reluctantly crouched down in the bulky, evil-smelling Nightbeast armour he had been forced to wear, stopping at the signal from Snatch and Girrolt who could see someone ahead of them in the darkness. He pressed himself into the deep, indigo shadows at the base of the sheer frost-glittering wall that encircled Candlebane Hall and felt a knot of disgust rising from his stomach at the senseless murder that was about to take place. The only purpose in it was to strike fear and panic among the city folk and give new life to the rumours that had been circulating since their last visit to the city, for the people must believe that the Nightbeasts really had risen again in Meremire Forest and were loose in the city. It would throw into doubt everything that the King had won at the Battle of the Rising. How he wished that the silent, swirling nightshapes would smother his shame forever, because he couldn't dredge up the courage to shout a warning as he listened to the soft crunch of the candleman's boots in the snow and saw the glow of his spark in the starry darkness as he drew closer, oblivious to the danger he was in, his clear voice singing out.

'Who calls the candleman to light them to bed?

Who calls the candleman to weave dreams in their head?'

Crimp wished he hadn't been in quite such a hurry to join this Honourable Company of Murderers. Why hadn't he realized that there could be nothing honourable about murder? Why hadn't he suspected the sinister intentions that lay just behind their façade? He didn't want the Chancellors back in power: he could remember how bitterly his father had spoken of them – he should have had the sense to realize that the Tunnellers couldn't possibly have been behind all these troubles. He had seen them often enough when they stopped at his father's forge to have their gardening tools sharpened – they were kind, generous, gentle people, for all their strange looks, not the marauding savages that they were now made out to be. But it was easy to be wise after the event, and he wasn't the only one to be drawn into the same trap. There had been dozens like him on the daylight he had reached the village of Deepling, searching for a way to join the Honourable Company of Murderers founded by the Chancellors' sons who seemed to be selflessly protecting the villagers and merchants who travelled the greenways, bartering their wares and preventing them from being killed by the Tunnellers and Nightbeasts who were rampaging the countryside. It seemed such an honourable thing to do, far better than doing nothing, but little did most of them realize what they were being drawn into until it was too late. By the time they knew what was really happening, death would be their only escape, Snatch would make sure of that.

Snatch was fanatical about secrecy and had gone to great lengths to emphasize the importance of everybody pulling together. He gave the impression to all newcomers that his one desire was to protect everyone, that he really cared about the ordinary folk, that his one purpose was to defeat the evil Tunnellers and their friends, the Nightbeasts. There hadn't seemed much wrong when he had suggested that they teach the merchants and villagers a lesson when they had steadfastly refused their protection. But Crimp had thought it a little strange when he had to dress up in Nightbeast armour and rob them to prove to them how vulnerable they were when travelling alone. However, his doubts and questions were laughed aside and he was made to feel an outsider and cajoled and urged to show his loyalty – and he really did want to be a part of this Honourable Company. It wasn't until after he had accidentally stabbed a journeyman to death when they robbed him of everything, even the clothes he stood up in, that he truly felt the horror of what was happening. Girrolt, who had been with him, had just laughed in his face and looked down at the dead man, then dipped the middle finger of his right hand into the victim's blood and smeared it across Crimp's throat whispering, 'Welcome to the Honourable Company of Murderers – you are truly one of us now and there is no turning back.'

Crimp shivered with dread, his hand upon the hilt of his dagger as the candleman drew closer. If only he could find the courage to stop this wanton murder. It didn't matter how many rewards or places under his sole control Snatch and his murderous friends promised him once he helped them seize power – he didn't want them. He didn't want this blood on his hands. He didn't want to see the faces of the innocent people he had murdered in the dark every time he closed his eyes but Snatch had a terrible hold over him: he was afraid, terrified, of what he would do to him if he refused. How bitterly he regretted that last argument he'd had with his father in the forge in the village of Muddle. Why hadn't he listened? Why hadn't he asked for wisdom instead of cursing him and calling him a silly old man who was scared of a handful of Tunnellers? Why had he accused him of jumping at his own shadow? He would never be able to hold his head up again, or look his father in the eyes, not after all he had done. He was a traitor and a murderer and he would be better off dead – but he didn't even have the courage to do that.

Snatch laughed softly and licked his lips in anticipation of the fear and terror that this killing would cause amongst the city folk, and where better to commit it than on the very threshold of Candlebane Hall? Silently he lifted his hand as the candleman drew level with the locked gates of the wall that encircled the Candlehall and the Towers of Granite. Starlight reflected coldly down from the long, curved, brittle Nightbeast claws that encased his hand as he gave the signal for his followers to pounce upon the unsuspecting figure and slit his throat, mutilating his body to make it look like a Nightbeast attack. But Squark, whom he had sent to keep watch from between the tall chimneys of the Gilders' Hall that stood on the outer edge of the seventh circle of the city, gave a sudden shrill warning that made Snatch hesitate and sent the rest of the murderous company skulking deeper into the shadows to wait until the danger had passed.

The candleman paused, holding his spark aloft. 'That's very odd,' he murmured suspiciously, frowning as he searched the steep, frosty roofs and the forest of tall chimneys that were silhouetted against the canopy of stars. He could have sworn he had heard the cry of a magpie coming from somewhere close by. A cold shiver ran up his spine and he pulled up the collar of his cloak as he prepared to move quickly away. He knew the omens. The cry of a magpie always heralded misfortune. But another sound rose up through the darkened streets. The sharp clatter of fast-moving horseshoes on frosty cobbles, getting closer, echoing between the crowded houses past the Honourable Masters of Barter, past the Haberdashers and Cloth Merchants. He could hear it more clearly now – it was two horses and they were in a hurry to reach Candlebane Hall or the Towers of Granite. He realized it must be somebody important, a messenger for the King or something, or the guards would never have opened the Stumble Gate and let them into the city at this late hour, especially with all those rumours of Nightbeasts roaming through the streets after dark. He knew that he had better be quick to warn the guards so that they would be able to open the gates in time.

'There ought to be a law against messengers and their like riding in when they please, disturbing a fellow in his work – and waking up honest folk and disturbing their dreams,' he grumbled, lifting his long, slender lamp spark and hammering loudly on the pitted, ironwood doors with its knuckled end as he called out for the guard to throw open the doors.

Snatch cursed and retreated a few paces, hugging the shadows, as the candleman reached up and trimmed the flickering lamps that hung in their iron baskets on either side of the archway. But he watched with sharp, cunning eyes as the guards answered the candleman's shouts. Keys grated stiffly in their frozen locks and the gates creaked and groaned as they were slowly pulled open, scraping and bumping across the cobbles.

'You lied to me, Grout, you treacherous, whining dog!' Snatch hissed from the darkness, barely able to contain his rage when he saw who the two horsemen were who rode out from between the last of the houses. They passed so close to where he hid before they disappeared through the gates and into the courtyard of Candlebane Hall that he could not be mistaken.

The taller, stouter, well-armed figure with the straggly, untidy beard, thick with frost, was that wretched horseman, Breakmaster: he recognized him from when he had burst into the Learning Hall with the King demanding to know the road to Cawdor. And the other one with the longbow slung across his shoulder with two quivers of arrows hanging from the cantle of the saddle fitted the description of Greygoose, the Captain of Archers. But why had the Loremaster lied? Why had he told him that both riders had deserted the King when here they were as large as life riding in through the gates and up towards Candlebane Hall?

'Those horses have travelled a long, unforgiving road,' Girrolt whispered in his ear, pointing to the dark patches of sweat that stained their shoulders and the burrs and thorns clinging to their manes and tails that they could just see in the lamplight.

'Yes, I could strangle a dozen merchants to know where they have been. There's something strange going on that we need to know about. Come on, we'll do our murdering somewhere else tonight and see if we can't squeeze the truth out of somebody. I want to know where that treacherous horseman has been before the grey hours touch the sky: somebody must have been witness to their comings and goings.'

Snatch drew the others away into a dark, evil-smelling alleyway that would lead them down into the poorer, lower circles of the city.

*　　*　　*

The Company of Murderers silently retraced their steps along Blackbone Alleyway at the back of the Learning Hall as the dawn hours began to lighten the sky, their hideous armoured shapes barely disturbing the shadows or leaving a trace of their passing. Nothing showed from the orgy of killing that Snatch had insisted they commit amongst the crowded hovels of weavers and tallow-makers in the lowest circle of the city save for the occasional, careless claw-scrape in the dirty, trampled snow or scattered spots of congealing blood that dripped unnoticed from their claws. They had been successful in their quest to strike terror into people's hearts.

Crimp trailed along miserably at the rear of the company, sickened by what he had just witnessed and been forced to take part in, and for an instant, just as the others slipped furtively through the back door of the Learning Hall, he had looked over his shoulder along the dark, empty alleyway and thoughts of escape had filled his mind. He half-turned, but hesitated, afraid but desperate to make a break and run for his life. His heartbeats were pounding in his chest, the blood was thundering in his ears. It was now or never. He took a step, the nightshapes swirling around him, but then he felt a hand grab at his arm. Its grip tightened and he was forcefully pulled stumbling over the threshold into the scullery.

'You're not thinking of leaving us now, are you, Crimp? You're not thinking of betraying us, are you?' Snatch's voice was loaded with malice as he drew the boy close to him and his pupils shrank until they were murderous pin-points of light.

'No . . . no . . . of course not . . . I was only looking back to check that nobody had followed us. I would never betray the Honourable Company of Murderers, you must know that, never . . . never . . . never . . .'

The words ended in a gasp of terror. He knew Snatch would kill him on the spot, slit his throat in one swift movement, if he guessed at half his secret doubts. He tried to laugh, to disguise his revulsion at the murders. There were no doubters in this company. But the sound came out like a betraying, high-pitched squeal as sweat trickled down the back of his neck, wetting the Nightbeast skin that he wore, releasing its evil, putrid smell and making it stick to him. For what seemed an age those ruthless eyes seemed to bore into his soul. Crimp trembled and hunted for breath in the dancing lamplight.

One by one the others in the scullery fell silent and edged backwards. They knew their leader's moods and watched with baited breath. Snatch frowned and shook him slightly. He couldn't understand it. He had never been wrong before. But no matter how much he searched he couldn't find that doubt he had sensed in the boy when he had hesitated at the entrance to the scullery. Perhaps he had been telling him the truth about turning to check that nobody had followed them. Perhaps . . .

Girrolt's light touch on his arm suddenly distracted him.

'Shouldn't we hide all the gear we've brought with us along with the Nightbeast armour? It shouldn't be lying around here when the new daylight breaks, should it? We don't want prying eyes and wagging tongues betraying us, do we?'

Snatchpurse blinked and nodded. He let go of Crimp's arm abruptly, snarling after him as he hurried across the scullery to squeeze in amongst the others, 'Let that be a warning to you, boy: don't go getting any ideas about running away. I'll be watching you more closely in future – much more closely.'

Snatch turned on his heel, leaving Girrolt to organize the hiding places for the company; there was plenty of room in the warren of rooms and cubby-holes at the back of the hall, and he strode into the Learning Hall. He had a score to settle with Grout for lying to him about Breakmaster and the Archer. Clearly neither of them had deserted the King. A familiar stale smell caught at the back of his throat as he passed beneath the low archway that opened into the vast, gloomy Learning Hall. The odour of chalk and slates, dusty vellum, quills and ink. It brought back echoes of his childhood. He paused for a moment, letting his eyes grow accustomed to the dark, and his face hardened as he caught sight of the Loremaster sitting at his desk, hunched down amongst tottering piles of his precious books and scrolls, mumbling and muttering to himself incessantly as he scribbled frantically. The ink spluttered from the blunt tip of his ragged quill to leave purple spots across the uneven surface of the crumpled parchment he was writing upon in the feeble light cast by the single candle at his elbow.

Thoragrasp rose hastily to his feet from where he had been lounging, watching the Loremaster from the shadows, but Snatch motioned to him to be still, pressing a finger to his lips as he approached silently. He wanted to surprise Grout, to make him jump out of his miserable skin. Snatch knuckled his fists, his lips compressed into a thin puckered line of anger. He would teach him to lie. The candle flame stirred at Grout's elbow, making him pause and wrinkle his beak-sharp nose. He sniffed at the cold, stagnant air in the hall. Suddenly he caught the reek of rotting Nightbeast skin and heard the dry rattle of its leathery scales behind him. Letting out a frightened gasp he twisted around to find Snatchpurse towering over him, his face dark with anger, his fist raised to strike him down.

'You lied to me, Grout! That horseman and the Captain of Archers are still loyal to the King – I saw them ride in through the gates of Candlebane Hall,' he hissed as the Loremaster shrank back in his seat.

'No . . . no . . . I did not lie, I must have made a mistake, I must have listened in to the wrong conversation. I would never knowingly lie to you, never. But wait . . .' he cried, barely pausing for breath as he stabbed a desperate hand towards the parchment. 'I have found out more about the secrets of Cawdor – dark, sinister things that have been hidden so cleverly in my books of lore that I almost missed them completely. Listen – once, in the daylights of the first Granite Kings, Elundium stretched far beyond the Emerald Mountains and the last lamp at Underfall, all the way through the petrified forest to the shores of a limitless ocean, or so my books reveal, and Cawdor was a place of sunlight and beauty. There is no mention of it being the dark side of morning, but a place where the golden ships of Carth and the vessels full of silks and spices from Minios traded their wares, where the huge reed boats of Gnarlsmyre rode the waves and their swarthy Marshlords haggled and bartered at the harbour walls. In those far-off daylights a great citadel rose upon the black marble cliffs above the waves. It had soaring spires, battlements and towers, quiet, shaded courtyards and vaulted halls, festooned with rare and beautiful stone orchids gathered from the petrified forest. It was a place of song, laughter and peace. But then, one awful night, when everything slept, the Eretch invaded the great citadel.

They crept soundlessly out from beneath the eaves of the petrified forest and rose up out of the soft sea mist, engulfing everything, weaving webs of shadow through the rigging of the ships in the harbour, darkening and possessing each person they touched. By the time the first fingers of the new daylight were lightening the sky, the Eretch had shrouded Cawdor with the dark side of morning and nothing but the echo of what it had been still existed in the thunder of the surf that beat up against the black marble cliffs.'

Snatchpurse gripped the Loremaster's arm as he paused for breath and forcefully twisted the voluminous folds of his sleeve to draw him closer to him. He laughed harshly in his face, making the thin candleflame that glowed between them dance and flutter on its wick, spilling hot wax across the crumpled parchment that Grout was holding. 'That is nothing more than one of your Learning Hall stories! You won't fool me with such embroidery, Grout. The Eretch indeed – what a name to conjure up in the dark. You will have to do a lot better than that if you want to avoid the beating you deserve for lying to me!'

There was a cold menace of purpose in the threat that brought fresh beads of sweat oozing from Grout's high, bony forehead. 'It's the truth, I swear it is. I've written it all down for you, it's all here in my books, I promise. I haven't embroidered one word of it. The Eretch are grave devils, the remnants of the Gabare wraiths that were the first evil that Krulshards released from the deepest, blackest chambers of the City of Night to fight against the Granite Kings. Their purpose was to devour Cawdor and shroud it in the dark side of morning. The books say that their presence shadowed the brightest daylight.'

'Truth!' Snatch hissed, his anger boiling up as he sent

a pile of books crashing to the ground with a sweep of his free hand. 'How dare you speak to me of truth when all your tales in the Learning Hall are exaggerated – when the truth is tortured by your tongue? Oh yes, you thought we hadn't heard how you lied, but word reached us even in exile of how you recount those last glorious daylights of King Holbian and his retreat from the city to the children who sit at your feet, how you poison them against the Chancellors and paint them as traitors who looted the treasury and then deserted the King, fleeing to save their own skins, leaving him defenceless as the Nightbeasts swarmed over the walls.'

'No . . . no . . . it's not true! I try to tell how justly your fathers governed Elundium during the times of the Granite Kings. I even make the children recite your fathers' names so that they are familiar with them for when you seize back what has been stolen from you; but the truth is so frowned upon and I am forced to tell them what a hero the King is and . . .'

Snatch waved the Loremaster into silence, sickened by his whining, when he suddenly wondered if there might be a grain of truth in the story, for he was attracted by the sound of the Gabare-wraiths. 'The Eretch – do they still rule in Cawdor? What do they look like – what became of them? You don't suppose they're still there, do you? And if they are, would they be foolish enough to give food and shelter to the Tunnellers? Tell me everything you have found out before the new daylight breaks – everything, come now, hurry!'

Snatch released the Loremaster's sleeve and patted him almost affectionately as he waited for the answers. Grout swallowed nervously, his adam's apple jumping erratically in his scrawny neck.

'Oh, yes, I'm sure they still inhabit Cawdor, most certainly if it is still shrouded by the dark side of morning, because Krulshards never brought them here, no, he must have forgotten all about them as he turned his attention to breeding Nightbeasts in the City of Night ready to overrun Elundium. From what I have been able to discover they wouldn't have wanted to help the Tunnellers, no, quite the opposite in fact. You see the Eretch's power lay not inside them, exactly, but in their ability to seek out those hungry for power: they could scent corruption, rage and anger or those eaten away by a secret envy and then they would silently inhabit their souls, feeding them with darkness, filling them with evil. From what we know about the wretched Tunnellers there is no place for the Eretch to find a way inside them, no room for envy or ambition – nothing at all.'

'But why wouldn't the Eretch just kill the Tunnellers the moment they arrive in Cawdor?'

Grout gave a small, high-pitched laugh and put his long, thin fingers together as he tried to explain. 'Because they're grave-devils, weak, indistinct, translucent figures, distorted creatures of the night with no form or substance. They have no real power to do anything: they are barely glimpsed, or if they are they are seen as fleeting shadows, pools of darkness – unless they have a body to possess, and from what I have managed to uncover, the people of Cawdor whom they invested with evil powers died out long ago and passed into the mists of history leaving only the remnants of the Eretch to roam the ruined battlements of Cawdor, forever shrouding it with darkness.'

'And these Eretch – they need people, right?' There was something intriguing to Snatch about the power the Eretch possessed, something he might be able to use.

'Yes, yes, they have no power without a host; but I wouldn't advise you or anybody else to embrace the Eretch – no, certainly not. You should let me learn a lot more about them, remember they are grave-devils, evil creatures from Krulshards' darkness. And . . .'

A sudden loud, hollow knock upon the outer doors of the Learning Hall cut short Grout's speech and he almost jumped out of his skin as he inhaled a frightened gasp of air.

'I am undone! All my treacheries have been discovered: I will be disgraced, flayed alive for helping you!' he cried, cowering in his chair, clutching at the throat of his gown.

'Shut up, you spineless fool! Go and open that door before your miserable whining gives us all away,' Snatch hissed at him, violently hauling the Loremaster to his feet as he propelled him towards the doors.

Grout stumbled and tripped as Thoragrasp appeared out of the shadows and pushed him forward. He let out a strangled sob of misery as he hurried through the gloomy hall. He had always known it would come to this in the end, and all because of that moment of weakness when he had allowed the Chancellors' sons to bully him into helping them.

'You're one of us, Grout, we won't let anybody harm you,' Snatch called out softly from where he had hidden. 'Now remember your dignity and demand to know who it is who dares to bother the Loremaster, calling him from his bed at this dreadful hour, before you open the door. Go quickly and keep your wits about you. Don't worry, we'll be listening to every word!'

Grout swallowed and tried to clear his throat in readiness to give his voice authority before he reached the doors. 'Who disturbs the Loremaster?' he demanded, only to hear his voice come out in a thin, dry crackle as his fingers reached for the bolts.

'It is Greygoose, Captain of Archers, Loremaster. I beg a little of your wisdom at this early hour.'

Snatch's interest sharpened as Greygoose gave his name. 'Open the doors, Grout, let the Archer in and try to coax out of him where he and that horseman so mysteriously vanished to,' he whispered from the shadows.

Greygoose continued, 'I am so worried about the whereabouts of my son, Eider, I'm at my wits' end, Loremaster, and I seek your knowledge.' Greygoose allowed Grout to hurry him in through the darkened hall and sit him in exactly the right place beside his desk so that Snatchpurse could easily eavesdrop on every word.

'Oh, yes, Eider, I remember him, such a nice boy, one of my favourites,' Grout lied, trying to draw the Archer out. 'Yes, he was always so helpful here in the Learning Hall, it is such a pity he got himself into trouble, mixing with bad company, I've heard, not that I pay any attention to such rumours, you understand. I had such high hopes for him. I suppose you and Breakmaster have been out searching for him? Only I haven't seen you in the city recently.'

'Well, no, not exactly,' Greygoose hesitated, his conscience pricked by the promise that he had made to King Thane, along with the rest of the council, that he would not reveal to anyone the purpose or destination of the journey that he and Breakmaster had just undertaken. He knew the King didn't want anyone to know where Elionbel and Krann had been taken and he didn't want to risk the safety of the tower on Stumble Hill: but he just had to find out all he could about Cawdor, to know if a road really existed through the Emerald Mountains and if he'd had a chance of reaching the dark side of morning, or indeed, whether the place of legends really existed at all. Surely it could do no harm if he just asked the Loremaster, for he seemed harmless enough.

Greygoose glanced anxiously around the gloomy, empty hall. All he could hear were the gnawing of the rats amongst the dusty scrolls and books, the sharp scuttling of their feet as they hurried into the shadowy corners and the crackle of the frost upon the windowpanes. 'You must swear not to divulge anything I tell you – not a word, not to anybody – do you understand?'

Grout's bushy eyebrows rose in mock surprise that he should ever dream of doing such a thing and he disguised his cunning smile behind his hand as he reassured the Archer that anything he said in that room would go no further, that the four walls of the Learning Hall would mark the end of the conversation.

'Of course all your utterances are safe with me, Greygoose. Who else could be near enough to hear us save the rats? Why even the King himself comes to me from time to time when he has grave matters to unravel and I have never, never revealed one syllable. Discretion is my watchword. Now, tell me, how can I help? Is it tied up with the journey that you and Breakmaster have just returned from?'

Greygoose wrestled with his conscience for a moment longer and than leaned closer to the Loremaster, sure he could trust him completely, but he still lowered his voice to a conspiratorial whisper.

'Eider was seen along with that crippled sweep's boy riding with the Tunnellers who escaped from the cellars beneath Candlebane Hall. The messenger who brought us news of them rode with Breakmaster and me in our escort to Stumble Hill and told me that he was part of the company of Gallopers who pursued the prisoners, that they tracked them past the last lamp of Underfall to the entrance of an ancient road that led up into the Emerald Mountains. When I pressed the man for where the road went he told me that it once, so legend has it, led to Cawdor on the dark side of morning. But I know he knew no more than that. I'm so worried, Loremaster: what has become of Eider? Is there really a road through the mountains or will they all perish?'

'Wait, wait, you go too fast. Start at the beginning. Where does Stumble Hill fit into this story? I thought you had ridden out in search of your son who was riding to Cawdor? How extraordinary. Yes, now start at the beginning, what did the messenger tell you? And please speak up, for I am a little hard of hearing.' Grout darted an anxious glance across the Archer's shoulders as he caught a glimpse of Snatch creeping closer.

Greygoose frowned but reluctantly began again, this time telling the Loremaster everything from when the messenger had arrived in Candlebane Hall with news of the Tunnellers' flight, to the decision that the Queen and Krann would be safer in the tower on Stumble Hill until the troubles were over. He had just finished telling him about the greater part of the journey when he paused for breath. Grout was well pleased with what the Archer had told him and he was about to hurry him on his way with a vague description of Cawdor, just something innocuous that would satisfy his curiosity, when Greygoose suddenly told him about the ragged column of people they had encountered upon the greenway near the tower on Stumble Hill who were trudging their way through the snow in search of Cawdor.

'Well, let me tell you, Loremaster, they were the strangest sight I have ever seen – blocking the road ahead of us they were, shuffling so slowly and purposefully through the snow. There must have been hundreds of them, dragging their few meagre possessions on crude wooden sledges or carrying them in sacking slung across their backs. And there were women and children too – but the oddest thing was . . .' Greygoose suddenly stopped, the words frozen on the tip of his tongue. He half-rose from his chair, his hand upon the hilt of his dagger. 'What was that noise? Did you hear it?' he hissed in alarm, twisting round to search the shadowy hall and upsetting his chair as he did so.

Snatch, who had crept almost close enough to touch the Archer's back, couldn't contain his gasp of surprise at what he had overheard and barely had time to duck down behind an upturned bench and freeze in its shadow as the Archer's sharp eyes passed over him.

'Oh, it's nothing, my good Greygoose, nothing for you to worry yourself about. We are completely alone, you can be sure of that, alone save for the vermin of this city of course.'

Grout's lies came easily as he tugged lightly at the Archer's sleeve and righted his chair for him. He knew that he did not dare to face Snatch unless he could get the Archer to reveal more about this ragged army and he laughed to put Greygoose at his ease, sweeping a hand across the Learning Hall. 'I have had such a plague of rats in here since food became so scarce in the city. It's such a pity Eider isn't here with us, he was so good at catching the vermin. But you were about to tell me – was there something odd about those travellers? They were journeying towards Cawdor you say?'

Greygoose frowned but nodded reluctantly as he resumed his seat. The hairs on the back of his neck prickled and again he looked behind him. That noise hadn't sounded like rats to him, no, more like the sudden, startled gasp of somebody standing right behind him. But there was no one lurking in the shadows: he had twisted around too quickly for them to hide. He looked carefully into the Loremaster's smiling face and wondered, for a moment, would Grout have lied? Could he have hidden somebody in the Learning Hall? Then he decided that Grout was probably the most trustworthy person in the city: he had to be if the King came to him for counsel in these troubled times. Greygoose leaned forward, dismissing his lingering doubts and gripping the Loremaster's arm fiercely.

'You are going to find this hard to believe, but that ragged mob were travelling through the depths of winter with no more of an idea where their journey's end lay than do I; they knew not if they were ever to reach it and, to make matters worse, they had hardly a morsel of food to share between them or decent clothes upon their backs. They had nothing – nothing to eat and nothing to keep the weather out when we came upon them.'

'But why? Whatever possessed them to set out on such a journey?' Grout interrupted, his eyebrows raised in speculation.

'That's the ridiculous part of it!' Greygoose laughed without the slightest trace of humour in his voice, 'They are following some madman of a blacksmith who'd had a vision. He says Nevian, the Master of Magic, miraculously appeared in his forge in the village of Muddle and forewarned him that his skill to forge arms and armour was needed in Cawdor. Apparently he was told to make the journey without delay, travel through the deepest winter, gathering all those along the greenways' edge who had the courage to journey with him. He was told to take nothing but the tools of their trades and the clothes they stood in. Nevian even promised to provide for their journey telling the blacksmith that the Warhorses, the Border Runners and the Battle Owls would watch over them. Now have you ever heard anything so stupid in your life before? Grout – how could their journeying to Cawdor – if such a place exists at all – help the King? I don't hold with magicians and I say the people are sure to perish once they wander past the last lamp of Underfall – if they even get that far. And anyway, there's nowhere around there to beg for food and shelter and they looked close to starvation when *we* came upon them. Many of them would probably have died if Lord Kyot had not been beguiled by their story and thrown open the doors of Stumble Hill to them and filled their bellies with hot broth and the Lady Eventine given up all the warm winter clothing the Tower could spare . . .'

Shouts, running footsteps and a rising tumult of voices suddenly broke the frosty dawn silence outside the Learning Hall. Grout jumped and quickly pulled away from the Archer, urging him to go, to slip out of the hall before anybody discovered he had been there.

'But what of Cawdor? Does it really exist beyond the legends? Is there a road through the Emerald Mountains? Could Eider have found it and survived?' Greygoose cried as Grout tried to hurry him towards the doors.

'Yes, yes, yes, I am sure there is a road – if it says so in my books of lore then it must have existed once, mustn't it, no matter how overgrown it has become. I am sure Eider's safe and I will search out news of the road if I have time tomorrowlight. The boy is bound to have found somewhere to shelter for the winter: he always seemed to lead a charmed life, no matter what trouble he got himself into. But listen – what's going on outside the doors?'

Greygoose paused and turned, tilting his head as he caught the faint words of the crowds as they streamed past the Learning Hall. He gave a startled cry as he reached back into his quiver and took an arrow out. 'Nightbeasts have attacked again during the night. They have been murdering and mutilating in the lower circles of the city under the cover of darkness close to the Stumble Gate. The people are converging on Candlebane Hall and demanding that the King protects them.' Greygoose's face was blanched a deathly white. 'You don't think they crept in through the gates when they were thrown open for us to ride through, do you?'

Grout wrung his hands together in mock dismay, crying out, 'Oh, what a disaster! What a calamity!' And he deftly threw back the bolts on the door and pushed the Archer out into the street.

'Swear to tell nobody that I came to see you,' Greygoose whispered across his shoulder into the closing door-crack.

And he just caught a fleeting glimpse of the Loremaster's cunning eyes as he heard him reply, 'My lips are sealed.'

Snatch was filled with a gnawing worry at the unexpected revelation that the King still had loyal friends, albeit a band of ragged peasants, nobodies and beggars from the villages along the greenways' edge. Despite everything they had done to discredit him they still believed in him. He had been a fool not to take the rumours of somebody stirring up trouble in the remote villages more seriously, and the thought of it overshadowed the delight he should have felt at the chaos and terror the murderous activities that they had carried out during the hours of darkness were spreading through the city folk. There was little pleasure in the sneer that thinned his lips as he watched the jostling crowds through a spy-hole he had rubbed in the feather-trails of frost coating the windowpanes.

'This throne-stealer will have no allies – not a single one!' he muttered, hate filling his breath, before turning sharply and calling for Girrolt, Huxort, Krush and the rest of his trusted, inner council to join him in the hall. A stunned silence settled over all of them as they listened to Grout recount everything, word for word, that the Archer had told him.

'We must pursue these turncoats, these king-lovers, with all haste. We must ride them down, kill every one of them before they have a chance of reaching Cawdor and joining up with the Tunnellers,' Snatch urged, the moment Grout had finished speaking.

'You can't. You heard what the Archer said – the greenways were blocked by fresh blizzards only moments after they struggled through on their way back to the city. It has been some days since they came from Stumble Hill and the weather has become worse. There will be no passage through the Emerald Mountains until the spring now,' Grout interrupted sullenly.

'But surely following them at all is hardly necessary, surely there's a chance that the Tunnellers never reached Cawdor, after all it's the hardest winter any of us remember,' Huxort commented, secretly weary of the killing.

'Yes, he could be right,' Krush added quickly. 'Surely those rebels will never get through the Emerald Mountains in this weather. All we are likely to find are frozen corpses if they're silly enough to try.'

'We would be mad to try to follow until the snows are gone. Nobody really knows if there is a road through the mountains at all or whether Cawdor actually exists beyond the legends in those books that Grout is so fond of,' Thoragrasp muttered, adding darkly, 'Anyway what's the point in it all, they can't do anything to harm us, can they? Nobody can hurt us: we control most of the villages and the people are too frightened to travel without our protection. Why, even the King has become a virtual prisoner in Candlebane Hall by all accounts, deserted by most of his warriors and hated by almost everybody else. Even his Queen and her creature, Krann, have fled to the safety of Stumble Hill. Surely we have riches enough to last us the rest of our lives without robbing any more and . . .'

'Shut up, you stupid fool. This isn't about riches! The Honourable Company of Murderers wasn't formed to fill your pockets – or have you forgotten our purpose already? We are going to seize back the power and dignity stolen from our fathers!'

Snatch's eyes had rapidly shrunk to pinpoints of rage as he listened to the half-hearted excuses for not pursuing the rebels.

'We control nothing, you fools, nothing at all,' he shouted, bubbles of spittle breaking out on his lips. 'Don't you understand what could happen if that ragged company of king-lovers reach Cawdor and the Eretch invest them with their power? They could sweep back across Elundium and drive us back into exile in a blink. Then everything we have achieved will be lost.'

Snatch paused for breath and grasped Grout by his sleeve, pulling him roughly into the centre of the council, prodding a hard finger into his bony chest, making him cough and wheeze. 'You are supposed to be the fountainhead of all knowledge, Grout, the wisest person in the Granite City. You have unearthed the secret of the Eretch and told us how they brought the dark side of morning to Cawdor; now tell us this – will those rebels reach Cawdor? Will the Eretch give them their power? What shall we do to stop them? Shall we follow them now or stay here and continue our reign of terror until the snows melt?'

Grout swallowed nervously, sure that whatever he said it would only serve to enrage Snatch further. 'I . . . I don't think the Eretch would have much use for the King's friends . . . no, my guess is that they would probably try to destroy them as they would have tried to destroy those Tunnellers – that is if they managed to reach Cawdor. But as to the possibility of the ragged company reaching journey's end . . .' Grout paused and glanced anxiously around the gloomy hall. 'There's magic tied up with them, from what the Archer told me, yes, yes, they will reach the doors of Cawdor all right, and I wouldn't follow too closely in their footsteps if I were you, not with Nevian watching over them.'

'Magic! Surely you don't still believe in all that Nevian nonsense, do you, Grout? I would have thought that you, of all people, would have known better,' Snatch laughed, playfully slapping the Loremaster between his narrow shoulderblades, hard enough to send him tottering forward amidst a gale of laughter from the others.

'Magic, magic, who's afraid of magic?' Squark mocked from Snatch's shoulder, compounding the Loremaster's misery. The breath had been knocked out of him and he had to clutch precariously at Krush's shoulder to stop himself falling to his knees.

Struggling to regain his balance, Grout sucked in a shallow breath and quickly hooded his eyes to disguise his loathing. Once more Snatchpurse had stolen his dignity, once more he had made him look like a fool, but he would get his own back, and he forced a smile and swallowed his anger as Snatch continued, so cocksure, so convinced that he had the world in his pocket.

'No, you can be sure it won't be magic that protects those king-lovers, but luck might be with them and they might just stumble on the ancient road through the Emerald Mountains, they might just find it still open. The worst of the weather which was close on their heels may have shut the high passes behind them, and it is just possible that they will reach Cawdor. But as to visions in a blacksmith's forge and colours in a rainbow cloak – that's just nothing but fairy stories, the sort of fantasy you weave here in the Learning Hall. Grout, you of all people should know better than to try and frighten me with it. I'm not even sure the old magician had any real power beyond simple conjuring tricks. Anyway, whatever it was that he kept beneath that silly rainbow cloak is gone forever, vanished into thin air at the end of the Battle of the Rising. You don't just have to take my word for it, there were thousands of warriors who saw him disappear and he hasn't been seen anywhere since, has he? Unless you take that ridiculous blacksmith's story seriously but you don't, do you, Grout?'

The Loremaster hesitated nervously, wringing his hands together. Magic was, and always had been, a part of their lives. It was woven through every book of lore, threaded through their history, it was in the air they breathed, in the wind and the sky, carried by the silent, swirling nightshapes that brought the darkness each twilight.

Magic was unpredictable: nobody knew who it would touch and when it would appear, Nevian had been its master, and probably still was whether they could see him or not, and Grout feared the magic touching him.

'But who has fed those ragged travellers and kept them alive in the deepest winter? The greenways are no place to wander without protection, so who has looked after them if Nevian has not?' Grout whined in a small, frightened voice. He fully expected Snatch to strike him again, only in anger this time, but instead he laughed dismissively in his face.

'They are beggars, Grout, nothing more, and they have probably survived this far by stealing. Why, if the truth be known they have probably beguiled everybody they met upon the road with this ridiculous story about the magician protecting them and have looted their property the moment the people's backs have been turned. And who is going to lift a hand to stop them if they tell everyone that Nevian is protecting them? Let's face it, the villagers jump at their own shadow easily enough, so nobody's going to go chasing after them to get their property back, are they – just in case all those stories about magicians are true after all. The rebels have been very clever, but we'll catch up with them once the snows melt. We'll teach them a lesson,' Snatch swept his hand across his inner circle, sneering. 'Magic is dead and gone – forever, Grout – it went with the passing of the Granite Kings. Go on, boys, tell him, tell the Loremaster. Girrolt, Huxort, tell the old man we're not afraid of any silly magicians!'

Snatch frowned as he looked around the circle. 'Well?' he demanded as they shuffled uncomfortably, avoiding his eyes.

'I . . . I . . . I'm not really sure,' Girrolt eventually answered, speaking for the others. 'I wouldn't want to mock Nevian or any of his magic just because nobody's seen him since the Battle of the Rising. He always was one for turning up unexpectedly, and remember what he did to those warriors on the Causeway Fields who refused to pledge their allegiance to King Thane? Surely you haven't forgotten the look of those two old Marchers who helped the Tunnellers, how gnarled and twisted their fingers were and the rough bark-like texture of their skin? And that was ages after he turned them back into warriors. No, I wouldn't want to laugh or dismiss the power of magic. Not yet anyway.'

'You fools! You're all weak fools, the lot of you,' Snatch muttered, glaring at each one of them in turn, but voices in the street outside caught his attention and he strode across the hall to peer out through the melting patterns of frost on the windowpanes. He could hear the talk from the people hurrying past and it was all of the atrocities they had committed during the night. They were clearly voicing their discontent with a King who did nothing to protect them, who kept himself safely locked up in the Towers of Granite while they risked being murdered in their beds.

Snatch smiled to himself, licking his lips. There was work to do here in the city. Cawdor could wait until the snows melted, then he would prove he was right to the others, the doubters. When their swords and daggers were wet with the blood of the king-lovers he would show them that the power of magic had faded forever.

Hurrying back, he shed the last remnants of the Nightbeast armour he wore. 'We will go amongst the people dressed as they are and fuel their discontent; we will spread all sorts of rumours about the Tunnellers and

306

the Nightbeasts. We will tell them that the tallow-houses are almost empty and soon darkness will smother the city during the dead hours of night. We will tell them that their Queen has fled with that dark creature of hers while the city people are trapped here to starve and die. Yes, there is plenty of work for the Honourable Company of Murderers to do in the city and where better to start than Candlebane Hall in the very presence of the King himself?'

XI

To Confront
a King

THANEHAND PACED restlessly backwards and forwards through the flickering, smoky, dawn light of the Candle-hall. Breakmaster strode beside him despite his weariness, the frost and snow from the long journey back from Stumble Hill still clinging to his beard. Thane had let out a huge sigh of relief to hear that Elionbel and Krann were safely within the tower but he had become restless and perplexed by the horseman's account of the ragged hordes they had encountered trudging through the snow near the tower and the strange story they had told him of their journey. Thane had seen a glimpse of hope in the story of the ragged company and had refused to allow Breakmaster to go until he had questioned him more thoroughly on the matter despite the hour.

'Were any of them warriors or carrying arms perhaps? Why is Nevian leading them to Cawdor – surely he must realize that they are needed here in the city? Whatever skills do they have? Why didn't you tell the Master of Magic how desperate our situation is? You did see him, didn't you?' Thane barely paused for breath and didn't allow the horseman to get a word in before the barrage of questions started again. 'Why Cawdor? How can the fate of Elundium rest in that far-off place? What did Nevian have to say about that?'

Thane suddenly turned sharply as the doors of the Candlehall were flung violently open and the captain of the guards appeared briefly before a handful of the soldiers who normally protected the outer gates of the upper circle of the city burst through, their swords drawn. An icy draught blew along the aisle making the thin, blue-white candle flames dance and sway, wildly distorting the shadows they cast and sending the nightshapes swirling up into the darkened rafters.

'Nightbeasts were abroad in the city beneath the cover of darkness, my lord. They have been murdering and mutilating close to the Stumble Gate. The city folk are in uproar and crying out for protection – they are converging on the Candlehall. We must seal the upper circles of the city against them and lock them out before they overrun Candlebane Hall and the Towers of Granite.'

'No, I may not have the warriors to guard them or the means to capture those creatures but I will not have the people shut out and left defenceless. I will not have them feel abandoned to face those beasts alone.'

'But there are not enough of us to defend both the Candlehall and the Towers of Granite, for more guards have deserted their posts during the night, my lord. There are barely enough of us left to protect you if the people riot or try to take the law into their own hands,' the captain warned as the first of the city folk began to appear between the open doors.

Their cries for protection, their anger and distrust, faltered as they saw him in the candlelight standing upon the high dais in front of the throne, his arms outstretched in welcome, beckoning them to enter. Their anger shrank further and became a disgruntled, mumbling suspicion, cloaked in silence as they edged uncertainly forward, expecting the guards to drive them back at each footstep.

Thane sighed wearily. He was at his wits' end to know what he could do to stop the dark canker of fear and distrust that was spreading through his people. Where had he gone wrong? What had happened to this better life he had promised them? And why, if Nevian was so sure that the fate of Elundium would be decided at Cawdor hadn't he come to him and revealed his strategy? Why had he abandoned him to stumble blindly in the dark? He looked down at the city folk as they shuffled closer, spreading out to fill the aisles between the tall slender, fluted candle-stems and despite all the troubles that beset him his heart was full of pity for them. He had wanted to give them their freedom and a life unshackled from their fears; he'd had such high ideals and yet he had somehow failed them and allowed all their old terrors to creep back, only this time they were much worse. The great barns and storehouses were almost empty of food, their harvests had been allowed to fail, the people of Elundium were close to starvation and all because of their fear of these creatures of the night. There was nothing he could do to halt one footstep of the ruin and chaos that was relentlessly threatening to engulf them. His own larder was as empty as everyone else's, for he had been quick to cancel all banquets and feasts and had everything that could be spared from his kitchens distributed amongst the most needy.

He realized suddenly that there was still something he could do. It was such a little thing but it would give his people comfort during the dark, dead hours of the night. He leaned down and called to the captain of the guard and spoke softly to him. 'Lock the doors of the Towers of Granite. Do it quietly and discreetly and order your men to return to their posts. Breakmaster will stay here beside me, I will not be harmed. Let the people move unmolested through the Candlehall. Go, there will be no trouble.'

Thane straightened his back as the captain of the guard turned away and faced the swelling crowd, sweeping back the folds of his thick, winter cloak to rest his hand upon the hilt of his sword. A thousand pinpoints of light shimmered and reflected from the hammered silver rings of his mail-shirt surcoat as he called out in a strong and steady voice, 'From this daylight Candlebane Hall shall remain open to all of you during the hours of darkness. It shall be your refuge and it will be filled with light. A sanctuary for all until I have purged the city and all Elundium of those foul creatures who haunt the black hours. I will catch them and destroy them: no dark hole or crack or hiding-place will be overlooked. There will be no stone left unturned. You have my word, a solemn pledge.'

Low murmurs of approval began to ripple through the smoky candlelight and Thane used the moment to press Breakmaster to tell him exactly what Nevian had said to him in the tower on Stumble Hill and why the fate of Elundium should rest in such an unlikely place as Cawdor.

'But that is what I have been trying to tell you, my lord,' the horseman whispered. 'I didn't see the Master of Magic at Stumble Hill, nor had anybody else in that ragged horde. Nobody had seen him except for that blacksmith who was leading them – Quencher, I think he called himself. And from his account the Master of Magic only appeared briefly in his forge charging him to journey to Cawdor and to gather up all those loyal to you, my lord, along the greenways' edge. But I couldn't make much sense out of the man's wild ramblings – he told me about visions of the rainbow cloak and the power of magic but it really wasn't clear. Why risk such a desperate journey – and through the Emerald Mountains of all places – to go beyond the last lamp of Underfall in the depths of winter? Why go to find a place that nobody can say for sure really exists beyond its place in ancient legends? And for what? To forge armour for those prisoners who escaped from the cellars beneath the Candlehall, to fashion saddlery and harness for them to use and to cobble new boots for them to wear? I'm telling you, sire, the whole thing sounded so ridiculous, why they will probably stumble upon the frozen corpses of those miserable prisoners in some high mountain pass if they're lucky enough to survive that long.'

Breakmaster paused and cast a troubled eye over the heads of the crowds, glancing at a small knot of newcomers who were hurrying through the doors, roughly jostling and pushing their way forward. He shook his head and resumed his story. 'I tried to get the blacksmith to turn his ragged company around and journey back to the Granite City but he would have none of it: he kept insisting that Nevian was guiding and providing for them, taking them to the one place in all the world where the fate of Elundium would be decided. But whatever that was supposed to mean is beyond me.'

'I wonder . . .' Thane murmured, lost in thought, reaching back into his memory to that last, brief moment when Nevian had appeared, a pale, translucent wraith in the Towers of Granite. What was it he had said? What could he remember? *Beware of false friends and be slow to judge those who are brought in chains before you.* He had been forewarning him that the prisoners were innocent and it had sown the seeds of doubt in his mind but now this new piece of news meant that those prisoners had survived, that somehow they would live through their journey through the Emerald Mountains and they would reach Cawdor. It seemed that there they would prepare to return and fight, but how could they help him? How could they decide the fate of all Elundium from that far-off place?

A burst of harsh laughter from the back of the Candlehall cut through the smoky atmosphere and made Thane blink and spin round as a voice called out mockingly, 'What use will this Candlehall be for sanctuary if it's swallowed by the darkness? Tell us, great King, where will the light come from if the tallow-houses are empty?'

Thane stared at the restless sea of faces that stretched away from him in the flickering light. The voice that had just shouted out sounded familiar, it tugged at faint, far-off memories, but before he could begin to place it another voice jeered.

'Perhaps the King is offering us the use of this Candlehall because he has no further use for it – because he is going to run away to Stumble Hill just like his Queen Elionbel and that dark creature, Krann, who have taken wagon-loads of food and enough tallow with them to last two lifetimes.'

Gasps of disbelief and distrust rippled through the crowd and other voices, fuelled by what they had heard, called out that they wanted to know how he intended to light the Candlehall and demanding that the Queen show herself to put an end to the terrible rumour of her flight to safety.

'Perhaps our Queen has thrown in her lot with those Tunnellers who escaped,' sneered another voice.

'I think we should pay a visit to the storehouses and break them open to find out the truth!' goaded Snatch from the back of the hall.

Thane stepped back a pace, his face a deathly white. How could anybody have known that Elionbel and Krann had journeyed to the tower on Stumble Hill? Who could have told them that the tallow-houses were almost empty, for he had sworn the Master Tallowman to secrecy. Surely nobody could really believe that he would have stolen from his people? Again he hunted amongst the faces of the crowd – were his enemies here inside the Candlehall? Were they standing amongst the very people he strove so hard to protect?

Breakmaster's face grew thunderously dark at the cries of mistrust. He gripped the hilt of his sword and drew it from its scabbard, sweeping the blade aloft and making the crowd shrink back as he advanced. 'How dare you question your King? Why the echo of his voice as he offered you the sanctuary of this great Candlehall has barely faded among the rafter beams before you are doubting his sincerity and calling him a thief. Get out! Get out, all of you! And as for the doubters let me tell you this, I saw the Queen myself only . . .' the old horseman hesitated, the lie choking in his throat, '. . . only three nights ago.'

'No . . . no . . . you do not have to lie, old friend,' Thane urged, gripping Breakmaster's arm to restrain him. 'At least let us keep our dignity and hold on to the truth. There is little else left to us these daylights.'

Thane lifted his head and called out to the milling crowds as he tried to stop them from leaving the hall. Perhaps if they heard the truth it might just stop them from rampaging through the storehouses and looting what little food there was left to last them through the winter.

'Wait! Be still, my people, listen to me. Yes, it is true that your Queen has journeyed to the tower on Stumble Hill but it was to take Krann to safety in these troubled times, remember he is only a child. Elionbel took nothing with her, merely a few guards and a couple of servants,

317

simply provisions for the journey. I will not desert you in this time of despair, I promise you that I will protect you here in the Granite City. My sword arm will grow weary in your defence, to my last breath, just as I promised the light of the last lamp here in Candlebane Hall is yours. Everything that lies in the storehouses will be shared out equally. Wait . . . listen!'

Thane fell silent, letting his hands drop helplessly to his sides. Clearly his words were falling on deaf ears, and seemed only to be fuelling the people's distrust. He could hear it on every side as the crowd streamed out of the Candlehall and into the strengthening daylight intent on looting the storehouses.

'There . . . what did I tell you? Lining their pockets at our expense.'

'Leaving us to starve to death while they live off what should be ours.'

'Come on, we have to look after ourselves.'

The muttering grew louder.

'Imagine it, sending his Queen and her dark creature off to safety with all our food while we starve and get murdered in our beds.'

Snatch watched the rising tumult from the back of the hall and a triumphant sneer filled his face. He had never imagined that just a few well-chosen lies would have such a devastating effect. He seized at the moment and pressed home his attack as he called out, 'It is hardly surprising this happened, for this King is not a real King, or had you all forgotten? He is nothing but a lowly candlecur. He is a throne-stealer. He stole the crown from King Holbian's death-bed on the Causeway Fields, didn't he? Why should he not steal the food from your mouths?'

In an instant a deathly silence spread throughout the

Candlehall. People stopped and turned to stare at the King. And then the first whispers started to rise against him. Eventually someone shouted.

'Throne-stealer!'

Then Snatch cleverly reminded them that they had all been better off when the Chancellors governed Elundium. Then, at least, there was food to eat and folks could sleep safely in their beds at night. Almost before Snatch's words had died away and he had ushered his followers out of the hall to start the looting a chorus of voices were calling out, echoing his demands that a return of the Chancellors would be the only thing that would banish their fears. The crowd became ever more restless as it fed itself on its own rumours, multiplying the fears that they would starve if they were not the first to help themselves. They began to move towards the doors, their voices now raised in anger. They were jostling and barging, pushing their way out. The slender candle-stems trembled and swayed as they threatened to topple over in the sudden rush and surge of panic.

Breakmaster, his face now purple with rage, shouted for the guards that Thane had so easily sent away, but his voice was lost in the mêlée and he turned desperately towards the King. 'We must do something,' he began, only to let his voice falter into silence as he saw that Thane was standing frozen upon the dais, his face pale and trembling as he peered into the gloomy shadows at the far end of the hall. Breakmaster followed the King's gaze to a single, tall figure concealed in the shadows.

Snatchpurse realized suddenly that the King was staring directly at him and he stepped back hastily, keeping his face hidden. He laughed softly to himself and mocked, 'Soon you will have nothing, candlecur, throne-stealer,

319

nothing at all!' And then he vanished, slipping in amongst the last of the city folk, squeezing through the doors.

'It's no good chasing him, Breakmaster, he'll have melted into the crowd and disappeared long before you reach the doors, and he's not the only one. But I caught a fleeting glimpse of him and at least now I think I know who our enemies are.'

Breakmaster drew closer to Thane and glared darkly around the almost empty Candlehall. 'You know who is behind all these murders? You know who is leading the Nightbeasts?' he asked in a hushed whisper.

'Why, yes, it has to be the Chancellors,' Thane replied grimly.

'The Chancellors? But that would be impossible,' Breakmaster exclaimed. 'They fled the city, they abandoned King Holbian and the people, stealing everything of value that they could carry with them. They left only moments before the Nightbeasts breached the outer walls. I should know, I was at the King's side. Surely they would never dare to show their faces here again. There was talk that they had sold their souls to Krulshards and that they had aided the Nightbeasts, for they were meant to have shown them the secret ways of the City. Surely the people would stone them to death for what they did?'

'Would they?' Thane laughed bitterly, directing their footsteps to the Towers of Granite and unlocking and locking the doors of the tower securely behind them before he continued. 'The city folk seem to have very short memories. You heard them cry for the Chancellors' return just now, didn't you? I know it was fuelled by their fear and stirred up by those hecklers but I am not so sure they wouldn't welcome them back with open arms if it meant a full belly and an end to these nightcreatures that prowl through the city.'

'But how could the Chancellors possibly provide food for the city, or promise them anything, for that matter? King Holbian banished them into exile and the last anybody has heard of them they were ekeing out a pitiful existence somewhere in the wilds of Meremire Forest, not that it doesn't serve them right after what they did.'

'Yes, yes, I know all that,' Thane muttered bleakly as they reached his chamber. He strode across to the window and rested his hands on the frosty sill and looked out across the frost-white roofs of the city. 'But how else can you explain away seeing Snatchpurse and, I think, at least half a dozen of the other Chancellors' sons at the back of the crowd goading them on just now?'

'What?' Breakmaster cried angrily. 'As if we don't have enough trouble to cope with without those evil, conniving, no-good, thieving creatures creeping back into the city. You don't think you could have been mistaken? There are so many rumours about – somebody would have been bound to have seen them – and none of the guards have reported them entering the city. Surely there isn't a single person who would welcome them into their house, not after what their fathers did. Are you really sure it was them, my lord?'

'You ask me if I can be sure?' Thane replied, turning sharply on the old horseman. 'Surely you don't think I could ever forget those Chancellors' sons? Don't you remember how they hated me, how they hunted me through the city crying out for my blood, how they chased me out of the Learning Hall enraged because Nevian had magically appeared out of the dusty shaft of sunlight? Don't you remember all the trouble I caused by crying out for the truth? You surely cannot have forgotten how all this began when the Loremaster beat me and mocked my humble beginnings and told me that Bravepurse had ridden Amach, my grandfather's horse, at the Great Battle of World's End before the Gates of Underfall.'

A ghost of a smile hovered on Thane's lips as he remembered the gasps of horror, the sudden silence that filled the Learning Hall as Pinchface, the Loremaster, was forced to tell the truth, and the look of rage on Snatchpurse's face and the hatred in the faces of the other Chancellors' sons as they heard how their grandfathers, whom they had thought brave and fearless, had in fact cowered and hidden in the city, too afraid to face the black terror of the Nightbeasts.

'Yes, I am sure it was Snatchpurse I saw hiding in the shadows of the Candlehall. And I think I saw Huxort and Girrolt, but I cannot remember the names of the others who were with them on the morning they chased me out of the Learning Hall. It seems so long ago now, almost as though it belonged to another life.' Thane paused and gazed thoughtfully out across the white, glittering rooftops towards the dark forest that smudged the hazy horizon line and suddenly it all made sense to him.

'It has to be the Chancellors behind all these troubles. Think about it, Breakmaster! Who else in Elundium has more reason to hate me or what I have tried to do to give the people a better life?'

'You're right, my lord. How blind and stupid I've been – of course it must have been the Chancellors who have been behind these troubles all along. No doubt they feel the time is right to seize the throne. Yes, and now I come to think about it there has been a smell of their intrigue in just about everything that has happened. I should have listened to Marcher Ustant when he said the Tunnellers were innocent. Who else could have stirred up the people against you so successfully? And as for blaming all those atrocities on the Tunnellers – all those murders, all that stealing . . . Why, that's typical of their cunning ways. But wait a moment, there was something else I wanted to tell you about. I heard a lot of rumours about some Honourable Company of Murderers, or some such strange name, on the journey to Stumble Hill. An innkeeper told me they offered protection to travellers, but he didn't expect we'd be needing it, being so heavily armed. I thought they might be a band of loyal Marchers and I tried to find out more about them so that I could find them and bring them back into the city, for we need every loyal man we can get. But then I became very suspicious when nobody could, or would, tell me anything about them. You don't suppose they're connected with the Chancellors in any way, do you?'

Thane nodded slowly and thought for a moment. 'Yes, I do: it's too much of a coincidence – what better way to gain control over the people than to pretend to be protecting them on the one hand and robbing those who shun their protection on the other? And doing it all in disguise so that they can blame it on the Tunnellers. They must have friends here in the city, people who shelter them and who know what they are doing. There must be traitors here in the very heart of the Granite City.'

'But what about the Nightbeasts? How did the Chancellors find these new creatures? How did they draw them into their treacherous plots? We destroyed the last of Krulshards' beasts at the Battle of the Rising and anyway surely nobody would shelter those creatures? I thought the people were too terrified of them.'

Thane thought for a moment and then suddenly laughed harshly. 'There are no new Nightbeasts, Breakmaster. There never have been, it's all an illusion. Think back to when the prisoners escaped from the cellars beneath Candlebane Hall. The guards swore that the courtyard was swarming with Nightbeasts, didn't they?'

Breakmaster nodded.

'Well,' Thane continued. 'Remember that fragment of one of the creature's armour that Errant discovered trapped in the grating that covered the secret passageway? It didn't have any strength in it at all – it was withered and rotten and you could have easily thrust your spear through it. I remember thinking at the time that it was more like one of the armoured scales belonging to one of the dead creatures who had lain for ages on the battlefield, forgotten, before we threw it upon the funeral pyre.'

'You mean the beasts who swarmed through the court-yard – the creatures who carried our those murders last night in the lower circles of the city – are dead?' Breakmaster frowned, scratching his beard.

'Not exactly, no,' Thane continued slowly. 'They might look like Nightbeasts, especially in the dark or if they waylay you upon a lonely stretch of greenway, but they're not really Nightbeasts at all. No, my guess is they are Snatchpurse and his friends dressed up, cleverly disguising themselves in the rotting hides of those creatures. Although I have no idea where they could have found the rotting carcasses, for I thought we had scoured the battlefield at the Rising and the countryside for leagues around it for all the bodies before we built the pyre.'

'Why, yes, of course, and we would have been none the wiser if Errant had not discovered that piece of armour – how clever. I suppose some of the smaller Chancellors'

children must have disguised themselves as Tunnellers –
that would explain how they create havoc in so many
different places at the same time. I remember thinking
that it could not just be one group of Tunnellers when
it was reported.'

Breakmaster paused, lost in thought. 'But why did
Snatchpurse and his friends risk their lives coming into
the city that first time? Surely they couldn't have come
here to free the Tunnellers who had been brought here
as prisoners and locked away in the cellar beneath the
Candlehall to await your judgement.'

'Yes, my guess is that is exactly what they came here
for but not to actually give them their freedom. They
couldn't afford to have them running around protesting
their innocence any more than they could afford to
have me lock them away. That might have made the
villagers wonder who was really behind all these troubles.
I think their intention was to capture them and take
them far away from the city and then kill them and
bury their bodies where nobody would ever find them.
That way they could go on committing all sorts of crimes
in their name.'

Breakmaster nodded vigorously. 'And that would explain
why Ustant died defending the stairway down to the
cellar. He was trying to stop the Chancellors getting
to the prisoners. And that is why there was blood all
around the courtyard, I knew it wasn't Nightbeast blood!
We must warn the people of their treacheries. I'll send
out criers without delay and every guard we have. We'll
have those Chancellors' sons rounded up and bound in
chains within the hour.' The old horseman turned and
strode towards the doorway of the chamber but Thane
called out to stop him and beckoned him to the window

where he had been keeping a watchful eye on the crowds as they streamed away from Candlebane Hall.

'Look down there. Snatchpurse and his friends have seized control of the crowds: they won't listen to reason now no matter what truths we tell them.'

Breakmaster gripped the balustrade, his knuckles whitening. He watched helplessly as the mob rampaged through the narrow, winding lanes and alleyways, over-turning carts that were in their way and breaking windows, beating anybody who wouldn't swell their ranks, burning and looting as they made their way towards the store-houses. Their chants and wild shouts rose on the thin, icy morning air. Quite suddenly the crowd began to split up and began burning and looting in every direction. Breakmaster saw the danger they were in if the crowds took control of the city.

'We can't stay here and do nothing, my lord. We must rally the few loyal men we have and fight our way down to the Breaking Yards and ride to the tower on Stumble Hill.'

'I think it may already be too late for that, look!' Thane warned, pointing down to where the handful of grooms who lived in the Breaking Yards must have heard the cries of the approaching mob and thrown open the doors to all the stables. They had saddled their own horses and were riding for their lives following Esteron and Beaconlight through the open gates of the city and out onto the greenway.

Shouts and the sound of armoured boots running across the cobbles outside the upper circle of the city made them both crane their necks to look down and see the few guards who were still loyal to them running for their lives, retreating before the angry crowds. The last of the fleeing guards slammed shut and locked the gates in the face of the mob. The thick, ironwood gates trembled and shook beneath the fury of the assault as the frenzied crowd hurled sticks and stones over the walls and demanded that the throne-stealer give them back what he had taken from them.

'We are siege-locked – trapped, my lord,' Breakmaster cried out in dismay as he watched the crowds blocking every lane and alleyway with upturned carts and rubble they had torn from the buildings in the upper circle of the city. Their escape was impossible.

Snatchpurse's head suddenly appeared above the top of the high wall that surrounded Candlebane Hall and the Towers of Granite. He had not intended moving so fast but the mob had seized the city and he had seized the moment: the victory was his. He looked up, searching out the window where Thane was standing, and then scrambled nimbly up the wall, his face a gloating mask of triumph. He jeered above the shouts of the crowds who were assaulting the gates.

'You and that silly magician, what idiots, what fools, to think you could steal what belonged to the Chancellors. Candlecur, you will soon have nothing, do you hear, nothing – even the skin you stand up in shall soon be mine: I will nail it above the Stumble Gate as a lesson for all to see that the Chancellors once more rule Elundium.'

Greygoose suddenly felt sick with the realization that the Loremaster must have revealed his confidences to the figure now standing on the wall, the one who led all the heckling in the Candlehall and who now knew everything he had divulged to Grout. The Archer crouched at the high window with tears of shame in his eyes. He saw a single chance to redeem his betrayal and he reached back into his quiver for an arrow. He nocked it onto his bow-string with trembling fingers and drew back the feathered flight to rest against his cheek as he took aim.

Despair and helplessness filled Thane's heart and he looked past the gloating figure confronting him out towards the distant horizon line and suddenly Nevian's words made sense. He was powerless, siege-locked within Candlebane Hall. Perhaps the fate of Elundium would, after all, rest in Cawdor with a handful of Tunnellers.

Snatch saw the King's eyes stray past him towards the horizon and sneered. 'Don't expect any help from that miserable crowd of ugly little goblins. They may have escaped to Cawdor but we will put them to death the moment the snows melt.'

Greygoose moved slightly to get a clear shot and Snatch caught a glimpse of the sunlight glinting on the arrow blade a moment before it was loosed. Snatchpurse laughed as he ducked out of sight and the arrow struck the top of the wall where he had been standing and spun harmlessly away into the gloomy courtyard below. 'You will have nothing, Throne-stealer – nothing.'

XII

The Fall of Cawdor

THE RESTLESS sea surged and thundered in grey-green waves against the sheer, black marble cliffs of Cawdor, breaking and boiling up in huge, drifting plumes of salty spray while high above its crumbling towers and wind-riven battlements the sea birds wheeled and cried, haunting the sky and cloaking the strengthening sunlight with the fleeting shadows. Winter lingered on in the high passes of the Emerald Mountains, reluctant to release them from its frozen mantle, but the pale green shoots of spring were beginning to speckle the retreating snowfields around the walls of Cawdor, and soon life began to stir at winter's end under the dark, sombre canopy of the petrified forest. Blackbirds and song-thrush started to break the eerie silence and to build their nests amongst the thick tracery of hanging vines and creepers that were interwoven through the lacework of branches. Everywhere new flowerheads started to form and then burst open, spilling their heady fragrance into the air, brightening the gloom with their large, fragile petals of azure, primrose and saffron colours.

Spring had come early to Cawdor, penetrating the dark side of morning with new hope. Drib hurried through the shadow of the gate arch into the outer keep of the fortress, his fishing boots, specially made to give him a safe purchase on the slippery rocks, echoing on the cobbles, and he paused to allow Oaktangle and the others to go on ahead of him towards the kitchens with the fish they had just caught. He carefully lowered the basket of trout he had been carrying, their iridescent scales glistening like silver in the sunlight, and stretched his aching back. Then he wiped the trickles of sweat from his forehead and sat down on an old bench to rest for a moment, savouring the spring air and resting his back against the smooth, wind-worn stone wall as he soaked up the warm sunshine and listened to the bustle of industry and the laughter in the voices all around him.

A lot had happened at Cawdor since he had stumbled back shivering and exhausted from that first perilous fishing expedition. The others had been furious that he had risked his life climbing down the sheer cliffs on his own without even a rope, especially Sloeberry who thought he had been lost forever. But they had been quick to forgive him as they tucked into the first proper meal that they had eaten for a good few daylights. However, the lack of food had not been their only worry as winter deepened. The sensation that something evil haunted the fortress intensified and even Berioss, who had at first denied it, had to admit that he had begun to hear whispering voices in the dark, cold nights which sent shivers up his spine. And what could have caused the collapse the tower roof that the Tunnellers had repaired on their arrival at the ruin? It had tumbled down one stormy night, possibly because of the weight of a heavy snowfall, but no matter what they did to patch it up they could not seem to prevent it from leaking. And then finding fodder for the horses had become a serious problem and they had been forced to let them roam freely during the daylight hours to forage for themselves, but they looked pitifully gaunt and thin and no one rode unless it was absolutely necessary.

They were faring no better themselves. Their warm winter clothes taken from the armoury on their flight from the Granite City had proved to be more for show than for hard use and had begun to fall to pieces as the weather worsened. They had neither the thread nor the means to weave new cloth, and to make matters worse as it grew colder every blade they possessed became blunt from the constant need to cut wood from the petrified forest for their fires. They had no stone or grinding wheel to sharpen them, nor the oil of the black ebony tree to rub into their armour to prevent it from rusting in the damp, salty air. Even Eider had been forced to give up hunting for hares and rabbits in the forest as the arrows in his quiver dwindled away and he had to admit he did not have the skill to fashion new ones.

Berioss had toiled tirelessly, putting his strength into every task no matter how small. He was determined that they would survive and every daylight, no matter how tired the company became, he insisted they practise their skill at arms. He remembered the promise he had made to Nevian, the Master of Magic, and was determined that they would be ready to ride out in the name of justice and honour once the snow melted, but of late, as their situation worsened, he had taken to muttering to himself – 'Knights of Cawdor indeed, how Nevian expects me to do anything, anything at all when we are reduced to little more than beggars . . . We are simply ekeing out a pitiful existence here on the dark side of morning. We are not really living.'

Then, one black night as the wind howled and shrieked through the ruins and the surf thundered up against the cliffs and shook the foundation of the fortress, as if in answer to his muttered complaints, the door had burst open and beyond the threshold had gathered hundreds of frozen, desperate figures. As Berioss and the Tunnellers had sat in complete surprise their leader, Quencher the blacksmith, had shuffled forward and many of his followers had crowded through the doorway behind him.

Through the icicles in his beard he had spoken: 'We come in peace. Nevian, the Master of Magic, has been our guide and he has protected us on the long, hard, unforgiving road through the Emerald Mountains that we followed in our search for Cawdor. The magician told me in a vision that I was to gather from along the greenways' edge all those who were still loyal and loved their King, that their skills to forge hot metal, to build and cobble, to weave and mend were in great need in Cawdor. He told me that the fate of Elundium would be decided in the great citadel that stood upon the dark side of morning.'

As he had spoken Quencher had let his eyes travel quickly from the small group huddled together around their fire as they cooked their meagre supper in the flames. They looked as ill-clothed and wretched as his own followers. He looked up from their ruined fire hearth to the dereliction of the tower they inhabited; he looked along its broken rafter beams to the leaking roof and his shoulders sagged wearily. Clearly this could not be the place they sought, for these people were surely not the ones who were to decide the fate of Elundium. Disappointment weighed heavily on him. For a moment as they had stumbled out from beneath the eaves of the strange, petrified forest with its luminous, frozen orchids into the unbroken snowfields and had seen the glint of the sea in the distance and caught a brief glimpse of a huge fortress that lay ahead of them, the moon had ridden clear of the storm clouds and their spirits had soared. But now, standing in its only habitable tower he could see that it was not journey's end after all.

'Could we beg a corner to rest for the night and shelter from the storm . . .' he continued. 'We would ask nothing more of you save the directions to Cawdor. If you know of the great citadel that Nevian told me stands upon the dark side of morning and guards the margin of our world?'

Berioss and the whole startled company rose slowly to their feet as the ragged, frozen figure spoke. The old Marcher took a step forward, his hand still on the hilt of his sword, his face a mask of surprise as doubt made him ask, 'Are you saying that Nevian appeared in a vision to you? He told you to find us? He guided you through the Emerald Mountains in the depths of winter? But that is impossible. The high passes must have been blocked with snow. How did you survive? What could you have possibly found to eat?'

Quencher's eyes had momentarily flashed with anger. 'Do you doubt the power of magic? How else would we have made such a journey or known where to tread if we had not found a clear path of footsteps to follow? Sometimes they took us over the drifts and through glistening icy tunnels but always they were strong and clear and kept us on the road to Cawdor. As for food each night we would find the fruits of the forest in neat piles beside the road and kindling laid ready for our fires. And during the darkest nights when the wolves howled and closed in around us we would glimpse the Battle Owls and the Border Runners from the light of our fires as they patrolled and protected us.'

There was a commotion behind Quencher as more of his followers pushed their way into the tower. Malthera hurried through the crowd to stand at her husband's side.

'So this is Cawdor – the place we have journeyed so far to find?'

Dozens of voices cried out in dismay, echoing her disappointment as they saw the ruins but Berioss laughed suddenly and strode forward to embrace Quencher.

'No, I do not doubt the power of magic and yes, this is indeed Cawdor, the Citadel of Shadows, the great fortress that stands upon the dark side of morning – your journey's end. Come in, come in all of you, come out of that dreadful weather. Drib, Eider, Oaktangle – stoke up the fire, Sloeberry, Damask, Mistletoe – prepare what food we have for our guests.'

In the long, dark winter daylights that followed their arrival the sense of an evil presence seemed to diminish, to shrink into the background and lose a little of its menace. Cawdor was gradually transformed and a new, but smaller, fortress slowly grew up out of the ruins. Stonemasons rebuilt the crumbling walls of three of the towers which accommodated everyone, the stables, storehouses, kitchens and the gatehouse were rebuilt and a new, low curtainwall was constructed to encircle them and protect them from attack. Carpenters fashioned new floors and roofs, built chairs and tables and made beds to sleep upon while thatchers discovered dense reed beds in a nearby stream and skilfully thatched the tower roofs and made them weather-tight. Huge piles of windblown firewood were gathered from the forest and stacked up near the hearths of each tower. Warreners journeyed into the surrounding countryside and set traps for hares and rabbits and fishermen wove nets to fish from the quay that Drib had discovered on that first fishing expedition. Potters and tinkers set about furnishing the kitchens with pots and pans while the weavers' spinning-wheels turned and the cobblers bent over their lasts. Eider was able to hunt in the forest after the fletchers cut him new arrow shafts and flighted them with seabird feathers. All daylight long the smoke billowed over the blacksmith's forge, sparks fizzed and crackled on his anvil and new weapons and armour were forged as the sweet music of his hammer rang out.

Drib smiled and stretched out his crooked legs, wriggling his toes luxuriously in his new fishing boots. The arrival of Malthera, the blacksmith's wife, had changed his life completely. The pain of her son, Crimp's, disappearance had left such a gap in her heart that she had immediately taken to mothering Drib, scolding the others if they let him carry the heaviest bundles of firewood or if he didn't have a warm seat at the fire. He wasn't always first to sit at meal times but she made sure he was rarely one of the last. She had been so insistent that when the cobbler fashioned his new pair of boots he had done them very carefully, taking pains to make sure they supported him correctly and helped with his crooked legs. He couldn't remember much about his own mother beyond the frail image of her amidst their grinding poverty after his father's death: he had been so young when he had been sold into servitude and there had been no love or kindness in his master, Sweepscuttle's, household. Sometimes Malthera's motherings embarrassed him in front of the others, especially in front of Sloeberry, but secretly he quite liked the way she watched over him and made him feel as if he belonged to the Quencher family.

Berioss listened with growing concern to the travellers' tales about the famine and chaos that had Elundium in its grip and it didn't take him long to guess that Snatchpurse and his murderous friends must be behind it when he remembered how the Chancellor's son had started all that trouble at the inn at Deepling and had driven their small company away from the village. He must have spent his time spreading evil falsehoods while his friends murdered and spread anarchy to bring down the King.

Berioss had drawn Quencher aside: 'Now I understand why Nevian appeared to me on that first daylight when we arrived here. I know why he pledged me to prepare our small company to ride out in the name of justice and honour in the dark daylights that lay ahead. Yes, our King has great need of us: we must be ready to return to Elundium when the snows melt.'

Quencher had laughed and gripped the old warrior's arms fiercely. 'You have my promise that new forged weapons and armour, new saddles and boots – everything your warriors will need will be ready in time. The Knights of Cawdor shall lack nothing.'

The sound of horseshoes clattering on the cobbles in the stable-yard made Drib jump quickly to his feet in guilt, for he should have delivered the fish to Sloeberry in the kitchens and gone to saddle his horse, but a smile softened his face as he saw Sloeberry lead Sparkfire out through the archway from the stable-yard towards him. She had obviously tired of waiting for him for she had saddled and bridled Sparkfire and tied a small, neat battle plait into his forelock so that he was ready for Drib to practise his mounted skill at arms. His sword was hanging in its scabbard from one of the strange horns of leather and stuffing that protruded from either side of the seat. The master saddler, Flock, had fashioned the strange saddle especially to fit around Drib's crooked legs and it made him as secure in the saddle as any Galloper. Silkstone swooped down onto his shoulder.

'Why didn't you warn me?' Drib whispered to the owl as the horse snorted and arched his neck, his ears pricked and alert. Silkstone flew from Drib's shoulder and alighted on the cantle of the saddle to preen his flight feathers. The bloom of spring shimmered and rippled across the horse's flanks and tiny sparks danced away from between his newly shod hooves and leapt across the cobbles.

Drib felt his smile widen as Sloeberry approached and he quickly raked his fingers through the tangles of hair that fell across his forehead and straightened his jerkin as he brushed away the stray strands of seaweed that clung to it after he had scrambled across the slippery rocks earlier in his search through the rock pools for the largest fish. He knew he was smiling foolishly and his cheeks were flushed, but he didn't care. He loved Sloeberry and the joy of seeing her never failed to quicken his heartbeat. Her beautiful, slender face with its large, round eyes that always held so much warm laughter for him framed by strands of dark, silken hair seemed to glow in the sunshine. Her voice was so full of soft, musical whispers as they shared their secrets by the fireside each night. From that first moment when they had met in the cellars beneath Candlebane Hall he had known he was in love with her. She made him want to laugh, to cry, to shout with joy and tell her everything that he knew. He wanted to show her all the things he loved and he remembered so clearly how he had flinched inwardly at that first meeting when her eyes had travelled down to his crooked legs and he had feared a look of disgust or pity before being dismissed with a cold glance that would tell him he didn't count for anything. But it hadn't come. Her eyes had been full of smiles and warmth and from that daylight onwards she had made him feel so special never chiding him if he couldn't keep up, never mocking him for slipping uncontrollably in the saddle before the saddler had made him that strange seat that made him equal to other riders. She had always been there to help and encourage him. One daylight, he had secretly promised himself, when these troubles were all over and they had proved to the King that they were innocent of the treasons they had been accused of, one daylight when they were all safely back home in Elundium, he would pluck up the courage to tell Sloeberry of his love. He couldn't tell her now, not because of his crooked legs but because in the Granite City he was nothing more than a penniless chimney sweep's apprentice. He had nothing, not even a scrap of barter to his name. But perhaps he could convince Breakmaster to give him a job in the stable-yards – he didn't care how lowly or humble as long as it gave him the chance to earn enough to buy his freedom from Sweepscuttle, his master. Then once he was free he would be able to tell her of his love, perhaps even to ask her to marry him. But these were fragile, far-off dreams.

'I am sorry, I let the others go on ahead while I have been sitting here daydreaming. I should have carried the basket through to the kitchens for you,' he began to apologize but Sloeberry laughed softly and shook her head but there was a troubled look in her eyes.

'It doesn't matter, I can do it in a minute. Let us sit here for a moment, I want to talk to you.'

She reached for his hand and their fingers lightly entwined as she drew him back down onto the stone bench. Sparkfire snorted and tossed his head impatiently, setting the bit-rings jangling. He could hear Berioss's deep voice and the sounds of the other horses as their riders gathered in the inner courtyard around the quintain. Drib took hold of the reins and calmed his horse as he looked into Sloeberry's troubled eyes.

'What is it? What shadows can you see to spoil the sunlight?'

Sloeberry shivered and tightened her grip upon his hand, searching for the words that would explain to him the feeling that she had that something terrible was about to happen.

'I don't know . . .' she murmured, biting her lip. 'I just keep getting feelings, a sense that something is not right, that something is going to happen. But it seems so silly when I'm sitting here with you in the sunlight and we're so safe and secure. We're so far away from the famine and despair of Elundium and now the others have arrived and the fortress has been rebuilt.'

'Perhaps you're worried because Berioss talks of little else but our return to Elundium – of battle and strategies, of marching and columns now that the snows are melting.'

'No, the feelings of dread are about here – about Cawdor,' she started, but Berioss's impatient voice boomed out, cutting her short and making Drib leap to his feet.

'Drib, Drib, where are you? Come here at once, we're going into the forest, we're not jousting with the quintain. Where are you? You're keeping the Knights of Cawdor waiting – as usual.'

'I'm sure we're perfectly safe but we'll talk again tonight, I promise: I'll see you by the fire,' he grinned, shrugging off her worries as he climbed up onto the bench and awkwardly into the saddle, fitting his crooked legs snugly around the horns before gathering up the reins and expertly pivoting Sparkfire and cantering off towards the others who were waiting for him.

'And there's something else,' she called out in a worried voice taking a step to follow him as he rode out beneath the stone archway. 'That strange feeling, that we're being watched, being haunted by something evil that has been with us since we arrived – the voices, the shapes – they've all gone. They suddenly vanished last night just as the sun set.'

'But that's wonderful news, isn't it? It's good to be free of those wailing wraiths finally,' Drib laughed, skilfully reaching down as he rode past the spear stand and taking a spear to hunt with.

'Oh but is it? Is it really?' Sloeberry muttered, picking up the heavy basket of fish, 'I'm not sure, not sure at all.'

Snatchpurse stood on the edge of the petrified forest savouring the power of the Eretch that he could feel pulsating through his veins, breathing in their darkness as he watched the dawn break over Cawdor. A sneer of impending triumph puckered the corners of his lips. Everything was working out far better than he had imagined. The throne-stealer was siege-locked in Candlebane Hall with only that old fool of a horseman and a handful of his faithful followers to keep him company and from the mood he had left the city in they would starve to death before anybody lifted a finger to help them. And as for that ragged band of king-lovers who had gathered together and thought they could help him by journeying all the way to Cawdor in the depths of winter – what fools they were. They couldn't have been more helpful in aiding the Honourable Company of Murderers to catch the Tunnellers if they had tried. They had trampled a path through the high passes of the Emerald Mountains that even a blind man could have followed and it led them straight to the ruined doors of Cawdor.

Snatchpurse smiled. Even Grout, whom he had thought incapable of telling the truth, had for once not lied about the Eretch and they had bestowed *such* power on him. Dusk had begun to gather beneath the trees as they had reached the edge of the forest the previous evening and they had caught their first glimpse of the citadel. Cawdor lay mostly in ruins! Girrolt and some of the others had been eager to storm the fortress immediately but he had stopped them and urged them to wait as they watched the wispy, elongated, shadowy shapes that were streaming out of the fortress and gliding up across the windswept headland towards them, drifting effortlessly through the trees as they did so. Slowly they had surrounded them in deep pools of darkness and their wailing cries had echoed through the forest.

'Remember what Grout said, remember the strength and power the Eretch possess. Stand perfectly still,' he had hissed.

And so they allowed the Eretch to possess them.

Snatchpurse had stood trembling, the remnants of the Nightbeast armour still clinging to his outstretched arms, and had thrown back his head in ecstasy and felt the power course hotly through the pores of his skin. His flesh crawled and itched almost painfully beneath the forgotten remnants of his armour and suddenly the rotten scales had changed their colour, turning to mauve and then through violet to deepest indigo. They glistened wetly and clung so tight that they felt as though they were forming a second skin. He had gasped and staggered back, his hands pressed hard against his throbbing temples as spectral images, far beyond his wildest, darkest dreams of power, filled his head. He greedily devoured the cries of the starving and laughed at the tragedies he had instigated while still hungry for more. His body swelled and pulsed and he became dizzy, spinning around and around, aware of the slightest sounds. His ears were assaulted by the scratch and scrape of insects burrowing through the ground beneath his feet; he could hear the crack of stone and the creak and sway of the millions of trees and branches that surrounded him. He shook and trembled as he cried out and slowly the power of the Eretch flowed through him, possessing him and flooding his soul with evil.

Huxort had suddenly screamed and run forward bursting through the others to clutch at Snatch's arm, frantically waving his other clawed hand in front of his leader. 'Look, look, I can't get it off!' he sobbed, slashing at the claw, smashing it against a tree trunk in desperation as he shuddered with the pain. 'I had forgotten to take it off and now look at it – it's grown into my hand. The Eretch have made it a part of me. What shall I do?'

Snatchpurse couldn't believe what had happened and he stared at Huxort's claw, reaching out to twist and turn it as he tried to pull it off. His friend began to scream with the pain and he looked down at his own forgotten remnants of armour. He made to pull them off but he couldn't even push his fingernails beneath their edges, for the shiny, armoured scales had grown into his skin; they had become a part of him. He heard grunts and tortured howls and he turned to stare in shocked silence at the rest of his followers. Almost all of them had been possessed to some degree by the Eretch and the pieces of Nightbeast armour that they habitually wore to disguise their murderous deeds had fused with their skin and grown into their bones, hideously distorting them and revealing the beasts that had grown up and now dwelt within them.

Snatch looked around, helplessly overwhelmed with regret, cursing his own stupidity as he remembered too late Grout's warning that the Eretch were grave-devils, evil creatures from Krulshards' darkness who might, through their possession, take far more than they gave. But the regret lasted only a moment before the voices of the Eretch welled up inside his head, filling him with persuasive whispers, convincing him that his friends were not hideous creatures, half-human, half-beast, but strong and beautiful, invested with power beyond their wildest imaginings. With a power that was theirs to use and control.

'Test them. See if we speak falsehoods.' The voices were soothing and soft.

Snatchpurse had looked curiously from face to face but then he laughed. It was true: his friends had grown in stature and their armoured scales and spiny ridges that now grew across the tops of their heads and their jagged teeth held a strange and powerful beauty.

'*We* are the new Chancellors!' he suddenly cried. 'Our fathers were nothing – mere shadows, worms that crawled through the dust compared to the power that we shall wield. And those who doubt us will soon cower before us and not a breath in all Elundium shall be drawn that does not worship us!'

His pitiless voice echoed for leagues beneath the silent, petrified trees, shrivelling bark and cracking stone. 'Tomorrowlight,' he whispered, licking his lips and drawing his friends close around him. 'Tomorrowlight Cawdor shall be ours!'

The Honourable Company of Murderers waited impatiently, hungry to kill, watching the sun rise blood-red out of the morning sky, watching it slowly burn away the thin wreathtails of mist that veiled the ruins of Cawdor. Snatchpurse strode forward lifting his arm to give the signal to attack, but suddenly he hesitated and then stepped hastily back beneath the trees, merging with the dappled shadows as he motioned to his followers to keep out of sight. He had spotted a small but well-armed company of Tunnellers led by the old Marcher Berioss, as they rode out of the fortress and cantered swiftly up across the windswept headland towards them. Snatch counted heads as they rode past his hiding place and disappeared into the forest.

'What could be better! By my reckoning that's almost all of those wretched Tunnellers – they haven't left anybody to protect those turncoat king-lovers and their families. The killing is going to be easy.'

His sneer soured into a scowl as he caught sight of the little crippled boy riding with the owl perched on his shoulder, the one who had loosed the arrow at him during their escape from the cellar underneath Candlebane Hall. The boy was laughing and talking excitedly to a taller boy who rode beside him with a bow slung across his shoulder as if he didn't have a care in the world. Hateful memories welled up as Snatch touched the place on his chest where that arrow had struck him and he remembered the second time the cripple had got away from him below the armoury, helped by that ugly little female Tunneller and those Nighthorses. He quickly searched the riders and saw that she wasn't there. He'd teach Drib to laugh, he'd teach him to be so carefree: he'd teach them both when he got his hands on them.

'Remember,' he hissed fiercely, just loud enough for his followers to hear. 'That one, the crooked boy, is mine – and hat ugly little female Tunneller he is so fond of. She must be down there somewhere in that fortress. Just make sure you leave them both for me. Now, let us go and kill.'

'Kill! Kill!' The Honourable Company of Murderers chanted as they swept down across the empty windswept headland.

One by one they clambered over the steep causeway, falling silent as they slipped unseen through the unguarded gatehouse, their swords and daggers drawn in expectation. Snatchpurse brought them to a halt in the outer keep, his face a mask of pleasure. He stroked Squark's chest feathers and sent the white magpie to fly across the ruins and bring doubt to all who saw him.

'Listen to those treacherous turncoats busily making things for their beloved King! What fools! Come on, boys, we'll soon turn their laughter and songs into screams of terror,' he sneered, leading the way through the main archway.

Eerie webs of darkness began to spread out around them, muffling their advancing footsteps. The seabirds fled from the sky overhead and the thunder of the surf as it rushed up against the black marble cliffs was suddenly stilled and died away to a whisper.

Quencher paused, enveloped in smoke from his fire, and glared towards the open doorway of his forge with his hammer poised above the anvil. Something was wrong. Flock, the saddler, suddenly frowned and glanced up from the saddle-clamp gripped firmly between his knees, a threaded needle in his hand, as he heard the harsh, mocking voice of a magpie that seemed to cry, 'Run . . . run . . . run for your lives!'

The fishermen's wives who were sitting in a noisy circle weaving a new net suddenly fell silent and looked around the sunny courtyard. Everything was growing dark: there were sinister shadows beneath the archway and they were spreading across the cobbles towards them.

Sloeberry gave a cry of distress and let the fish-kettle slip from her fingers to clatter onto the floor of the kitchen. The other women turned towards her.

'Listen, everything has gone silent and it's getting dark. Something must be terribly wrong,' she whispered, hurrying to the open doorway only to gasp and stagger backwards and turn to slam the door shut. But it was too late.

The courtyard, corridors and towers swarmed with vile, half-human creatures. The citadel was overrun, its defences breached. Everything familiar was vanishing beneath smooth webs of darkness. Shouts and screams of terror rent the silence as everyone tried to run for their lives.

'Nevian, by all the power in your rainbow cloak – help us, Nevian ... Nevian ...' Quencher shouted, his long-handled hammer gripped firmly in his hands as he ran out through the billowing smoke. 'Nevian – we are under attack!'

Nevian was engrossed in his tower deep in the Emerald Mountains, constructing his storm engine to control the unpredictability of the weather, when he caught the faint far-off sounds of the blacksmith's cries of distress.

'Cawdor – under attack? But what can I do to help? I can do nothing, my power to intervene in the troubles of man are all but spent.'

He frowned, 'But I must do something, I cannot just abandon them. Grannogg, guard the tower!' he cried to the ancient Lord of Dogs who was stretched out, fast asleep across the fire hearth.

Grannogg barked and sat upright as Nevian gathered the fading colours of his rainbow cloak about his shoulders and hurried through the doorway.

Sloeberry was knocked to the ground and trampled as the attackers filled the kitchens. She struggled to unsheath her dagger only to have it knocked from her hand. She heard a vaguely familiar voice cursing in the darkness. Strong hands reached down and grabbed her and roughly dragged her outside.

'At last I have you, you ugly little goblin,' Snatch spat in her face as she was thrust in front of him. He grasped her by her hair and lifted her up off her feet. She saw clearly his face through a mass of moving shadows that filled the courtyard: there was no mistaking those mean, murderous eyes, for they had loomed over her in the inn at Deepling moments before he had struck her. And she had caught a glimpse of them in the shadows in the courtyard of Candlebane Hall when they were brought as prisoners into the city. But now they were inhabited by a darker, more menacing evil, one that she had not seen before in them. Now they were filled with the evil that had once haunted Cawdor.

Snatchpurse laughed cruelly into her face. 'Now you will watch and enjoy my victory here at my side before I torture you and make you dance,' and he twisted her hair, dragging her head back painfully and forcing tears from her eyes. He gloated and sneered as he made her watch his company pursue the people who had trudged through such terrible hardships to help them. There were people fleeing helplessly in every direction; children screamed and cried out for their mothers who were knocked to the ground. Precious possessions were scattered and dropped in their desperate bid to escape.

'Hurry, damn you, hurry and kill them all. Don't let a single one of them escape. I want to set a trap for those Tunnellers who rode off into the forest and it must be ready before they return,' Snatch cursed impatiently.

'We can't see anything through these swirling shadows!' Huxort shouted back, stabbing and hacking at what he thought was the blacksmith's body only to find his blade cutting empty air.

Snatchpurse's triumphant sneer suddenly turned into a snarl of rage as faint, elusive rainbow colours swirled and flowed through the gloomy darkness, gathering around the fleeing people, protecting them and drawing them together as it guided them out through the gate arch towards the forest.

'I knew you wouldn't abandon us, Nevian!' Quencher shouted, wielding his hammer at the hideous, shadowy figures that surged all around him as the soft, muted colours of the magician's cloak enfolded him.

'Run – run for your life! Make for the forest – take everybody who is still alive with you. Use the last few moments of my power to get everyone into the safety of the trees. I thought my magic was at an end but something – some new evil – must have revived a little of it. My sight is failing – I cannot see what causes these infernal shadows – run – run!'

Nevian's voice faded as the colours melted and began to disappear.

'Look! Look at the colours of his rainbow cloak! We are all done for now, I told you Nevian's magic wasn't dead and gone. I told you his magic would get us, didn't I!' Girrolt wailed, cowering in fear.

'A curse on magic! A curse on all your fears! There is no real power in that cloak of colours. Look, look at it now, it is fading away. Now, hurry, damn you, hurry, and kill all those who haven't already escaped. Go!'

'Run – make for the forest!' Sloeberry shouted as she struggled to break free but Snatch dragged her with him as he slashed and thrust wildly with his dagger, trying to cut down the fleeing people ahead of him. The broad back of one of the fishermen's wives loomed before him through the shifting darkness as she struggled to scale the curtainwall and he raised his dagger to lunge at her. The blade jerked forwards and Sloeberry made a desperate grab at his arm, biting his wrist. Snatch gave a shriek of pain and the blade flew from his fingers as her teeth cut through the skin. He turned on her savagely, striking her across the face and cutting her cheek open with a raw weal. Her head snapped back and a sudden explosion of light and pain filled her skull. The sound of Snatch's voice, the screams of terror and the panic all around her seemed to roar in her ears, and then darkness folded over her but through it she thought she could hear the thunder of hoofbeats on the Causeway and the shriek of Silkstone stooping down from a clear blue sky. But the webs of shadows had engulfed them and then the sounds faded into soothing blackness as she slumped unconscious to the ground.

Drib let Sparkfire drop a little way behind the others. He wanted to be on his own for a moment, to breathe in the fresh, fragrant air and listen to the sounds of the forest all around him. He smiled, half closing his eyes, the reins loose upon his horse's neck. It felt so good to be alive. The forest looked different, less menacing and much more friendly than it had the first time they had ridden through it, starving and almost frozen to death from their long ride through the Emerald Mountains in search of Cawdor. Now those same, stark, winter trees were softened with dappled, leafy shadows, squirrels leapt from branch to branch and birdsong sounded from the thick, new undergrowth; there was a profusion of brilliant flowerheads that hung down from the vines and creepers and brushed gently across the top of his helm, perfuming the air.

A shout from ahead made him sit up straight in the saddle, cast his daydreams aside and grasp at the reins. Through the trees he saw that the others had halted and dismounted in a sunlit clearing. Berioss, Oaktangle and Eider were crouching down beside a huge, fallen oak tree and were examining something. Drib guessed they were probably on the track of a Nightboar and he rode slowly into the clearing and dismounted with them. Berioss frowned and shook his head resting his hand on the rotten bark of a fallen tree for support as he rose stiffly to his feet.

'Well, I certainly don't know what to make of them, but there is one thing I am sure of, whatever made those tracks were here very recently. They can't be more than a couple of hours old.'

He brushed his hand across his forehead and stepped back to allow Drib to peer down at a mass of strange, huge, seven-toed footprints that filled the soft earth around the fallen oak.

'And don't tell us you think they belong to giants, Drib: we don't want any of your Learning Hall fairy stories until we're safely back in Cawdor,' Eider muttered, and there was more than an edge of caution to his voice as he drew an arrow from his quiver and nocked it onto his bow-string, carefully searching the dense undergrowth that hemmed them into the clearing.

'No, of course I wasn't going to suggest any such thing!' Drib began crossly as he straightened up and Silkstone suddenly flew up from his shoulder, but his words trailed off into silence as he stared at the bright purple streaks on Berioss's forehead where he had rubbed his hand after resting it upon the fallen oak.

Memories of that first hunt when he and Eider had been chasing the Nightboar through the forest came flooding back. He had thought there was something familiar about this clearing and the fallen tree and now he moved closer, peering at the rough, wrinkled surface of its bark, and he saw that it was covered in thousands of tiny, dark purple, bell-shaped toadstools. He remembered how he had accidentally brushed the fingertips of his battle gloves through the fragile fungi and watched them burst into clouds of purple dust that melted into the snow when he had climbed up onto the fallen tree to remount Sparkfire and catch up with Eider. He glanced further along the tree to where some of its branches towered high above his head and he saw that the fungus had been carefully scraped away as if by huge fingers.

'Eider!' he hissed, turning sharply towards him. 'Do you remember those enormous, hairy creatures who followed our sledge after we had tied the carcass of the Nightboar onto it?'

'I thought I told you that I don't want to hear any of your stories!' Eider muttered.

'No, listen,' Drib cried, turning to the others. 'There was something about the one who leaned over me when I lay on the sledge, the one that tore off my glove: something didn't make sense to me then but it does now.'

'Well, what is it? Spit it out, Drib, before you have us all jumping at our own shadows,' Berioss frowned.

'Well, I only caught a glimpse of it but I distinctly remember that it had too many fingers.'

'I told you, I told you it would be one of his ridiculous stories, didn't I? Come on, let's get going.' Eider gathered up the reins of his horse and put his foot in the stirrup ready to remount.

'But the number of fingers the creature had is very important!' Drib replied indignantly pointing down to the mass of enormous footprints in the ground around the fallen tree. 'Whatever made these tracks also had too many toes. It has to be the same creatures who attacked the sledge and I think I now know why. Look at the way those toadstools have been scraped off the bark of the tree, look, up there high above . . .'

Silkstone suddenly reappeared, stooping fast into the clearing, shrieking and hooting as he flew over their startled, upturned faces. Drib let his explanation go unfinished as he listened to the owl's frantic cries. The colour drained from his face.

'Cawdor is under attack. Silkstone says a darkness smothers everything and he could hear screams and cries from the people. Come on, we must gallop back now!'

He made a wild grab at Sparkfire's reins as he scrambled up onto the fallen oak and clouds of purple dust erupted all around him as he threw himself into the saddle. With shouts of dismay the others vaulted onto their horses and cantered out of the clearing, spurring their mounts in and out of the trees, oblivious to the thorns and low branches, the tangle of vines and creepers that hung down and impeded their path. Galloping hard, their bit-rings jangling madly, they burst out of the forest and streamed down across the headland at breakneck speed. Smoke and fire billowed from three of the towers and hung in a thick pall above the stricken fortress.

'All is not lost. Look, down there, many of our people have managed to escape!' Oaktangle called out as they drew closer.

People were fleeing, running in every direction, escaping from the fortress with blood running down their faces. Some were limping, some crawling, others were clutching terrified children.

'Make for the forest – hide among the trees! Oaktangle, go with them, stay and protect them!' Berioss shouted as they galloped past.

Oaktangle reined in his horse and pirouetted him, slowing to pick up two of the children before galloping towards the eaves of the forest. Drawing together, the rest of the company breasted the steep causeway in a thunder of hoofbeats.

'Keep together. Remember everything I have taught you!' Berioss cried, but his voice was lost in the black, boiling shadows filled with half-human shapes and creatures of the night that swirled all around them, engulfing them as they rode through the gate arch into the outer keep.

With a roar of triumph and chanting, 'Kill! Kill! Kill!' Snatchpurse and his followers, driven on by the power of the Eretch, surged forward to overwhelm the small company of Tunnellers, assaulting them from every side. The Nighthorses reared and plunged under the force of the attack. Damask and Mistletoe were cast to the ground as their mounts fled in terror.

Berioss saw their peril as they staggered and tried to climb dizzily to their feet. He leapt to the ground ready to defend them, gripping the hilt of his long, double-edged marching sword firmly in both hands. He urged them to get in close behind him as the light of old battles lit his ancient eyes. He strode forwards, scything a glittering arc with his sword, cutting through the boiling shadows. His blade shivered in his hands and smashed through outstretched claws as it sent up showers of bright sparks in the darkness. But there were too many for him to fight alone. Damask and Mistletoe vanished beneath the restless shadows, and step by relentless step the creatures drove him backwards through ruined courtyards and over broken walls until he teetered at the top of the crumbling, black cliffs. The heels of his armoured boots protruded over the edge and his back was to the thundering surf that pounded the rocks below. In desperation, with riven helm and a notched and bloody sword, he made his final stand. The light in his eyes had not dimmed nor did his voice falter as he cried out his love of his King and the beautiful sunlight that he knew still shone above the dreadful shadows.

'No amount of evil can dim the ordinary people of Elundium, the ones you have cheated and tricked, the ones you have lied to. One daylight they will rise against you, mark my words, Chancellors' spawn. And you mark this, and mark it well: one day the Knights of Cawdor will rise victorious from my ashes. You will not win.'

For an instant his attackers hesitated, lowering their weapons, troubled by his words. But Huxort charged through their ranks and spat in his face.

'Be gone, you useless relic, you king-lover – nobody can help you now. Your words don't frighten us!' And with a mighty thrust of his dagger he pierced Berioss's breastplate and the blade stuck fast as he drove the old warrior backwards over the cliff edge to plunge to his death on the rocks below. His attackers surged forward, laughing and jeering as they peered over the edge to watch him fall.

Berioss's sword flew out of his flailing hands and his voice became a wailing scream as he tumbled over and over. 'Nevian, I have failed you but by all the power in your rainbow cloak please do not desert me now. Help me, Nevian, help me . . .'

He grasped desperately at the soft, crumbling, windworn ledges and storm rills, sending up clouds of seabirds each time he struck the cliff face. His fingers became torn and bloody as he snatched at the cliff in desperation, but forgotten threads of magic still dwelt deep within his bones, magic from an age ago when Nevian had cursed him, one amongst many warriors who had refused to pledge themselves to King Thane upon the Causeway Fields. It was powerful magic that had once turned him into a tree to wait and watch upon the greenways' edge until the King should call for him. Now the magic stirred and came to life, coursing through his veins. His armoured boots swelled and split apart and his toes spread out into a strong mass of grasping roots that gouged at the soft marble and burrowed into a dozen fissures, clinging to a narrow ledge, taking root and breaking his descent as they took hold. His breastplate shattered to reveal a trunk of ancient, weatherworn bark, thundercracked with age and strength. His hair and beard became a tangle of vines and his arms and fingers grew, twisting and dividing into a gnarled, sparse canopy of branches.

Dark, uncertain mutterings rippled through the murderers who peered down from the top of the cliff.

'Where has he vanished to?'

'I don't know, all I can see is a weird, old tree half way down. Look at it, clinging onto that narrow ledge. I swear it was never there a moment ago.'

Some of them drew back from the edge in fear.

'You're right, it wasn't. But wait, look, there's Huxort's dagger sticking in its trunk. How in blazes could that have got there, for it was stuck in the chest of that old Marcher? How can that be?'

'It could only happen by magic . . .' somebody began, but Huxort cursed him into silence.

He ordered them back to the fortress harshly: 'There is still plenty of killing to be done, remember nobody is to escape.'

Then he glanced back over the cliff edge at the ancient tree that clung there and laughed. 'There is no magic here, or anywhere else in Elundium. We are the only power that matters!'

Eider spurred Nightshade forwards beneath the gate arch loosing arrow after arrow into the hideous, half-human shapes that suddenly swarmed towards them, swallowing the daylight as they filled the outer keep. Fear and doubt momentarily gripped his heart as the light failed and froze his fingers to the bowstring. Nightshade sensed his terror and reared, spinning round and bolting away, carrying Eider out across the causeway and up through the fleeing people to gallop deep into the forest. Eider wept and cursed his fear as he tore at the reins but there was nothing he could do to check the bolting horse. For leagues Nightshade galloped until exhaustion slowed his pace in the shadow of the Emerald Mountains. Eider dismounted and looked back at the great distance they had covered and he threw down his bow, overwhelmed with shame. He had deserted his friends in their moment of greatest need and he knew it had been his fear that had made his horse run away. Collapsing onto the ground he covered his head and wept, oblivious to the slender figure of a young woman who watched him from the undergrowth.

One thought and one thought alone drove Drib and filled him with dread as he galloped across the causeway and hurled his spear into the seething hordes that surged forward, roaring and chanting all around the small company: he had to rescue Sloeberry, – nothing else mattered. He had to hope beyond hope that she was still alive. He hadn't seen her fleeing with the others who had managed to escape towards the forest. He knew that when the fortress had been attacked she would have either been in the kitchens or sitting in the courtyard in the sunshine gutting the fish he had caught earlier. Drawing his sword and shouting her name he tried to force a passage through the roiling crowd; he spurred Sparkfire against the mob trying to burst through a sea of hideous heads and the forest of spears and swords that thrust at him through the webs of darkness. He thought he caught a glimpse of her pale face in the kitchen courtyard and he cried out her name again.

Sparkfire heard the urgency and the despair in Drib's voice and he reared up, his nostrils flared, his ears flattened back against the side of his head as he struck out at the seething mass of shadowy figures and tried to force a path through them. Claws tore at his flanks and cruel blades hacked at his proud, arched neck. Blood ran down his withers and his shoulders were white with the sweat of battle. Drib twisted and turned, secure in his new saddle. He slashed and stabbed frantically with his sword at the hands and claws that reached out to pull him down.

Cruel laughter suddenly rent the shadowy air from

beneath the kitchen archway and he could hear Snatch-purse shout, 'Leave the crooked boy, he is for me to torture and kill! He is mine, mine alone!'

The screams and shouts calling for his blood abruptly died away into silence as his attackers drew back leaving a clear, narrow path to where Snatch stood filling the archway, dangling the unconscious body of Sloeberry by her hair, which was caught in the clenched, armoured glove of his left hand. Drib could see blood oozing from the gash in her cheek where the Chancellor's son had struck her.

'Now I have got you both and victory is surely mine!' he hissed, relishing the look of despair in the small boy's eyes as he lifted his left hand, shaking it violently before he cast Sloeberry aside to slump onto the blood-stained cobbles where the boy could see her.

'How long I have waited for this moment. Your King is siege-locked, starving to death in his Granite City, and that magician who was so fond of helping him steal what belonged to others has faded to nothing. All your friends will soon be dead: you are done for. Listen, cripple, listen to the silence. We have thrown that old fool of a Marcher over the cliffs – there is nobody left to help you now, nobody at all. Even that precious owl of yours has been chased off by Squark, my magpie. You're all alone . . .'

Girrolt suddenly burst through the archway from the direction of the gatehouse shouting breathlessly, 'Almost all the king-lovers have managed to escape and even those left in the fortress are using those infernal shadows of the Eretch to evade us. That cursed Archer broke free and galloped into the forest and now nobody can find a trace of those two little Tunnellers who were thrown from their horses.'

The gloating mask of triumph vanished instantly from Snatchpurse's face and was replaced by quivering rage and furious anger. 'Follow them, pursue them, scour these crumbling ruins for those Tunnellers. Every last one of them must be killed.'

'We have chased them, followed them as fast as we could, we have searched every corner of this fortress, but once they got into the forest they vanished. We could search forever and not find them.'

Snatch thrust Girrolt aside and grasped an iron-spiked mace from Crimp's trembling, clawed hands, failing to notice the revulsion on the boy's face. Crimp's lips were silently mouthing his mother's name and hot tears of shame and horror were coursing down his cheeks. He felt dizzy and sick from the sudden shock of coming face to face with her in the thick of the fight and he had almost thrust his brutal dagger at her before he realized who it was. He had seen her startled look of recognition and then she had suddenly disappeared in the swirling colours of the magician's cloak as he had come between them. Crimp didn't know what had happened to her after that but he was sure that his blade had struck her, for there was blood on it. He raised his clenched, clawed hand to strike at Snatch but he had moved away and the crowd was pressed in all around him. Snatchpurse felt his victory was melting, crumbling into ashes before his eyes, and yet still the voices of the Eretch that possessed him goaded him to take his revenge and punish the crippled boy. Drib saw the look of triumph melt from Snatch's eyes and heard a ripple of doubt pass through the hordes who pressed in around him. He felt a surge of joy. Not all his friends were dead. He had seen Damask and Mistletoe get thrown to the ground and now he had heard that they had escaped, and beyond hope he knew that Sloeberry was still alive, he saw her stir while she lay, thrown aside on the cobbles, and he heard her cry out his name. Memories of the vision that Nevian had given to him of his father defending the gates of the city, hopelessly outnumbered, filled his mind, giving him the courage he needed. He tightened his grip on the reins and raised his sword, spurring Sparkfire forward and crying out defiantly as he charged at Snatch, 'The Knights of Cawdor are not defeated – not while there is breath left in my body!'

A roar of laughter and cruel taunts erupted all around him and drowned out his voice.

'What can a cripple do? Look at the way his legs stick out from the saddle. One blow and he'll fall off. These Knights of Cawdor are nothing.'

Snatch stepped out of Drib's path and swung the mace against his sword to disarm him. The blade shattered and the hilt flew from his hand. The blow numbed his fingers and sent shivers of agony up his arm as Sparkfire pirouetted, kicking out to keep the space around him.

'Come on, crooked boy, surely you can do better than that!' Snatchpurse jeered, swinging his mace again and striking Drib's injured arm before he had a chance to draw his dagger.

Drib gasped with pain as the bones cracked and tears filled his eyes. Sparkfire sensed the terrible danger he was in and reared up, leaping for the gap in the crowds where Girrolt had burst through and taking Drib out of Snatch's reach as he lifted the mace again. The mob scattered in confusion and Sparkfire used the moment to break through and canter out beneath the gate arch onto the causeway.

'Stop him! Don't let him escape!' Snatchpurse screamed in rage as he realized that the boy was getting away. He gripped the mace in both hands and swung it around his head, hurling it after the boy across the heads of his followers.

The mace spun round twice before it struck Drib hard on the back of his head, splitting his helm and sending it tumbling away across the causeway into a ditch. A searing light burst through his skull and he clutched desperately at the empty air, his scream of pain swallowed by the shadows. His mouth snapped shut and he slumped forward, as limp as a rag doll, rolling from side to side but kept securely in the saddle by the horns of leather and rolls of stuffing that held his crooked legs in place. Sparkfire gathered speed, nostrils flared, taking him up across the empty, windswept head and towards the eaves of the forest. Brambles scratched at the horse's neck and shoulders and threatened to entangle his legs and quickthorn spikes dug into his flanks as he forced a passage through the dense stands of undergrowth. He leapt over hidden streams and scrambled up muddy banks as he galloped through the gloomy, airless grooves and leafy glades until gradually the sounds of pursuit faded away far behind him and everything was silent.

Breathing hard and white with sweat he slowed the pace and eventually stopped. It was getting dark and nightshapes were silently drifting through the trees, lengthening the shadows. Sparkfire snorted to try to waken Drib but the boy didn't stir but lay unconscious, sprawled along his neck. Sparkfire snorted again and then suddenly froze. The whites of his eyes were clearly visible in the thickening gloom as his nostrils filled with the strong earthy odour of rotten leaves and moss. He heard soft, musical whisperings in the air around them and then a twig snapped and then another. The horse tilted his great head, his ears flattened, but before he could move away the undergrowth rustled on either side of him and three, huge, hairy figures suddenly emerged, surrounding him. A large, strong, seven-fingered hand grasped the bridle, preventing his flight. Sparkfire neighed just once and the stood still, steam rising from his sweating flanks. Drib was motionless, slumped unconscious in the saddle.

The Yerrak had been following the horse through the forest, keeping watch on Drib, waiting for the moment to return his glove that they had accidentally pulled off in the snow. They had watched the destruction of Cawdor in horror and had followed Sparkfire in his flight. Their leader reached out and gently caressed Sparkfire's neck and shoulders, running his fingers over his trembling flanks. As the horse gradually relaxed they all joined in, their gentle voices rising and falling in a calming, musical whisper that echoed the soft murmur of the wind amongst the leaves or the sigh of clear water running over pebbles. There was a gentleness in their jet-black eyes, a tenderness in their voices and their touch that told Sparkfire they meant no harm. His whinny of fear became a nicker of fretfulness as he stood reluctantly, unable to escape.

Umm, the leader of the Yerrak, bent anxiously over the boy, holding out the crumpled glove that he thought was Drib's hand, eager to return it and free his people from persecution for the crime of stealing it. Reverently he smoothed out the fingers one by one as he spoke. His deep musical voice begged Drib's forgiveness as he told him that they were truly sorry for stirring up the shadow of the Eretch and causing the destruction of Cawdor by the stealing of his hand. Umm frowned as the boy didn't move. He touched his shoulder, his voice rising, but he could not make the boy stir.

The two others crowded forward. At first they touched Drib gingerly and then prodded at his torn halbert. Umm

364

lifted his broken arm and then cried out in fear, pointing at his bruised and blackened fingers. Turning to the others he whispered, indicating that the boy must have the power of magic in his veins, to be able to grow a new hand when it had been torn off. Hastily he let it fall back.

'He is cruelly injured. He may die,' the third Yerrak called out after running his fingertips over the ugly, oozing wound on the back of Drib's head. He sniffed at the drying blood and covered his own head with his hands, terrified at what might happen to them if the boy died.

The Yerrak drew back with troubled eyes and squatted down in the gathering darkness, whispering to each other in sad, frightened whispers, rueing the day they had accidentally taken the boy's hand. They needed his forgiveness, without it the shadows of the Eretch would never fade away.

'Surely if there is magic in the boy then the magician who lives in the tower that looks down over the whole world will know how to heal him. He will be able to make it better,' Umm suddenly sang out in a strong, booming voice that made Sparkfire snort and the birds fly from their night roosts. He grasped the horse's bridle in his strong hands as he stood up.

'But can you ever find the tower?'

'Yes, of course, by leaf and branch I will – I must. But you two must go back and search through the forest and make sure no harm comes to the boy's friends and watch over them until I return,' he answered, heading towards the steep shoulders of the Emerald Mountains that were already bathed in moonlight.

Snatchpurse cursed in a black rage, striking out at those closest to him, making them scatter and scramble out of his way in fear as the crippled boy vanished amongst the trees. The very purpose of their long journey through the Emerald Mountains, the sacking of Cawdor, all his plots and schemes to overthrow the King and seize back what their fathers had lost, would come to nothing if any of these Tunnellers and king-lovers lived to tell the truth.

He was well aware how easily the people could turn against them. He knew that many of them had secretly hated their fathers, the Chancellors, when they had ruled Elundium.

'Nobody must find out that we are behind all the ruin and devastation until we have overthrown the King and seized the throne.'

Sharp spear-tips stabbed and prodded Sloeberry to her feet. She was cursed and kicked and forced to stumble forward out of the ruined fortress. Tears blinded her eyes and blood oozed from the harsh bindings that had been tied around her wrists. She looked up and searched the empty, windswept headland and the dark, silent eaves of the forest for any sign of Sparkfire and Drib as she was dragged and prodded helplessly along. One tiny spark of hope was kindled amongst the ashes of her despair – there was no sign of either of them. They must have reached the safety of the forest, they must have done.

'I love you, Drib, I'll always love you no matter what these people do to me,' she whispered to give herself strength as the Company of Murderers closed in around her, jostling and pushing her as they cursed her to move on faster.

Snatchpurse swept his hand dismissively across the fortress as he strode out onto the Causeway. 'Reduce these ruins to rubble. Raze them to the ground, and then scour the forest for any sign of those traitors. Come, we must hurry, there is a King to topple in Candlebane Hall and rich pickings for everyone in Elundium!'

Epilogue

Night silently drew its smoothing shroud over Cawdor and moonlight softened its dereliction. All that could be heard in the silvered darkness was the restless sigh of the waves breaking against the black, marble cliffs and the mournful whisper of the wind combing its fingers through the deserted ruins, fanning the dying embers of the fires that had consumed it until they glowed a dull red. A splintered door creaked eerily on riven hinges and then hung, still and silent in the moonlight.

The wind gently stirred the tangled mass of vines and creepers woven through the branches of the gnarled old tree that clung perilously to a narrow ledge halfway down the cliff-face. The trunk shivered as Berioss awoke to find himself transformed by the forgotten threads of Nevian's magic into the tree, and images of those last, desperate moments of the fall of Cawdor filled his mind. Everything he had striven to achieve lay in ashes. He had failed Nevian, he had failed them all. Despair and desolation swept through him and a large teardrop formed and began to trickle slowly down the weatherworn bark. The wind fell away to nothing and in the sudden silence Berioss thought he caught the faintest echo of the magician's voice deep within him.

'Remember, Marcher Berioss,' it whispered. 'Remember: where there is life there is always hope.'